OBITS
AND
MURDERS

A newspaper story set in Chicago

OBITS
AND
MURDERS

A newspaper story set in Chicago

JERRY CRIMMINS

OZANAM PRESS
Chicago

Published by Ozanam Press, 7759 W. Berwyn, Chicago, IL 60656

Composition by Point West, Inc., Carol Stream, IL
Jacket design by Ben Yonzon

To my wife, Dottie O'Hara Crimmins

OBITS
AND
MURDERS

A newspaper story set in Chicago

PROLOGUE

The late 1960s, West Side of Chicago

"Speaking of dangerous women, whaddya make of those three raven-haired temptresses that just walked in?" said Herbie, stirring his drink at the far end of the bar on Division Street near Laramie Avenue.

Sam Nash and John Flannery laughed.

"First generation Italian, probably all related. They go around like that. Scared their brothers'll find them here," said Nash.

"They should be on Taylor Street," said Herbie.

"And they know it, too," said Nash. "That's why they act so lost."

From the far end of the bar, on the short leg where the bar ran to the wall, the three young men had an easy view of the front of the tavern.

"They're not Italian," said Flannery. "Too dark."

Herbie coughed into his drink then wiped his face. "Too dark? Flannery, an Italian that's too dark is a Negro."

Nash smiled. He enjoyed this sort of conversation, and he got high on the camaraderie of guys he had known all his life when he journeyed back to the old neighborhood.

Nash was a reporter for the City News Bureau of Chicago, 24 years old, low on cash, but with the world by the tail.

"I'm telling you they're not Italian, Herbie. How much you wanna bet?" said Flannery.

Herbie leaned over to talk past Nash to Flannery. "I don't trust you, Flannery. You probably brought them here personally and told them to say they were Jewish. Why don't you tell us what you think for free?"

"Based on my experience, I would say Greek," offered Flannery.

"Greek," said Nash, nodding and pondering this possibility. There was a reasonable number of Greeks on the West Side of Chicago, and they had their own school, Plato School, and their church at Harrison Street and Central Avenue, but Nash did not know many of them, and he did not know of any Greek girls who came in Marty's. He took a big swig from his beer bottle.

"Greek. Yeah, could be Greek," said Herbie.

"The one in the middle is Maria Kostakis," Flannery added. "She used to work in that little food store that used to be on Harrison owned by her parents. Too bad you didn't bet me, Herbie."

"Whose turn is it? said Nash.

"Yours," the other two responded in unison.

"Okay, order us a round on me. I'll be right back."

Nash was already a little lit, although it was only 9:30, just enough to be a little braver than he was when sober. He maneuvered through the crowd gathering for a Friday night in Marty's.

Some of those in the bar still lived on the West Side, in the more western and northern portions of it. Others had moved away but came back every week because this was where their friends were. The neighborhood they grew up in was shrinking as blacks continued their expansion out of the inner city. The neighborhood, as they knew it, would soon disappear. This gave the young people even more reason to come back.

Nash approached the three Greek girls who were standing and cautiously observing about 10 feet inside the door as people jostled by them in all directions.

"How do you do, ladies? I believe you're new here. I wish to offer you the hospitality of the house and buy you all a drink," he said. A beer in Marty's was only 25 cents, before the inflation caught up with the war.

The tallest one, who Nash knew to be Maria Kostakis, smiled and said, "What are you, the official greeter?"

"No, but I'm sure the management would approve of my buying you a drink. They like to sell drinks here." Nash was expansive and smiling broadly. He stood 5 feet 10 inches tall with wavy black hair, blue eyes, and wide shoulders.

Maria shrugged. "Sure," she said, ignoring her shorter companion who gave her a gentle elbow and shook her head barely perceptibly. Nash caught this action out of the corner of his eye because it was the standoffish one who was the prettiest. She wore her dark hair behind her ears, showing little earrings, and her trim figure looked beguiling in a print dress under a light coat. It was the end of April.

"We'll have to step out of the doorway, ladies. If you'll come to the end of the bar, I can clear some space there." Nash had his left arm out in a symbolic gesture gathering the three girls together, and with his right hand pointed to the place where he had left Flannery and Herbie.

"Thanks. We'll stay here if you don't mind." This was the prettiest one talking.

"I'm just trying to be helpful. There's a lot of married men here and other people with unsavory reputations. My friends and I are single and savory." Nash said this directly to the cutest one and could not help but suddenly smile a real smile when he saw the coldness in her eyes. Her hostility struck him as funny. This was a result of being 24 and having experienced these glacial looks a few times before.

"We want to look around a bit. Thanks," she said.

"I'm just an ordinary guy, girls. My friends are ex-convicts, but they're nice. Forgers. High class, you know?"

"Thanks very much," said the cute one as a dismissal.

"Katerina?" said Maria, rolling the R.

Katerina was already moving past Nash's right side away from him. Nash watched her go by.

Oh, well, he thought. "Some other time ladies." It did not pay to drag these things out. Bad for the ego and bad for the reputation.

He went to the john before returning to Flannery and Herbie, saying hello and having brief conversations with half a dozen people on the way there and back. When he finally slid through the last knot of people, he was surprised to find Flannery and Herbie entertaining the three girls.

"Nash, it was kind of you to leave so much money on the bar," said Herbie.

Nash looked at the prettiest girl, who was actually beautiful, but sullen. There was a slight Eurasian cast to her face and in the shape of her dark eyes.

"Thanks for the drink," she said deadpan. She was holding a Coke.

"We wanted to meet your friends, the forgers," said Maria cheerfully. The third girl giggled. "And I knew I'd seen this guy somewhere before." Maria indicated Flannery. "He used to come in the store."

Nash let Flannery and Herbie tease the girls and make the funny remarks. Maria, who had a lot of personality, could have held up the girls' side by herself. But the giggling one helped a lot because her laughter encouraged Nash's companions. After a few minutes, Nash excused himself and went to the pool table in the back.

"Who's got the winners?"

4

"Gene and whoever."

"Who's after Gene?"

"You if you want," said a guy Nash did not know chalking his cue.

"Okay. I'll be over there."

He went back, but kept an eye on the pool table. When his turn came, he said to Katerina, "You want to play pool?"

She didn't, but he persuaded her, counting on the possibility that she'd be polite for brushing him off earlier and then drinking her Coke on his money. He had to teach her, of course, which gave him an easy subject for conversation. She appeared to tolerate the whole business, declining to warm up.

Nash had found that if he concentrated, he could still sometimes shoot pool for short periods as he had learned to do in two pool halls on Madison Street, one a storefront, the other attached to a second floor bowling alley. From age 15 through 18 Nash had devoted himself to learning to shoot pool because he thought it was something a man should learn. He eventually tired of the discipline necessary to be very good, but he still played for fun.

In Marty's with the adrenalin rush that came with performing for a girl, Nash sunk all the stripes but one by the end of his second turn before he noticed something surprising. His partner was trying very hard.

"C'mon, Kate, let's get this one," he said as she took aim at the nine ball lying near a side pocket.

He was just keeping up the chatter as in any sport. Leaning on his cue, he was barely paying attention to what she was doing. If the opposition let him, he'd get the nine ball the next time. But she took so long he was forced to look. She was rigid with determination, and her eyes were burning a hole in the end of her cue. The fingers of her left hand were holding the cue point too tightly, refusing to let it slide.

They were playing 8-ball in which one pair of shooters tries to sink the seven, solid colored balls while the other pair goes after the seven striped balls, leaving the 8-ball, the odd one, for last.

As he figured, she tensed up more when she finally shot and her left fingers deflected her aim. She struck the cue ball a glancing blow and it dribbled away.

"That's okay, Kate. We'll get it the next time." She did not look at him. She glowered at the pool table.

The opponent whose turn came between Nash and Katerina sank only the two ball, leaving one solid up, the five. Nash quickly dispatched the nine and the eight, ending the game. He had to do it. He wanted to get the balls back on the table.

"That was just practice, Kate. Now you and me are going to get down to business. Let me see your stick. Sometimes you need to put chalk on the end so it doesn't slide off the ball."

"I don't think that's the problem," she said testily.

"Ahh, you never know."

While a new set of opponents racked up the balls, Nash leaned over the table to take a practice shot, aiming across the short side of the table. "Come here, Kate." He made her act as his right hand, and he gave her the butt end of his cue. "Shoot it." She did. The ball came back. He set it up. "Aim with your right hand for now. Shoot it so it comes straight back." It wasn't easy because she was determined to keep from touching him, but she did it. Then he grasped the butt end of the cue along with her and slid it back and forth.

"See, you don't squeeze the end of the stick. Use your left hand as a loose gun sight or a bow, like a bow and arrow."

"He'll give you a different demonstration later, honey," said someone on the fringe.

Nash gave the man a quick, fierce look. "Hey, jagoff."

Nash sunk the twelve ball on the break, then left the ten sitting directly in front of a corner pocket at the far end of the table. On his next turn, he sunk the thirteen then hit the nine ball gently so that it rolled to the lip of a side pocket and stopped, poised to go in. "I'm getting robbed here. That shoulda dropped," he said.

Katerina eventually sank both of them. He noticed each time this seemed to satisfy something in her and she loosened her hard tension at least for a second. Once, he thought he saw a tiny smile of achievement that was very brief. But she always seemed to look at the table, never at him.

Moving both teams' targets around, Nash managed to keep the game going long enough for Katerina to sink one more ball before they lost.

"That was a good beginning you had there, Kate," he said as they maneuvered back through the crowd toward their four companions. "You're gonna be a hell of a pool player some day."

"I'm really looking forward to it," she said sarcastically.

Geez, what a ball buster, he thought, without reference to pool. Nevertheless, he had liked the way it felt when he was teaching her to shoot, and she sure was a looker.

The girls left at 10:30. The next Friday, they showed up at 9 o'clock. Herbie, who had begun drinking in the late afternoon, was already in the bag and had been wondering for an hour and a half why Nash had come back two Fridays in a row. Nash generally came back to the old neighborhood every other week.

"Look who's here," said Nash.

"Who? Oh. Hey, Sam, iz dat why you're here?"

"Yep."

"Oh, yeah? What iz dat? Dat's . . . . What izdat?"

"Interest," said Nash starting off in their direction.

This time Nash tried to monopolize the conversation in the group. He told his best stories from the news business. The news business was not regarded as being particularly glamorous then, nor did the City News Bureau pay much, but it was interesting. At first, he spoke mostly to Katerina trying to establish something. She responded by making cutting remarks to him, to each of which he would smile.

"Why are you always grinning?" she said after a while—as another putdown.

7

"I'm thinking dirty thoughts, Kate."

This earned him a disgusted grimace. He switched tactics and spoke to her sister, Soula, and her cousin, Maria, as well as Flannery and Herbie, all of whom were genuinely interested and even asked questions. Out of the corner of his eye, Nash snuck occasional looks at Katerina and saw that she really could smile at the funny parts if she thought no one was looking. He also watched Maria, who took a proprietary interest in her beautiful, but morose, cousin.

By observation, Nash deduced that when Maria stared at Katerina, it was because Katerina was staring at Nash, which was what he was working for.

"It's gonna get more and more important in this town to speak a second language, like Spanish," said Nash.

"Or Negro," interjected Herbie.

"Yeah, I understand Negro, but I don't speak it too well. You girls all speak fluent Greek, I'll bet," Nash added. It gave him an opportunity to look at all three.

"Yes." "Yes." "Yes." And he finished his survey looking in Katerina's lovely face. Caught unawares, she had, for the first time, a soft expression for him without the hint of a wisecrack. He lingered only for an extra heartbeat so as not to spook her. Then he looked at Maria and said, "Maria, where did your parents reopen their food store?"

As Maria picked up the conversation, Nash waited until Katerina was watching her cousin so he could look back at Katerina. He did it often enough to let Katerina know he was looking at her, but never for too long. She eventually looked him back.

"Wanna play pool?" he said softly while the others talked.

"No, thanks," she said in the same voice he had used, calmly, looking up at him.

"Okay," he said, and he held her eyes until she got embarrassed—plain, girlish embarrassment which Nash was very happy to see and which was even more fun than he had expected.

Maria said suddenly, "I hate to break up this party, but we gotta be home early. Katina? Soula?" The sisters nodded. Nash figured "Katina" was the short form.

Nash quickly proposed that they all stop for coffee at the White Castle on North Avenue and Central. It took considerable convincing because Maria was antsy. But Herbie was drunk and impressionable, and Flannery, who was on leave from the Army, and Soula were having a good time, so Nash put the idea over.

Walking out the door, Nash said, "Can I give you a lift there, Kate?"

"No! Why do you call me Kate?"

They were on the sidewalk. She was walking away with her sister and her cousin.

"Because it's easier for me to say."

At the White Castle, always crowded when it got late on the weekends, there was no table available for six of them, so Nash and Maria sat at a smaller one away from the others, a situation somehow arranged by Maria. She was relaxed and in a confiding mood after one and a half beers, and she told him some things about Katerina.

"Why is she always cutting me down?" Nash asked. He was curious, not overly concerned. It seemed like something that could be handled in the long run.

"Because she doesn't expect to see you again, Nash, and you keep at her. That's her way.

"You know, Sam, you're a nice guy so I'm going to tell you something. My two cousins," she pointed with her head, "only go out with Greek boys. They're from Greece only 10 years; they're from a very small village; and their parents are very strict. My parents are, too, but I was born here and I can handle them."

"So what are they doing out with us?"

"I have taken it as my job to show them the world a little bit. I could get in a whole lot of trouble because I shouldn't be here either. Katerina is 19 and Soula is 22. Katerina goes to college, but she just goes to school on the bus and comes right home. I thought they should see something. I was curious, too. So I took them to Marty's twice to see it. That could be it." She shrugged. "The only reason my cousins aren't married is their father scares even the Greek boys away so far. So you get what I'm telling you?"

Nash understood Maria meant the girls were not for him to go out with. He chuckled. "I think Sam sounds like a Greek name, don't you?"

"Yeah, you're Greek," said Maria, meaning the opposite.

The next two weeks, Nash came back and the three girls did not. Nash was working nights with Thursdays and Fridays off, living in an apartment with another City News reporter in a popular, congested neighborhood on Surf Street on the Near North Side. He resumed his former habit of visiting Marty's twice a month. He continued to think about Katerina mostly because of her looks and also because he was intrigued about what was inside her. He knew she had the guts to attend Chicago Teachers College. Maria had explained that Katerina was a tough one who chose this on her own and got her way after numerous fights with her parents who could not understand why a girl wanted to go to college.

It was six weeks before he saw them again, walking in the front door of Marty's. He had just about stopped thinking about her, having decided she was one of life's crazy events that were not to be repeated. Now here she was again. Was she looking around more boldly than usual or was he only imagining it? From across the room, her eyes scanned right past his face quickly with no sign of acknowledgement, then they came back for a second. She looked away and stopped scanning to talk nonchalantly to her sister and her cousin. The trio did not come in Nash's direction. Flannery had gone back to the Army which Nash had left not too long before. Herbie was playing pool that night.

Damn, Nash thought, considering the trio. Am I going to do this again and stick my neck out? Being a loser did not appeal to him. The girls appeared content where they were. Nash simply stared in their direction, waiting. For a long time, half a beer, he stared in vain. When he was tiring of it, Katerina's head turned in a perfectly normal manner to look around and her gaze came to his spot. He looked at her with what he considered to be no expression. She saw him looking and turned away as if she were displeased. Nash finished his beer and punched the wooden rim of the bar lightly trying to decide if he should order another. He gritted his teeth and started towards them.

His travel from the far end of the bar to the spot where he had last seen the Greek girls seemed to him to take half an hour. And the place was not that big.

Every few feet in the crush, he met an old classmate, or someone from Moore Playground, or someone he had played softball with or against, all these people jammed back to back or arm to arm with no path, and they all had spouses or girlfriends or boyfriends to introduce him to.

"Holy Cow. Sam! This is the guy, Sally, who used to bump into girls with me when we ice skated at Moore Playground. Remember that, Sam, accidently running into the girls with your arm out chest high? It was about as big a thrill as a guy could have."

Or he met a young woman. "Sam. Sam. We hear you're a news reporter now. That sounds neat. Tell us about it."

Nash did not understand. He knew a lot of people on the West Side, but some nights he came in Marty's and didn't recognize anybody except the bartenders and Flannery and Herbie. He began getting physically nervous. Trying to fend off conversations, he looked sideways to where the girls had been, and they didn't seem to be there anymore. He suddenly realized the girls might have gone out the door. They left in Maria's car. Why the hell had he waited anyway? What was the big deal?

"Hi, Sam," said Paul Lawlor easily as Nash tried to slide by. "Who's here tonight?"

"Paul....I'm trying to find a girl."

"Oh. Good luck."

Nash was already one body past him. "She used to be right there where you are."

He got to the door and the door was opening and people were coming in and they weren't there. What the hell? Should he go out on the sidewalk? Then he heard Soula giggle. Damn it, there they were to his left standing near the window at the other end of the bar. He slowed his movement and tried to slow his breathing and quell the annoying pressure in his chest. He slid over to his left and saw that the girls were being entertained by a burly, red-headed man a few years older than Nash who Nash knew was very funny. The red-head sat with his back against the bar, and the girls were ranged in front on him, Soula and Maria smiling and laughing and Katerina, the farthest away from Nash, wearing her usual stone face.

So there she was and he could get this over with. But he seemed to have come down with the Asian flu because his head was light and he couldn't get his insides to slow down; they were going too fast. There was this pressure in his chest, lung congestion? And he felt all over disordered and fearful as if something was going to fall on his head while he was feeling crummy and he couldn't get out of the way.

He didn't want to walk around behind the group and approach her because that would be too obvious to everyone and embarrass her. He found himself standing and listening to the redhead's stories and jokes and even laughing a little in the right spots. She glanced at him several times as if he were scenery and kept returning her attention to the red headed man.

Once Nash lifted his hand as a gesture showing he was about to say something, but the punch line came and laughter and the chance was lost. The red-headed man began setting up a joke that required him to ask the girls questions. "All right, Maria, you're Maria, right?"

"I'm Soula. She's Maria."

"Okay, Soula, honey. . . ." The red-headed man's question even provoked laughter, and Soula was slow to answer. There was a pause.

Nash simply wanted to know, but now he really wanted to know.

Her name had been going around in his head more than he had admitted to himself, and he had gone to all this trouble, and he had to do something soon because for some completely unrelated reason he was about to have a heart attack. At his age!

So he said over the background noise, across five feet, using Greek pronunciation, as clearly as he could:

"Katerina."

All eyes in the group turned to look at Nash including the bystanders who had been attracted by the redhead's storytelling. He saw her tense.

"Can't ya wait for the punch line, buddy?" said the red-headed man as a joke more than a rebuke.

"Sorry," Nash held up his left palm to keep the redhead out, keeping his eyes on Katerina.

"Do you want to shoot a game of pool?" he said.

This appeared to be an extremely funny question, and everyone laughed happily. Several remarks were made from the crowd. Nash did not decipher them.

She shook her head slowly, looking at him.

"I got a game coming up. It's mixed doubles like in tennis. I need a girl." (I sound so normal, he thought. Why is that?)

She looked at Maria, so Nash looked at Maria, and Maria was looking at him. What was Maria saying? Was it pity? Or, 'I told you.' Was she laughing at him?

"Hey, what the hell is this?" said the redhead. "I never heard of mixed doubles in pool games. But that's good bullshit, lad." Everyone laughed at this because it was true. When he realized what the redhead had said, Nash turned to silence him. Somebody had gotten in his line of sight. Somebody's hair. Oh. Where was she going? She was running away.

"She's going to play the game without you, pal," said the redhead to more laughter.

Nash turned quickly to his left. She was standing next to him.

"Katerina?"

She looked at his face. She looked nervous, too. Scared even. He didn't want that.

"What's the matter?" he said.

"Do you want me to play?" She really seemed to be unsure.

"Yeah. I asked you. Whadjyou say 'no' for?"

"I don't know. You are. . . . "

She was puzzled about something, and Nash was confused himself. So he just started her off in the direction of the pool table in the rear. "You better take a bodyguard, lady, judging by the look in his eye," said the redhead loudly behind them.

"Where the hell have you been?" said Nash after they had advanced a few yards in the crowd with Katerina walking directly in front of him. The question sounded harsh, but he couldn't help himself. He was just running at the mouth. "I've been practicing your damn name."

She stopped and turned full around. "You have?"

"Yeah," he smiled what felt like a silly smile. "It's hard for me to say."

"Samm,"—he thought he was going to melt; she had never said his name before—"I don't mind 'Kate.' I can get used to you saying that, Sam." She actually smiled, but he was already bowled over by the music she put in her voice for the first time.

They got embarrassed from looking at each other and she glanced over his shoulder. Nash remembered that he had ignored Maria and Soula. He turned and saw Maria on her tiptoes trying to follow them by sight. When Nash got her eye, Maria put a hand over her face and shook her head from side to side. But she was peeking out through her fingers.

1

The Chicago Chronicle

The early 1980s

"There's a bomb in the Mutual Building, and it will go off at 10:30 p.m."

"Did you put it there?"

"Yes."

"What part of the Mutual Building are you blowing up?"

"The cafeteria."

"Where's that?"

"I'm not going to tell you."

"Why are you doing this?"

"You can find that out."

"Oh, sure. But what if we don't? You want everybody to know why you did this, don't you?"

15

"Maybe. I can't talk anymore. Are you the editor?"

"Yes. Are you going to blow up the whole cafeteria or just part of it?"

"The whole thing." Click.

Georgia Krolikowski hung up next and laughed. "That was a bomb threat," she said.

"I'm glad you answered it," said Red Phelan, the night city editor. "Sound legit?"

Krolikowski shrugged. "It didn't sound like a Puerto Rican liberator if that's what you mean. But how can you tell, really? I'll call the cops."

"When can we expect this?"

"Ten-thirty in the Mutual Building. It's ten-fifteen."

Phelan made a mental note. No other action was necessary except calling the cops. Bomb threats were tiresome.

Although Georgia Krolikowski said she was the editor, she was actually a reporter for the Chicago Chronicle. Late at night, every other caller wanted to talk to "the editor" or the "city editor" or the "night editor" or the "editor-in-charge." So whoever took the call pretended to be the boss. The copy clerk on the switchboard—when he was around—was the editor, too.

Phelan, the bona fide night city editor, resumed trying to balance his personal checkbook. He was pleased he had not answered the bomb threat. The police always called back at least once to talk to whoever received the call. Often they phoned twice, and the same story had to be repeated to different sets of cops.

The routine always took longer than it should have because the average bomb threat did not make sense. So, the police couldn't understand it, and they kept asking questions trying to force some logic into it.

Phelan knew Krolikowski would handle it properly. She would be patient. Play the game out.

Scratching the side of his head with his pen, Phelan felt uneasy, unfulfilled and bored. There was no news. For a second, he wondered what the other guys were doing—the other papers. When things were popping, he could guess. But in a vacuum, trouble could occur. Somebody might jump on a silly story and make it out to be World War III.

Forcing this hint of anxiety from his mind, Phelan concentrated on his checkbook. Had to keep up with chores.

Phelan ran the city desk for the Chronicle from 4 p.m. to 11:30 p.m. When he arrived at work at 3 p.m., the first edition, the afternoon edition, was just going onto the street. Real afternoon papers no longer existed in Chicago at this time, but the three surviving morning papers were still publishing one edition for the homebound commuters.

When Phelan sat down, there were 20 to 30 stories on the Chronicle's local schedule produced or promised by the day shift or carried over from the morning editions. Four to six of these stories were usually in flux and needed to be done again with reactions, updating, correcting, addition or subtraction of detail. By the time he went home, Phelan was happy if he offered four new stories, including a couple good ones, either from the beat reporters at the end of their day or produced by the small night crew. All the stories could not fit in the paper, even allowing for the old ones that died. Some stories were almost always left out. But that was the business.

On this Monday night, Phelan had offered only one new story. The doping session at 5 p.m. when he informed the news editors what he had or expected to have was dull. The candidates in the upcoming primary election were dutifully throwing stones at each other, and the governor's opponent, Havranek, was surprisingly nearly even with the governor in the polls. That was interesting, but had already been said. The election was two months away.

Havranek had shown himself to be a clever user of the media, but he had had an off day on this particular Monday and failed to excite much interest with his white paper on reform of state insurance regulations. The story would be fairly widely used, but would not get great play, Phelan guessed. Wisecracks, vituperation, and screams over alleged scandals had played better and Phelan suspected this would not be lost on Havranek. At any rate, it was still too early for the candidates or the media to reach fever level.

The wires were dull, too, Phelan was aware. The national and foreign desks read their schedules in the doping. It was early January, and Chicago and the world were still recovering from the holidays.

By this time, the 3-star edition was nearing lockup. Phelan finished his checkbook and looked at the clock. It was 10:35. His relief, Bill Nordstrom, had arrived. Nordstrom was allowed an hour to read the papers and the latest stories about to be in print before he took over.

"Any noteworthy explosions?" Phelan asked Krolikowski.

"Nope. Want me to call?"

"No."

The police and fire radios were going, and Phelan knew he would have heard something. His reporter in police headquarters had the same radios. Phelan felt momentary sympathy for the police prowling around the Mutual Building. They knew they were being taken advantage of by some jerk, but they were probably a little nervous, too.

"A still and box alarm for an explosion at 702 N. Orleans," said a slow, clear singsong on the fire radio. No urgency. The fire alarm operator didn't know if it was true. He was just reporting a phone call received by the fire department and the sending of the troops.

"Call the Mutual Building, Georgia," said Phelan.

"That's not this one," she said. "That's a mile away, I'll bet."

The Mutual Building was on Wabash, north of the river. The address of 702 N. Orleans WAS a mile away.

"Might be an echo," said Phelan. "Just call them for the hell of it."

Explosions downtown sent sound waves rattling among the tall buildings. An explosion sometimes was reported a half mile from where it actually happened, Phelan knew. So why not a mile?

Phelan got up from his chair and walked swiftly into the photo

18

lab carrying a scrap of paper on which he had written the intersection as reported on the fire radio. Two photographers were watching a basketball game on television.

"Who's up?" said Phelan.

From a couch, photographer Tony Rago said, "Me, I guess. What is it?" Rago was not enthusiastic. News photographers rarely are. Too many false alarms.

"The fire radio has an explosion at Erie and Orleans. Take Georgia with you. It's not verified, but it's a slow night."

"Yeah, okay," said Rago with reluctance in his face and voice. He moved slowly. Rago was as good a news photographer as there was in Chicago. He liked news. He liked to take pictures. But he would not get excited until there was something to get excited about. He went without resistance because he and Phelan understood each other.

Rago knew Phelan wouldn't send him unless it had to be done—except for those times when Phelan was having a bad day and guessing wrong. That was all right, too. Everybody had bad days.

Phelan walked back into the city room, stepping into the slot of the horseshoe-shaped city desk. He asked, "What did they say at the Mutual Building?"

"No explosion there that they know of," responded Krolikowski.

"Go with Tony, Georgia. You're going to 702 N. Orleans."

Krolikowski dutifully fished in her bottom drawer for a notebook, and only half her head showed above the desk as she tried to draw Phelan out.

"You think this might be something?" she said.

She was puzzled at Phelan's great interest in a unverified report of an explosion only a few seconds old. People called up the 911 emergency number all the time to report things that never happened.

"I think there's no news," said Phelan.

Rago, carrying his gear, was leaving. Krolikowski left her seat at the outside rim of the horseshoe, took her coat off the back of her chair, and fell in behind Rago.

"Let me know on the car radio if you hear something," she said.

Krolikowski was 29 years old with medium length brown hair, good features, and a superb body. She didn't seem to give much thought to these qualities unless they were useful for getting the news.

There was no hint of charm school in her walk or the angle of her chin. But sex appeal she turned off and on like a light bulb.

Phelan punched out a call on his phone to the press room at 11th and State Streets in police headquarters. He punched only four numbers because the phone he wanted was on the Chronicle's extension. It was an in-house call to a phone 14 blocks away.

"Hold on a second," said the man at the other end. Phelan became aware that the noise out of the phone was the same as the noise from his fire radio, and he heard it in hi-fi:

"...Emergency. Give us a 2-11. Send some ambulances here. We've got a few people down. And send a flying squad. This is a building collapse with a lot of broken windows around.

"Battalion 2," said a voice with a hint of irritation, "How many ambulances did you say you wanted? And are any of those people down firemen?"

"No firemen. Send four. And get police here for traffic control."

"The police are being notified, Battalion 2. Was that an explosion?"

"Looks like it."

"Ten...Four." The response was dragged out by a man in the main fire alarm office who was always near exasperation. Phelan recognized the voice from years of listening.

("So," thought Phelan, "the Mutual Building was a crank, but this is legit.")

"I take it you heard that," said Henry Pierce, the evening police reporter, over the phone. "It ain't the Gold Coast."

"Yeah. Go to work on it, Henry."

"I am." They both hung up.

Phelan looked around for a warm body. One experienced reporter, Kemper, was sick, but Phelan had let this slip his mind for the second time of the evening, until he noticed for the second time that Kemper wasn't there.

With a sinking feeling that he quickly pushed out of mind, Phelan turned to Brian Forrest, nephew of the financial editor, master's degree in journalism, and a new reporter for the Chronicle. Forrest was sitting to Phelan's right on the rim of the horseshoe, his ears perked like a dog for a whistle.

"You know what the criss-cross is, Forrest?"

Forrest nodded yes.

"Go get it; find out what this is supposed to be, and call there."

Phelan wrote the address on a piece of paper and gave it to Forrest who hurried away. Although he was 22, Forrest could still pass for a teenager. His plastic framed eye glasses looked like something his mother had picked out for him when he was 11. He appeared well fed with baby fat collected around his ribs making a small roll at his belt line.

Phelan knew he should now tell the news editor something. It was already 10:45, only 45 minutes before deadline and past the time when the news editor liked to hear what to expect for the 4-star.

But Phelan didn't want to dope this until he had a handle on it. A small thing could be doped early. It was going inside. If he doped this now, this story would be pointed inside due to fuzziness of facts and lack of catastrophe. By the time he got enough to make it page one, it would be too late to call back the horses. ("We'll bring it out next edition.")

Phelan smelled something. So he sat.

Forrest had found the odd looking phone directory in which phone numbers were listed by address instead of by name.

"What do you want me to call now?" asked Forrest willingly.

"The address. What's listed at that address?"

"Rio Grande Lounge."

"Call 'em."

21

"The lounge?" protested Forrest. "That's the place that blew up."

"Call them anyway. If anybody answers, ask them what happened. Interview them," said Phelan, feeling silly. This was elementary, and he had already told the kid twice.

"Want me to call next door?"

"No. Call the address first."

"Why?"

Instantly, Phelan's eyes widened; his blood rushed; and his back stiffened. But he clamped down on the reaction.

"Forrest," he said in a low, hoarse voice, "Make the call. Maybe the first address we got is wrong. Maybe it really happened down the block."

He wanted to say, "Don't be so damned stupid," but he knew he couldn't talk that way to young reporters any more. They couldn't take it. Phelan was 46 and had seen many.

Forrest began punching the numbers, simultaneously shaking his head to show he was not intimidated.

"The line's busy," he said.

"Call it again!"

Phelan was trying to sort out the chatter on the police and fire radios to see if anything came over about his explosion. He wished Forrest would pick up the ball and run with it.

Phelan knew a busy signal could be caused by a down line, but it could also mean something else.

Forrest kept punching buttons rapidly, then hanging up, then trying again, and Phelan knew the busy signal persisted. He let it go on longer than necessary to break Forrest in. Krolikowski would be on the scene in half a minute because it was close by. Krolikowski and Rago would dig up any witnesses if there were any to be had.

"One-forty to city desk," said Rago's voice on the radio.

"Go ahead," said Phelan into his desk mike.

"Phelan, this is a pretty good blast. Lots of ambulances coming in here. Windows busted. Hey, I can see it now. The building is completely down!"

"Fire Department asked for four ambulances," responded Phelan.

He added, "What's the neighborhood look like?"

"Shitty. Big old buildings that might be warehouses; taverns and a hot dog stand. Closed."

"Tony, I want you to take a few pictures and head back for the 4-star. We'll try to make it. Craig will relieve you. You hear that, Craig?"

Craig Bowman, the second photographer watching the ball game, heard the conversation over a speaker in the photo lab.

"I'm going," he said into the lab mike.

"Georgia," said Phelan into his mike, "I want to hear from you by 11:05." This gave Krolikowski 15 minutes.

"Ten-four. We're getting out now."

Phelan turned to Forrest. "What are you doing?"

"The line is still busy."

"What's the number?"

Forrest recited a number ending in 7610.

Try 7611 and 7612," said Phelan.

Phelan knew that the chances that the Rio Grande Lounge had an alternate and consecutive number were miniscule. He didn't care. He got up and walked in the direction of the news desk—the desk where stories were put into the paper and taken out, where the location was decided and often the size.

Automatically, Phelan classified this as a gas explosion. No bomb would make the building collapse unless the bomb came from the Air Force. The experience of the Weather Underground in New York who blew up themselves and brought a building down he considered an abberation.

Phelan felt his adrenaline coming up and enjoyed it. The phenomenon failed him occasionally as events became repetitious. Despite the touch of excitement, he spoke to the news editor in the relaxed manner he had long practiced.

"Don, we've got what appears to be a gas explosion in a tavern on Orleans Street, and there are a number of injuries. I can't say how many. No one dead so far, but I wouldn't be surprised. The joint should have been open. Now it's completely blown away."

"Yeah?" said the news editor, Don Karpis. "How much do you have?" Karpis was interested, but not sure it was page one because nobody was dead.

"Not more than I told you," said Phelan. "I'll get a call at 11:05. With a little luck, we should be able to give you six inches for the 4-star. And Rago is coming in with pictures. He'll be a little late. My guess is the story is going to be worth page one."

Phelan knew the facts he had presented weren't worth page one, but he pushed the story anyway. Four people should not have been on that street which was not for window shoppers, and there was scant traffic. They had to come from the tavern. And if there were four...?"

"Orleans and what?" asked Karpis.

"Erie. A warehouse district."

Karpis interest fell.

"Well, maybe if we get a picture, we'll put that on one and refer to the story," said Karpis, meaning the story would be inside. The current page one picture was the President with his arm around a visiting head of state—expendable. But there was no easy, six inch story hole on page one. It would take...

"HEY! Somebody answered! There's somebody in there!"

Forrest had suddenly appeared at the news desk demonstrating, in Phelan's view, Forrest's essential qualities of ignorance and assertiveness.

"He's talking to me!" continued Forrest. Although he was the youngest person in the room, with the exception of the youngest copy clerks, Forrest stood and shouted directly at the news editor, who was sitting down. Forrest ignored Phelan, who was standing.

24

Phelan turned cold and stiff. The news editor frowned. But each was interested despite himself.

Phelan was slow to act, concentrating on controlling his annoyance and not touching Forrest. Forrest began to slide between the two men until Karpis put his hand up and stopped him.

"Thank you," said Karpis as a dismissal. Then, to Phelan, "What is he talking about?"

"He says he's stuck." Forrest mucked on. "It's a great story, but we better help him." Forrest looked from one man to the other, amazed that they weren't catching on.

Phelan at length seized on a non-violent approach and spoke.

"Forrest, go right back there and interview the guy. Right now. You'll be famous."

"OK," said Forrest, backing away, his teeth shining. "But we better do something."

"We will," assured Phelan with a profound nod of his head. Turning to the news editor, he said, "You heard him. It's news to me, too. I hope he's not talking to someone in Skokie. I better go back." Phelan started walking away, then turned.

"If it's true, make it 9 inches."

"Could be a hell of a story," said Karpis across 15 feet.

"A prize-winner," responded Phelan sarcastically.

Karpis laughed. He assigned the story, mentally, to run over the roof, that is, across the top of page one over the main headline and story. It would be the number two story. The lead story just below it with the giant headline was a predictable but "significant" piece about violence in Lebanon. The indictment of two city inspectors would be pushed inside. But Karpis was leery so he did not change page one immediately.

Phelan took the long way back to the city desk, past the water fountain; took a drink, straightened up and walked into the horseshoe. He was six feet tall, even, but his stocky build and wide-set legs made him look a little shorter.

Forrest was talking on the phone and scribbling too fast. Phelan thought Forrest wouldn't be able to read it.

"This is legit," said the only other person on the rim, Paul Youngman, 58, rewriteman. Often depressed. Sometimes funny. Phelan had been saving him to write the blast story.

"I listened on the phone when this boy was giving you the happy news," said Youngman.

"How do you know it's legit?" asked Phelan.

"The guy on the phone is coughing and panicky. Says he's in the basement. Who the hell else could it be? You told Forrest to call there."

"Do you know this guy's whereabouts so we can tell the Fire Department?"

"Yes. I just did that."

"I'm counting on you that somebody is in there, Paul; otherwise we will be embarassed."

"We could wait a couple days 'till they dig him out, and then say we knew it all the time."

Phelan gave up.

"All right.....COPY!" he shouted, turning away from Youngman.

He quickly turned back.

"Paul, this guy's not hiding from the noise, is he?"

"No," said Youngman.

For an instant, Phelan had a picture of a man in a building near the explosion who thought he was in mortal danger and was cowering in the basement. Youngman's attitude convinced Phelan otherwise.

"Hey, you," said Phelan to the approaching copy clerk. "You know where Gentile's desk is at?"

The copy boy nodded.

"Go in his top, left hand drawer and get out his tape recorder and a couple tapes and bring them to me. And fish around in there for a black wire thing with a rubber suction cup attached. It's a micro-phone."

As the copy clerk left, Phelan glanced at Forrest who was agitated and couldn't sit still, even bent over. Forrest was talking loud enough for Phelan to hear, but the conversation was not immediately decipherable, and Phelan deliberately made no effort. He was keeping his distance. ("Have to do something about that guy," he thought.) He meant Forrest.

Suddenly, he looked at the clock. Eleven-oh-seven. Where was Krolikowski?

The copy boy came back with the items and dumped them on Phelan's desk. Phelan stepped over to an empty desk on the rim and took the phone off its hook. He attached the suction cup mike to the earpiece; plugged in the mike; stuck a tape in; and hit "record." He punched the line on which Forrest was talking.

This was electronic eavesdropping and against the law. But Phelan didn't think it would become a federal case.

Phelan wondered momentarily what was on the tape that was being erased and recorded over. Then he dismissed the thought.

"Phelan! We have to help this guy," whined Forrest loudly. "Phelan!"

Phelan looked at him out of the corner of his eye, then rose and stood right in front of him, forcing Forrest to look up.

"Yes, Forrest, we do," said Phelan calmly. "Put the phone down a second."

"I can't. We should help him get out. He's in real trouble. Did you call the Fire Department?"

"Put the phone down, Forrest. That's an order. And cup the mouthpiece." Phelan figured he hadn't said, "That's an order," in 14 years on the desk. Ridiculous.

Forrest did as he was told, but stiffly, and said, "Let me call the Fire Department."

"We already did that," said Phelan slowly. "Now listen. Whoever this guy is you're talking to..."

"His name is Earl McCoy."

"Well, that's good. You got his name. Now shut up for a second. Whoever this guy is, he seems to be in real trouble."

"HE IS! You talk to him." Forrest held out the phone.

"NO. And I told you to cup that." Then Phelan started to talk faster, but not much. He suddenly felt deadline pressure.

"Keeping it simple, Forrest, this guy's in trouble, but you are not. And you will never get him out. The firemen will, if anybody. You are just talking to him. So be decent and be calm. Relax. Now where is he?"

"He's in the basement!!"

"Be calm when you're talking to me, too. Calm. Where in the basement?"

"In the back. In a corner. He thinks it's the northeast corner."

"That's what I told the Fire Department," Youngman offered.

Phelan glanced at Youngman, then turned and shouted to the switchboard. "You heard from Georgia?"

"She's on zero."

"Well you gotta fuckin' tell me!"

"I shouted it out," said the copy boy defensively.

Phelan turned to Youngman. "Paul..."

"I'll take her," said Youngman, putting on his headset.

Phelan felt better for a second. He turned and looked into the crazed eyes of Forrest, whose face was red.

"Aw shit," said Phelan abruptly. "Paul, you take the victim."

Youngman shrugged and put Krolikowski on hold. Then he punched the victim's line. Forrest's jaw dropped.

"Yeah, Paul," said Phelan to himself. "That's right. Forrest...."

"Hey, what the hell," sputtered Forrest.

"Forrest, you're going to write a story. Just cool it. Talk to... Hang up on that McCoy character. Youngman has him. Now you talk to Georgia. Take perfectly legible notes on your typewriter so I can read 'em. But before you do that, tell me quickly what you know about this guy's problem. Make it simple."

"He's in pain. There's something on his lef—the right leg. He says he's sitting on the floor, and he thinks the ceiling is in front of him."

"What does that mean? 'The ceiling is in front of him.'"

"I don't know. That's what he said. He said he can touch it but can't see it. It's dark."

Phelan guessed that the first floor had collapsed into the basement everywhere except in McCoy's corner. There, the floor may have formed a lean-to, trapping McCoy, and the basement ceiling was now an angular wall in front of him.

He paused for only a second, then said:

"Okay, Forrest, take the story from Georgia. You're gonna write it, so get it straight."

As Forrest punched Georgia's line, Phelan imagined that she would be angry, but he dismissed that thought in favor of some others. The time had come to weigh the situation, to judge it as he was paid to do.

Phelan did not like this situation. Too much emotion. He preferred to report events, not to be involved in them. He was forced to surrender his best rewriteman (only one actually) to talk to the poor soul in the basement. Wouldn't be fair to have Mr. McCoy spend his possible last moments talking to a jackass like Forrest. The story Forrest would produce would be poorly written, perhaps awful, but that could not be helped.

Nevertheless, the final rewrite for the 5-star, the last edition, would make great reading and look good if Phelan could avoid anything suggesting exploitation of the victim. This was touchy, he knew well.

He got up and walked quickly toward the news desk.

Phelan did not think beyond "touchy," but for him this meant problems of good taste, gruesomeness, ethics, lawsuits, even McCoy's life. It was a long way from the 1920's when anything went in the news business.

"Don, it's true."

"You sure?" said Karpis.

"Yeah. Youngman's talking to him now."

"OK, if Youngman believes it. I'm putting it over the roof. You gotta give me 10 inches."

"We will. We're gonna be late, and the story will not sing, but the facts will carry it. We'll make it."

"You better move. It's your deadline right now. This guy gonna die?"

"I don't know."

Karpis shook his head; then he threw the design of the new page one into his "out" tray. He had been holding it up.

Phelan walked quickly back into the horseshoe, feeling his engine revving up to high gear. This really had to move now. No jacking around.

"Georgia wants you," said Forrest.

"You got everything?"

"No."

"Well, get it all before I talk to her. Fast."

"Phelan?" It was Youngman.

"Damn! Yes, Paul."

Phelan was looking at the clock rather than Youngman. He had to look at the clock a long time to figure out what time it was. He finally deduced it was 11:21, nine minutes before the formal deadline.

"Phelan, get ready. Take it easy. This guy wants a priest."

"Son of a bitch!" Phelan hit himself in the forehead with the heel of his right hand.

"Take it easy, Phelan."

"Paul, we'll do it. We'll do it," said Phelan, controlling himself.

"CALL THE CATHEDRAL!" he shouted to the switchboard. "Keep ringing until somebody answers. Then I want 'em."

Phelan looked at Forrest who was still taking notes. ("Never make it," he thought.)

30

"You ought to listen to this guy, Phelan. I don't know how much longer he's gonna talk," said Youngman. "Just pick up five."

"Yeah, you're right. All right." Phelan was becoming resigned to blowing the story. "But you talk to him, Paul; I'm just gonna listen."

Phelan punched five and picked up his phone. He heard Youngman say:

"We are getting a priest, Mr. McCoy."

Then came another voice which sounded older than Youngman's.

"You guys are gonna hep me nowuh, aintcha? Ma sister...she knows who ta cawll...."

Phelan expected background noise, but there wasn't any.

"Ma sister...You git her...."

"We're getting a priest from right near here," said Youngman, "then we'll call your sister."

Phelan hung up, then turned and whispered to Youngman.

"That guy's a hillbilly. What's he want a priest for?"

A Baptist minister would be more like it, Phelan thought. Youngman shrugged.

Forrest put his phone down, and Phelan's mind leaped.

"Gimme those notes. Now. Now."

Forrest handed over the piece of paper from his typewriter, but Phelan gave it right back.

"Forget it. Start writing. On the computer. Slug it BLAST. The lead says 'This many people were killed or injured Monday night in an explosion at thus and so which rocked the neighborhood.'"

"I want the survivor in the second graph. 'Only minutes after the blast, The Chronicle phoned the place, and....' One more graph on him, then run out Georgia's stuff. Put quotes from McCoy on the bottom. Ten inches total. Do your best."

Forrest scribbled as fast as he could on a piece of paper to re-member what Phelan said. Then he began typing on his computer terminal. As he typed, the words appeared on the screen.

"Any byline?" said Forrest as an aside. He kept typing.

"Fuck the bylines," said Phelan.

Phelan picked up his phone and punched one. He meant to hit zero, but didn't notice.

"Georgia...."

"Excuse me? This is Father Givens at Holy Name."

"What? Oh, yeah. Father, we wake you up? I'm sorry. Here's the reason. We have a man on the phone here who is trapped in a collapsed building and in a desperate situation. He wants to talk to a priest. The only way you can do that is to come to our city room. Right now. That's it."

"Does he want to go to confession?"

"I don't have the faintest, Father. As you can imagine, things are pretty hairy here. The guy's life is in danger. He wants a priest. So I called you. Wanna know where we're at?"

"Well. All right. Give me directions."

"Fifth floor. Chronicle Building. On Michigan Avenue south of the river."

"I know where that is. Maybe I should go to where this man is?"

"Not a chance, Father. He's under a ton of junk and you can't get to him. We've got him on the phone, amazing as it seems. You coming?"

"Yes."

"Thanks. I'll see you." Phelan punched zero.

"Georgia?"

"Phelan, what the hell! Don't you want this story? Trying to talk to you is..."

"Shut up, Georgia. Have a heart. Forrest fill you in?"

"Yes. I don't think I believe it."

"Who cares? Now shut up a second and let me think."

Phelan sat back and rested the phone on the desk, still holding it. He let his eyes go out of focus so he wasn't looking at anything. He mentally checked his insides. No pain. No indigestion. Breathing all right.

He enjoyed the momentary relaxation. He was actually resting. He was high.

The sensation of being high on excitement made him think of his friend, Nash. Some of Phelan's colleagues, after a certain number of years and too many deadlines, concluded that the news gathering part of the business, particularly chasing spot news on deadline, was for kids. Nash was one who professed to think that way. "If you're 40 years old and you're not at least city editor or some kind of privileged reporter above the pack, you should have the sense to go on the copy desk or find a different line of work," Nash liked to say. Phelan wasn't city editor and he was never going to be a privileged reporter, but he still, once in a while, enjoyed the game. He felt sorry for Nash who was approaching his own, self-imposed deadline, the age of 40.

After 10 seconds, Phelan allowed himself to return to the business part of his brain and found it cluttered. He let it settle like snow in a paperweight.

Phelan did not know what he was going to do next, but he wasn't worried. As soon as he started talking, it would come out. Another two seconds.

"All right, Georgia. The firemen know our situation here?"

"Yeah, the chief told me. I thought you guys had flipped. But there is one missing it turns out. The owner, before they hauled him away, said everybody, him and three customers, cleared out when they smelled gas, but it blew right away. These four got hit with airborne stuff, but the firemen said they're gonna live. They forgot the sweepup guy in the basement."

"How much is standing?"

"Damn little. But there's a piece of wall in one corner. You know, a little on the side and a little on the back, and they meet. Not more than 15 feet altogether," she said.

"All right, you're doing a good job, Georgia. Keep it up. I want you to go in the alley and see if there's a line running from the back of that wall to the telephone pole."

"Of course there will be. There has to be."

"I know, but I want you to look for it. Have Craig take a picture of it."

"Okay, if they'll let me back there. They're sensitive about that. I think they're sending for a crane, maybe two."

"You're in for a long night there."

"That's okay. This is a hell of a story for me. Not bad at your end either."

"I don't know about that. I'll talk to you."

"Okay," she said with a cheerful lilt. "Hey, wait, Phelan. Everybody knows. They'll be calling you."

"Fuck 'em," said Phelan.

"Hah, hah," said Krolikowski.

They both hung up.

Phelan looked at the clock again, and this time he grasped it immediately. Eleven-forty-five, 15 minutes past formal deadline. He knew he was going to push things pretty far. After Forrest's story cleared the city desk, it would be up to the copy editors, the composing room printers, the makeup editors, and the pressmen to do their jobs in less time than normally allotted.

This put a lot of pressure on all of them, but Phelan thought that sharing the pressure was only fair. The real hangup would be the computerized typesetting machines. The people could speed up, but the machines had only two speeds—normal and slow. They were slow when a lot of stories had to be done at once. Phelan hoped the national and foreign wires were still dull so that he had little competition for the attention of the computer.

The switchboard sang out: "Fire Department on four."

Phelan answered.

"This is Chief Jorczak. We understand you are in contact with a man who may be inside the restaurant that collapsed."

"Yes, chief. This is the night city editor. Our best information is that he is at the rear of the building on the north end, east corner. His right leg is stuck and apparently he can't free it. He says the ceiling is in front of him, which I take to mean it has fallen down near him, but not on him."

"What's on his leg?"

"He doesn't know, chief. There's no light. By the way, that's a tavern, if it makes any difference."

"OK, a tavern. You're sure he's in there, I suppose."

"He's there, chief. He didn't call us. We called him. What's it look like?"

"Part of the rear wall is standing, but the rest of the building has come down. The first floor appears to run down hill from the rear. He's probably under that. It all depends on his condition. We have to move slowly so as not to knock the whole works down on top of him. And it might happen anyway. You will use common sense, of course, and just tell him we're getting him out, but it will take a little while. We've had the gas turned off, and the fire is out."

"How bad a fire?"

"Minor. We used a hand pump. He has a chance. We'll get him out. I may have one of my men call you back. If you learn more, pass it along. We may want to keep a direct line open to you later." Click.

Putting down the phone, Phelan glanced at Forrest and saw that he was struggling. Fingers not moving. Face screwed up. About as expected.

"Move, Forrest. Type anything."

Phelan turned to Youngman.

"Paul?"

"Yeah?"

"What's the latest?"

"He hasn't said anything for a minute or two as far as I can tell. He was fading before that and starting to talk jibberish."

"Ask him a question."

"I asked him lots of questions, Phelan. He's not talking. May be unconscious."

"Maybe he dropped the phone. Where'd he get it anyway?"

"I don't know. Maybe he did drop it, but I didn't hear it."

"Can we shout at him and get him interested? Don't want him to go into shock or something."

"Maybe we should. But if it was me, I'd wish to hell you'd leave me alone."

"We can't do that, Paul. Perk him up a little. Get him talking."

"You're the boss, Phelan. You do it."

"Paul!" But Phelan couldn't think of anything else to say. He and Youngman stared at each other.

"Paul, you look at Forrest's story when he's done, which better be in three minutes. Make sure it's okay and move it. Tell Karpis when it's gone."

"What are you going to do?" asked Youngman.

"Just put your headset down."

Youngman took his headset off very slowly, like an old man.

"Don't blow the connection," he said.

Then Youngman swiveled his chair, poked Forrest, who sat next to him, and motioned impatiently with his hand, signifying, "Come on. Come on."

Phelan punched the line McCoy was on; picked up his own receiver with his left hand and with his right hand reached over and unplugged Youngman's headset so there would be no extra noise on the line. Phelan did not put the receiver to his ear, but held it away, resting his left elbow on the desk. He felt like he was about to jump into a cold swimming pool.

Then he moved.

"Hey, aaaaaaaa, McCoy?" he said into the voice piece.

Nothing. Faint background noise.

"McCoy, this is the Chronicle; the guys you were talking to. Speak up. We need to know your condition. What's happening?"

Phelan had an urge to quit, to step away. ("Leave it alone," he thought. "Take care of the story.")

Phelan took the phone from his ear and stared at the wall 20 feet beyond him. For a moment or two. Then he decided to just do the right thing. He put McCoy on "hold," something he would never allow anyone else to do. He walked to the switchboard and picked up the phone there—it was just 15 feet to his right outside the horseshoe. He punched McCoy's button and faced away from everyone in the room.

"McCoy!" he shouted. "McCoy! Answer!" in his best sergeant's voice.

Heads popped up around the room. The city desk was getting carried away again. Always rowdy there. No control.

"McCoy, the priest is gonna be here soon. Now get your ear on this phone and start talking. Wake up! What do you want me to tell your sister! Hear that? Your sister! Wake up!"

Then Phelan put two fingers of his right hand into his mouth and whistled as loud as he could into the phone. He was a good whistler. He whistled the standard, three-note, "come-here-doggie" whistle over and over. He thought the high pitched whistle might carry through the receiver even if McCoy wasn't holding it.

Then he filled his lungs, suppressed a feeling of being foolish and the natural fear of the eyes at his back, and shouted as loud as he could into the phone:

"MC COYYY!"

Someone tapped him on the back. He listened for a human sound in the receiver; found none; and turned around. A copy boy was behind him.

"Mr. Karpis told me to tell you to stop that," the copy boy said. "That's all he said."

"It's OK," responded Phelan.

Phelan made a small bow toward Karpis and waved, then walked back to the city desk.

"It's gone," said Youngman.

Phelan felt guilty. He had never before sent a page one story to the copy desk without reading it himself. So he read it now in the computer. Halfway through, he had a disquieting thought.

"Paul, call 2080. Give them the number that Forrest called. The one we got through on, not the one in the phone book. I just want to verify it. We've got the firemen risking their limbs on the assumption that this number is the Rio Grande Lounge. If it is, fine. If not, I've shot myself in the foot. I should have double checked this sooner. The phone number and the address have to match."

Phelan thought Youngman might fight. But Youngman looked abruptly worried himself and obeyed right away.

In Chicago, 2080 were the last four digits of a phone number to call the telephone company's name and address service, the reverse of directory assistance. Given a local phone number, the operator at 2080 would supply the name and address that went with the phone number, as long as the customer had not requested anonymity. Reporters used 2080 frequently.*

"City News is on one and the Ledger is on four," sang out the copy boy on the switchboard.

"Tell them, 'No comment. Too busy,'" said Phelan. "Any news organization that calls, tell them the same thing."

Phelan picked up his phone and dialed zero for the company operator. "Lobby guard," he said when she answered.

"Lobby," answered the guard momentarily.

"This is Red Phelan on the city desk. There is some possibility that TV crews and reporters of various types may want to come up to the newsroom tonight. Tell them all we're sorry, but something will be arranged for tomorrow. Be polite, but don't let anybody in. There are no problems up here. You have nothing to worry about. I'm just trying to avoid a nuisance."

"Okay, sir. What is your name again?"

"Phelan, night city editor. P-H-E-L-A-N."

"Your first name?"

"Red."

Phelan's thinning, curly hair was the color of copper wire with gray mixed in. As a boy he had been a carrot-top. His first name was Fergus.

---

*The number has since been changed to 796-9600.

"Okay, Mr. Phelan."

"But if a priest comes, let him up."

"A priest. Yes, sir."

Phelan called city editor Aaron Solomon at home. Solomon was still up. Phelan gave him a brief rundown.

"I want the phone line to that tavern kept open all night, if necessary," said Solomon, "until they find this guy. And I want somebody listening to it all night. I want a reporter and photographer to stay at the scene all night."

"Right. That's what we planned on." The orders were elementary, but Phelan understood the city editor had to give some orders just as he would have done in Solomon's place. Phelan relayed the official instructions to Nordstrom who was waiting to take over. It was past time.

"It's all right, Red. They match," said Youngman, referring to the phone number and the address.

"Thanks, Paul," said Phelan.

The priest came three minutes later, talked quietly on the phone for a while to McCoy; heard nothing; blessed the air near the receiver; then said he was going to the scene.

Phelan had discreetly turned off the tape recorder and unplugged the microphone when the priest picked up the phone.

In the last edition, Youngman subbed out Forrest's crude story. He added a lot from Krolikowski's second and third calls and from Henry Pierce in police headquarters. Pierce, who had the names, ages, and addresses of the victims, was irate that nobody would talk to him earlier.

At 5 a.m., firemen worked their way down to McCoy's cage and took out his body. A doctor pronounced him dead on the scene. The priest administered last rites. Phelan, who had gone to the scene after leaving the office, watched with Krolikowski as the TV lights came on and the electronic flashes popped.

"Shit," said Phelan. Then he touched Krolikowski and added,

"If you're going back to the office, Georgia, tell them to hang up the phone."

Krolikowski turned and smiled on Phelan in a way, he was surprised to see, that was meant to comfort him.

McCoy was pronounced dead a second time in a hospital emergency room. But all the Chicago papers were in the trucks or on the street with McCoy still alive. There was no edition until 10 hours later. Radio and TV had the story for a while, and they led with what the papers lacked, the fatal outcome.

After sunup, a man from the phone company climbed down a ladder into the hole. The phone sat on a chair against the back wall of the basement. The receiver was on the floor. Firemen had hosed the blood away. The man from the phone company, standing in the wreckage, hung up the receiver, dialed his office, and someone answered.

Phelan had gotten home at 6 a.m. He had dug a six-pack out of his refrigerator and gone down to his basement. At 7:30 a.m. his wife came down while the kids were eating breakfast.

"I heard about it on the radio," she said. "He's dead."

"Yeah, I know. If the office calls, tell them I'm asleep. They'll probably want to know why we had such a fucked up story in the 4-star."

"So what? Red, honey, you know that each shift always claims that the other shifts are screwed up."

"Yeah," said Phelan. "But one of us is right." He laughed.

She rubbed his head.

2

Nash

Sam Nash, a veteran reporter for the Chicago Chronicle, woke up with his clothes on. He turned off the alarm on the floor and laid back on the couch feeling tension in the back of his neck; his scalp was crawling, and the long muscles in his arms and legs were rigid. He felt very afraid, but he didn't know why. He decided he'd better think about it. He closed his eyes.

He drank too much the night before, but he was all by himself, so he probably had not done anything ridiculous. Perhaps he had screwed up at work; but there was nothing recent that he could think of.

He had not fought with his wife because he hadn't seen her in more than a week. The crisis in the bills came next week, not this week. And the kids were okay, he assumed. He hadn't seen them in more than a week either, which made him feel guilty. Nash had entertained the kids every weekend, almost, in the two and a half months since he and his wife had separated. Since he was nearly single, he should at least have a weekend to himself once in a while, he thought.

So, what, he wondered, was he afraid of? That the Chronicle was going to fold and he'd have to find a job? He had feared that for years, he knew, and that fear had no sting anymore. It looked like the Chronicle was holding up better than he was. The paper seemed to be a survivor, imperfect but permanent. Then maybe he was afraid just to get up. That was very possible. Maybe he should take a day off, he thought. The rest would relax him. Sleep rejuvenated him. He turned over on his side to face the back of the couch, and he wished he had a blanket.

Thirty seconds later, Nash began to slide his rear end off the couch, then his legs, until gravity caused him to fall on the floor. His left arm remained on the couch for support. From this sitting position, he slowly got onto his knees and put his face in the center cushion, vaguely hoping to shut out all sensations.

He felt ill and miserable and fearful. In his malaise, his posture reminded him of when he was a little boy kneeling at his bedside saying his morning prayers.

"Okay," he thought, "God, help me to go to work and stop being afraid, at least for a while, and become rich and famous or at least to keep my job or to find a better one." Some other, more personal things, Nash could not mention to God.

He stayed in place for a minute, trying to go to sleep. In the back of his mind, an image began to form of Sam Nash running for the El train because he was late. Part of him knew he was wasting time, and this gradual awareness ruined his efforts at sleeping. He staggered to his feet and the battle was decided.

Nash saw that the quart of whiskey on the end table was not capped which struck him as wasteful. He could not at the moment figure out what evaporated from whiskey, but he was sure it was the best part. He capped it and wondered where the glass was. Stepping back, he found it on the floor next to a wet spot on the rug.

When he bent down to pick it up, his head hurt so bad that he stumbled a little sideways and said, "Ow!" Elevating his head, he did a knee bend to pick up the glass. The spot on the rug smelled of stale whiskey, but the generic cola he mixed it with would have worse long term effects, he imagined. Probably bring bugs.

He carried the glass and bottle to the kitchen; put the glass in the sink with some other dirty dishes and the bottle in the cabinet over the sink. Nash always cleaned up his drinking apparatus as soon as he woke, just from habit, although he did not live with children any more.

In the shower, Nash wondered what the hell was making him scared again. He was glad he had not surrendered to the urge to take a day off. Once he started giving into that urge, he would open a gate he didn't want opened.

"What a relief it must be to be dead," he thought. He stood with the hot shower spray on the back of his neck.

When he left his basement apartment, Nash was dressed in the business attire common to male newspaper reporters and office machine repairmen: "no-iron" shirt and tie, cheap sportcoat over cheap slacks, but tasteful, solid colors, green over brown, and his trenchcoat with the winter lining of synthetic fuzzy stuff. He also wore boots to cope with the snow. It had not snowed during the night, and the sidewalk in front of his building was clear, but there had been so many small snowfalls that some of the burghers of the Jefferson Park neighborhood had grown weary already of shoveling it. Packed snow covered several sidewalks, and there was mush and ice in the gutters mixed with road salt.

From the three-flat where he lived in the basement apartment, it was only two blocks to the busy Jefferson Park El and bus terminal.

When Nash and his wife had separated, he tried to maintain some sameness in his life. He took an apartment less than two miles from his family on the Northwest Side and a short walk from the terminal that he had formerly reached by bus each morning. He still took the same El line to and from work.

Before he entered the tunnel leading to the fare booths and the trains, Nash put a quarter in the Chronicle's newspaper box at the entrance and took out a paper.

The top story on the front page was, "Man trapped in tavern blast cries for help." The story ran the width of the page. Below it was the Chronicle's official "line story," the one the editors supposedly deemed most important.

New Beirut raid
charges escalate

In larger letters, this ran across four columns of the six column front page. This main headline was almost halfway down the page, so that to read the story, Nash would have had to turn the paper over.

He checked the headlines in the windows of the Daily Ledger and the Morning Post to see what they had. The Post said:

Trapped tavern keep
prays to be rescued

This headline, which had no competition on the Post's front page, ran over a large picture of what seemed to be the scene of the explosion.

Across the top of the Ledger, the headline said:

Study raps property tax reform plan

The Ledger's official line story was broadcast in taller and wider type just above the middle of the page. Nash could not decipher it. The bottom of the letters fell below the window in the newspaper box. But Nash knew it would be some Washington speech or the wholesale price index.

He walked into the terminal to catch his train for downtown.

As he did every other morning, Nash rushed for one of the single seats at the end of each car. He had difficulty reading the Chronicle in a double seat because he had to jostle his neighbor to turn the pages. The single seats were taken, so he settled for the window half of a double seat. He nestled down and shrunk inside his clothes a bit to create some inner air space and keep warm.

He left his newspaper on his lap unopened for a few minutes. When the El pulled out and ran beneath the overpasses of the Kennedy Expressway, he looked at the dirty walls. In between overpasses, he looked at the embankments of the Kennedy, the sunken expressway which carried the El in its median. Where the snow had melted, bottles, cans, papers, and other garbage were sometimes exposed, although the surface was usually just dead grass.

He looked at the low, concrete walls separating the expressway from the right-of-way for the El tracks and saw the many flaws, chips, cracks and scaling from the weather. But they were still rock solid and would stop any car, probably any truck.

Everything Nash saw out his window was strange and new and sharply etched, like scenery on a new planet.

That's how he knew he had a bad hangover.

Nash had no intention of reading the Chronicle's line story, "New Beirut Raid//Charges Escalate," unless the El broke down in a tunnel and he was trapped with nothing to do for hours. He knew the Chronicle was imitating the Ledger by stressing a story of international significance, or one that looked that way, even when a great local story was available.

The tavern blast story, under the bylines of Georgia Krolikowski and Brian Forrest, started out:

> *"One man was trapped in the basement of a collapsed building in the downtown area Monday night after a massive explosion which brought down the building and injured four other persons.*
>
> *"A Chronicle reporter reached the trapped man by*

phone only minutes after the two-story, brick building with a tavern on the first floor was ripped by the explosion.

" 'Tell them to get me out of here,' said the victim. The victim in the basement said one of his legs was trapped under debris, and he was bleeding.

"The other four injured persons were believed to be the tavern owner and three customers who were struck by flying objects after they ran from the tavern just before the explosion.

"Fire officials said they suspected a natural gas leak as the cause of the blast.

"The man who was trapped. . . . "

The story excited Nash. It was only fair that a spectacular spot news story like this one should fall to his paper, he felt. In the competition to investigate public officials and private ripoff artists which had come to dominate the news, the Chronicle always finished third. It did not have the money and could not spare the staff.

Nash also liked how the Chronicle got it. A reporter had called up the building even though it had collapsed. Nash knew his old friend and mentor, Red Phelan, had a hand in this.

Nash daydreamed about outlandish telephone happenings that he remembered. One of his favorites was the coup pulled off by Don Harris of WGN TV and radio in 1970. A guy with a gun had surprised the president of a South Chicago Heights bank at home, taken his keys, and opened up the bank. The bank president untied himself and called the cops, and Harris heard the alert on a police scanner. Harris phoned the bank.

"I'm the so-called bank robber, I guess," said the dejected voice that answered. Realizing that his plan had fallen apart, the robber had then threatened to shoot himself, but reporter Harris had argued with him while recording the conversation. Near the end of the tape, another voice from a distance broke in.

"All right, get 'em up! Hold it right there! Freeze! Get your hands up, up, UP! Put it down! Put it down!"

Nash would never forget the animalistic authority in that loud, repititious voice. The cop was telling the robber to take the gun away from his own head.

The incident was still vivid in Nash's mind because he had been fairly new then. He had made WGN play the tape for him over and over so he could get the story exactly right. What a wonderful way to make a living, he thought at the time.

This guy in the basement was even better. What a story! Nash wondered what had happened to him. The story left him in the basement.

Before the train got to Clark Street, Nash read as much of the local news as he could then left the paper neatly on the seat when he got up to leave. Maybe if somebody picked up the Chronicle on the train, they would like it and buy it in the future, he thought. The Chronicle, like the Post and the Ledger, could never stop, even for a day, searching for new readers because current readers were always dying or moving.

The walk up the stairs to Clark and Lake Streets made Nash breathless. He inhaled air deeply as he walked along with the rest of the rush hour crowd. He looked in the window of a rental car office to see if the pumping blood made his face red, but he could not see himself.

By the time he got near the Chronicle Building on the west side of Michigan Avenue south of the Chicago River, his breathing was normal, and he began to feel as if he might survive this hangover, too. His glands and organs responded to the daily routine; the vitamin capsules he took at home were being absorbed. Something resembling his proper chemical balance was being restored. He was hungry.

The Chronicle Building was five stories high and did not look as if it would survive long against the encroachment of skyscrapers in the neighborhood. Illinois Center, a chain of steel and glass high rises across the street on the east side of Michigan Avenue had blocked out the light of the sun rising over Lake Michigan. On the west side of Michigan Avenue stood a few old skyscrapers that would probably survive as landmarks. But the smaller buildings gave off silent suggestions that their time was past.

"Two chocolate donuts and a large coffee."

The first floor sandwich shop was just a small room with a line of people moving through. Nash paid and would eat at his desk.

At 9:10, he approached the city desk on the 5th floor after leaving his coat and hat in the locker room.

"Nash here," he said. Albert Miller, the day city editor, sat in the same slot of the horseshoe where Phelan sat at night.

"You look like hell, Sam," said a voice from the rim. This was assistant city editor Bob Wolfram. "No offense. You just look like you had a bad night." Wolfram smiled.

"Happens to the best of us, Bob."

"Yeah, and to you, too, Nash," said a man on the other side of the rim, one of the rewritemen who chuckled at his own joke.

Changing the subject, Nash said, "Hey, how'd they get through to that tavern last night? Damn, I loved that story."

"The number in the criss cross was 7610 and they called 7611," said Miller as he poured boiling water into a cup containing a tea bag. Miller had his own electric tea pot on his desk. A formal man, he always sat up straight with the sleeves of his long-sleeved blue shirt rolled up to avoid soiling them with ink from the newspapers.

"It appears the owner is a bookie and he needed two lines. Business was good. He kept his books in the basement where he had an extra phone. The janitor just happened to be next to it. He went down there to get something a moment before it blew. He sometimes lived there."

"How is he?" Nash could not endure the sound of a radio in the morning.

"He's dead. He bled to death," said Miller.

"No shit. It would have been better if he lived, if we saved his life."

Miller shrugged. He didn't mind talking about it once or twice because he was fascinated by the story, too. But he was tired of having the same conversation with every reporter who checked in.

"Listen, what are you doing today, Sam?" said Miller. There were five or six piles of paper on his desk, each a collection of memos, announcements, news releases, letters, wire service copy, sorted according to his own system. He also had two lists of events.

"Nothing urgent as yet," said Nash. "Solomon wants to see me about something. He told me yesterday. But I don't know what it is."

"I know about that. What else?"

"I suppose I could start that Sunday story they asked for on the proliferation of animal protection groups. The Sunday people want me to find an 'Adopt a Mouse' program or something similar."

"That's cute. First give me about six inches on this power outage on the IC."

"Sure." Nash took the scrap of City News Bureau copy from Miller. Miller returned to his preoccupations.

"An obit for you," said Wolfram who leaned across the desk and handed Nash a note with a name and phone number on it. Nash stepped outside the slot and around the rim to talk to Wolfram.

"So what are we doing today with the guy in the basement?"

Nash liked Wolfram because Wolfram kept in touch with what was going on, was always relatively cheerful, but did not try to fool the reporters or parrot the words of the top editors.

"Well, first we have to feed the ladies and gentlemen of the tee-vee." With the top of his pen, Wolfram pointed at the TV crew standing on the opposite side of the horseshoe—a young woman producer, a cameraman, a sound man, and a duded up reporter. They were planning their next move. Nash thought the reporter could have used a lesson from Wolfram on how to look casual to take the edge off the suit and haircut. Wolfram also dressed for success.

"This is the third crew of the morning. I figure we'll get four more."

"I saw them when I came in. Four more?"

"Yeah, Channel 9 is one. Two, five and seven make four, and the three networks. Seven."

Nash had forgotten that the three network channels, two, five and seven, often sent two crews on a story of national interest, one to do the local news and one to do the network news.

Channel nine was an independent channel.

"You won't get all seven," opined Nash. "It's not that big a deal, and somebody, somewhere has got to get the bright idea of using the same crew for two versions."

"Ahh, but what about cable?"

"You're way ahead of me, Bob."

"After they all shoot THE phone," Wolfram pointed to the phone on his right, "and a little office background, Solomon is going to hold a press conference at 10, I hope over by sports." Sports was empty in the early morning.

"Enough of that. What are WE doing?"

Wolfram lowered his voice a little, and Nash leaned over.

"Mary Stern is transcribing the tape of our conversation with the guy—they taped him—and she's going to write a story off it, all quotes. Abramowicz is doing the police and fire angle, the bookie stuff. There might be another short sidebar on who the guy was. If experience is any guide, the stories will be terrific. Then they'll combine them all into one mishmash for the final on the grounds that the paper is too tight."

"And ruin it," agreed Nash.

"Can't have space without ads, Nash. You know what they say."

"And you can't have ads if you don't give people a reason to buy the paper," responded Nash.

"Same old baloney."

"Routine."

"And they haven't even done it yet."

"But we know they will. So—what's the latest?" asked Nash.

"Circulation was up a little in December compared to this time last year, about 500 papers."

"What? Up? When's the last time that happened?"

"Oh, two years ago, maybe. It happens. The bad part is ad lineage was down again."

"Keep a stiff upper lip, Bobbo. I was a pessimist long before you. You and I can remember one September when the word was we would be gone by Christmas. That was four years ago. I remember two different Mondays when we all heard they were gonna lock the doors on Friday. That was last year and the year before. My theory now is that there is a bottom beyond which newspaper circulation in general won't go, a hard core of people who still read. With all the papers that have gone under, maybe we've reached the bottom. And we're still here."

"So we've won the race. We're home free."

"Exactly," said Nash. "You have a lifetime job."

Wolfram gave Nash a raspberry.

"Excuse me? Excuse me? Sir?" Nash looked up for the female voice and saw the tv producer talking to him from across the horseshoe.

"Would you pick up that phone there and talk on it," she said. "We'd like to have someone talking on it. You work here, right? On the city desk?"

"Not me, ma'am," said Nash. "I sell death notices."

Nash escaped, carrying both pieces of paper Miller and Wolfram had given him. He heard Wolfram say at his back, "He's the publisher. You should grab him." Nash dropped the papers on his desk behind a pillar and went to the john.

In the guise of combing his hair, Nash examined his face in the bathroom mirror. His face was getting puffy and his eyes were bloodshot. He bared his teeth and saw that his gums were receding, but at least no worse than usual. His hands were pale and not too steady.

The overall impression was so bad that Nash reached into his shirtpocket and pulled out his first cigarette of the day.

3

Victoria

The phone rang as Nash was halfway through his first donut and perusing the sports section.

"Nash," he answered.

"This is Victoria. I've called before, but you people didn't listen to me. It's happening again."

Nash wrote "Victoria" on a piece of paper out of habit. He started to write what she had said—"called before"—when something about her tone of voice stopped him.

"Is that good or bad, Victoria?"

"What?"

"Forget it. What's your problem?"

"There's illegal drugs in the Pittman Center in Elmhurst. (This was a private mental hospital, Nash knew.) The staff give the patients all kinds of unnecessary things to keep them crazy or doped up. LSD and stuff like that. I caught onto them, and I called your paper, but nobody would believe me. I quit there and went to the Ruggiero Clinic, and the same thing was happening. I never let on I was telling anyone, although I told your paper. I got out just in time."

"What would you like us to do?" asked Nash, putting his feet up on his desk and crossing his legs at the ankles. He sipped his coffee from a plastic foam cup. He preferred paper cups because they tasted better, but they had gone out of fashion.

"I'm at the Read Center now, and it's the same thing." Read was a state hospital.

"What do you do there, Victoria?"

"I'm a patient."

"Same problem again?"

"Yes, and they know I know. I went to see the doctor this morning, and something started coming under the door."

"What did?"

"Some microwaves, I think. They tried to get me in the doctor's office."

"What about the doctor? Wouldn't they be getting him, too, when the microwaves come under the door?"

"He's immune or something."

"How did you get away?"

"I asked the doctor if I could leave the office and I left. They didn't expect that."

"Has this ever happened before, the microwaves coming under the door?"

"No. It's worse here. And they probably know I'm talking to you."

"All right, we'll look into it, Victoria. Where can I reach you?"

"During the day I'm usually in the day room." She gave him the number. He took it down from force of habit.

"Okay. We'll call you if we need more information."

"You don't believe me, do you?"

"Well, I have my doubts."

"None of you people believe me."

"I'm listening to you, Victoria. That's something."

"Yeah, I suppose. Okay. What's your name? You're nicer than some of the others."

"Sam Nash. I've got to go now, Victoria."

"All right. Goodbye."

Nash stepped around his pillar and walked toward the switchboard. One of the switchboard operators, an adult woman, saw him coming and pointed to the city desk as the instigator. Nash turned to the city desk.

"Which one of you guys is a friend of Victoria?" he said.

All five people in the city desk, Miller, Wolfram, two rewritemen, and Mary Stern were talking on the phone. Wolfram looked up with a gleam in his eye, pointed to Nash, and mouthed without saying it, "You."

"She said she misses the one who used to talk dirty to her," lied Nash. He strolled away.

At his desk, Nash finished his donuts and begin riffling through pieces of paper he had piled under his desk calendar. Some were typed sheets from memo pads. Others were handwritten notes on scratch paper. Still others were newspaper clippings, long or short, with scribbles on them. All were long-collected assignments from various editors. Nash figured they spewed out assignments like Johnny Appleseed scattering seeds from a sack.

"The street sweepers do not come around as often as they used to on the Near North Side," read one. "Are these machines breaking down or wearing out or is it a budget cutback or political retaliation? Do a thorough study of 'How Clean is Our City?' Can we make comparisons to other cities? How about the suburbs? Copy due...."

In addition to the Day City Editor, the assistant city editor, and the Metropolitan Editor, Nash was subject to assignments also from the Sunday editors. And, since the Chronicle had cut back on its features staff, he occasionally got assignments from the daily "Chicagoland Scene" section and the Sunday "NOW" section.

The street sweeper assignment had been due two months earlier. Nash had ignored it because he knew the city desk would never give him time to do a "thorough" study of how clean Chicago was and he refused to fake it. Instead of throwing the assignment away, he kept it because he enjoyed it. An editor, who lived on the Near North Side, thought somebody on the staff should find out why the street sweepers didn't come down his street as often as he imagined they did in the good old days. Such personal peeves were a common inspiration for assignments, in Nash's opinion.

He anticipated receiving an assignment some day from some editor saying, "Why doesn't my doorbell work? Have landlords stopped fixing doorbells? Is this a common problem in the city? What about the suburbs? How about Detroit? Copy due..."

Nash soon found what he was looking for, a note on half sheet of bonded paper, imprinted with "From the Desk of Robert Simonet," the executive editor.

Nash's phone rang again.

"Nash."

"I have a collect call for Mr. Sam Nash."

"Who is it from?"

"Victoria."

"THE Victoria?"

"What is your last name, Ma'am?"

"Moreechee," said a distant voice.

"Make her spell it, operator," said Nash who was feeling mischievous.

"M-O-R-I-C-I."

Nash scribbled it. He imagined it was Italian or Romanian.

"Sir, did you get that?"

"Yep."

"Do you want to pay for the call?"

"Not really, but I'll take it."

"Go ahead, Ma'am."

"Mr. Nash?"

"Hello, Victoria. I didn't know you called collect."

"Can you help me?" said a whining voice.

"Victoria, I already helped you," said Nash patiently. "I listened to your story when nobody else would."

"Mr. Nash, this is very important. You're a nice man so I'm going to tell you. There's something really strange going on here."

"What do you expect? You're in a nut house."

"Hey, I've been in these places before, and I'm telling you there's something very weird about this one."

For that moment she sounded sane, Nash thought. This did not surprise him. Some nuts were good at introductions.

"Okay, tell me what it is fast, Victoria. I've got work to do."

"Some man got shot here yesterday."

"Shot with what," said Nash in a flat tone.

"With what? A bullet, I think, and a gun. It made a lot of noise."

"I dig it, Victoria. Who shot who or whom? Did you see it?"

"No. We were in the dayroom and we heard this commotion and then a big bang down the hallway. A couple of us went to see, but Johnson got in the way. He blocked the hall and wouldn't let us go down there."

"Who's Johnson? One of the nuts?"

"No. He's an aide here. Nobody likes him. But wait. You don't think I saw anything, but I did. I ran all the way around the other way. The others were too afraid to do it. And I looked down the hallway. They were dragging this guy by the feet. One of the doctors was dragging him and another aide I don't know. The gun wouldn't go into his back pocket."

"Whose pocket?"

"The aide. He poked it in there one way and another way, but it stuck up. Then he put it in his pocket on the side of his pants. The aide called me a bad name, but the doctor just told me to go back in the dayroom, and I did."

"How many times have you seen this happen before, Victoria?"

"I don't think I ever saw that before."

"What other crimes have you seen in your career?"

"Oh, lots."

"Like what?"

"Oh, people stealing and rapes. I almost got raped once, but not here. You won't put that in the newspaper, will you?"

Nash closed his eyes and sighed. In his experience, a good nut could talk sanely for half a minute before he or she started to babble and gave it away. A few could go for three or four minutes, once in a while 10, but the long-faking variety were rare and usually highly educated. Nash wished Victoria would expand her story a little more so the mystery could be solved.

Trying to speed up the outcome, he asked, "What did the gun look like?"

"It was shaped like an 'L,' a capital 'L' but a small one."

"Not a little 'L' but a small capital 'L.' Um hmm. Yes?"

"Yeah. Not like a stick."

"And after you saw this, they just let you call me up and tell me about it, right? Why didn't you mention this the first time you called instead of that jazz about the microwaves coming under the door?"

"I don't know."

"Gimme a reason."

"I don't know. I guess...I had to know if I could trust you."

"And you found out Sam Nash would listen to anything, right? All right, what in heaven's name happened next?"

"Johnson sat down in the day room and everybody's afraid of him. He stayed until we had to go to bed and he flirted with Doreen like he always does."

Nash waited.

"And then what?" he said momentarily.

"And today I called you."

"That's what I said, Victoria. They just let you call me."

"No. They don't know. I snuck down here to one of the doctor's offices. This doctor is never here."

"Is this the place where the microwaves came under the door to get you?"

"You don't believe me, do you. Nobody ever believes me."

"Victoria, do you often imagine things that are not really there?"

"Sometimes, maybe."

"Like the microwaves coming under the door—in the shape of golden rays, I suppose—that was malarkey, wasn't it?"

"I'm not sure. But it wasn't golden rays; it was a big, brown envelope."

Nash hit himself in the head with the heel of his right hand. Then he said, "How could that hurt you?"

"I don't know. It just made me nervous."

"And this guy getting shot; shall we forget about this?"

"No. This is real."

"All right, what did they tell you, the people that run the place? Did they say, 'Sorry about the disturbance, folks, we're making a movie?'"

"They didn't say anything. Nobody said anything about it."

"What about the patients?"

"They didn't see anything. They only heard a noise. And they don't believe me. I wouldn't believe some of them."

"Who got shot?"

"I don't know. Just a man. I couldn't see much because the aide was in the way. But they were dragging him by the feet, and he was wearing gym shoes."

"What was he wearing besides that?"

"An ordinary shirt and pants."

"What color?"

"Brown pants, I guess. I don't remember his shirt. Maybe yellow. It looked like a knit shirt. I couldn't see his head or his face. They blocked my way."

"Coat and hat?"

"No coat. Will you come to see me, Nash?"

"Not likely. Can I give you some advice, Victoria?"

"Sure, You're my friend, Nash."

"We've never met, Victoria. My advice is to do nothing and say nothing. This is our secret."

"So you believe me this time, don't you?"

Nash wasn't sure. It bothered him that she continued to sound so sane. His broad rule was there was no limit to what a crazy person might dream up. But he thought he might make a phone call later if nothing was happening.

"I wouldn't say I believe you, but I'm willing to check on it."

"What if they ask me? What if Dr. Crawford asks me?"

"Who's he?"

"He's the doctor who was dragging the man's feet."

Nash felt a slight chill.

"Well, let me say if I was in your position, Victoria, and if any of this were true. . . ."

"It IS."

"I know. Then I would act very stupid. . . I would. . . Hell, I don't know what I'd do, Victoria. Are you smart?"

"Sometimes I was in school, but not always."

"Well, if you really saw anything, there could be lots of explanations. But just to be on the safe side, insist that you didn't see anything—only if they ask you—or start talking some nutty gibberish like some of your friends must do there. You see, Victoria, now you've got me talking nutty. I'm acting like this might be true. It's contagious, Victoria, and I don't want to catch what you got. But I'm going to check on this for you."

"Are you coming to see me, Nash? It's not contagious."

"Is that what this is all about, Victoria?"

"If I'm in danger, you should come to help me."

"Who said you're in danger?"

"You almost did. You told me to keep my mouth shut or talk nutty."

"Did you make all this up just because I thought I might come to see you?"

"Never did. But I've got to go. If I'm absent too long from the day room, somebody will rat on me. Are you going to investigate?"

"I might. I mean, of course, I'm not a cop, but I'll ask around. I'm probably as goofy . . . I'll check on this if I can do it without getting you into trouble. How's that?"

"Um Hmm."

"What?"

"Um Hmm."

"Don't expect miracles."

"AAAAAAAAAHHHHHHH."

"What the hell was that?"

"I was just relieving my tension. The doctor says it's okay to scream if I have to. It's such a relief to be able to tell this to somebody. But I've really got to go now. Goodby, Nash."

Click.

Nash hung up and shook his head vigorously to clear it. The things a person runs into in this business, he thought. He decided if he inquired into Victoria's story, he'd have to be careful that nobody on the Chronicle found out. It would be embarrassing.

To bring his mind back to comfortable reality, he decided to do what he'd been told to do.

He made a phone call to the public relations office of the Illinois Central Gulf railroad. After the call, he wrote on the computer terminal alongside his desk:

"A downed electrical line on the Illinois Central Gulf commuter tracks that delayed 600 riders during the morning rush hour was expected to be repaired and operational for the home trip, a railroad spokesperson said Tuesday."

He went on for four more inches then hit the "end" button. The words rolled up off the tv screen from the bottom and disappeared. The computer digested them, then ordered itself to print the story on a small printer resting on one corner of the city desk.

The IC commuter trains to the South Side and south suburbs are electrically operated by trolley-like wires that run above the trains. The lines occasionally fall down, especially in winter.

Nash approached the city desk and told Miller, "I could only get five inches out of the IC."

"Fine," said Miller.

"I need your obit, Sam," said Wolfram. "We're short of obits."

The first afternoon editions of all three dailies got on the street at 3 p.m., but the Chronicle's deadline was 11:30 a.m. The various editors constantly ragged the staff to get their copy in early to avoid a glut at deadline.

After calling the undertaker at the phone number Wolfram had given him earlier, Nash wrote the obituary. He wrote that the deceased was a manufacturer's representative, which Nash figured to be a salesman, for 35 years for a firm that sold power tools. He was an Army veteran of the Pacific Theater in World War II, and he had a wife, two sons, three daughters, and eight grandchildren.

Nash had difficulty remembering which survivors were the sons and which the daughters. "Lolo. Who was that?" Victoria's account of the supposed shooting at the mental health center was distracting him.

"What if it's true?" he thought. "Have to be a lot of good shit surrounding that event." But Nash could count great stories that had fallen through using the hairs of his well-thatched head. There was no need to do anything about it at the moment.

He called the undertaker back to find out who Lolo was.

4

After he hit the "end" button and the obit rolled up off the screen, Nash scanned his desk for the half sheet of bonded paper "From the Desk of Robert Simonet." Simonet was the executive editor of the Chronicle. His note, typed by his secretary, said, "Pete, could we cover the luncheon of the Childhood Foundation Tuesday in the Hotel Continental? Thanks for anything you can do. R.W.S." Pete was Ralph Peterson, the managing editor. Attached to the memo was a letter describing the event.

Peterson had scribbled on the memo, "Aaron, take care of this, R.P." Aaron was Aaron Solomon, the metropolitan editor. Solomon had written, "Al, who have we got for this? A.S." When his turn arrived, Al Miller, the day city editor, wrote, "Nash," in large letters with a red pen, circled the name and threw it in his out basket. Nash had received the well-used note the previous week. He got up and walked to the morgue to get the clips on the Childhood Foundation.

When he came back, his phone was ringing and he picked it up. "You've got a lunch to cover for Simonet today, Sam. Miller told me to remind you." It was Wolfram speaking.

"I know all about it."

"Also your wife's on the phone. She said she called your desk and you weren't there."

"I was in the morgue."

"Do you want me to switch her over?"

"Tell her I'm out, thank you, Bob."

"Sure, pal. You coward. She sounds like a nice lady."

"I'll tell her you said so."

"Whoa...Okay."

Nash started to read the clips on the Childhood Foundation, but Wolfram's jest bugged him. Every since City News, Nash had made it a point not to be afraid to call anybody, or, more precisely, to be willing to call anybody even if he was afraid.

[This may not sound like much, but the news business requires quite a few phone calls over time that are embarrassing to make, or uncomfortable, and sometimes dreadful.]

Nash got up and got a drink of water, then emptied his ash tray in a garbage can. He sat down, put the end of his pen in his mouth, chewed it for a moment, then he picked up the phone and punched the number. She answered on the second ring.

"Sobieski and Sobieski." Such a sweet voice, thought Nash. The music of feminine tones.

"This is Sam."

"How nice of you to call back, Sam. I thought you were out."

He detected only moderate sarcasm.

"I came back."

"I need some money, Sam. We still owe St. Monica's $50 from the fall semester, and they want the spring semester paid in full immediately."

"I'm working on it."

"I need it now, or at least very soon, Sam. And I've got the anesthesiologist from Bobby's hernia operation calling me every other day. He wants his $400. He collects his own bills, a very nasty man. And to TOP IT ALL OFF, I just found out that you skipped the December mortgage payment."

"I had to pay the Master Charge or they were going to take us to court."

"I told you those things create illusions. We could have got by without it. What have we got to show for it, Sam?"

Your last two birthday presents, he thought, and your anniversary present, and I borrowed money on it when we weren't getting by.

"I have a large bill, now partly paid off."

"Fair enough. I think I know what part of that was anyway. When are you going to pay the mortgage?"

"I went to the bank yesterday and applied for a bill payer loan. Not counting your car and the house, I figure we need about $4,500 to pay off everybody. We should know in a week."

"Are they going to give you the loan? What did they say?"

"The loan officer wanted to know where my column appears."

"Oh, shit. I sure hope you get that."

"Me, too."

"How are you these days, Sam?"

"Me? Uh..." [How am I?] "I'm fine." She hadn't asked him how he was since they had separated. "How are you?"

"Are you eating? Anybody that drinks like you do has to eat or you'll burn out your stomach lining."

"I'm trying to pay attention to it. How are you?" he asked again.

"Not bad. Not great. I may have to get another sitter. Kim is not getting along with Mrs. Kolarick's daughter."

"That's too bad. Maybe it will work itself out."

"Maybe. I'll handle it."

"You've done pretty well picking the sitters, Kate."

"Thank you," she said softly, sounding so grateful it was as if he had just bought her a Porsche. The things she could do with her voice, thought Nash.

"Is there anything else, Sam? I have to go."

"No. I'll pick up the kids Saturday."

"Be sure now. I don't want to get them excited if you aren't coming."

"I'll be there."

"Do you need anything, Sam?"

Aww, don't do that, he thought. I'm not going to answer that question.

"I'll see you Saturday, Kate."

"Goodbye, Sam. Eat your meals."

Nash hung up and stared at his desk, resting his face on his fists. He was trembling slightly. He thought, She pushed a couple of my buttons and I fell apart. Why did she do that? He opened his hands and massaged his face to make it look as if that's what he had intended to do if anyone was watching.

Oh, fuck, he said to himself, and he took a long, deep breath. Then he remembered he was supposed to do something. What was it? Nash turned in his chair to look in a glass-partitioned office at the side of the newsroom. The office belonged to metropolitan editor Aaron Solomon, and he was sometimes in it. This time he was, and Nash got up and started in that direction.

Solomon had been city editor of the Chronicle until six months earlier. One day a note had appeared on the bulletin board signed by the managing editor saying Solomon would henceforth be the metropolitan editor. At the Ledger and the Post, the city editors had been renamed metropolitan editors years before. At those papers, other people were then named city editors, and the city editor job became subordinate to the metropolitan editor.

The usual public announcement ran like this: "The change reflects the growing influence of the suburbs while retaining a special emphasis on the city."

At the Chronicle, the process was simplified. Solomon's title was changed and that was it. The staff assumed no one was appointed city editor because the new city editor would have wanted a raise.

Nash knocked on the glass. Solomon was sipping coffee out of a plastic foam cup and reading something on his desk. He glanced up. "Yeah. Come on in, Sam." Solomon was an intense man with curly brown hair of the steel wool sort that never seemed to grow out or need combing, but thinning at the temples. He was halfway educated as most people in the Chicago news business were. The highly educated seemed to lack aggression, but less than halfway was not viable. Solomon was self-conscious about what he didn't know, and very confident of his knowledge of current events. A little shorter than Nash and better dressed, Solomon had a karate chop conversational style when talking to reporters that gave the impression he was a man with many things on his mind and little time. This was the impression he wanted to convey, because reporters, in his opinion, frequently just wanted to gab.

Nash had watched Solomon develop this style and admired his adjustment. As a new city editor, Solomon had started out being friendly and understanding to all—until he was wide-eyed with frustration and confusion after a few weeks. Since his change, he had the attention span of a telephone operator, except in special instances when he symbolically closed his door. At 39, Solomon and Nash were the same age.

Nash sat down in a hard back chair on the opposite side of Solomon's desk. The metropolitan editor opened his middle drawer and took out a piece of white paper without needing to search for it.

"What do you know about Alderman Colucci?" asked the metropolitan editor.

"Only what I read in the papers," responded Nash. Solomon was gazing into his coffee cup.

"This stuff tastes pretty good, Sam. How do you account for that?"

"They put half a cup of monosodium glutamate into every urnfull of coffee downstairs."

"Die with a good taste in your mouth. Well, tell me what you know."

"Chosen in a special election to replace somebody who was convicted of taking bribes. Lesniak? First alderman from South Water Market. Used money from his family's produce business to run. The typical fear of mob connections."

"Okay. But he has a pretty good image. Got help from the Democratic organization in his campaign, then sided with the mayor against the organization in the budget dispute. People think that's a sign of great character."

"They do?"

"Yeah, sure. Some people do. IVI types. Our editorial writers." The IVI was the Independent Voters of Illinois, a liberal group drawing membership from Hyde Park and the North Side lakefront wards.

"Know anything else?" said Solomon.

"No."

"Check this out." He handed Nash the piece of paper. "I'd like to have it for Sunday if you can do it, Sam." Solomon stood up.

"Can I read it?"

"Sure. Take your time. I've got to go to a meeting. Check to see how many other aldermen have a lot of relatives on the city payroll. We've done that before. Let me know tomorrow how it looks." Solomon was already at the door. Nash, still seated, gave him a military salute which he knew would annoy Solomon. Solomon had one leg out the door.

"You know how to handle this, Sam. That's why I'm not going into great detail." He walked away.

Nash read the memo.

"Phone call from anonymous caller 9:30 p.m. Monday. Ald. Colucci has a host of relatives employed in his office and on the city payroll. Caller said she has been waiting for some newspaper to write about this. 'You're letting him get away with it. Why?' she said.

"She identified them as Carol Barski, Mary Losurdo, and Bill Martin, all of whom work in his office; Vincent Colucci, who works for the city dept of economic development and just got a big promotion from the mayor; and Lucy Malek, who works in the corporation counsel's office. Barski is supposed to be the alderman's sister; Martin is his nephew; Losurdo and Malek are in-laws; and Vincent is his brother. Caller spelled all the names except the alderman's which she assumed I knew. She added that Martin sells dope and has been arrested several times for this and should be in jail. If there's any truth to this horrifying situation, it would seem we missed it because they all have different last names except for Vincent."

The note was signed by Paul Youngman.

For a fleeting second while Solomon was in the doorway, Nash had thought of telling him about the possible shooting in the mental health center. But he knew it would be foolish. Solomon would want to know what, exactly, he had. And Nash had nothing. Nash was accustomed to keeping strange things under his hat, and Solomon had enough under his.

Solomon was right about the memo. Nash knew how to handle it. Call up the alderman and ask him.

5

Nash went back to his desk behind one of the round pillars, two feet in diameter, that stood along the north and south sides of the newsroom. He supposed these pillars were to give the newsroom a stately appearance. He doubted that anything so massive was needed structurally. The only thing above them was the roof with a skylight in the center of the room. The newsroom was quite spacious and 18-feet high. The whole effect was imposing, Nash thought.

The best thing about this particular pillar, which Nash gave a friendly pat every day, was that it made it impossible for the city desk to see him. He was thus sometimes spared extra obituaries or the tedious typing of stories dictated over the phone. These tasks were normally assigned helter skelter to whoever came into the line of sight of the city desk.

Nash tried to remember how he would have reacted to the Colucci assignment when he was starting out. "Holy Cow! Nepotism in city government, and I'm going to expose it." And shortly, "You won't believe it, boss. It's all true and we got him nailed!" The editors would smile at him and at each other. Nash had once thought these glances the editors exchanged in his presence were their silent way of saying, "Hey, this kid is sharp." Now that he was the same age his editors once were, he realized they had been saying, "He thinks this is brand new. Remember when you felt that way, Harry? It's cute."

This time it was just an assignment. It was a story on its face, Nash admitted. But how many times had this story been done? Ten times? Twenty? Different names. Different aldermen. It was too easy. Was this work for a grownup, he found himself wondering again? Be serious. You need the paycheck. He was probably feeling physically negative, he thought. Alcohol induced depression.

Nash phoned Colucci's City Hall office and his neighborhood office and left messages in both places because the alderman was not in.

Then he read the clips on the Childhood Foundation. The clips showed the foundation was concerned about child abuse, neglected children, conditions in the Audy Home—the local jail for juvenile delinquents—and conditions in other juvenile prisons in the state.

Last year's luncheon featured a local Catholic priest, a black man, who had adopted a child and urged other blacks to adopt orphans. The year before, child abuse statistics were discussed. They were going up, naturally.

Nash read the stories and noted that the Chronicle had congratulated itself in a three-year-old clip for receiving an award from the foundation for a series on child abuse. Nash felt he knew all he needed to know about the Childhood Foundation. He stuffed the clips in the envelope and went back to the morgue for clips on Ald. Colucci. After reading these and some more of the sports section, he looked at the clock. The luncheon started at noon and the speeches at one. If he was going to mooch a free meal, he liked to walk there leisurely and arrive at about 12:40. Latecomers always got served immediately at these affairs, and he could eat with a minimum of small talk. Nash did not like to talk to people at luncheon and dinner meetings although a little conversation was unavoidable.

He put the morgue envelopes in his middle drawer and pulled a half used notebook out of the same drawer. He checked to be sure he had a pen in his pockets. He had two.

He stretched, picked his sportcoat off the hook he had personally screwed into the plaster pillar and stuffed a long, narrow notebook into the inside pocket. As he turned away from his desk, putting one arm in the sportcoat, his wife slipped into his blank mind and he became instantly tense and perplexed. He winced. His marital or unmarital situation was the sort of mess that could throw him for hours if he indulged it, and he was supposed to be working. To shake it off, he forced himself to think of something else. Wasn't there a book called, "Murder in the Mad House," he thought? He pictured a paperback from long ago on a revolving rack in a drug store and tried to imagine a cover. Then he thought, putting the other arm in the sportcoat, I wonder what's for lunch?

Still, Kate stayed in his consciousness.

6

Nash walked through the doors of the main ballroom of the Hotel Continental on Michigan Avenue north of the river noting that this was the third name for the hotel since he had known it. He stepped a few yards into the ballroom and waited. A waiter with a napkin on one arm glided over from the side and said, "Ticket, sir?"

"Not yet," said Nash.

The waiter shrugged and glided away walking a little like Groucho Marx. Without removing his overcoat, Nash stood and looked around. It was a good crowd of about 400, he guessed, about half female, above the average ratio for downtown luncheons. The crowd was distributed at round tables with white table cloths on a red carpet, eight people to a table. At the rear fringe of the crowd, several diners turned in their seats to stare at the stationary figure of Nash. But Nash was not in a self-conscious mood.

He was thinking—purposely, to avoid the continuation of other thoughts—about what bank he would go to if the first one turned him down. And he wondered if perhaps there had been a shooting in the Read Mental Health Center that had been reported in the normal manner.

He stood like a man waiting for a bus.

In a few moments, a young woman in a skirt and business top, which to Nash meant a high necked blouse with a large satin bow and some kind of jacket that complimented her skirt, rose from one of the tables off to the side of the last row and approached him with a big smile.

"Can I help you?" she said.

"Yes. I'm from the Chronicle. My editor asked me to cover your luncheon."

"Oh, wonderful." Nash knew she would be pleased. "What did you say your name was?"

"Sam Nash."

"How do you do? I'm Joyce Fisher. Do you want to check your coat?"

"No, thanks. I'll just hang it on the chair."

"Any place in particular you'd like to sit?"

"Wherever you want."

"Well, how would you like to sit with us, then? We've got an empty space. We were hoping you were coming. I think you can still get lunch. Have you eaten?"

Joyce Fisher was blond, bubbly and very efficient, just what Nash wanted. He let her lead him to his place.

"Mr. Nash, I'd like you to meet Mr. Parker, our director of public relations. Mr. Nash is a reporter for the Chronicle."

Parker got up bending over and trying not to lose his napkin. He appeared to be a very ordinary, middle aged man who did not pretend much. His mixed brown and gray hair had obviously just been cut by a standard barber. His suit, of middling expense, was basically brown with a muted plaid pattern. On a Northern European face, he wore the practiced expression of a man who was used to pleasing people.

"How do you do, Nash? We're mighty glad you came." He extended his hand and smiled with true gratitude. "Do you want something to eat?"

"I asked him, but he didn't answer," said Miss Fisher.

"Sure. Whatever you're having," said Nash.

"Its boneless chicken breast. It's not bad. Sit down. Sit down. Why don't you check his coat, Joyce?"

"He wants to keep it with him."

"Oh, in case you've got to make a quick getaway, huh? Like go to a fire or something. Ha Ha," said Parker.

"It saves me from waiting in line later and leaving a tip."

"Ah, very good. Well, you've met Joyce, and these five people are friends of ours who are also active in the foundation."

"Don't stop eating on my account," said Nash.

A waiter came by and asked Nash again for a meal ticket to show that somebody had paid for his meal. Nash looked at Miss Fisher sitting next to him. She produced a ticket and gave it to the waiter.

"He'll have chicken," said Parker.

"Very good, sir."

"Excuse me, what did you say your name was?" asked another woman at the table. She appeared to be in her late 40's or early 50's, but she had a cherubic face and the clear, shining skin that comes with good health and no bad habits.

Her hair was tightly gathered in an old fashioned bun at the back. She wore department store clothes of respectable style, but not stylish. Nash thought she looked like a nun or somebody who worked in a hospital.

"Sam Nash," he said.

"Where does your column appear?" asked a man in his 20's sitting next to the woman.

"I don't have a column. I just write stories. The kind you see on any page."

"What sort of news do you cover?" The young man was wearing an expensive, dark blue, pin stripe suit and sported a mustache to make himself look older.

"Anything and everything. Whatever I'm assigned to or I trip over."

"You cover sports, too?" the young man inquired.

"No, not sports."

"He's general assignment. You're general assignment, isn't that right?" said the middle aged woman.

"That's it," said Nash.

"My brother was a newspaper reporter for the Toledo Blade. Now he has a public relations agency there. He said he couldn't make any money in newspapers."

"I can understand that." Nash smiled his best smile.

The waiter returned and slipped a salad plate in front of Nash, then one-handedly cleared a space for Nash's main course plate with deft but noisy bangings of silver, plate, and glassware, and set down the main course, too.

Serious thinking made Nash hungry, and he plunged into the salad. He was thinking, despite distractions, about Victoria's story. A small, 'L'-shaped gun could be construed as a description of an automatic. Automatics were made in straight lines in the barrel and the grip while revolvers, as everybody knew, had curves in the cylinder and curves in the grip. The description of the aide trying to stick the gun in his back pocket afterward also suggested to Nash that the gun was small, possibly a .25 or a .32. Suddenly Nash wondered if this episode had just been on television. He decided to read the TV listings going back a week, including the soap opera summaries. While he thought of this, it soon occurred to him that there were so many shootings on television, three or four a show sometimes, that no listing would ever attempt to describe them all. He shook his head imperceptibly while leaning over his salad plate and let his thoughts move on.

Victoria had plenty of reasons to make the story up—a whole

universe of reasons, he assumed, because nothing was off limits to the insane. But could she steal it or make it up and still keep the details so sparse? At the very least, he thought, a spinner of yarns should include a motive for the shooting. But she didn't.

Nash polished off the salad down to the last scrap, grateful that the conversation went on around him. He was on his second bite of chicken, when Miss Fisher, apparently thinking it was impolite for them all to ignore the reporter, asked, "How long have you worked at the Chronicle, Sam?"

Nash swallowed. "Fourteen years or almost a decade and a half."

"It's about the same, isn't it?" Parker smiled.

"Yeah, it's a long time either way," said Nash.

"I worked 16 years for the old Daily News," said Parker. "I used to chase around all day like you. Maybe we chased around even more in those days."

"You might be right," answered Nash. He thought of what the old reporters had told him about taking the street car to stories and the shortage of telephones. Then Nash realized Parker was not that old, so Nash did not know what the hell Parker was talking about.

"The last story I covered, or the last decent story, was the Mickelberry's fire. Do you remember that?"

"Sure. Big explosion. Hell of a fire." The Mickelberry's fire occurred in a sausage factory in 1968. Friends of Nash's had covered it, and he had read about it avidly.

"If you don't mind my telling an old newspaperman's story...."

"No. Go ahead. I'd love to hear it," said Nash, who resumed eating.

"That was near where I lived then. We lived in Canaryville. I heard the first fire engines, but I chose to ignore them. You know how at first you'll chase any fire truck down the street, but after a while, you don't want to? It's usually nothing."

Nash nodded.

"When I heard the big explosion, and I was still in my car—I was on my way home from the early rewrite shift—I had to go.

"When I got there—couldn't have been more than 10 minutes after it happened—son of a gun, that was devastation. The building was half gone, and the vanished half was all over the neighborhood. People were still on the ground, knocked down hard and couldn't get up. Some were dead, including some spectators.

"The ambulances hadn't got there yet, and they were carrying people away on boards and ladders or using their fire coats like stretchers. So I pitched in to help a little bit—after I made a phone call.

"Good for you," said Nash appreciating Parker's presence of mind to call the office.

"I remember there was this one photographer shooting everything. I think it was Don Casper. I forget which paper he worked for then. It surprised me to see him because I thought I'd be the only newspaperman there so early.

"A police car drove up with a flat tire. They loaded three injured firemen inside, and drove off, flat tire and all."

"No kidding," said Nash.

"I wrote down a description in my notebook. Mounds of bricks with firemen crawling on them, throwing bricks this way and that, looking for people. Cars were burning. The building was still burning."

"You sound like my brother," said the angel-faced woman.

"Well, to make a long story short," Parker talked to the whole table this time, "What happened is a gasoline truck had an accident in the alley, and the gas ran out of the truck into the basement of the factory. It caught on fire; the workers on the upper floor ran onto the roof; the firemen went up to rescue them; then it blew up."

"Some of those people on the roof were killed?" asked the young man with the mustache.

"Yes. Firemen, too. Eventually, eight people died and 70 or 80 were injured.

"At the Daily News we were past the end of our press run so we couldn't be satisfied with the simple description. We had to have that plus 'How it really happened,' the usual afternoon paper lead the next day. The morning papers always had it easy. Disasters seemed to fit your schedule better. But I got an interview with the gasoline truck driver in the hospital that night, and I had half of page one to myself the next day."

Nash found he was interested. And Parker's monologue made it possible for Nash to eat. Parker seemed like most reporters Nash had met, ready with stories of their wild days, tales that might be a little exaggerated although exaggeration was not usually necessary. Nash knew he often indulged in this himself when drinking or even once in a while in the office talking to the youngsters.

"Right after that, I quit," said Parker.

"Because of Mickelberry's?" asked Nash.

"Yes and no. I ran around like crazy that day. My stomach was killing me; I had an ulcer. Too much drinking and smoking. I used to get so wound up, I had to drink to come down. We didn't have a huge staff at the Daily News, not like the Ledger, and a rewriteman really busted his butt. My impression is that you guys are a little tamer now in your personal habits, and that's smart."

Nash said nothing.

"After Mickelberry's, I realized that was as good as it was going to get. I wasn't going to Washington or Europe. I wasn't that kind of reporter. My two kids were starting to grow up, and I didn't have any money. That's all changed, of course. Newspapers pay a lot better today."

"Yeah, they do, especially the Ledger and the Post," said Nash. Nash was surprised Parker could tell his personal story so easily in front of the whole table, especially the drinking part. He must have conquered drinking pretty thoroughly or he wouldn't be so free to bring it up, Nash decided.

"You guys at the Chronicle are the step-children in the wages department, huh?" said Parker.

"Seems that way."

Nash scraped up the last of the mashed potatoes by running the heel of his fork against the low, circular ridge that broke up the smooth surface of the plate. A waiter arrived with a tray of desserts. Nash turned down a chocolate sundae and waved to another waiter he saw going by with a pot of coffee.

One table was the same as any other to the man with the coffee, so he filled the cups at Nash's table. Parker began talking to the nun-nurse about her brother in Toledo. Nash lit a cigarette and assumed a pose of listening. Five years earlier, Nash thought, he would have instantly classified Parker as an old windbag who chose to hide in public relations because he couldn't cut it in the news business no matter what he said. Searching for a judgement this time, Nash came up neutral. Life was longer than he had thought, and you couldn't play baseball forever.

He checked his watch. He had been at the luncheon almost 20 minutes. The tinkle and crash of spoons, plates, knives and glasses all around him was like a weird modern symphony. The loudness always rose to its peak when the waiters were taking away the plates. Through the chaotic noise came a rapid "dink, dink, dink, dink, dink," which stood out because of its regularity. The conversation dipped quickly and the waiters tried to be a little more quiet.

The man standing up at the head table on a dias at the front of the room banged a little longer with his spoon on his water glass then spoke tentatively into his microphone.

"Hello? FFFFFFFFF. (He blew in it.) Can you hear me? Yes? Good."

The speaker smiled a malicious smile, perhaps unintentionally.

"I want to welcome all of you here today to an event that is rapidly becoming a tradition, I think, in Chicago. This is only our eighth year, but the Childhood Foundation has become a force to be reckoned with. If you'll look around you and at our head table here, I think you'll see as big a collection of movers and shakers as can be found anywhere in the city today."

He smiled again, this time more evil than before, and began to introduce the head table.

"Most of these men here. . .and women. . .need no introduction. But it is protocol. It gives me enormous pleasure to introduce the governor of Illinois, William Beal."

The governor, to the speaker's left, took a bow to applause. Nash moved his chair sideways to the table to stretch his legs. He took out his notebook and pen and pretended to get ready for work so the people at the table would not bother him. He knew the real speech would not begin for another five minutes.

Doodling on an empty page, he reran the same string of thoughts he had had a few minutes earlier. Assuming for the heck of it that Victoria's story was true, how could it be verified?

If the shooting was for a legitimate reason, it would come out by itself in the normal manner. Nash could not see much possibility of a legitimate reason. Robbers, rapists and general maniacs at large were stupid, and one might even assault a mental hospital. But the picture wasn't right. If a street maniac got shot by a hospital security guard, a doctor would not drag the mope away by the feet afterward. The mope would rate a stretcher and an ambulance, all the best the state could offer. And the half dozen cops who would clomp around later would be impossible to miss, even for Victoria.

Nash doubted the security guards carried guns in a mental hospital anyway. Who were they expected to shoot? The patients? But that part was easy to check out. And if the guards did not have guns, the gun was there for no good reason.

Assuming it happened, the shooting was most likely not in the line of duty and was a crime on the shooting side. If so, the shooter and any accomplices would not report it. So who could he ask? Dr. Crawford? That would put Victoria in the middle.

The alleged involvement of a doctor did not faze Nash. He had once covered the trial of a doctor for shooting and killing another doctor over professional and personal jealousy. That shooting was performed in the hospital where both doctors worked. As for doctors in mental hospitals, Nash had a low opinion of them. There were a few saints, he assumed, but the rest, especially in state hospitals, he considered to be dubious.

What did they do with the body? Put it in a trash barrel, or a box, and took it someplace at night, probably. Could cause talk, but it would work. What if the victim wasn't dead? If the guy was hospitalized anywhere it would lead to exposure unless he agreed not to talk, which would be surprising. Putting him in the mental hospital's own infirmary and perhaps drugging him unconscious was no solution. The staff would know a gunshot patient did not belong there.

If the victim was wounded and the shooters were determined to keep it quiet, they would have to kill him, Nash concluded. Or, if they were reluctant to administer the coup de grace, they would have to try something freaky, like tying him up in a private house and waiting to see if he recovered. But if he did, he would tell.

That left the obvious. Nash was looking for a dead man that nobody wanted to talk about. Nash's authority for this supposed killing was an inmate in an insane asylum. He scratched his head with the back of his pen. The knowledge that he had taken so many mental steps to arrive where he began was paradoxically comforting. Nash's standard practice was to line up all the dumb questions and ask them in order. He'd done it. But he was stuck for the next step.

He could call the police. The police were not choosy or put off by improbabilities. If a Chronicle reporter called with a story like this, they would laugh privately, but they would check it out. The simplest approach for the police would be to go to the hospital and announce they wanted to see Victoria because she had reported a shooting. The police would take the simplest approach, as he would in their place.

But Nash felt he had given Victoria a promise not to involve her in that way, and he could not control what would happen once he called the cops. When the cops left Read, she would still be there.

He could forget the whole thing. But if this thing ended up in the news under somebody else's byline, his regrets would be titanic. He could not fool himself by pleading boredom if he got scooped. Nash thought of the five or six UFO reports he had listened to sincerely and followed up with a few phone calls to their logical dead ends. He had enjoyed them all, and he wouldn't mind doing it again. One of those would be legitimate some day. There was still the possibility that everyone in town already knew about this shooting except Nash, but Nash doubted it.

"Seriously, ladies and gentlemen," said the luncheon speaker whose name Nash got from the letter attached to Simonet's memo, "I do not think I exaggerate when I say there is a crisis today...."

Nash began taking notes. Before putting his thoughts completely aside, he tentatively settled on the usual motive that police and reporters assigned to offbeat shootings, a motive that stood up more than half the time if the cases were solved.

If this really happened, it was dope.

7

Nash started the easiest way he knew. After leaving the luncheon at 1:20 p.m., he hunted up a pay phone and called Area 5 Violent Crimes. If any kind of shooting, even accidental, had been reported in the Read Mental Health Center, Area 5 had the geographic jurisdiction and should have been notified.

"Nothing like that recently or even in a year that I'm aware of, pal," said the sergeant.

Then, in case there was a state regulation that might have kept out the Chicago police, Nash called the state police. The state police professed no knowledge. Finally, Nash put some more money in the phone and called Wolfram. "Bob, I've got the speech from the Childhood Foundation to write for Simonet for the 3-star. Before I come in, I'm going to take a little trip over to the morgue for a different story. I'll be in the office in an hour and a half."

"Whose morgue?"

"The county's. It's not for tonight."

"I need obits. Find out who might want a nice obit in the morning Chronicle."

"I'll post a notice. 'If you're dead, call Bob Wolfram.'"

Nash felt a little sorry for Wolfram. On the table of organization, Wolfram was a boss, although a minor one. He had a quota of small obits to fill, but reporters often brushed aside the obits Wolfram assigned to them.

Nash went into the subway at State and Grand savoring the funny, irresponsible feeling he usually had when traveling around at mid-day on a story that was not assigned and was, at the beginning, nine-tenths imagination.

He wondered how many people would consider what he was doing honest work, checking out the ravings of an insane woman about a shooting not because he intended to arrest anyone but because he wanted to write a story in the newspaper and make a name for himself. Even to newspeople, he knew, this was pretty far fetched. Yet here he was, foot loose and fancy free, going to the morgue.

He forgot he had been pretty much tired of his job a short while earlier.

When the train came, he got on a middle car that had only three other passengers. At Washington Street, he got off, walked through the tunnel to Dearborn and took a B train. This train carried a pretty good crowd, two-thirds black. He noticed one old white woman who was smiling for some reason and carrying her shopping. Nash watched her strike up a conversation with a black teenager sitting next to her who reluctantly, but respectfully, answered her questions from his slouch as if she were his grandmother and he had no choice.

At Polk Street, Nash got off and walked west down a row of tall, red brick structures, collegiate looking but too tall. The buildings were part of the city's medical center which served people from all classes and the bulk of the poor. The surrounding area was booming with new hospital structures, and it occurred to Nash that medicine was a good racket.

The building at 1828 W. Polk St. contrasted with the others. It was low, three stories, constructed of yellow bricks dingy with age. A sign on what might be termed the front lawn, a rectangle of black dirt, named the building. Another sign taped to the front door said:

"Identification of deceased persons is restricted to the hours of 12 noon to 8 p.m. daily."

He passed more signs on stands in the hallway and glanced in a darkened room to the right of the hall. It was empty. This was the waiting room for the fearful. Nash noticed the furniture in this room was still wooden church pews up against the walls, minus the kneelers. A color TV had been added to the room. He had not been in the morgue in years.

On the second floor he talked to a nice-looking, overworked secretary who never questioned that he was what he said he was, Sam Nash from the Chronicle. He examined the "daily case ledger" of violent, unusual or temporarily unexplained deaths reported to the Medical Examiner during the previous 48 hours. Then he want back 24 hours further just to be sure.

He would have been glad to find any death from any cause in a local mental hospital, or any gunshot death on the far Northwest Side, for something to start with. None of the entries fit. The ledger entries could have been wrong. Most were wrong in one detail or another because they represented the first slapdash report of a death phoned in by a harried cop, nurse, or hospital clerk. But if one of these dead people was Nash's man, there was no way to tell it. He counted seven homicides in those 72 hours.

8

Nash had not expected to find any deaths related to the Read Mental Health Center—he was just eliminating the obvious again—but he was still disappointed. It would have solved the mystery. Back in the Chronicle office he wrote 12 inches on the speech at the luncheon of the Childhood Foundation in 50 minutes. The topic was the exaggeration of juvenile crime by the media. Nash fantasized while reading his notes that some 15- and 16-year-old psychopaths had appeared at the doors to the ballroom, armed, and refusing to let anyone leave.

Nevertheless, he wrote the story straight, as if it made all the sense in the world, because that was the assignment, and speech stories were easy.

Finished, Nash lit a cigarette, put his feet up on the desk and resumed thinking. Other reporters around him were plunking away at their terminals or talking on the phone. Nash tuned out. In addition to writing about innumerable violent crimes, Nash had investigated a few before, some police brutality cases which did not always turn out to be police brutality, and a few especially interesting murders. A truly gripping murder that made the city desk a sucker for any new development for days on end was rare. There were only two or three a year.

While trying to extract from his past investigations some hint of how to proceed on the Victoria matter, Nash was struck by the difference. On the other occasions, he had always begun with a shopping basket full of information: the name of the victim which followed easily to the victim's relatives, friends and neighbors; also police reports, witnesses, cops to talk to, assistant state's attorneys, sometimes private lawyers or public defenders.

In the asylum shooting, he had no victim, no relatives, no reports, no cops. After 10 minutes of fruitless thought, he mentally composed a headline:

"Big Time Reporter Helpless in Murder Probe."

He picked up the phone, still with his feet on the desk, and made a call. The person he wanted was not available, so he left a message and returned to rumination.

"I'll give you the benefit of the doubt and say you're thinking of a lead."

Nash looked up and saw Mary Stern, the Chronicle's day rewrite-woman. Stern was over 60, gray haired, with a slim figure and a classy, once beautiful face that sometimes lost its softness in the tension on the desk. Once divorced and once widowed, she was the oldest female reporter or newswriter still on active duty in Chicago.

"Just thinking, period," said Nash. "I already wrote today's epic."

"Pure thinking, eh? You should do that in the john, Sam, so nobody sees you."

"Why? Who's around?" Nash took his feet down. Stern filled the empty desk top space by sitting on it, showing legs under her wool skirt that once gave men palpitations.

"The usual people. But in the old days, Schuman would pay a guy off in a trice if he saw him doing nothing with his feet on the desk."

"Yeah, and you could get fired for whistling in the newsroom, too. But you happen to have struck on the very subject I was thinking about, Mary. I'm in the market for a little advice from that direction."

"What direction?"

"The old days."

"If you're wondering whether a girl kissed or worse on her first date, the answer is 'No,' and I still don't."

"You still date?"

"Sometimes."

"Could be expensive to date you if it takes so long to get a kiss. But it might be worth it."

"You're sweet, Sammy."

"That's nice to hear. If I might brutally change the subject, I want to investigate a murder, or what I think might be a murder, from the ground up. Nobody knows about it so there's no reports to work with and only one witness. I never did anything like this."

"Who is the dead party that nobody knows about?"

"The dead party is missing. I don't know who he is or where he is."

"How do you know this party is dead?"

"My witness works for a certain institution, and she says she saw three employees of that institution shoot a man and drag the body away. I apologize for being so vague. These are government employees, but not very significant ones."

"Where do I fit into this?"

"I thought you might give me a hint of how reporters went about this in the old days when crime news was half the ballgame."

"I covered City Hall."

"Yeah, but you knew the old police reporters, like the two guys who broke the Leopold and Loeb case."

A look of insulted astonishment crossed Stern's face. "Gimme a break. Holy cow, Sam!" Her hands went to her hair checking for anything out of place. Then she adjusted her blouse. "That was the 1920's. I was a girl reporter in the 1940's. I ought to brain you."

"Sorry. Your correspondent didn't mean that the way it sounded. I was just using them as an example. You're still a girl reporter, Mary."

"I wish. Boy oh boy, you never know who your friends are. Okay, I knew a few of the old police reporters, characters all if they were any good. But you worked with one of them."

"That was different, Mary," said Nash, looking away. "Fred Hughes and I never did a murder together. With Hughes I was always looking up records in City Hall and Springfield. He knew where the fishy stuff was as far as municipal graft. But I don't think he's the guy I would consult for this."

Stern saw that she had touched a nerve. "He treated you like his personal copy boy, so you're mad at him. He treated everybody here the same way, Sam. Still, he had great tips. He knew so many people. And Hughes was a good police reporter for 20 years before they invented the title of chief investigator for him. I keep his address and phone number back at the desk for the Press Vets dinners."

"Is he goofy by now?" Nash was half hoping.

"He's not senile, if that's what you mean. He's still mad at the world like he was in his last years here. After his son died, he hated the young. Are they going to give you some time for this, like a week?"

"No, no. I just have to fit it in between things. Don't tell anybody, Mary. It's a little silly."

"You up to dueling with the old fart again?"

"If we could use guns. Did I ever tell you how we did the parking tickets?"

"Ahhh, what should I answer?" Stern shifted her fanny back and forth on the desk, swinging her legs lightly as a school girl. Nash guessed she was trying to restore the circulation cut off by the pressure of the edge of the desk.

"You say, 'No.' On a certain Tuesday, Hughes tells me a policeman is going to testify before the grand jury about some ticket fixing, and Hughes wants me to go with him out to Criminal Courts. I was interested to see how we were going to get this because the grand jury was secret. I was relatively new. So we get out there, and there's two grand juries meeting, one in the grand jury room and one in a locked regular courtroom on the sixth floor in the late afternoon. We can't get near the usual grand jury room, so we go up to the sixth floor, which is deserted by 3:30, and we wander around until we hear mumbling. We go to the side door of the courtroom, and Hughes tells me to put my ear to the crack between the double doors. I thought, 'This is reporting?' So I listen. Hughes' hearing wasn't good enough. And I tell him what is being said."

"What was the scandal?" said Stern. Nash could see the sparkle come into her widening eyes, a sign either of true interest or a woman's way of appearing interested when a man was talking.

"Your eyes are very blue, Stern."

"The pot calling the kettle blue. You're forgiven, Sammy. What was the scandal?"

"This cop testifies that police in the First District are under orders not to ticket any cars parked by the car hikers working for a couple well-connected restaurants in the North Loop no matter where the car hikers park 'em. That was basically it. Hughes was underwhelmed. Even I was. But the managing editor was hot for this story. He apparently was mad at one of those restaurants. They pressured him to pay his tab, or something. So Hughes and I and a photographer go out that night and find cars parked all over the North Loop, on the sidewalks, in the alleys. No tickets, of course.

"We write the story and run the pictures, come out four square in favor of the parking laws. And—as you knew they would—the next morning after the story appears, the police hustle over here and ticket every car, truck and bicycle parked near the Chronicle. Then that night, same as always, the cops show up at our loading dock to get their free papers. We gave them their free papers as usual."

"Why not?" she said.

"I know. That's the point." Nash smiled wider. "This was only a year after all the police reporters in town used to give their parking tickets to Hal Newberg who kept them in a shoe box. When the shoe box was full, Newberg would go over to Traffic Court and have all the tickets dismissed as a press privilege. That went back a long way."

"Why did that stop?"

"People started to abuse it, parking illegally on a date, or outside a high rise where they lived, every night all night. And the times were changing, too."

"Do you want Hughes' number?" she said in a smoky voice.

"What the hell," he said.

After visiting Mary Stern's post, Nash wrote a quick list of the phone calls he wanted to make for the rest of the day:

Colucci

Hughes

Animal

Flannery

Bryce.

His mind was working the way it should, he thought. All the effects of the hangover had worn off or been burnt off by the day's activity. He called both of Alderman Colucci's offices again and left more messages. No hints, simply, "Sam Nash of the Chronicle called," and a phone number.

He passed up Hughes and dialed the Illinois Coalition for Animals Rights, the group suggested by one of the Sunday editors as the central focus for the animal story. He spoke to somebody who said she was their "media person," and he set up an interview for 9 a.m. the next morning. Then he dialed Hughes.

9

"Hellohohoh."

An old lady answered.

"Is Fred Hughes there?"

She went to get him.

While waiting, Nash held the phone in his left hand and started clearing his desk with his right hand. Except for the space where Stern had sat, there were newspapers all over in piles of four, five and six. Grabbing as many as he could with one hand, he began dropping them in a neat pile on the floor. The pile was about a foot tall when a voice came on the line.

"Yeah. Who is this?"

"Sam Nash at the Chronicle, Fred, you old bastard."

"Let me pause and absorb this. The young Sam Nash. Did you win the Nobel Prize yet?"

"Sure I did. And the Pulitzer, too. Don't you read the papers?"

"I must have missed it. What was it for?"

"An in depth probe of jay walking."

"What causes you to disturb my idyl here, Nash? I assume the Chronicle is paying for this call." Hughes' voice was gravelly with phlegm, and he began clearing his throat seeking a normal tone. The sound was harsh and irritating, but Hughes made no effort to cover the phone.

"I have an unusual murder I would like to look into. Can't expect any help from the cops. Believe it or not, I always admired your style, Hughes." Most of the stories Nash had done with Hughes were quite serious.

"I suppose you are a private detective now, trying to prove some asshole innocent who the cops know is guilty. Forget it. The cops are probably right."

"The cops don't know about it."

"A murder the cops don't know about. Kehack. And you aren't telling them, Nash. Gonna save this all for yourself. If you haven't lost all your marbles, go to see Lupa. Is he still head of homicide?"

"He's a deputy superintendent now."

"Even better. Tell him I sent you."

"I don't have enough to go to any cops yet."

"I thought that would smoke you out. This is the sort of phony story pretenders do. Who is missing?"

"Why don't I just tell you what I know and we'll start from there."

"Do I have to listen to this?" said Hughes, suddenly near choking. He had a whistle in his voice.

Nash was tempted to say, "No," and let it drop. Instead he said:

"Yeah, you do. For old time's sake. For all the stories I did the work on and put your byline first."

"Ho! Kaharrgh. I suppose that makes sense to you, Nash. Since we're talking turkey here, I'll tell you straight that you don't have it as an alleged investigative reporter and you never will. Hockhh. If you ever had it, you wouldn't have been working so long as my leg man. You would have got your own stories like any real reporter.

When's the last time you were on page one, Nash? A week ago? A month?"

When he began asking these questions, Hughes' voice grew weaker and rose an octave as if his windpipe was constricting.

"That clears the air, Hughes? Shall we get down to it?"

In sidestepping the attack, Nash felt the return of a familiar pattern of dealing with Hughes, without nostalgia. It was like returning to sixth grade. He hated sixth grade.

(Nash did not mention that after Hughes' retirement, Nash had asked to be a general assignment reporter.)

Hughes paused, a myopic bull who has lost sign of the matador. Then he said in a low, clear voice:

"You are still a dumb son of a bitch, Nash, but you are persistent. I'll give you five minutes."

"What's your big fucking hurry?"

"Never you mind."

Nash told Victoria's story briefly, pretending it occurred in a regular hospital and Victoria was an employee.

"Nash, that couldn't be simpler. Take your source to the police and make a deal that you get the story. Offer your services, too. They probably won't know you."

"My source won't go to the police."

"Twist your friend's arm. Tell him, or her, you'll have to nail her fanny, too, for obstruction. You can figure that out for yourself, Nash."

"Let's just assume there's a good reason for things to be this way."

"How many people were in on this murder besides your alleged source?"

"My source is not involved. Two orderlies and a doctor."

"Does your source watch a lot of soap operas?"

"That is a problem I have considered. I'm not 100 per cent sure this happened, but there are enough clues in the description to suggest something did go down. I want to check it out. It's just a side job."

"Have you got names?" Questions seemed hard for Hughes, pushing his voice into the upper register again.

"I got two of the names including the doctor. I can get the third one, I think."

"And the time of day and the location?"

"Yeah."

"No motive?"

"No. I'm assuming dope."

"Haahhhg. Uhhh. Dope is all over like warm shit today. Anyway, the motive doesn't matter at this stage. The sensible thing to do is to go to the cops with your source and the names and let them try to scare somebody, one of those three names. You know if your source is too shy to go to the police, you have no witnesses. And it sounds like you have no body."

"Right. Yes."

"You have diddly. Fucking air."

"Give me one, original, Fred Hughes idea."

"For old times' sake. You see, Nash, somebody has to scare one of those three into talking. And not you. They'd see right through you. Police are good at scaring people. They have badges. Since you refuse to use them, call up the head of the hospital and make him do it."

"Okay." Nash waited to see if there was more.

"Kaharg. You say you're about to go to the police with this astounding story. But somebody told you the administrator of this place was a fine fellow, so if he'll tell you what he knows, then you'll be assured he is not a party to this coverup."

"And if he doesn't know anything?"

"Give him the three names and the description of the alleged event. Tell him you're going out on a limb. When the paper gets reports like this, we usually just refer them to the police. Of course, you have no idea if any of this is true. An employee of his approached the paper. Avoid making accusations in your own name.

"Tell him you'll give him 24 hours, 48 hours at most. And afterwards, you and he will go to the cops together."

Nash resumed throwing newspapers on the floor. "I may try that," he said, but he doubted it.

"I ain't through yet. Mind you, I'm just winging it here. The head of the hospital probably won't learn anything. Even more likely, he will tell you to get laid. He knows commander so and so, and if you want to sit down with them and talk about this ALLEGED report, that would be the proper way to handle it."

"Back to there again," said Nash.

"Then you DO sit down with commander so and so and the administrator and give them the name of your source. Maintain your dignity, and you won't lose your job. If it doesn't pan out, you will be an idiot. But that, Nash, is not so bad. So you shook up the jagoffs at Malpractice Memorial. Good editors won't mind that. They get a kick out of it.

"What happens to the source?"

"How do I know what happens to the source?" Hughes' voice was weakening again. "Either your source was telling the truth or she wasn't."

"What if I gave my word, Fred?"

"Oh, crap! What if somebody got murdered, Sam?"

"Thanks. You're going to be late for the races or whatever?"

"Card games. That's what we do here. Ahhemmmm. I almost lost my wife in a big pot the other day."

"Yeah, right." Nash laughed.

"Do me a favor."

"What?"

"If you follow my advice, let me know how this comes out. If you don't, don't call me no more."

"Deal. Want me to say hello to anybody here for you?"

"No. Just keep the paper going until after my funeral."

"When is it?"

"I haven't decided."

Nash hung up and put his feet on top of the desk again. The relationship hadn't changed in the five years since Hughes' retirement party, the last time they had spoken. Nash had worked with Hughes for three years and had finally decided Hughes was a human category all to himself.

One memory stood out as Nash tapped the base of his ballpoint pen on the desk. He and Hughes and two other reporters were having lunch at the Press Club. In the middle of the meal, a short, muscular, Italian type with a bald head, wearing a casual knit shirt and tailored slacks that cost more than Nash's one suit approached Hughes. He put his arm around Hughes and sat down next to him ponderously.

The two conversed softly, ignoring Nash and the others and shared a few laughs about some secret. Then the muscular guy left.

On the walk back to the office from the Press Club, Hughes had reached into his pocket and pulled out five $100 bills. "Just what my brother needs to put down on a new car for his brood."

"Where'd you get it, Fred?" one of Nash's companions had asked, as expected.

"My friend, Albert. Didn't you see him pass it under the table? His union went out on strike, and he asked me to keep it out of the paper. Was easy. Wasn't news anyway."

The other reporters' mouths hung open. Their chief investigator! Nash knew Hughes well enough by then to understand he was an actor who liked to maintain his aura of mystery and unpredictability with small incidents. The $500 had probably been Hughes' own money. But you never really knew with Hughes.

Nash doubted there was a reporter left in America who would pull such a stunt anymore.

Hughes' advice on the story was very good, Nash recognized as he finished piling the newspapers on the floor. He let the pile get sloppy because he refused to take his feet off the desk. Nothing fancy with Hughes. Economy of effort. Quick results. Hughes would never conceive of something as outlandish as putting an undercover reporter to work in the hospital. That stuff was for the Ledger or the Post. The Chronicle could not afford it even if the facts justified such a production.

Nash also knew he would not follow the advice. It was too risky to expose Victoria for a routine inquiry. She was an inmate there. But Hughes was right about one thing. It was foolish to keep the cops totally out, a conclusion Nash had already been leaning toward. That was where Bryce came in.

Nash got out of his chair and carried a pile of newspapers that came up to his chin to a gray, plastic garbage can on wheels that was lined with a plastic bag. He tried to remember when he had begun treating Bryce as if Bryce were—despite his manner and reputation—an ordinary, uncertain, insecure person who wanted to be liked the same as everybody else. Bryce never seemed to mind. Nash noticed it was 4:30. He dropped the newspapers in the garbage can, and they split the bag.

10

Nash picked up the receiver and, for the second time, called Clarence Bryce, the chief of the criminal division of the Cook County State's Attorney's Office. He had to wade through two secretaries to get him, but this time Nash was successful.

He asked, "Did you get my message?"

"Some crackpot called here wanting to know if the answer was: 'Mr. Green—in the hall—with the knife.' That, I assume, was you, Nash."

"Come on, Clare. I'm a serious journalist. I think it was Miss Plum anyway. Listen, I've got a favor to ask."

"And I have one for you."

"Good. That always makes it easier. I think you might enjoy this."

Bryce had been chief of the criminal division for five years, a long run. The State's Attorney had changed, and the new State's Attorney was of the opposite political party, but Bryce was kept on because of his reputation in the office. Nash and Bryce had known each other since Nash had been assigned to cover the Criminal Courts Building years earlier. When they first met, Bryce was short and husky and arrogantly tough in the manner of a certain number of young trial lawyers. Now Bryce was short and massive, but nasty only when he wished to be.

Nash told him Victoria's story and added his reasons for believing it had a hint of credibility to it along with his guess at a motive. Bryce took the story seriously right off, which Nash considered odd. The story begged for a joke; but Bryce seemed preoccupied.

"Did she tell the police approximately the same story she told you?" asked Bryce, missing the point.

"As I said, she hasn't talked to any cops. She's pretty vulnerable to be going around making public accusations. This was told to me in confidence, and I was going to investigate it until I realized a curious thing."

"What was that?"

"It's easier to let you do it."

"Of course, Nash. You are beset with many weighty concerns besides this one."

"That's the truth." Nash had just concocted an idea for his own investigation, but the idea required a lot of time. There was no need to tell Bryce his scheme.

"I'll have to call up the director of the state Department of Mental Health to ask if we can see their girl," said Bryce. "I don't know anybody personally at DMH, and they're not one of our most cooperative agencies. But I think we will reach some agreement. We'll have her transferred, if necessary, and we'll find out if there's anything to this."

"Hey, uhh, Clarence, that's perfect, but don't you think this is just a little bit funny? Unbutton your shirt collar. It's pinching your neck again." Nash could picture Bryce in his long-sleeved, white shirt, the only type of shirt he ever wore, with his fat neck garrotted by the collar.

"My neck is fine. Joanne is purchasing custom made shirts now. As for your other question, EVERYthing is funny to the ladies and gentlemen of the news media, Nash. If you wish, my personal theory is that they are running a white slavery racket at Read, sending insane but beautiful women to Palestinian terrorists in return for a pledge that they won't do anything on Sundays. How's that? It's all orchestrated by the State Department, and the guy who got shot was an intrusive newspaper reporter."

"You may be right, Clarence. That has real possibilities. Otherwise, what time are you usually leaving the office these days. Wanna have a drink?"

"Too late. Seven or seven-thirty."

"Be cool, buddy. You can't try all the cases yourself. The young guys are just as smart as you were."

"You are snidely implying that I am no longer as smart as I was. I haven't tried a case in more than a year, so there may be something to that. Let me tell you today's box score, Sam. Judge Hardhead Clifford threw out two-thirds of our evidence against the animal who killed the two cops last summer. Our best witness flipped in the Bonnie Logan rape and murder, the one on the El tracks. One of my assistants was threatened with contempt if he doesn't stop complaining about the number of continuances granted to every lawyer who happens to be a friend of Judge Wishaw. And we've got a serious grand jury investigation that is going to hell because suddenly everybody has a slightly different story."

"The Christmas turkeys disappeared from the County Jail again."

"No. Alderman Finnegan misbehaved. You don't know about that for now. Most of these things are my problems. . . .When did the Christmas turkeys disappear from the County Jail?"

"Before your time, Clarence. Before my time, too."

"As I was saying, perhaps you could distinguish yourself among your ilk by performing a rare, selfless good deed. I would like the Chronicle to 'lash out' at Judge Wishaw on your front page. That's a newspaper term I've always enjoyed. I'm asking you to speak up for the story. Wishaw thinks his courtroom should be a calm port in the storm for his old legal buddies. Our witnesses are paying the price. We bring them in on firm trial dates, and he keeps kicking the cases over."

"Clare, complaints about continuances and delayed justice are not exactly original, page-one-type news. What happened to two-thirds of the evidence in the cop-killing case?"

"Technical problems with the search warrant. Murray gave Anderson chapter and verse on Judge Wishaw, an impressive study we've put together. Call me tomorrow...just a second." Bryce began talking to someone else and Nash could hear only half the conversation. "Tell Banks I want the witnesses in here tomorrow. All of them.... Don't let Banks slip away. Tell him he has to stay all night, if necessary, to round them up. I'll be here to check on him." Bryce came back on the line. "Call me tomorrow, Sam, and I'll let you know if we got in to see your maiden in distress. I've got her name written down here. There's an outside chance of difficulty. On Judge Wishaw, what do you think you can do for me? I want to see that son of a bitch buried."

"Custom made shirts, eh?"

"Yes. Joanne keeps hoping I'll join a respectable law firm soon. Dress for success."

"Anderson" of whom Bryce spoke was the Chronicle reporter assigned to the Criminal Courts Building, 26th Street and California Avenue, where Bryce had his office. Nash wondered how Bryce would react if Anderson's story did not get in the paper at all.

"I'll exert my enormous influence on your behalf, Clarence," said Nash, adding, "Let's get drunk."

"That's basically a reasonable proposition. Maybe next month. Goodbye, Sam."

There was a guy who could use a vacation, thought Nash. Then Nash called the phone company's name and address service to check the phone number Victoria had given him. He kicked himself for not doing it hours sooner. The number belonged to a pay phone in the Read Mental Health Center. He was relieved enough to light another cigarette. Only one name was left on his list, Flannery. He decided to postpone Flannery to another day.

Nash was beginning to get concerned because he hadn't heard from Ald. Colucci. But how could Colucci call back when Nash was on the phone all the time? To kill a few minutes and give Colucci a chance, Nash summoned up Anderson's story on Judge Wishaw in the computer by asking the computer for anything written that day by Anderson. Nash read the story. For what it was, it was good, Nash thought. At 15 inches, it was too long for its news value in the next day's Chronicle and too short to explain with ease the judge's handling of four or five court cases. But the information was there in the short form for those who were interested.

Nash released the story, and when his mind wandered, he thought of his wife. He winced, then closed his eyes. When he forced himself to think of something else, he got a new idea.

"Jose, watch my phone, would you? If anybody calls, I'll be right back."

Joseph Gentile, an Italian whose nickname was Joe, not Jose—except to Nash—was typing on his terminal at the desk next to Nash's. He waved without looking up. Nash went quickly to the morgue and signed out three envelopes of clips on the Illinois Department of Mental Health.

On the way back, he approached the city desk horseshoe. Phelan was standing in the slot, arranging his work. He seemed subdued, not his usual top sergeant self, Nash thought. Phelan seemed, for the moment, old.

"That was a hell of a story you had last night, Red. Once in a lifetime."

"It was for him," said Phelan who picked up his wire basket full of stories and story schedules and started to turn away.

"Hey, Red, I wanted to ask a favor of you."

"You see what time it is?" Phelan nodded at the clock on the east wall. It was 5 after 5.

"Did you get a story from Anderson about a judge named Wishaw who gives out too many continuances?"

"I doubt it will get in the paper. Hurry up. What do you want?"

"You think you could get it on page one?"

"Sam," Phelan looked at him incredulously, "have you been drinking? Not a fucking chance. I warned you before as a friend, and that was when you only drank after work." Phelan started walking towards the conference room at the north end of the office.

"Red, where do you get off with that shit?" said Nash who caught up and walked alongside him. "Did I tell you you look old today?" Nash was going to add, "past your fucking prime," but he restrained himself. "No, I didn't because it has nothing to do with my request."

"If I look old, it's because everybody gets old, Sam. Get the difference?"

"I'll give you two good reasons to get that story in the paper, Red. Number one, it's a public service. If you read it, you know that, although perhaps we are all too jaded to give a shit."

Phelan ignored him.

"Number two, the guy who wants us to get it in the paper is a good friend of ours in the state's attorney's office who has helped this newspaper a lot in the past and will again in the future. We owe him."

"Nash, if you ever follow me across the room like this again, I'll knock your teeth out."

Nash stayed with him step for step.

"That's a legitimate story, and it's NOT MY STORY. I really appreciate your professional manner, Red."

"We're friends, so lay off." Phelan obviously meant this.

"Think of the story, Red, just the story. You know a worthwhile story when you see one. You're the best night city editor in town."

"Don't say that again. Anything could happen within reason."

Nash knew this meant the story suddenly had a chance to get in the paper. "Now please leave me be."

Nash let him go. He mulled over Phelan's last words: "Please leave me be." What kind of way was that for Phelan to end a fight?

11

A short while earlier, after five hours sleep, a shower, and a breakfast of salad, baked potato, meat loaf and canned peas prepared by his wife, Red Phelan had started to feel a little better about the tavern blast story and the man who died.

He had noticed, humbly pleased, that the meat loaf was whole, and the baked potato had been cooked only once. Phelan usually ate for breakfast whatever his wife and children had eaten the night before. His baked potatoes were often reheated in a pot with a little water. This gave the potatoes the consistency of a crisp apple or an unripe peach as opposed to the fluffiness of the just baked variety, but he never complained. Phelan liked potatoes in all their forms except french fried.

Margaret Phelan had gotten dinner ready by 2:30 p.m., trimming her own plans accordingly.

"Good meal, babe," said Phelan when he had finished.

"I thought you looked a little wacked out. You need your strength. Here, I got this for you."

She handed him a Chronicle that she had walked two blocks to buy from a Chronicle box at the bus stop at 103rd and Pulaski.

"What's this?"

"The 5-star. It looks good to me. I read the story. It's just like it sounded on Wally Phillips although they didn't read it all." Phillips had an unusually popular morning talk show on WGN radio. The Chronicle edition that Margaret had purchased was the last edition. They received an earlier edition by home delivery for which they paid like any subscribers.

"Paul Youngman writes a good story," he said. "It's too bad the guy died."

"Youngman writes a good story because he's got a good boss."

"Of course. But I had nothing to do with this."

"Sure you did."

"After I told him to write it, I turned the desk over to Nordstrom and I left. Youngman did it because he's a damn good newspaperman when he wants to be. From the old school."

"Youngman wouldn't even be there if it wasn't for you. Didn't you tell me they wanted him out, but you held onto him?"

She poured the grease from the meat loaf pan into a milk carton, holding the carton over the sink to catch the drips.

"Yeah. That was too bad. Unnecessary. We took that three weeks vacation and he drove Wolfram nuts. But it was a case of the editor, Wolfram, not knowing how to handle somebody. You can't push the old boys around. You have to find out what grooves they run in and try to accommodate them. You do that, and they'll go all out for you."

"That's what I mean. He wrote that story because you saved him. Admit it, Red. You're great."

After squeezing liquid dish soap into the pan, she placed the pan in the sink and ran hot water in it.

"If you're satisfied, I'm satisfied," said Phelan.

From the sink, she turned and faced him with her legs in blue jeans wide apart, her hands on her hips and her breasts jutting out under her blouse.

"I'm satisfied, Phelan," she said with a smile.

"C'mere."

"No. You better go to work." She turned to face the sink.

He left the kitchen table and went to the sink, putting his arms around her from behind and cupping her breasts in his hands.

"You going to be staying up late to watch a movie tonight, woman?"

"If there's anything good on."

"What if there isn't?"

"I might read a book."

"I should have got you that Agatha Christie book you wanted." She put her head back on his shoulder and enjoyed his hands.

"I got it already."

"Good. Don't read too fast."

"Now you go to work. When are you going to see one of Kevin's basketball games?"

"Saturday? I didn't want to upset him when he was sitting on the bench. Is he any good starting with the big guys?"

"See what you think."

"Who would have guessed? I never played basketball."

"That might account for some of it."

. . . .

Phelan felt even better about the tavern blast story when he looked at the final editions of the Ledger and Post in the office. The Ledger had the story and a picture below the fold on page one, and the Post had it as the line story. For quotes from the victim, both were forced to say, ". . . told another Chicago newspaper in a telephone interview," and they lifted whatever they could from Forrest's 4-star story.

Phelan knew the home delivery Ledger and Post did not have a word about the blast. He had seen them the night before. He

108

thought of the home delivery readers who got the Chronicle's 4-star. They were the only subscribers who could relate what they heard on the radio or TV in the morning to their newspapers. [The final editions at all three papers were almost entirely street sales.]

A clean beat on a spot news news story of this dimension was rare. It had even occurred to Phelan that he might hear a compliment or two from his bosses. This unguarded notion would normally have made him wary as soon as he had it. But the lingering picture of his 42-year-old wife with her hands on her hips and her chest stuck out had temporarily smoothed his suspicious edges.

As always at the beginning of his shift, Phelan had settled in his "hiding place" at a table at the far end of the locker room, an expanded version of what had formerly been the coat room. There he read newspapers, story dupes, memos, schedules of events, and laid tentative plans for the evening. During his reading period, Phelan hid far away from the city desk to avoid reporters who might start bothering him prematurely and to make sure his predecessor was not tempted to leave early. Everyone knew where his hiding place was, but custom dictated that he not be disturbed.

"Phelan, Mr. Solomon wants to see you."

Phelan was startled. And he was instantly annoyed like an animal who is surprised while eating. The copy clerk who had spoken to Phelan from the entrance to the locker room saw the flash in the night city editor's eyes and fled.

Trying to imagine why a copy girl had come to interrupt him, Phelan found himself thinking for a second time that he might hear some nice words. This time he was surprised at himself and forewarned by the foolishness of the idea. He gathered up his pile of newspapers, other papers, and his story schedule, walked out of the tile-floored locker room and across a rug the length of the newsroom until he entered Solomon's office without knocking.

"You want to see me, Aaron?"

"I'll call you back," said Solomon into the phone. "Yeah, Red. What did you bring all that for?"

109

"If I put it down someplace, it might get lost."

"Suit yourself. You can put it on the couch if you want. Get the door, would you."

Phelan closed it.

"I have to tell you, you and your people did a great job last night with the explosion and the guy who was trapped. I haven't seen any reports yet, but I'll bet you sold some extra papers on the street."

Solomon did not deal with Phelan the way he dealt with reporters. Phelan and Al Miller were Solomon's two chief assistants. What they did decided in a large measure whether Solomon succeeded or failed. Also, Solomon was aware of the difference in age and experience between himself and Phelan.

"We had a little luck," responded Phelan. "We were about due. Youngman wrote a nice story for the 5-star which made the whole thing work. We were hoping the guy wouldn't die."

"I know what you mean in all the ways. It's a funny business we're in."

"Sometimes it is."

Solomon leaned back in his flexible, swivel chair scratching his curly head with his right hand, obviously stalling. Finally, Solomon said, "Why don't you put that stuff on the couch and sit down."

Phelan placed all his paraphernalia in a neat pile on the fake leather couch on the side of Solomon's office and sat down on the cushion next to it. Solomon swiveled to face him.

"I want to say something to Youngman about his story. That was your idea to call there, right?"

"Sure."

"Simple but beautiful. I envy you that one."

Phelan smiled. Solomon meant it.

"If I forget to say something to Youngman, you tell him I liked his story. Tell him anyway. It won't hurt."

"Be better coming from you, Aaron."

"I'll try to remember." Solomon made a note to himself on a small memo pad but continued talking. "Thanks for calling me last night. I think you handled it as well as could be done. One thing. Don't be too hard on Forrest. The new reporters are not like you and I were, thick skinned."

"Did he complain to his uncle, the financial editor?"

"Yes. And his uncle mentioned it to Simonet."

Phelan's jaw dropped. "Fitzpatrick took a complaint from that child—about getting yelled at by his boss—to the executive editor?"

"Yes."

"Did Simonet have the sense to boot them both in the ass?" Phelan considered Fitzpatrick incompetent and devious, but Fitzpatrick was Simonet's most loyal ally, his eyes and ears for rumors.

"Take it easy, Red," said Solomon. "Simonet understands your problems."

"What problems?" In an unconscious gesture, Phelan closed his left eye half way and stared at Solomon with his right eye.

"The usual night shift stuff. New reporters a lot of the time; unhappy reporters who think they're in exile; short staff if the going gets hot."

Phelan had been sitting well back, sunk in the couch. Now he sat up on the edge. "When did this subject come up? Anything I should know about? I seem to be missing something."

"Simonet was inquiring today about how the night shift works, especially late at night. I told him how valuable you are to me and the paper."

"Whoa. Thanks for that. I would have thought he had some idea of what I do here by now. He's been here eight years."

"Now he knows."

The growth of Phelan's suspicions could be observed in his expression.

"There's one more thing I have to mention concerning last night," Solomon continued. "Then we'll go on to other matters. I probably don't need to ask, but whose decision was it to tape the guy in the basement last night?"

"It was my decision, and I did it physically, too. When the FBI comes, I'll surrender."

"That's a state law. You know that."

Phelan was unimpressed. Solomon swiveled toward his desk and picked up a large piece of lead from the composing room, one of his paperweights.

"Well, it made Simonet a little nervous this morning when he found out. He had a bad experience with that once—when he was managing editor?"

"I remember it well," said Phelan. "But that was a criminal case. Simonet got personally involved in one of our rare investigations, and he was way over his head."

"He doesn't see much difference, and I'm not sure I do."

"That's bullshit, Aaron, if you'll pardon the expression."

"You can't tape people in Illinois without their expressed knowledge and consent unless you go through certain procedures."

"I called the state's attorney up and got permission."

"Come on."

"Just kidding. Listen, Aaron..."

"Now you need a court order," said Solomon, "not just permission from the state's attorney."

"Who says? I don't recall that. But what I was trying to say is that Simonet taped a copper in the act of shaking down a tavern owner and then used the tape to accuse the cop."

"I know."

"And he bragged about the tape in the paper which brought the ACLU and the Post down on us proclaiming that the Chronicle is not above the law."

"The copper is probably shaking somebody else down right now as we speak," said Solomon. "He got off."

"I thought they at least fired him."

"They did. He filed a lawsuit and won his job back. Without the tape evidence, which was inadmissible, the city had no case. We didn't print the end of it. It was long after."

112

"All right," said Phelan. "We're not accusing anybody. We're not bragging about a tape. We're just using it as a tool to help somebody's recollection. And we're keeping it very quiet so as not to offend anybody's sensibilities. It's a total non-issue, Aaron. Tell Simonet to relax."

"It's not quite that easy, Red." Solomon lifted the paper weight about a foot off the desk then put it down heavily. "If there could possibly be anyone who didn't know about the tape from office conversation—and that's the kind of stuff that gets in gossip columns or the Reader [a weekly with a large circulation]—then Gentile took care of it, complaining loudly that you used his tape without his permission."

"Was anything on it?"

"An interview with a mountain climber that ran in the paper three months ago. Just don't tape without the consent and permission of the person at the other end. You and I know it's the little things we have to pay attention to, Red, like spelling names right and asking permission to tape."

Phelan nodded, but Solomon noticed Phelan's face darkening and settling into contempt.

"Okay," Solomon softened. "You know you deserve better than this because you did an extraordinary thing last night and did it well."

"Under the prevailing circumstances, Aaron, would you have asked that guy, 'Sir, may we tape this conversation?' "

"I might."

Phelan snorted. Solomon laughed. "I don't know. You were there. I wasn't. Simonet insisted I lay down the law on taping; so that's done. And that is the law."

Phelan shook his head from side to side as if in exasperation and sat back.

Solomon relaxed, too. "Is there anything you can think of we could have done for that guy that we didn't, Red?"

"Did we send flowers?"

Solomon grinned and shook his own head. "Red, help me out here. I listened to the tape, and everything seemed...fairly respectable. We have to be careful of lawsuits in this situation."

"The tape probably shows the usual chaos. We looked out for the guy, I'll tell you that. Give the tape and the stories to the lawyers and see what they say."

"Simonet doesn't want the lawyers involved. They're a pipeline straight to old man Schuman." Solomon was obviously uncomfortable. He would have preferred to avoid that subject. "There are some hard feelings from the eavesdropping case years ago. I don't know the whole problem." Solomon waved his hand. "Forget that. Simonet is under a lot of pressure. What I'm going to tell you now is not to be repeated. I trust your wife so I guess you do, too. But nobody else."

Phelan nodded. Solomon sat up straight again and put his arms on the desk.

"The official baloney is that Mike Schuman has given us a promise of one more year at the minimum. The truth is, we've got six months to show substantial improvement, especially in advertising lineage, but circulation would be nice also. Maybe we won't get the whole six months. We're going to have some new ideas starting Sunday."

Mike Schuman was the son of Carl Schuman, publisher and patriarch of the family that owned the Chronicle.

"Okay," said Phelan. Everybody knew another campaign was being planned.

"Promotion is going to launch a blitz, and we're going to launch 'The New Chronicle.' New makeup. A new personality. A remodeled product to attract the advertisers and the upscale readers the advertisers like."

Phelan rolled his eyes.

"You better be careful, Red." Solomon paused. Then he continued his speech. "A lot of the staff will adopt your attitude. I know you've seen these campaigns before, but you may not see one again if it doesn't work. A little dog doo has always been a part of this business. I'm pushing certain ideas, but we'll have to see what happens. The final decisions are going to be made tonight."

"I'm behind the new program, seriously," said Phelan. "What choice do we have?"

"Mostly this will involve makeup. Certain quarters have boundless faith in makeup," Solomon continued. Phelan well understood that this meant type faces, page design, headline sizes, story configuration, and the display of pictures and charts. "Features is being tuned up which it certainly needs. Locally, we may try for more news features and scoops and let the Post and the Ledger have the city budget."

Phelan was suddenly interested.

"When you go in there, tonight, Aaron, stress one thing. This is my offering from 25 years experience. We try for scoops; we try for good features every day. Give it our all under the new program. And when we've got 'em, we HAVE to play them well. Back in the paper won't do any good. You've got to be proud of what you do. Equally important: When you don't have them—if a story doesn't work out the way you hoped—you don't force it. That's where we can lose credibility. We come back and try again the next day."

"I'll mention those things," said Solomon.

"Better stress it or they'll be looking for a bombshell a day."

"I'll do my best." Solomon paused. "This is the last shot, you know." The "new" Chronicle's trial period was really much shorter, Solomon knew. The paper would be lucky to survive three months. But this was not the story he was authorized to tell.

"The three-star doping?" said Phelan.

"What?"

"The doping session." Phelan pointed to his watch. It was fifteen to five.

"Shit. Yeah." Solomon stood up. "I need you on the team, Red." He pointed at Phelan. "I want you on the team."

Phelan narrowed his eyes at this. "Be straight with me. Does Simonet want me out?"

"The taping really bugged him," said Solomon. "Then I think Fitzpatrick's whining about his nephew came at the wrong time. I can handle it, I'm pretty sure, if you do your part."

Phelan touched his forehead with incredulity. "You never know," he said. He shook his head again. Then Phelan gathered up the tools of his trade while Solomon came out from behind the desk. Before they went out the door, Solomon told him, "Pay attention to any suggestions or criticisms from Simonet just in case they don't come through me. Even be enthusiastic if you can."

Phelan chuckled with a note of bitterness.

Solomon added, "You're the best night city editor in town, Red."

In truth, Phelan was the oldest night city editor in town. The job consumed and exhausted those who held it, including younger men and women who had lasted much less time than Phelan.

After leaving Solomon's office, Phelan conferred with day city editor Miller and got a five-minute rundown on most of the latest stories, possible stories, the locations of the staff, and sundry orders that resisted categories. Because there was no time, the summary was too quick. Phelan began to arbitrarily assign lengths with his pen to the newest stories on the schedule as Miller left, based on either what Miller had said or on five- or six-word summaries next to the slugs. Phelan could change the guesses later. At least he could change some of the guesses. But he had to have lengths for the stories on his schedule to give to the news editors in the doping session. Two slugs had no summaries, and Phelan, who was in charge, did not know what these stories were. He would wait to see if they were around somewhere or if they turned up later. He rose from his chair.

In his career, Phelan had been through unexpected demotions, missed promotions, and lateral moves based on the whims and fortunes of his superiors. But he felt he was losing his resilience for these insults. He knew he would get very angry later when he had time to think. They wouldn't fire him, he supposed, probably just push him aside again into something demeaning, editor in charge of cleaning the bathrooms. There was another problem nagging him. What was it? The Chronicle was going under! That he was sure of. The paper was through.

"That was a hell of a story you had last night, Red," said Nash accosting him. "Once in a lifetime."

"It was for him," said Phelan.

12

Nash went back to his desk reasonably satisfied. If Phelan got the story in someplace, obviously not on one, Nash thought—that was only to get Phelan's attention—then Nash could pester Bryce about Victoria. Simple, really.

"Nobody called," said Gentile.

"Thanks."

Nash began skimming through the clips on the Department of Mental Health looking for the name of any employee who had filed a sex discrimination suit against the department, or any kind of lawsuit, or the name of a union agitator, someone on the inside who might be willing to talk. This was in addition to another, somewhat absurd, idea he had concocted for performing his own investigation. Nash had learned not to be afraid of absurd ideas. They were just ideas.

He did not find any useful names in the clips, but he continued to read them anyway because some told strange stories.

"Hi."

Nash looked up to see Georgia Krolikowski standing next to his desk with her left hand on her hip and a cocky, "Aren't-you-going-to-notice-me?" expression. Nash noticed. She was wearing a dress.

"Couldn't find a thing to wear, eh, Georgia?"

She turned, flicking the skirt. "I like it. Don't you?"

She was wearing a simple, fancy dress with a deeper than normal neckline for the office, although her breasts were hidden, and a short string of pearls. The dress was a cross between innocent and alluring with the effect depending almost on the wearer's facial expression. He could see now that Krolikowski was unsure.

"Knowing you, there's something daring about your white dress. I can't put my finger on it. You're not wearing underwear. Is that it?"

"Don't be a jerk," she said looking around.

Nash grinned. Krolikowski was making him uncomfortable—her neck was quite lovely—but he was willing to endure it.

"It's not white. It's cream. The thing is, it's almost like an evening dress." She pointed to the lace trim on the collar.

"Take the pearls off," he said.

"The pearls are okay. Pearls are in. You are a big help."

Then Nash realized what was wanted from him. It had nothing to do with the news business, or the dress's place in the office, or Nash's knowledge of fashion. Realizing this, he said:

"You look terrific, Georgia."

"You think so?"

"Guys will be drooling. Me, too. But not while you're standing here."

"My boyfriend picked it out. He's going to meet me for lunch tonight, and he wanted me to wear it."

Nash knew her boyfriend was a Chicago policeman. "You're uncomfortable, but you're wearing it anyway."

"Obviously."

119

"Well, I wish you luck." The way he said it, and the way he smiled at her made Krolikowski blush.

"Don't get carried away, Sam."

"Wouldn't think of it. Turn 360 and give me the full effect."

"I can't do that here."

"I'd say you were capable of doing anything you wanted."

Krolikowski represented to Nash the paradox of the hotshot female reporter. She was smart by instinct—this was unfakeable in a reporter; she liked hard work; she understood news; she could make people talk; she could write. He had watched her mature into tremendous confidence while she continued to be permanently insecure. Good reporters were all like that.

The paradox was that Krolikowski sometimes wanted to be appreciated by men solely as a female. When she did, she didn't want her professional reputation to interfere.

"Yeah?" said Krolikowski. "If I'm so capable of doing anything I want, how do I get off the night shift?"

"It'll happen, Georgia. And when it does, you'll miss it. You'll find that everyone on days feels unloved and unappreciated by the bosses."

"I'll risk it."

"Interesting story you had last night."

"I was on the fringe. I wish we could have helped that guy. But it reminded me of the mine disaster you and I worked on downstate years ago. I still think about that."

"I think about it, too."

They stared at each other for a few moments, teasing. Nash recalled there had been a sudden sexual chemistry between them at the scene of that story, a chemistry that was almost visible in the air. The result was that they both acted with such propriety that it finally became funny. Looking back, Nash wondered if he should have behaved in a different way.

"Okay, 360, right?" said Krolikowski. She did a turn adopting a model's aloof expression. When she finished, she was facing Nash again. She tossed her hair and walked away.

Nash whistled.

"Thank you, Georgia," said Gentile in a mocking tone from the desk directly behind Nash. After Krolikowski was several yards away, Gentile added, "Maybe you should go after that, Sam."

Nash stiffened, grimaced and raised his right hand without turning around. "Don't bring it up, Joe." Nash meant the subject of his separation, and he knew that Gentile knew what he meant.

"Sorry."

"It's okay."

"What are you working on?"

Nash turned around to look at Gentile to take the sting out of sudden rebuke. "Nothing yet. I'm just killing time waiting for a call back and checking some clips." He showed the clips in his hand.

"What do you know about the Lake County Board?"

"Only what I read in the papers, Joe."

Nash smiled meaning he knew nothing in the way of background or names that could help Gentile with whatever he was working on. With heavily forced concentration, Nash resumed skimming the rest of the clips on the Department of Mental Health, going back five years. Then he picked up two he had put aside because they interested him, and he read those carefully.

Despite his distractions, he began to get the tingling sensation a reporter gets when he is mechanically pursuing an unlikely story, if only to kill it, letting anything and everything interrupt him, when suddenly the story begins to seem possible.

Of the two clips that aroused his interest, neither suggested employees of the Department of Mental Health were inclined to homicide. But the clips did suggest that if a crime occurred in the department, DMH employees sure as heck could cover it up. They were ready, willing, and able to cover things up, and they were experienced.

The first of the two curious stories, both several years old, told how mental health officials had concealed from the police the whereabouts of a male inmate accused of sexually assaulting a female inmate in the Madden Mental Health Center in suburban Maywood.

The hospital security department had reported the sex attack to the local police department, but afterwards, the doctors repelled all efforts by police to arrest the attacker, claiming that revealing his location would violate his right, as a state mental patient, to confidentiality. The doctors secretly transferred the attacker out of the Maywood hospital to another state hospital 25 miles away to frustrate the cops.

Nash noted, with a grin, that the doctors did not reveal the whereabouts of the alleged sex attacker "until three weeks after he died" when he got drunk while out on a pass, then passed out and froze to death on the grounds of the Elgin State (mental) Hospital. The doctors had been hiding the guy for six months from the date of the sex attack. They claimed their conduct was justified by a revised state mental health code. The new code contained a patients' bill of rights including a strong provision guaranteeing the patients confidentiality during and after their stay in any state mental hospital.

This provision obviously had been added to assure people who suffered mental breakdowns that their records would not later turn up in the hands of blackmail artists or the press. But DMH officials had interpreted the law to mean they were duty bound to hide an alleged sex offender from the cops. Give a bureaucrat an excuse to suppress information, and he will suppress everything, Nash concluded.

The second story told how mental health officials had tried to conceal embarrassing information from a federal grand jury, citing the same justification about the patient's right to privacy. At the maximum security mental hospital in downstate Chester, where many of the criminally insane were held, the doctors had once had custody of a madman who had been transferred there from a U.S. veterans hospital. In the veterans hospital, he had killed another patient in a terrible manner, but had been found innocent by reason of insanity.

Despite a continuing history of bizarre and very aggressive behavior in Chester, mental health officials had decided to release this madman into society. U.S. marshals seized him at the last minute, and a federal grand jury was asked to investigate with the object of preventing the incident from happening again. State mental health officials thumbed their noses at the federal grand jury and refused to turn over records of the madman's conduct in maximum security. They even refused to tell the feds, who were holding the man, what medicine he was supposed to be taking. The excuse given was protecting his privacy. The story showed that DMH officials were eventually forced to give in to the federal grand jury. The grand jury finally issued a scathing public report.

A strange bunch of people in DMH, thought Nash. He felt certain that if Victoria's shooting really happened, DMH officials were dealing with it in their own, secret way.

Nash put his feet up on the desk and read more clips, mostly dull treatises on the department's lack of money and staff. He had to remind himself that the only information he had on any shooting at the Read Mental Health Center was Victoria's word which was only fractionally better than nothing.

His phone finally rang.

"Sam Nash, this is Ray Colucci calling. I've been trying to get through to you for quite some time. Your phone is always busy. You must be a hard worker."

This was reasonably true.

"Sorry about that, alderman." Nash pulled his feet off the desk, grabbed the note from Youngman and opened it. "Listen, so we don't beat around the bush and waste your time, I called because I'd like to talk to you a little about the number of relatives employed in your office and on the city payroll. My editor gave me a list of names. This won't take too long. We can start with Carol Barski, B-A-R-S-K-I."

Colucci begged off until the next day, as Nash thought he might. After he got his ducks in order, Colucci would see Nash alone Wednesday afternoon in Colucci's office where the atmosphere was more conducive to baloney than on the telephone.

Colucci would tell the truth as far as he had to, Nash imagined. The smart guys never denied what the newspapers could prove. Only dumb people did that. It was very time consuming to prove X was a relative of Y. If forced to go that route, the Chronicle would get annoyed and would make the story bigger, playing up the ridiculousness of Colucci trying to hide the situation. A wise politician understood these things, and Nash judged that Colucci was wise.

Nash was getting thirsty and wanted a drink. The inside of his mouth was dry, and his cigarettes were starting to become boring. A shot and a beer would change that. Two stories in one day, the IC commuter delay and the luncheon speech plus the start of the Colucci story, plus a start on a long- longshot project involving Victoria; such steady endeavor made Nash feel virtuous.

There was one thing he wanted to do before he left. He opened his notebook and found the phone number for the day room at the Read Mental Health Center and called it. The first person who answered was a female who giggled when he mentioned the name.

"You her boyfriend?" she asked. She giggled again. Someone else took the phone. Nash repeated that he wanted Victoria Morici.

"You won't find her here anymore," said a tremulous male voice. "She was discharged this morning, I think. I saw somebody gathering up her belongings. We'll miss her. She was really crazy."

13

At 5:30, Katerina Nash stuffed her Kleenex in her purse and fished for the car keys in the various compartments. She thought that the next time she bought a purse it would be one with a little hook on the inside for a key ring so she would not waste so much time looking for her keys. She put on her coat from the coat rack near the door, said, "Good night, Stan," to the younger Sobieski, and walked out the door onto Milwaukee Avenue. She sometimes worked until 5:30 because she was occasionally forced to be late in the morning, and she did not like to lose any hours.

Alone in the office, Sobieski junior said to no one, "Mmmmmmm-mMMMH!" and shook his head after the door closed. He thought again how intriguing Katerina Nash's trim figure looked, today in a skirt, yesterday in a sweater and slacks. When she wore her hair up as she did today, Sobieski could hardly stand it.

Mrs. Nash, who was called by her short name, Katina, by most people, had been phone answerer, second typist and general factotum for the father and son law firm for a year and a half. Sobieski junior had appreciated her ability from the start and the way she dressed up the office. He also like to look at her, but he could never comfortably gaze. Since he had broken up with his longtime girlfriend, Sobieski found that Mrs. Nash was getting under his skin. He wished she would act like an air head to break the spell. But her continued quiet attitude and poise added to her attractiveness. He wished she would quit the job, or, conversely, he wished she were available.

He had surprised himself by digging out her employment application to verify the story her ring told, that she was currently married. He saw that her maiden name was Demopoulos. The 30-year-old lawyer knew that Mrs. Nash was four years older than he was, and she had two children. But he didn't care about these liabilities.

For weeks, he thought he had detected by a word here and a phrase there that something was awry in Mrs. Nash's marriage. Finally, he couldn't restrain himself any more, and he asked Marlene, the legal secretary, "Have you ever seen Mr. Nash around here? I'd like to meet a real newspaper reporter."

"They're separated," Marlene told him straightaway.

Sobieski had began inquiring among his friends what principles of etiquette were involved in asking out a woman who was separated from her husband.

. . . .

Driving to the babysitter's, Katerina Nash was thinking she should be able to detect better whether Sam realized she had made the first move. Had her husband been away so long that she couldn't be sure of the meaning of his voice anymore? He seemed interested enough. He asked how she was after she asked how he was. But maybe he was only being polite. Enough was enough. Either he would respond...or life was too hard alone.

14

At 8:55 a.m. Wednesday morning, Nash stood in the lobby of the Old Colony Building, an ancient high rise in the South Loop, wondering if Bryce had sent someone to question Victoria Morici at the Read Mental Health Center, or to track her down if she really wasn't there. If Victoria turned out to be an ordinary lunatic with delusions, Nash knew he was going to have to undergo a lot of teasing. On the other hand, if Victoria's information was legitimate and led to the discovery of a serious crime, the State's Attorney's Office would get half the credit. This was fine with Nash. He knew he would get the exclusive story.

His appointment to interview a spokesman for the Illinois Coalition for Animal Rights for his assigned feature story was at 9 a.m. He scanned the building directory noting with familiarity, amidst the names of small businesses and small law offices, the citizens groups that gave the Old Colony Building its personality.

Alliance to End Repression
American Friends Service Committee
Amnesty International
Citizens Against Nuclear Power
Committee for a Nuclear Overkill Moratorium
Communist Party of Illinois
Illinois Coalition for Animal Rights
Illinois Right to Vote Committee
National Committee Against Repressive Legislation
No More Witch Hunts
Young Workers Liberation League

Perhaps, Nash thought, the tenants could all agree on the aims of Amnesty International, but probably not.

The Illinois Coalition for Animal Rights was on the fourth floor. Marble stairs led up, each with a shallow depression worn by generations of feet. Nash took the elevator, chauffered by an elevator operator.

Entering the coalition office by turning the door knob in a frosted glass door, Nash next encountered a rude shock. Much later he compared the experience to an allergic drug reaction he had suffered as a child that caused his fingers, lips, nose, and ears to swell up. In this instance, his visible body behaved, but his emotions boiled up.

The self-described "media person" for the coalition for animal rights who came to greet him inside the office was in her early 20's and said her name was Andrea Crocker. The combination of Crocker's swaying skirt and lovely rear end as she walked in front of Nash leading him to her desk was what jolted him and broke the dam. Crocker sat in a chair in front of her cluttered desk and directed Nash to sit nearby. When she crossed her legs, Nash nearly fell out of his chair. He wanted to call for help. (But at the same time, he didn't want to.)

Behind a business-like gaze, Crocker's manner was restrained in such a way that Nash knew she intended to provoke no more than a routine, positive reaction from him, for the cause, and for daily female self-assessment. He knew his overreaction came from within. This caused him to bite his tongue. He missed entirely her first few sentences while his eyes roamed up her legs to her rear end, up the curve of her back to the hair at the nape of her neck, across the top of her head and down her face to her lips, which were reading:

"...approximately 100 humane societies in the state today up from about 60 five years ago."

"Big increase," said Nash.

Crocker half looked up at him as if to say, "What are you up to?" She had auburn hair and a face of regular Anglo features highlighted by large brown eyes. Her yellow, high-collared blouse of the Puritan variety had vertical pleats that accented the angle flowing down to Crocker's full breasts, which stood out with spirit.

Nash could sense Crocker's blood flowing, her heart beating, and he had x-ray vision. Part of his mind told him he could communicate his sudden sexual energy through electromagnetism or mental telepathy. He could make Crocker want him and ready to submit by concentrating his silent will on her. Another part of his mind said this was a joke. But his body believed it and wanted to try it.

The rational part of his brain warned him firmly that Crocker was a stranger and a very young person sitting in a wooden swivel chair in a large office near a picture window talking about animal rights. Nash almost didn't care.

He forced himself to look at his notebook, and he wrote down something Crocker said. While he looked down, he opened his eyes as wide as he could and held them that way. Then he shut his eyes tightly and took a deep breath. He blinked a few times, then scribbled something more. When he looked up, Crocker had paused in her prepared remarks (which are not usually necessary in an interview.)

"Ahem. Yes," said Nash.

"This...is part and parcel," Crocker looked at him warily, "of the growing ethical interest in the real rights, just like human rights, of animals," she said.

"Who speaks for the bugs?" said Nash.

. . . .

The interview lasted an hour. After 10 minutes, Nash no longer had to secretly pace his breathing and managed to gain complete control over himself. As he did, he had the sense of living a high wire act over a pit full of powerful hidden impulses, boozing, and marital troubles. The duality made it humorous, and he concluded one should do this trick with pride and discipline. ("And now, ladies and gentlemen. . .") So he did a professional interview on animal rights.

By 10 a.m., Crocker was leaning as far back in her chair as she could, stretching, with her hands locked on top of her head. The posture showed off the roundness of her breasts under her blouse. Nash guessed he had won her confidence.

"Geez, do you really think you need all this?" said Crocker. "I feel like I'm talking to a shrink."

"You're released." Nash snapped his notebook shut. "I have four or five more interviews to do, over the phone. Then when I sit down to write, I usually have a couple more questions for you. So I'll probably call you again."

"Feel free," she said, looking at the ceiling.

"Due to my schedule, I may end up writing this at night after normal business hours. Would I be rude if I asked for your home number?"

From her stretch, she turned and gave him a suspicious look. "Are all Chronicle reporters as rude as you?"

Nash shrugged.

Crocker rose and walked around behind her desk to put distance between them and drop several papers. Adopting a non-committal expression, she gave him the number. Very young, thought Nash, suppressing a smile.

While leaving, Nash said, "Goodbye, Miss Burton." Crocker and

Nancy Burton were the only full-time employees of the coalition. An unidentified female had been in another small room throughout the interview, and at Nash's announcement, a plain face appeared in a doorway looking shy and embarrassed. "Oh, goodbye," she said, "and thank you."

Crocker walked him out. Nash estimated she was about 5′ 8″. Her wavy hair was past her shoulders, a little daring, against fashion. He imagined it would look great pinned up, to fall later. He had held back a step to get a last look at that combination of ass and swinging skirt. When Crocker turned around, he started talking to cover up.

"Uh, would you report me to my editors if I asked what you were doing Saturday night?" He had decided not to attempt this, but then he just said it.

Crocker politely turned him down and said she hoped it wouldn't affect the story. "Not a bit," said Nash, who added that he had enjoyed asking the question. He stepped out into the hallway. Crocker remained in the doorway, so Nash turned to wave politely.

"Call me," said Crocker in a low voice.

"What?"

"Call me," she whispered.

"Oh...Count on it," said Nash, nodding enthusiastically. When he reached the first landing going down the stairs, he turned and tipped his hat toward the closed door of the coalition office above him. He smiled and said, "To animal rights."

131

15

Nash looked at his watch as he left the Old Colony Building. It was 10:15. He knew he had an interview at 1 p.m. with Alderman Colucci. He hoped he would have the intervening hours to himself because he was rolling on the animal rights story, but he knew this luxury was doubtful. The Chronicle had not hired a new reporter in about a year despite the loss of five or six to other papers, or to television. The staff was getting thin.

He walked north on Dearborn Street. He was amazed he had a date, or almost, with Andrea Crocker. He hadn't even planned it. It was almost effortless. Saturday night was a rash choice, he realized. He had to take his kids for the weekend. But any weeknight would do.

For two months after he had left his wife, Nash had wanted nothing to do with women. Women who even seemed to flirt with him he tolerated only if necessary, restraining himself from punching them in the chin as a message to all crooked-walking females. Only a few female friends were exempt from his hostility, Stern, Krolikowski, one or two others.

But prolonged hostility was painful and bad for his digestion. When he decided to treat women merely as he would any other warm blooded creatures trying to survive, some of the hostility ebbed away. Soon his body began to speak up, and he knew it was only a matter of time before he risked himself again.

At the corner, he raised his head for the traffic. He had progressed 30 yards from the Old Colony Building. The wind was going down his neck. He adjusted his scarf as he crossed Van Buren, walking northbound on Dearborn Street, then quickened his pace and scanned. The Monadnock Building to his left on the opposite side of Dearborn was black and ugly but an interesting pile of bricks. It was one of the last of the old skyscrapers, without a steel frame, built by piling bricks and stones on top of one another until the pile was 16 or 17 stories up.

He turned to face his line of travel and saw a woman looking at him walking the other way on Dearborn. Why was she looking at him? She wasn't bad, thirties, appeared to have money. What did she think of him? Did Kate look at guys like that?

Nash realized he was going to have to make a decision sooner or later, most likely sooner. Here he was asking girls out. There was no question in his mind that he loved Katerina, but he could not stand living with her if she was going to fool around with other men, even if she convinced herself that she wasn't really.

If he lived with that, he would either end up killing somebody or turning into a twerp. And the guy he would kill by strangling would be that fucking candidate for state representative, Verbecke.

Kate had started stuffing envelopes for Verbecke two nights a week. He was a friend of a friend. "I have to do something, and politics is interesting," she said. "You've got an interesting job, Sam. What have I got?" As Nash had fully expected, the candidate flipped over her looks and started driving her home himself, calling her in to work at his little storefront on Saturdays and picking her up himself.

"All politicians and would-be politicians are on the make, even the littlest ones," Nash had told his wife. "Take my educated word for it. Verbecke is not just seeking your clerical assistance." But Kate was flattered and acted girly with the guy which drove Nash berserk. "I can handle him, Sam. He's no problem," she said. He was the same age as she was.

The crash came when Nash stayed downtown drinking one night and came home to find "the asshole" in his house, sitting at his kitchen table making eyes at his wife while the kids were asleep. Nash gave him the bum's rush, which put Kate in a huff.

"Sam, if I wanted to be married to a jealous fool who told me when I could go out and what I could wear, I would have married a rich old Greek with a big mustache. He wants me to do some position papers for him. I can do it. I'm a college graduate, Sam. I'm not as dumb as you think. I can work for a man in this country if I want as long as I keep it decent. Why can't I do something I want? Be something? I'm going to work for him and help him get elected."

Nash remembered opening a can of beer while she ranted and thinking it was good to let her talk. When she wound down, they would discuss the situation. He began pouring himself a shot to go with the beer.

"Okay, Sam, we might as well lay it all on the table. You're drinking way too much. I can't stop you. We're not getting rich right now, and I don't know how long that stupid newspaper of yours is going to last. If you're out of a job, you're just going to drink more. What then? We have two children. What if I have to support them, and you, and ME? I think you're losing it, Sam. I'm going on no matter what."

"Going on where?"

She had her hands on her hips and her face was contorted with anger or disgust. He could still see it. "I don't know where!"

He downed his whiskey in one drink. "Perhaps with Verbecke instead of me?"

"Oh, you son of a bitch."

"Now wait a minute, Kate. I want to explain something to you. Sit down."

"No!"

"All right. Stand up. I'll sit down." He sat at the kitchen table. "Remember nine years ago when I had a string of very good stories and Bobby was just a few months old? I wanted to apply to the New York Times and the Washington Post and the L.A. Times. You said you had to be near your mother. You didn't want to be all alone with the baby. So I didn't."

"Maybe you should have anyway."

"Now you say that. You're right. I should have. We'd all be better off, I think. I thought I was being a nice guy. I was stupid."

"I said I'd go with you. I never stopped you. Maybe you were just afraid yourself. If you weren't, do it now, Sam. And quit drinking. It shows in your face. Nobody is going to hire a boozer."

"I said I was going to explain something Kat-e-ri-na. I didn't finish. I didn't understand it then, but one of the reasons I was producing such great stories is that I got great assignments. Connolly was the city editor then. He thought I was brilliant, and he was right. Whatever was hot, I got it. If I picked up stories on my own, Connolly pushed most of those, too, because I was brilliant. But I was too closely identified with Connolly."

"I've heard this before. Then Knox came in and after him some other guy and then Solomon, and you're just one of the crowd. You refused to crawl and pledge homage. What a man. Bullshit."

"Now I'm too old to apply to the New York Times and the rest. I should be somebody by now to do that. Nine years ago, I could have claimed to be a potential somebody."

"Sam, you think that's some sort of unique story. Everybody's got problems. You stopped trying in my opinion. And you definitely drink too much. If you want to be a tragedy, do it on your own."

135

Nash could not let that pass. "On my own? Am I in the way?"

"You know what I mean. Sam, why don't you go see somebody about this? Or take up racquetball again. Go into television. Coach little boys' soccer....And let me do what I want."

"You want me to go away and leave the field clear for you?" He had intended to be clever and caustic, but he could not believe how silly he sounded.

"Noooooo!" An anguished look to heaven. "Euhhhh! Sam, you make me want to throw up. Damn you!"

Nash cringed. It looked like she meant it. He made her want to throw up. Kate went down to the basement, slamming the door to the stairs. Going up the other stairs to their bedroom, Nash thought how repetitious this fight was becoming. Now his wife was revolted by him at the same moment he was beginning to seriously doubt himself. Still a bit drunk, he packed two suitcases. He could not live with somebody who was sick of him when he already didn't like himself. He had to be his own best friend, save what he could. Why do this? he had thought. Just go to sleep. No. Out. Out. That's what he needed.

She was doing the laundry and smoking one of his cigarettes when he came down with his coat on. She hardly ever smoked. "I'm going to move out for a while," he said. She rolled her eyes and stood with her left hand in her right armpit, holding the cigarette in an untrained manner in her right hand. "We'll discuss the arrangements by phone tomorrow. I'm going to a Y for tonight."

"Go!" she said angrily. Then he saw her face becoming strained and reddening and her eyes glistening.

Nash was hard put to figure out later what he had expected to achieve by leaving home. What he did achieve was inducing a burning hostility in his wife coupled with what seemed to him as irrational behavior. She had the locks changed on the front and back doors of the house by a locksmith whom she paid in cash. Then she insisted Nash repay her even though Nash did not have the money. The bill was over $100, and Nash at the time was buying his meals on his Visa credit card. On the day that Nash got his own apartment and furnished it with a few Salvation Army furniture items, he tried to buy groceries on his Visa card and found that the card was charged to the limit even though it should have had $600 left by his calculations. He knew what had happened. His wife, who did not believe in credit cards, had purchased $600 worth of something probably by using an old Visa bill in lieu of the card. It was the sort of retaliation he expected. But his wife violently refused to admit she had bought anything.

When he spoke to her on the phone, she was consistently difficult to hold to a topic, hyper, and vituperative to the point that Nash began to worry about her mind. He felt guilty about this because he knew he had caused it, but he didn't know how to fix it because she did not want him back home. "This is not a hotel, and I am not a maid, or a prostitute, or your friend, or any kind of servant; and you stay wherever you want; sleep in the gutter and get run over by a garbage truck; but not here. You are the ex-father (the ex-father?), and you're doing a damn half-assed job of that which is what I expected. I hope you take out more life insurance and get a second job because you're not making enough to support us this way."

As always, she included some truth when she chose to lambast him. In earlier days, sometimes her angry insults had stopped fights, at least on his side, because he was forced to laugh and give her credit. But since their separation, Nash had found that what formerly rolled off his back, he couldn't take anymore. When Nash heard that tone of voice begin, he hung up; and he stopped calling her except when it was unavoidable.

Nash was walking east on Washington Street, back to the Chronicle. So it wasn't just Verbecke, he thought. Nash somewhere still harbored the idea he would astound the world. His wife did not. And he couldn't argue with her assessment.

Did he still have this idea? He was working on a general interest feature about "animal rights." Later in the day, he was going to interview an alderman about civic nepotism because the alderman hired his own relatives. Nash knew if he could keep his habits in order, he could do these sorts of stories for years. And he could join a health club, work straight hours, quit drinking and smoking, and fix up the house.

Could I do it? he thought. I don't think so, he answered himself. He feared he was not stable enough. If he wasn't chasing something spectacular, or pretending to, or hoping to, he would truly "lose it," as his wife said. He would lose his reason for trying.

But what could he do that was original and astounding?

Find out what happened in the Read Mental Health Center. He could do a few things without waiting for Bryce, who might take days. If the incident turned out to be a secret murder by public employees, that could be a hell of a story. It wasn't exactly astounding, but it was the best thing he had.

What else could he do?

Get laid. Definitely.

He also resolved not to nod in agreement with himself when he had these inner dialogues on the street.

16

Nash stopped at a phone stand in the lobby of the Chronicle Building near the elevators and made a call.

"Hello, Jose?"

"Yes."

"This is Nash."

"I figured that out, Nash. I recognize speech patterns of the underprivileged."

"No shit? A linguist, eh? Or linguini I believe you call it in your language. Before you respond, Jose, I have a favor to ask of you. I need to borrow your car to take a ride to the Northwest Side. I won't be gone long. It's for a good story."

"What's the story?"

"I'm going to meet one of my sources who's going to tell me about a hell of a scandal on the Lake County Board that's right under the noses of the press."

"Yeah. Yeah. Alright, I suppose I can let you borrow it. This isn't really about the Lake County Board, is it?"

"Of course not."

"I'm going to trade that car in soon. Keep it in mind. When do you want it?"

"Can you bring me the keys now? I'm in the lobby."

"Why don't you come upstairs?"

"If I come up, Miller will give me something to do."

"How do you know?"

"It's only natural. I won't be able to put any gas in your car because it will take most of what I have to pay your parking fee. I'll owe you whatever you think is fair."

Nash drove the Kennedy Expressway outbound to Foster Avenue, Foster to Narragansett, and Narragansett south to Irving Park Road. Gentile's car was a heavy, Chevrolet Monte Carlo with an old-fashioned, monster engine that burned a lot of gas. The engine hood appeared so vast in front of Nash that he felt sure someone would accidentally try to land a plane on it. For the last half mile of his trip on Narragansett, he was driving along the eastern perimeter of the mental hospital's spacious grounds which were bordered by a tall, black, wrought iron fence with points on top.

He turned right on Irving Park to approach the guard shack at the entrance to the southern perimeter. Everybody who lived on the Northwest Side and everyone Nash had known on the old white West Side was familiar with this institution although no one Nash knew had ever been in it. It was a landmark. Moreover, Narragansett was a fast through street, the best north-south street for miles around, so it was commonly used. In his childhood, Nash's mother or father had always pointed while driving and said, "There's the insane asylum."

Nash and his siblings were left to their imaginations because nary a soul was ever visible at the "insane asylum." In those earlier days, the institution had been called "Dunning."

The red brick guard shack at the entrance on Irving Park Road was big enough to house a small family of illegal aliens and had a tall, peaked roof and its own chimney. When Nash turned into the driveway, he became mildly perplexed. Nobody was in the guard shack. The big window facing him was gone leaving the shack completely open to the weather, and he could see right through the structure because the door was open on the other side. The windows slanting back to the right and left of the main window were covered with plywood. Shingles were falling off the roof. Nevertheless, a 10-foot tall, chain-link fence flanking the driveway was new. The gate across the driveway was open so Nash drove in and followed the road. Nash guessed this slovenly appearance and lack of a guard constituted a form of public relations. Like all state agencies, the Department of Mental Health was constantly complaining about budget cuts. The department's budget was not frequently cut; it was the amount of the yearly increase that was cut; but he assumed the department was putting on a show.

He could see buildings in the distance and had to guess this road would get him there on its circuitous path. The road was extraordinarily bumpy and breaking up. On either side of the road, dead weeds three feet high stuck up out of the snow, and in one spot along the road lay a dead tree branch 25-feet long. Very convincing, thought Nash. He came to a fork in the road and chose the left fork hoping it would take him to the vicinity of a red brick church building an eighth-of-a-mile away with a prominent steeple. He thought the church might be near the center of business.

When he got within a hundred yards of the church and the other buildings, he began to get an eerie feeling. The place was haunted. Nobody was around. Windows in the church appeared broken, not all of them, but enough, and the church was very obviously locked up. Pieces of plywood were nailed across the double doors.

He turned off the car radio and parked about 30 yards from the church, as near as the road went. (The engraved stone above the doors said "chapel.") The day was sunny, unusually bright with the sun's reflection off the snow. He could not hear a sound except the hum of the big engine.

The church, of plain American Protestant variety, was located on the left end of a group of four or five buildings of different styles and ages facing different directions in a disorganized manner. To his far right, a white brick, one-story building looked like a public school but with plywood in place of glass in many of the window panels. Directly in front of him was a red brick, two-story building, the right half of which was very old and the left half, newer. On the old half, the bricks were painted red and the paint was peeling. The newer half of this building had huge glass block rectangles in the wall to allow light in. In the middle of each of these was a tiny real window just big enough for a human to crawl through except that each was covered with metal mesh.

What a place to live, Nash thought! In his mind he imagined the inmates had sensed he was there, and they were screaming: "Help, you asshole! Help! Get us out of here!" But then, listening, he heard nothing.

Nash turned off the car and got out hearing only his feet crunch on the gravel road underneath the snow. He gazed all around and listened.

He was about to approach one of the buildings and knock on a door when he decided the panorama was not quite believeable. He got back in the car, turned on the ignition, and drove back toward the fork in the road. There had to be someplace else. Nash knew the populations of state mental institutions had dropped dramatically in recent years as the inmates were resettled in halfway houses in the inner city or issued shopping bags to wander. He supposed part of the Read Mental Health Center was empty.

He drove on the other fork this time. The alternate road led farther north past a stand of towering black elm trees at least one of which was dead and another of which was listing heavily ready to fall over. On both sides of the road, he noticed big tumbleweeds. They were dried out and prepared to separate from the ground and tumble if a strong wind should arrive. The road turned back west and led him toward the assemblage of old buildings again, this time

142

coming up in the rear of the first group of buildings and in front of a second group. He was on Main Street.

The first building he came to on the left was a fire house. The overhead door on the truck garage was rotting away, and in the second floor sleeping quarters, all the windows were broken out. On the right he passed an auditorium or gymnasium. Wood veneer was peeling off the front doors in huge strips. Past this building was a courtyard surrounded by the remaining buildings.

Twenty cars were parked in the courtyard. He thought, So this is really it, then.

A warmly dressed man driving a tractor pulling a cart with tools in it was coming towards Nash. Nash rolled down his window.

"Excuse me. Where's the business office for this place?"

"You want Read?" said the man, who stopped his tractor.

"Yes."

"It's on Oak Park Avenue, the other side. Just follow this road. This here is all closed up. Only maintenance people are left."

"This is abandoned?" said Nash.

"They're gonna build a college," said the man with a sweep of his hand indicating leveling.

Well, son of a bitch, thought Nash. He wondered how many times he had driven by this place thinking it was the nut house when the real nut house had been relocated four blocks to the west. He continued driving west on the same road, past more haunted buildings, at least one of which appeared to date from the 19th Century, then past much open ground until he crossed the next north-south street. On the other side of that street, Oak Park Avenue, at the end of a long asphalt driveway, he came upon the Read Mental Health Center.

The center was a spread of modern, one-story, white brick buildings each with a red-shingled, Mexican-style pyramid on top. (Nash imagined the pyramids had something to do with air conditioning. The hottest air rose into the rooftop pyramids in the summer.) The whole institution looked like a campus or a medical center. Glass doors to the lobby of the main building opened automatically like at a supermarket. The windows and glass doors were dirty and the lobby was dusty as befitted a state operation, but otherwise the institution was eminently presentable. Nash approached what appeared to be a box office and asked how to locate a certain patient.

"Go to medical records," said the man behind the window, pointing across the lobby. In medical records, a pretty young girl wearing a blouse with vertical light green and dark green stripes, suggesting an alligator, and black slacks, said, "Hello. Can I help you?"

"Do you have a patient here named Victoria Morici, M-O-R-I-C-I?"

"I'll look," she said pleasantly. She stepped away from the counter and began working a machine which held endless records on large index cards in trays. The machine moved the trays up, down and around and presented different trays to the girl continually as long as she pressed a button. She found the tray she wanted, released the button, and riffled through the cards.

"I can't find anything," said the girl after a few moments, turning to look at Nash. "Are you sure she's here?"

"Almost positive. I spoke to her here this week on the phone."

"Her card should be here. I'll try December." She went to a different machine, same type. "Nothing for December or November."

"What if she was transferred to a different institution or discharged altogether?"

"We should still have her record. What's her home address?"

"I don't know."

Nash was not entirely surprised by the absence of Victoria's records. This trip had seemed just too easy, and he knew from experience stories such as this did not come easy. The missing records could be a standard paper work foul up. But he also knew employees of the Department of Mental Health could hide patients. They had done it before.

"Patients are frequently assigned to the center nearest their home," said the alligator girl. "But if she were here recently, we should still show her."

"Can I call up the various state hospitals looking for her? Will they tell me?"

"No. But you can write a letter to the likely ones if you don't want to drive to each one. The director of each institution should reply. We're not allowed to give any information about patients over the phone."

"Can I talk to a Dr. Crawford here? He knew Victoria."

"Hang on a second." She picked up a phone and made a call from which Nash learned that Dr. Gerard Crawford was on vacation.

"Where'd he go?" said Nash. She hadn't hung up yet.

"Is he in town, Collette? The man wants to know. He's trying to find a friend of his and Dr. Crawford knew her. She might have been a patient here." She smiled. "Sorry. He's in Hawaii."

"Could I talk to her, whoever that is there?" Nash smiled stupidly and pointed to the phone.

"He wants to talk to you, Collette.... You'll have to come around behind the counter, sir.... I don't know.... She wants to know who you are."

"Sam Nash, a friend of Victoria Morici's." As Nash came around the counter, the alligator girl began to realize she might have made a mistake, Nash could see. What if he was a nut like all the other nuts here? Nash stopped looking stupid and tried to look official and purposeful like a new police officer or a young FBI agent. He took the phone and said, "When is Dr. Crawford due back from vacation, ma'am?"

"Why do you need to know that?" said a suspicious voice at the other end.

"Because I have to talk to him about a patient named Victoria Morici, about her location and other matters. It's important, to him as well as her, ma'am."

"I think you'll have to ask the administrators. What is your name?"

"Sam Nash. Did you yourself know Victoria Morici, Collette?"

The alligator girl looked very puzzled but more curious than afraid.

"Sir, what is this about?" said the voice on the phone. "There are many patients here. I might have heard of Victoria Morici, but I am not personally acquainted with all the patients so I could not say for sure. Who are you with?"

"I'm an acquaintance of hers. Have you got a guy named Johnson there, an aide? He might remember her. She talked about him."

"I'm afraid I don't understand this conversation, sir. There's no one here named Victoria Morici now. I'm sure they already told you that."

"Ask Johnson if he'd like to talk to me, would you, ma'am?"

"He's not here now."

"Sure. Of course. He works nights. Give him a message for me, would you?"

"Sir, I'm very busy."

"It's a short message. What's his first name?"

"Is that your message?"

"No. I just want you to put it on top. 'To Mr. John Johnson,' or whatever. What is it?"

"Just tell me your message, sir, or I'm going to hang up."

"Okay, tell Johnson that Sam Nash, N-A-S-H, a reporter for the Chicago Chronicle, came to see him. I want to talk to him about Victoria Morici and Dr. Crawford. Tell Johnson I hope Victoria is in good health and he can call me. Also, Dr. Crawford can call me." Nash recited his phone number at the Chronicle.

"You're a reporter?" said the alligator girl. "Now you've got me in trouble. You shouldn't be back here."

"I'm sorry. If anybody gives you a hard time, just tell the truth. You had no idea who I was. I'm also a friend of Victoria Morici's just like I said." Nash drew his notebook from the inside pocket of his sport coat, found a blank page and scribbled his name and number on it and added the words, "looking for Victoria Morici." He tore the page out and offered it to the girl. She pushed his hand away with both of hers. He left the page on the counter. "Just in case you hear anything. You really should have a record on her."

Stepping out the door of the records office, Nash saw a middle-aged female zombie in a sweater that was too big for her with messy hair shuffling along in slippers down the hallway past the lobby. She had been shuffling in the other direction when he first arrived.

Trying to decide what to do next, Nash walked briskly across the open floor to avoid appearing lost and came to a large table at the west end of the lobby, where the lobby and the hallway met. The table was covered with a dusty, transparent plastic hood, and under the hood was a model of the entire Read Mental Health Center with all the tiny buildings marked, showing all the dormitories as well as every other structure.

He thought, Now if I only knew where she was, I could just go see her and ask what is going on. He assumed security was relatively loose as in most hospitals. Or if I knew where Johnson worked I could come back to see him. If I knew which unit Victoria had called from, I could visit there and ask people questions.

He would like to have tried one of these gambits even though the expected results were limited. He couldn't hope for much from Johnson, and how much testimony from Victoria's fellow nuts was useful? He needed hard information, and he didn't know where to get it.

But Dr. Crawford definitely existed, and so did some guy named Johnson. That was important. What Nash had to do next was make many phone calls.

Nash was getting the feeling that this building held a story. He often thought stories truly existed, some of them; they possessed their own essence somewhere between corporal and spiritual. They were around. One could sense them in the air as he sensed something in the quiet of the lobby. They were a series of recollections waiting to be told, or a form of energy built up, waiting to be released.

When he glanced up, a pretty young blond, or a blond who could be pretty, came out a door down the hallway wearing a cloth coat and carrying a shopping bag. She looked as if she had just seen a ghost. Her face, which had no makeup, was pale, and she seemed ready to faint. Nash sympathized with her. It looked as if she had just come from a very bad visit with someone in the institution who was her burden. When she tossed her long, silky hair, swiped at it with her free hand and tried to assume her normal bearing, Nash could see this girl would be really something under different circumstances.

Nash thought he knew who was waiting for her. Standing in the middle of the lobby was a big, handsome, dark-haired boy wearing an Army winter fatigue jacket with his hands in the pockets of his sloppy blue jeans. His face was gentle and concerned. The overall impression he gave off was kindliness.

Sure enough, as the girl rounded the corner from the hall into the lobby, the two looked directly at each other and came together. The boy asked a question very softly to which she gave a weary shrug, and he took her bag. Nash imagined it contained the family burden's laundry. As the pair approached a security guard at a desk behind another window, the girl folded both her arms briefly around the boy's left arm and leaned on him, grateful for his strength. Then each hugged the other around the waist, their flanks touching. They were joined together from hip to shoulder, each with one arm around the other, when the boy spoke to the guard.

"She's checking out," he said.

Nash was taken aback. He had not expected to see a normal looking person in this place.

Another door down the hall opened with a bang. A security guard barged out and marched toward the lobby in a big hurry, seeming to be working up his official dander. Nash knew what this was. This was for him. To avoid the upcoming hassle, Nash strolled across the lobby and out the automatic doors.

17

By 4:15 p.m. the same day, Nash was beginning to feel that he needed to write a story. Sometimes when his brain became too full of information, he found that writing a story was a relief because he could get rid of some of the information and forget about it. He had his feet on the desk having just finished seven, relatively quick phone calls. In his notebook, he had an hour-long interview with Andrea Crocker that would have to sit for a while. In the same notebook, he had a 45 minute interview with Alderman Colucci plus the results of the phone calls he had just made to check out information supplied by the alderman and his staff.

Not reflected in his notebook, but occupying space in his brain, was the curious will-o'-the-wisp, Victoria Morici. She existed, then she didn't.

Nash glanced at the Chronicle in his lap, folded to show the story about Judge Wishaw that Bryce had been so anxious to see in print. The story was on the obit page and trimmed by about three inches.

One little push would have knocked it out of the paper entirely. Nash was grateful for small favors, but he didn't know how Bryce would react. Time to find out. He took his feet off the desk and called him.

"I did the best I could, Clare," said Nash. "I do have some influence. What you see is a good indication of how much. I think we got enough in to ensure that your prosecutor will be cited for contempt."

"Hah, my friend, that little asshole Wishaw won't do it now. He's on notice that somebody is watching him, namely the unblinking eye of the press. What happened to all my quotes, Sam? I had some nice things to say about delayed justice."

"That was the last three inches. Got trimmed for space. I think you're lucky. The story almost makes it look like our reporter, Anderson, is the outraged citizen."

"Well, thanks for your part. Is there anything you want? I have to get back to the war."

"Victoria Morici."

"Victim or defendant."

"Witness. The lady in the nut house I called you about yesterday."

"Oh, yes. Geez, I'm getting bonkers myself. Should have gone in the news business. I called the director of DMH myself. They're mulling over our request in that great nut house in Springfield. He called me back a little while ago and wanted to know where the police report is."

"There IS no police report."

"Easy. I know. I explained to him that we got the first call. He kept insisting on wanting to see a report. It's the nature of a bureaucrat. Now he says he's checking with his legal staff. We have to let him do that just to say we gave him a chance. If they jack us around too much, we'll issue a subpoena. But that's down the road."

"For the director of the Department of Mental Health?"

"No. For the patient."

Nash fidgeted in his chair and felt for his cigarettes. "What's all this bullshit about, Clarence? You're the cops. Can't you just go in there and find her and talk to her after a perfunctory phone call?" Nash was pretty sure he knew the answer, but he wanted to make Bryce say it. He hoped Bryce would be embarassed to be stiffed by a bunch of functionaries and motivated to roll over them.

"Hmmm. If we knew something had definitely happened and it was fresh, we might be willing to send some of our brutes and break a few doors down, figuratively, of course. We have to pick those occasions carefully. DMH became very touchy about letting anybody talk to their patients after the patients' bill of rights passed in Springfield. They were absolutely asinine at first, a couple years ago. Things have improved a lot. Keep your shirt on, Sam. We'll get in."

"How long will it take?"

"A day or two. A week. Two weeks. DMH is very inscrutable. But we are very persistent."

Nash sighed. "Clarence, things might have changed. I don't know if she's at Read anymore. One of the nuts told me she had packed up and left when I called the dayroom where they watch TV. I called the number that she gave me."

"Ah hah. I see. Where did she go, Sam?"

"I don't know. And I have a strong feeling they're not going to tell me. Judging by our past clips on DMH, these guys would hide Jack the Ripper if they thought it would make him feel better. In Victoria's case, who knows?"

"My knowledge of Read is somewhat sketchy, Sam. But I believe there are several wards and dayrooms. As to their history of concealment of patients, I know what you're referring to. They're not that unreasonable any more."

Nash had taken his cigarette pack out and he shook one loose, letting it fall on the desk. "Okay. There is another complication. Read claims to have no record of any Victoria Morici as a patient in the last few months. I was out there today."

Bryce snorted at the other end. "Now, Nash, now you're talking complications!" He laughed.

"I know. I said to myself that a lesser man than Clarence Bryce might be discouraged by this, but not Clarence Bryce."

Bryce was still chuckling. "Well, it's not all as bad as it sounds. I've already made the inquiry, so if she truly doesn't exist, the Department of Mental Health will have to say so. And while there's no law against bullshitting the press—I do it myself all the time—there are laws about bullshitting this office, if a crime is involved. Plus we have other ways of making their life uncomfortable. Are you sure that's her name?"

"That's the name she gave me, and she spelled it. And that's the name one or two patients knew her by."

"But she is a certified lunatic."

"I don't think we should be prejudiced about this, Clarence."

Bryce laughed again.

"I'll have to ask you to trust my judgement about this, Clare, at least until we go a few more steps. In my educated opinion, nobody makes up the alias Victoria Morici."

"I trust you implicitly, Sam, because of your standing in the community."

"Amen," said Nash smiling. He could imagine Bryce smiling at the other end.

"I'll do what I can," said Bryce.

"The faster the better, I would say. I don't know how long nuts can remember things, and I don't want her to get herself in a jam, either." Nash returned the cigarette pack to his shirt pocket.

"If we don't get to the scene of a homicide right away, delays after that don't change the situation a lot. But for your long term mental health, Sam, try looking at the situation this way. There are many homicides, many rapes, many robberies. We don't even know about them all here. If we miss a few murders or lose a few in court —and we do—there are always more. Nature is bountiful. Seen in this context, my role in the grand scheme of things is to prosecute malefactors who come our way in a proper, professional manner and avoid the temptation to become personally involved."

Nash cleared his throat loudly.

"I acquired this world view," Bryce continued, "in a series of conversations with our distinguished young first assistant, the most recent being this morning. He was disturbed by the mild thrashing administered to Judge Wishaw. Based on the first assistant's vast experience, he feels it may be counterproductive for us to feud with the judges."

"Did you get in trouble?" asked Nash.

"Piss on him."

"I see."

"If you feel your young lady might be compromised, perhaps we can speed things up a wee with DMH, but I can't promise," said Bryce. "We are very meticulous about procedure here." Bryce said he would call Nash back on Friday.

"Thanks," said Nash before hanging up. The conversation bothered Nash on two levels. First, he did not like the uncertainty over the fate of the voice on the phone he knew as Victoria. Second, he felt the customary nervousness that came whenever he had to rely on other people while pursuing a good story, or what might be a good story. Other people did not understand the importance of quickness, of being first, of staking a claim by getting something into print. Other people diddled around.

Nevertheless, Nash had a different story in his back pocket that needed attention. He scanned the room and saw Solomon coming out of Peterson's office. Nash walked quickly and intercepted him.

"Want to hear about our friend, Colucci?"

After dumping some papers on his secretary's desk, Solomon walked into his own office and Nash followed.

"Gimme the grim details."

"The memo is accurate. He confirmed it all. I saw him for 45 minutes this afternoon."

"Good."

"The story is a little offbeat."

"How?"

Nash sat in the hardback chair, and Solomon began shuffling papers on his desk, reading each one for three or four seconds in his right hand, then transferring them to his left hand.

"He says he hired his relatives with the public good in mind. They're all qualified, in his opinion. They don't make an extraordinary amount of money. And he says he's running his office on the Italian restaurant theory that you can get more work for less money and have an efficient organization by employing the family."

"I love it. He's a jerk. What's so highly qualified about the dope peddler?" Solomon looked up at the end of his question.

"He could be considered an exception. But he is supposed to be a college graduate with a major in accounting. Colucci says he pays the guy with the money the city gives him as an office allowance. This is interesting. The city allows $13,200 a year for a neighborhood office, rent, furniture, whatever. Colucci says he has his office in a building owned by his family and doesn't charge the city for it. He pays the money to his junkie or ex-junkie nephew. He's supposed to be detoxed now."

"That's all deductible somehow. So the story is just what we thought it was, nephew included." Solomon finished the pile of papers and turned them over, face down. "Write it. How much space will it take?" He had pen in hand ready to write down Nash's answer and end the conversation.

"Mmm. Fifteen to twenty inches. But I don't think it's exACTly what we thought it was. I think it lacks a bit as a slam dunk scandal. I stand by what I said earlier. It's offbeat, and the story should be, too. And we might want to ignore the drug part."

Nash braced for the attack by Solomon. Nash also wondered if he would have gotten farther in life by avoiding these situations.

Solomon dropped his pen. "Why, pray tell, would we do that?" He displayed only small annoyance, not yet convinced there was any real problem. Then he looked at his doorway. "Yes?"

"Mrs. Lentz is on the phone," said his secretary, a brunette about 35 who was in the middle stages of pregnancy.

"Tell her I'll call her back in . . . 10 minutes. I promise. And close the door would you, Eileen?" He turned back to Nash. "Some broad wants to sue us because she claimed we ruined her travel agency. We printed a picture of a building that burned down with the wrong address. Her address. As if people look at pictures of fires to decide what travel agent to use. So why leave out the drug part? I don't want to. I want to go with it. He's getting paid by the taxpayers one way or the other."

"Let me describe it for you, Aaron, rapidly. I said to Colucci, 'Did this nephew making $13,000 once get arrested for selling dope?' "

"It was twice or three times, wasn't it?"

"The memo says 'several times.' I said 'once' just to see what would happen. I like to start low and raise. Colucci says, 'Yes, that's true. Let me call him in here.' He had the nephew downtown just for us. Then he says, 'Tell this reporter about your narcotics background.' The nephew says he's been arrested twice for possession and once for selling. The possession was marijuana, a couple ounces; the selling was cocaine, five grams. He says he was acquitted in both marijuana cases because he had a good lawyer—and, in my opinion, because they were minor and the judge didn't want to bother. He pleaded guilty to possession in the cocaine case, although he admits he sold it to a guy who turned out to be a narc, and got probation. He gave me the names of the arresting officers in all three cases which I sure did not expect, and his probation officer. He's been on probation for six months and has gone through detox." This was more complicated to describe than Nash had expected, but he pressed on.

"I asked him if he thought he should be employed by the city. He said, 'I think I should be employed some place. I have to work. What's the point of trying to clean up your life if you can't get a job?' Colucci said he had prepared his nephew for this because he told him it might come up some day."

"So, we give them points for honesty and go with the story," said Solomon. Solomon was leaning back in his chair, looking up at the top row of cabinets on his side wall.

"We could. Just so we know what we're doing. I talked to the cops involved and the detox center and checked his rap sheet. He told the truth. Colucci claimed his nephew is fragile. He works well if left alone, but could not take any limelight, especially negative, says the alderman. He's 30 years old and has to make it or break it soon, be self sufficient or a problem child all his life. Colucci said he would leave it in our hands to decide if his nephew, who is paid with the rent allowance, is an important city official."

Solomon straightened and turned on Nash. "That son of a bitch. Maybe we'll decide his nephew should be an EX city official. Does he do anything or is he on a unique form of welfare?"

"We are led to believe he types and keeps the books for the alderman's office," said Nash slowly.

"And helps himself to a little, I imagine."

"There's not much he could take, and it would have to come out of one of the other salaries or the alderman's car allowance. Aldermen don't have expense accounts." Slower yet.

Solomon exhaled air through his nostrils with his mouth firmly closed, showing irritation in his eyes. "What about the rest of these relatives?"

Nash laid it out. Colucci's sister was his secretary, $22,000 and change. A sister-in-law was one of his aides, $13,250. His brother did indeed recently get a big promotion in the city department of economic development, and his cousin worked in the corporation counsel's office and had for a long time.

"What is so special about this story, Sam? I don't get it."

"Well," Nash felt pressured by Solomon and was annoyed by the feeling. They were both the same age. "If we don't count the brother and the cousin, both of whom worked for the city before Colucci ran for alderman, we are left with the three in the office, one of whom is paid with the rent allowance. If we don't count him, that leaves two. There are two others in the office who are not relatives, Lesniak's old secretary, who is now the assistant secretary, and a part timer. I can give you a good story. Some people will decide it is scandalous from Colucci's own words. Maybe many people. In my opinion, it's a judgement call. We can't ignore it. But I can do it in such a way that it's left up to the reader. Two of the three relatives in his office are making only $13,000, remember. I don't want you to expect the sinking of the Maine."

"Fifteen inches. And I want to see it before you give it to the desk. The narcotics arrests are definitely included. This is for tonight. That lady called back again and threatened to go to television if we don't print something."

Nash shrugged and started to rise.

"By the way, Sam. . . ."

Half up, Nash looked at his boss and saw Solomon examining him.

"You know I learned something about wash and wear shirts since my wife went back to work."

Nash sat down.

"You have to take them out of the wash machine as soon as they're done and put them in the dryer right away or they'll be wrinkled as hell."

Nash smiled, knowing whose shirt Solomon was talking about. "She taught you that?"

"She allowed me to learn it. Another thing. . . ." Solomon was going to say something else then dropped the idea. "You know how to do this story as well as I do. Go do it."

Back at his desk, Nash decided he should not have expended so much hot air dickering with Solomon in advance. He should simply have written the story and then negotiated.

He could have argued the case both ways. If one alderman got away with this "Italian restaurant" operation, 49 other alderman and other city officials would see this as a green light to hire more relatives.

Nash looked at his shirt. Hmmm. He had to make more phone calls. His stomach was bubbling and growling, and he lit another cigarette to calm it, the one that had been lying on his desk since he talked to Bryce. He made a little list:

Flannery

Animals

V. Colucci rep. (which stood for reputation).

He thought for a moment he might write another name down, "Kate." What would be the reason for calling her, he thought? Just for the heck of it and because I want to, he answered himself. He knew he was living in the past and acting as if this would be no big deal. What if she cut him short or did a number on him? He had a lot to do and needed to think straight. He ended the debate without a decision, but he left her name off his list.

18

"Rookie alderman Raymond Colucci, who has two relatives working in City Hall, has hired three more relatives to work in his ward office, the Chronicle learned Wednesday.

"Asked about the latest of the Colucci clan to go on the city payroll, Colucci said he intended to run his ward office like a family business, modeled on an Italian restaurant."

To Nash's eye, the story started out as a scandal then fizzled somewhat with the explanations in the bottom half, but people could make up their own minds. Nash was reading the story one more time before he left for the day. He already had his trench coat on his desk. He was anxious to get out, but he wanted to leave with the knowledge that the story was right and could then be forgotten if he wished. He read it fast in the computer.

Vincent Colucci, the alderman's brother, had turned out to be highly regarded, embarrassingly so, by several members of the business community whose names Nash got from a friend in the financial section. Nash could fit only two short sentences of praise for Vincent in the story, but he added it was an opinion "echoed by some others."

On Lucy Malek, Nash quoted Colucci saying, "She's my cousin. She's worked for the city for almost 10 years. What can I do about it?"

It was the first half of the story that Solomon liked, the list of names and salaries and relationships, each person with a separate paragraph marked by a black dot called a "bullet," and Colucci's description of why an Italian restaurant works so well. It was almost funny. Many Chicago readers enjoyed these stories and considered the relationship between the press and aldermen a form of sports.

Solomon had made only one suggestion on the next to last version. Nash replayed it in his mind because the outcome had gone Nash's way, something worth remembering.

"You left the nephew's arrest record too far down. Get some reference to it up high." Solomon had been standing behind Nash while Nash was showing him the story on his computer screen.

"What do you say we drop that, Aaron. The story's plenty good without it. Imagine the story without the arrests. It's good."

"It's better with it. Why so touchy, Sam? You have a relative who's a dope addict?"

"I admit this guy was, until very recently, a social termite, and he may be again, Aaron. But right now the guy just went through detox. That has to be difficult. He's got a job that pays no better than our copy clerks, and he's not bothering anybody."

"As far as you know."

"As far as I know. So?"

"So, I like that part, and you don't," said Solomon, who was pondering. "Why do I have the feeling this is going to come back and bite us."

"Because it probably will," said Nash, "nevertheless. . . ." He understood Solomon meant he was giving in.

"It's your story but my ass, Sam."

"I know."

"Shit. Take it out. I hope you're happy."

"Thanks."

Nash knew Solomon would not bring the matter up again unless it did "come back and bite." Similar decisions were made nearly every day. Once made, they were pushed to the rear by new conundrums.

Nash had given Colucci's nephew, a total stranger, a chance, he thought, done him a favor which would never be repaid. There was risk involved. Anyone who was arrested three times for dope, even if two of the arrests were for marijuana, had been very busy and could easily fall again. But Nash was content, and he thought maybe that was the payoff.

By this time, Nash was dying for a drink, or more precisely, two or three drinks for starters. He got up and told Phelan he would be in the Radio Grill if anybody had any questions on his story.

"The Radio Grill?" said Phelan.

Walking down the aisle out of the newsroom, Nash was feeling feisty, looking forward to sitting at the bar, having his shots and beers and getting mellow, and then. . . he would go home. This last thought detracted from his mood. The apartment was unattractive and sloppy. TV shows put him in a bad mood; they were so plastic. He had read all the books he could read for the time being. He could no longer get through a chapter. Living alone was grimy unless you made something out of it, Nash concluded. He had not. He decided to go to the Billy Goat instead where he could drink with friends, although he knew his money wouldn't last as long. By this time, he was standing in the aisle in an empty part of the newsroom between rows of empty desks. He didn't want to blow the mood. When you feel good, take a chance, he told himself. He thought of Kate warmly, thought of his kids, thought of everything that had once belonged to him. What would Kate think if he called her up and told her he was coming over, only to talk to her? She could say No. So what? He could charm her. Heh, no. She didn't buy it anymore. "Ah, hell," he said aloud. He looked up. Nobody was nearby. He didn't care if they were. He didn't want Kate to get angry and lose her bearings. That was the problem. He pictured the possibility of a real messy scene. Nope, she needed more warning.

So it was the Billy Goat. Then he remembered the goal he had set in the morning. This goal was in addition to ferretting out an expose about murder in a mad house. Once in his head, this goal wiped out everything. If Crocker turned him down, there were lots of bars to meet girls in. But he'd give Crocker a ring.

It was 7 o'clock. How could he call a girl up at 7 o'clock on Wednesday night? He decided to do it anyway just to break his inertia. He went back to his desk, got Crocker's home number and called it. No answer. He called the coalition, and they were both surprised when she answered.

"What are you doing there so late?" asked Nash.

"Well, uh, you put me behind. You took up the first hour of today. I have to get my newsletter to the printers by 7:30. You got a question?"

"Yeah, several. Would you like to have dinner?"

Nash was already looking around the newsroom trying to spot someone from whom he could borrow money.

19

The next morning, Nash sat at his desk reading the columnists on the opinion page and drinking his coffee. He intended, when he finished both, to hit the phone for more information on his animal rights story. He had the usual nag about Victoria Morici in the back of his head. One story was the sort that kept him employed. The other, he thought, might remotely turn out to be the winner of a journalism prize and get him a better job. Nash liked long shots. Several times a year, he pursued unusual notions for days at a time in between his ordinary work.

Suddenly, he brought one hand to his forehead to shade his face so no one would ask why he had started to grin or why he was blushing. The night before had flashed through his mind again.

Nash had picked up Crocker at the coalition office, after going home to get his car, and had taken her to a restaurant on Ohio Street that served, at reasonable prices, what Nash called the American menu. The menu was pioneered by Greeks. The restaurant was owned by Albanians. Nash had a turkey club sandwich deluxe, and Crocker had a Denver omelette.

The food was good. Nash liked it, and Crocker considered it to be historically important as well after Nash told her the menu had once been the dominant theme in Chicago restaurants.

Nash temporarily ran out of things to say, and Crocker seemed to be waiting for him, so he interviewed her again. He asked her two pointed questions about animal rights, which led, as he assumed they would, to her parents, which opened up her childhood. He coaxed her along with mere nudges until the sarcastic inner voice of his libido began chiding him that this line of conversation would never achieve the goal of taking Crocker to bed.

["I'm doing the best I can,"] Nash responded within. Crocker caught his drop in attention and immediately turned the conversation to him.

Nash told interesting anecdotes, as reporters do. During each one, Crocker asked a question or two seeking some revelation about the news business or about Nash.

He told her he was separated—because she asked, "Are you married?" She did not seem particularly disturbed by his marital status which surprised him. As Nash told his stories, Crocker became more and more relaxed.

She began to get a glow in her eyes that was not the proper wavelength and made Nash uncomfortable. It was reminiscent of a certain girl in a pony tail who used to gaze at him in class. But he also recalled dating a grownup girl who manufactured that innocent-appearing glow out of calculated habit, so he did not reach any conclusion. He discovered for sure that if he frowned or smiled too artificially, Crocker became anxious, like a kid. This made him guilty, so he resumed being fascinating.

Before she glowed too much, and before another glass of wine took the last of his money, he took her for a walk. An hour and a half later, he drove her home to her apartment on Lincoln Avenue just north of Jeff's Laugh Inn where Lincoln Avenue begins.

"I wish I could invite you up, Sam," she said, "but I don't know what my roommate's doing."

"Maybe your roommate's not home," said Nash, getting down to business.

"Maybe, but...." Crocker's face was strained. She gazed through the windshield, then suddenly said, "Oh, pull in there." A car was leaving a parking space.

They said nothing as he parked. When the engine was off, Crocker looked at Nash and said, "When do you think you're going to know where you're going?" He understood she meant his marriage.

"In a sense, I know where I'm going right now," said Nash. He put on a candid expression for the first time of the evening while looking into her eyes.

Crocker seemed paralyzed. Finally she said, "You sure do." She turned and looked out the windshield again. "All right. I'm willing to take a chance with you, Sam. Boy, these things move too fast sometimes. But not the first night, okay?" She looked at him.

Not the first night? Nash felt trapped. What first night? he wanted to say. What second night? This was just....

It was his turn to stare out the windshield. He could come back for a second night, go through all this again, and get what he wanted. This required long drawn out deception. Rejecting this idea, he knew he could still make a graceful exit with a smaller lie, namely that he would call her. Last, there was the dead fish of truth.

"Uhhh, Andrea, I don't think..." He cringed but he turned and looked right at her. "I don't think I'm ready to start dating right now."

"Oh," she said, dropping her chin. "Well. Thanks...Whoa!" The chin came up. "I don't recall your taking notes tonight." She sat up straighter and grabbed her purse which was hanging from her shoulder. "You are a little crude, aren't you? Is this common to newspaper reporters?" She opened the car door. "Thanks for the dinner!" she said getting out. "The American menu, no less. I hope you didn't overspend."

"Easy. Just a second," said Nash.

"I only did this for the damn story. You're a bit old for me, Nash, but I value the rights of animals. Maybe you should find a pet. On second thought, please don't. Good night, and don't call me."

"The point is. . ." He was speaking to the car door which was now closed.

He definitely was crude, thought Nash, sitting at his desk Thursday morning. He lacked patience, and as yet he had little desire to cultivate his own patience, tolerance, and cuteness all over again. Arching his eyebrows, he gave himself credit for not leaving Crocker in suspense.

He picked up the phone and started his calls on animal rights. Giving the phone book a good working over, he called public officials and groups mentioned in the clips, and he followed referrals from one person to another to locate knowledgeable people. He stayed on the phone almost continuously for four hours, immersed. When his ear hurt from pressure, he moved the phone to the other ear.

To keep his brain relaxed and agile, he mixed four phone calls to state mental health officials in that span, one call an hour. For those, he first stretched his neck and swiveled his head and then opened up a separate notebook.

At 1:30 p.m., he caught at the other end of the line the first potentially useful official, Dr. Vishnu Chandra, the director of the Read Mental Health Center.

"Dr. Chandra, we're investigating a report of a shooting—an attack with a gun—that allegedly occurred in your hospital earlier this week, a shooting possibly involving your employees, perhaps even one of your doctors. It hasn't been reported to the authorities, but based on information supplied to us, we think there's a good possibility it happened. What do you know about it? The victim was a man about 30." He made up the age. Nash used the straight-on approach because he decided he had already put Victoria in the soup, if there were any soup.

"I beg your pardon," said Dr. Chandra for the third time. "Who is thees?"

"I'll tell you again, doctor. This is Sam Nash of the Chronicle. That's a newspaper in Chicago where you live now."

"Sahm Nahsh, you say? Of thee Chicago Chraunicle? Thaht is thee news mediahh, is it naut?"

"Yes, it's the news media, to be exact, a news - paper."

"Wehll, Sahm Nahsh, you will hahf to coal thees number." He gave Nash the number of the department's p/r man. "I cannaut talk to thee news mediahh. It is agaynst our policy."

"Doctor, let's be serious. I am talking about a shooting with a gun that reportedly occurred in your hospital while you were in charge. If the report we have is true, it could be a serious crime. What do you know about it? I'm going to write down your answer next to your name."

"Excuse me? I theenk you have made ay mistake, perhaps. But you will hahf to coal thees number."

They went round and round and Nash could not budge him. Either the man felt safe behind his accent or he didn't know what Nash was talking about. Undoubtedly, Dr. Chandra had been instructed to refer all calls from the news media on any subject to the department's p/r man. That was the current style. Nash guessed this was especially true in this case because, like most foreigners, Dr. Chandra hadn't a clue as to what he should say or not say. Even if Chandra was in a jam, he would surely rely on the department to get him out of it, not Nash. As to the whereabouts of Victoria Morici, Dr. Chandra told him to visit medical records whenever he wished. Nash wondered how Hughes would have dealt with an Asian immigrant hospital superintendent.

After going to lunch and coming back, Nash took a shot at the top again. He called the state director of Mental Health, Dr. Charles Medaven, who was relatively new, according to the clips. New or not, Medaven carried on the department's tradition by the book. He was unavailable and he did not return Nash's phone calls.

As he started organizing his notes on animal rights and got ready to make a few more calls, Nash decided that on Friday he would phone every Morici listed in Chicago and suburban phone books and listed with directory assistance. He felt there was a 50/50 chance he could locate Victoria through relatives if she was back in society, or if she was in another mental hospital, or if she was still in the same place in a different ward. Bryce was taking his sweet time about this, thought Nash, but Bryce was up to his pectoral muscles in mayhem, so maybe that was to be expected.

Nash also had another idea for continuing to pursue the matter, an idea that was unusual even for him.

20

"I sent Maynard Marshall to find the burned-out family. They've gone to stay with somebody, but we don't know where yet. If we're lucky, there will be no need for another story. I wish, though, you had let Nordstrom handle the story and handle Forrest in this instance, Red. Just avoid trouble for a while," said Solomon. The metropolitan editor's eyes showed a plea combined with exasperation. "I guess you thought getting personally involved in this was more important than my suggestion to avoid trouble."

"Just doing the news, Aaron," said Phelan.

Solomon sat in his reclining swivel chair, his hands behind his back in parade rest position. He told people this stiff posture eased his occasional back pain. To observers, he also seemed to use it when dealing with other pains.

"What do you think has happened as a result of this little incident, Red?"

Thank God it's Friday, said Phelan to himself, sitting in the hardback chair in front of Solomon's desk. "It's difficult to know what to expect around here, Aaron, so I try not to think about it too much."

"That's interesting," said Solomon.

At 11:45 the night before, Phelan had sent Forrest to a blaze in a basement apartment on West Erie Street with possible fatalities. Phelan could have gone home then and turned the desk over to the midnight man, Nordstrom. But it quickly turned out the blaze had killed five people, four of them children. This was a major story, and Phelan did not trust Forrest to do it right. Moreover, Phelan knew that Forrest was dangerous to supervisors because of Forrest's relationship to the financial editor. Thus, Phelan had reluctantly stayed, annoyed with himself in hindsight for sending Forrest to what Phelan had hoped would be a simple story.

Forrest had called in with his information, but he had failed to carefully ascertain the full names and relationships of the victims, one of the most important aspects of any story regarding a fatal fire and usually the most difficult reporter's task in ghetto fires. Forrest was not certain if the woman who was killed was the mother of all the dead children. He assumed she was, which was of no use. Similarly, he had not asked the authorities and other people on the scene for the last name of each child. Phelan knew that among poor blacks, siblings frequently have different last names reflecting different fathers. Moreover, it was very common in poor black communities for a child to stay temporarily, or sleep overnight, in the home of a relative who was not the child's parent, or in the home of a family friend.

Instead of discovering basic information, Forrest had gone off on a tangent after a young woman at the scene, an angry relative of the victims, told him, "The firemen stole my money." The young woman told Forrest she saw a fireman going through coats in a closet on the second floor of the three-flat building, and the fireman had taken a $5 bill she had saved.

Both Phelan and rewriteman Youngman had refused to listen to this allegation and had insisted that Forrest go after the names and relationships of the victims. Phelan had stated that unless the accuser filed a police report, her allegation was to be ignored.

"I suppose I would have done the same thing as you," said Solomon as he and Phelan discussed the matter in Solomon's office. "But you could have left a memo, Red."

"Why? It's bullshit."

"Forrest left a memo. How do you know it's bullshit?"

"People lash out at the scenes of fire deaths all the time—or with a certain frequency," explained Phelan. He knew Solomon had not covered a lot of police and fire stories on the street in his career. It was basically nighttime stuff. "They accuse somebody of something. Somebody did this. Somebody was the cause of all this trouble. The police and firemen are usually the closest, and nowadays, ambulance drivers. Any accusation that comes to hand that allows people to express their emotions. She's really mad because her cousins—I think it's her cousins—got killed. But she probably hadn't absorbed that yet. They were dead before the Fire Department was called. It was one of those slow-building asphyxiation fires."

A fire that starts in furniture from a small ignition source, such as a cigarette butt or electrical sparks can smolder slowly and consume all the oxygen in an apartment before it is discovered when the hot gases break a window. Victims suffocate in their sleep.

"I see why you think the way you do," said Solomon, who leaned forward folding his hands on his desk. "But we don't really know her allegation is bullshit. We just assume that it is. It was in the Post this morning. They didn't play it up, but it was in the story, and they got a denial from the Fire Department. The girl was on TV this noon. What she describes is kind of a cold, rotten practice, if true."

"Did she file a police report?" asked Phelan.

"Not the last that we checked."

"Then it's bullshit. It shouldn't be on TV either. Shall we go up and down the streets of the ghetto collecting accusations? 'Hey, any accusations today? Turn 'em in; we'll print 'em in the Chronicle.'

That's what this amounts to. For that matter, you can get plenty of free accusations in my neighborhood or in yours."

"I understand. Equally to the point," Solomon sat back again, "Simonet does not. Forrest left his memo in the computer where people saw it. It was not a nice note, and, of course, it suggests you and Youngman are racist bastards without saying so. Simonet got wind of the talk around the office, that you spiked this part of the story. I don't think he saw the memo because he has no time to read our memos, but he saw the TV at noon and saw the Post. It is possible to develop a scenario in which Forrest is an aggressive young reporter and you are an old fogey editor. This is, fortunately, complete hogwash. Forrest is an idiot and you and Miller are my best assistants.

"But this would never have caused you or me any trouble if you had simply let Nordstrom handle it. Simonet doesn't know Nordstrom and has no bee in his bonnet about him. But—and it's just bad luck—Simonet does have a bee in his bonnet about you."

"I can't operate that way, Aaron." Phelan dismissed the notion with a wave of his right hand, but he was thinking inwardly that it was foolish to totally ignore office politics, and he, Red Phelan, did not do foolish things, and could this be a first sign of rigidity related to age? Phelan told himself he did not intend to get old, and he decided he would think about this.

"You say you don't operate that way, but that's exactly what you did," said Solomon. "You stayed there because you knew Forrest was poison, and you were protecting Nordstrom. Nordstrom is fine. He's level headed. He can make decisions. Let him take his own chances on the desk. That's why he's there. If Nordstrom had done this, we wouldn't have the tiniest headache because he would have been the second editor who had a little difficulty with Forrest, which looks better."

Phelan nodded. He could see the benefit of that, once again in hindsight.

"Okay," said Solomon, who relaxed and sat forward. "Now that you see my point of view, I'll have to admit I do remember being taught years ago by old McCarron that in instances of allegations of street crimes like that, especially petty crimes, we should check to see if the accuser filed a police report—because it's against the law to file a false police report, so that keeps 'em honest. It's a good rule, like waiting until a threatened lawsuit is actually filed. So you were probably right, as usual."

"There is another issue that is somewhat related," said Phelan, "a certain sophomoric cynicism in our young friend. This is not uncommon." Phelan had acquired his education in the news business, but it served for what he wished.

"You mean Forrest, because he instantly believed this allegation?"

"That, yes. It wasn't what I was thinking about, but some young people we get nowadays think they are superior to firemen and policemen and politicians, many of whom could have them for breakfast.

"But what I had in mind was: Don't we get the correct names and relationships of the victims when the victims are white?"

"Ohhh." Solomon's eyes widened. He looked aside, nodding, then looked back at Phelan. "You mean Forrest...?"

"It is possible to develop a scenario in which Forrest thought that correct names and relationships were more important with some groups than with others. I'm not saying this is what he thought. I'm just saying the facts could be construed that way if someone wished him ill. It would be closer to the truth to say he's immature. He's a spoiled nincompoop," said Phelan shrugging. "We get one once in a while. He just happens to have connections."

Solomon chuckled. "Okay, I see," said Solomon. "You understand why I had to send out Marshall."

"No problem. You had to once the matter was questioned. It'll probably be better for me in the end, at least I hope so."

"I think it will be," said Solomon. "I'll take care of this with Simonet. I already defended you at an earlier meeting today. I can't have guys like Forrest undercutting my key people. I'll defend you even better at the next meeting. Simonet doesn't always understand why things have to be done a certain way because of his non-news background." Solomon paused a beat. "I didn't say that."

Phelan nodded gravely and waved a hand, meaning, "Don't worry."

"He's a smart man, though. He'll listen to me," Solomon added.

"You're a damn good city editor, Aaron, or a damn good metropolitan editor."

"I'm learning," said Solomon. "The thing to keep in mind is that one of these days we're going to make a real mistake, a bona fide error. When it happens, we want to have some capital in the bank to bail us out. Right now, I'd say our bank account is about two bits. We're not overdrawn, but we have to build it up."

Phelan understood that "we" meant only Phelan.

"We build it up by avoiding any disputes that can reasonably be avoided," Solomon continued, "running the night desk the way YOU know how to run it, and agreeing to what Simonet wants when we start the new Chronicle next week."

"I don't know how much I can do about the bees in his bonnet, but I'll do the best I can, honestly," said Phelan.

"I know you will."

"I heard there's a rumor among the pressmen that the paper might fold after the primary election in March," said Phelan. This was only two months away. "Around here there's always rumors."

"We can't worry about those kinds of rumors," said Solomon, who made no denial. "We just go on like always, hoping for the best. I've been thinking of transferring Forrest to days."

"Georgia has been on nights two-and-a-half years. She's been doing a lot of work on her own time to impress you."

"Georgia's time will come, if there is time. I've talked to her."

Promises from editors to reporters were often worthless, Phelan knew. Some editors handed out promises like helium balloons at a grand opening. But he wasn't sure what Solomon's style was.

175

"If you want to take a chance," said Phelan, "leave Forrest on nights. This may be the moment he learns something. If you put him on days, he'll think he got away with his behavior."

"That what you really want?" Solomon sat back again.

Phelan nodded. "How'd Forrest ever get this job, Aaron? I thought we had a rule against nepotism."

"Fitzpatrick's ass kissing, principally. Also, he's not technically Fitz's nephew. Fitz's sister married Forrest's father, but Forrest was produced before that. How's your daughter, Red? The one with the eye trouble."

. . . .

As soon as he got back to the city desk horseshoe, Phelan started doling out assignments and rewrite tasks. He saved the last for his problem child.

"Forrest, do me a head obit on this judge. Four inches."

He gave Forrest a dupe of an ordinary obituary that had been written for the afternoon edition. It was only an inch long. At the Chronicle, a head obit was a story of at least four paragraphs that rated its own headline, "Judge Whoozits." There was not enough information in the original obit to stretch out to four inches, so Forrest would have to do some research and a tiny amount of writing. Phelan intended to start him through the fundamentals.

As he resumed his work, Phelan did not feel particularly secure in his job despite the results of the latest office tug-of-war. He never ceased to be amazed at the unpredictable manner in which people rose and fell in the news business.

At 8:15, reporter Maynard Marshall finally returned to the office. From thirty feet away from the desk, standing where Forrest could not see him, Marshall gestured to Phelan. He wanted to talk privately. Phelan weighed the idea, then decided Forrest would notice and think some conspiracy had been hatched to suppress the truth. He signalled Marshall to approach the desk.

Dressed in a new, medium brown trench coat, open now with the belt hanging loose, wearing a red knit tie over a shirt with a complimentary color pattern, Marshall looked like a magazine liquor ad or an advertisement for a haberdashery. A former police officer, Marshall had been persuaded to get into the news business by Chicago TV reporter "Surrender Sam." They had met on one of the many cases in which Surrender was accepting the surrender of a criminal on television and immediately struck up a friendship. (Criminals who surrendered on television hoped to receive better treatment from the police. Without the services of Surrender Sam, who had become identified with this practice, they feared they would get beat up.)

Marshall sat down at the top of the horseshoe on the outside rim, directly opposite Phelan, and put his elbows on the desk.

"Well, do we have a story to write for the 3-star?" said Phelan.

"Not unless there's business I don't know about," responded Marshall.

"What about this story in the Post?" said Forrest, holding up the opposition newspaper. He knew Marshall's assignment. "It's the same story I had, only I had it first."

Marshall glanced at Forrest, but spoke to Phelan. "She still hasn't reported this claim to the police, if that's what you want to know. You probably want to know that, too, Forrest."

"Well, she should," said Forrest.

"No, I don't think so. I wouldn't swear that the firemen didn't steal anything. That's been known to happen, in my opinion. But she didn't see any stealing if you ask me. In fact, I know she didn't."

"She told me she did! She saw the fireman go in her pocket."

"How old did you think this girl was, Brian?" Marshall was trying to be nice, but he came off condescending. This was the proper attitude anyway, Phelan thought.

"Nineteen or twenty."

"She's 15. Some girls look older, though."

"So what if she's 15?"

Marshall lifted his eyebrows and looked at Phelan. Phelan kept his face blank and tried to read the story on his screen. It seemed all right.

"Well, she hasn't had much experience of anything, Brian, and this fire killed her sister, three nieces and nephews, and another boy," continued Marshall. "I think she didn't know what to do or how to act or even what to think. She was very confused and upset, so she decided, 'Piss on the real world. Let momma handle that. And piss on all these stupid white fuckers in the rain coats who aren't worth a shit.' Then she put on her coat because it was cold with all the windows open, and she discovered these stupid white fuckers were evil, too, just as she suspected. So she said so."

"That doesn't mean what she said is a lie," responded Forrest. "She said she saw a fireman going through her coat. You're trying to say she lied to me, and the Post, and the television?"

"I didn't say she lied to you—exactly. She thought it was true. But she made up the part where she saw it. She admits that and considers it inconsequential."

The copy boy on the switchboard told Phelan he had a phone call. It was Kemper with the mayor's speech. All the mayor had said was welcome to the American Psychological Association and could they please analyze the Chicago press to find out what their problem was. The speech lasted 30 seconds. Phelan found it cute and worth two or three graphs. He told Youngman to pick up Kemper and write it. Then he phoned the news desk across the room to offer an item called "mayor." The news desk liked it.

Marshall and Forrest had continued the conversation without Phelan.

"I should add, Red," said Marshall, "that brothers and sisters sometimes steal from each other. She has two brothers and a sister who are still at home. She was giving one of her brothers the evil eye as we sat around and talked. I had the whole family there. This girl had her ass reamed out by her momma after I left, I can tell you that. Momma doesn't need this shit with her other problems. Whatever happened, we had nothing to go on, Forrest. And having seen that house, I truly doubt any fireman was going through the coats."

"Thanks, Maynard," said Phelan. Like most white news people, Phelan trusted firemen.

"Taking the TV, maybe," added Marshall. Phelan and Marshall both laughed. Forrest remained glum.

"Thanks very much, Maynard. I'm sorry we kept you so late."

"No problem." Marshall bounced up sending the chair rolling away on its casters.

Phelan found himself more relieved than he had expected. Because of the scare, he reminded himself that, just in case, he should start "hearing" each one of these incessant allegations again before he dismissed it.

He moved a story he had open on his computer screen, then said, "Paul, I'm going for coffee. Watch the phones."

"Call for the desk on zero," sang out the copy boy. Phelan picked up the phone out of reflex. "City desk."

"Uhhh, mister, where do I cash in my winning numbers?" It was a very old lady with a shaky voice.

"What numbers, ma'am?"

"Winning lottery numbers."

"Take them to wherever you bought them, or any place that sells state lottery tickets."

"But, I . . . I bought them from you people. They come in your newspaper. Can't I send them to you?"

"We don't sell lottery tickets, dear. The state does through stores. We never sold them. And we don't have any games in the Chronicle right now."

"I . . . I got them right in your paper. I cut them out. It says, 'Winning Lottery Numbers,' right on page two. I want to cash them in. Where do I send them? I . . . cut them out."

Good grief, thought Phelan. She was cutting out the little box on page two that reported the winning numbers in the state lottery every day. She thought that meant she was the winner.

"Will you send me the money?" she said.

Phelan looked at the clock. He was standing up. He had three stories to move in half an hour. He sat down again. "Let me explain, madam . . ."

21

A short while earlier, Sam Nash sat at the bar in the Radio Grill and poured beer from a 12-ounce bottle into a small beer glass. He took two good swallows. He kept an affectionate eye on the brown whiskey in a shot glass in front of him. The two liquids were a team and had to be appreciated together. Setting the beer glass down, he picked up the shot glass. He held it delicately and drank about half the whiskey, rolling it around in his mouth before he swallowed it. The pouring and drinking he did with his right hand. In his left hand, he held a folded computer printout of his latest story on the bar.

While writing this story during the day and early evening Friday, Nash had also attempted to phone every Morici with a listed number in Chicago and suburbs. He called them in batches of five at breaks in his writing, and he called some numbers two and three times because no one answered. Of the total of 29 Moricis who had listed phone numbers—listed either in phone books or with directory assistance—23 said they did not know any Victoria Morici.

Nash was suspicious of several of those responses because the speakers had sounded suspicious of him. Some, he assumed, considered him a bill collector, a common misperception. He knew also that his search had a built-in level of difficulty because relatives would be protective of a family whose daughter had been in several mental institutions and protective of the young woman, too. At six of the numbers, no one ever answered. He could call those numbers another time. Much more daunting, he had discovered that an additional 12 Moricis in the Chicago area possessed unlisted numbers. These were out of Nash's reach.

Nash had expected better luck. In fact, he had expected to be successful in locating Victoria's relatives. He would bet that half the Moricis in the Chicago area were related to each other. And despite the sensitive nature of Victoria's situation, he had hoped his telephone charm would get the job done.

His basic approach for those who wanted to know why he was calling had been that he was a friend of Victoria Morici's; he was a reporter for the Chicago Chronicle; Victoria had called him to tell him a story, an interesting story about the Illinois Department of Mental Health; and now he could not locate her at her old number. "Do you happen to know a Victoria Morici in your family?"

This approach, Nash hoped, avoided telling every Morici in a 40-mile radius that Victoria Morici was in a mental hospital, for those relatives who might not already know it.

Sometimes, he left out his occupation and the Illinois Department of Mental Health and simply described himself as her friend, which he felt was true enough. Occasionally, he said Victoria had asked him to do her a favor (by which he silently meant the story of the alleged shooting), and he was trying to do it, but he needed to talk to her again. He could not describe what the favor was, so this gambit was awkward. Nash had ceased telling lies on the telephone during his early days at the City News Bureau after he found that he disliked this approach.

Most people had not wanted to hear either a short or a long spiel. They said they did not know any Victoria Morici. Two said they knew a Vicki Morici. Of these, one refused to give him Vicki's number. When he located the other Vicki (if she was a separate person), the entire business was news to her. Moreover, she did not know any Victoria Morici. Her name was strictly Vicki.

The 12 Moricis with unlisted numbers represented a blow to Nash. He had not expected so many.

The whiskey he drank in the Radio Grill was very mellow because it was only 80 proof as were most whiskeys, trimmed from the former standard of 86 proof apparently to keep the price down. Nash preferred a higher alcohol content, but whiskeys with more alcohol cost more. This one was still good. The first jolt of the day gave Nash the same feeling of contentment he saw on other men's faces when they lit up cigars after a full meal or on women digging their forks into evilly sweet desserts.

He drank a little more beer, finished his shot in one more sip, then moved the empty shot glass toward the rim of the bar. When the bartender passed by, Nash lifted the shot glass to indicate another. He let the second whiskey sit, sipped his beer, and returned his attention to the computer printout of his animal rights story.

Nash had tried several different ways of making the animal rights feature into more than it was or as much as it could be, depending on one's point of view. His assignment was to focus on animal rights activities in Chicago, so he could not devote a lot of space to whales. He had tried the crisis approach in his mind, but nothing in his notes suggested any believable crisis that matched up with the accepted crises of the week. The funny approach also failed because, while it was easy to poke fun at animal rights groups, too much humor distorted the issue. Nash was not supposed to write for or against animal rights, simply about it. He decided the straight story he finally wrote was, on an interest scale, a five, but that it was the best he could do in a 25-inch overview.

He wondered if he might have done a better job if he had not interrupted himself periodically to make phone calls to Moricis. He doubted it. Interruptions in newspaper writing were routine.

He could have phoned Andrea Crocker while writing to get answers to a few questions, but he got the answers by other means. He decided that when he intended to get laid in the very near future, he would go to a singles bar, skip the dinner, and hope for the best. He was not yet willing to pursue females in his office because he did not wish to open himself up to anyone there.

Finished reading his story, Nash folded the computer printout and put it in his back pocket, then opened the Ledger to read his favorite columnists. Nash's bartender was a burly black man wearing a red sweater under a sportcoat he could never hope to button. It was cold in the Radio Grill. Nash kept his coat on. He had been in this bar on Rush Street south of Grand Avenue quite a few times, but he did not know the bartender's name, and the bartender did not know his. They never spoke except for the minimum. The bartender's look always suggested he suspected Nash of something Nash had done or was about to do. This made Nash comfortable.

Another bartender served the opposite end, a short, old white man with white hair who was crippled in one of his hips so that he walked with great difficulty, using his whole body to lift one leg, then taking a short, normal step with his other leg, and repeating. Nash guessed the old white guy was the owner.

The Radio Grill was a working man's bar, the sort of place where parking lot attendants bought their half pints on very cold winter mornings. It was several blocks south of and out of sight of the Rush Street nightclub district. Between the Radio Grill and the nearest cross street, Grand Avenue, stood a currency exchange and an old-fashioned diner. The block had so far resisted the surrounding real estate boom, but it was marked. Two decades earlier at a location only three blocks away on Hubbard Street, the Radio Grill had been a rollicking newsman's hangout, Nash had heard, until it had lost its lease and gone out of business. Nash guessed the owners of the current establishment, either the same people or somebody else, had kept the name in an attempt to win the newspaper people back. Despite the effort, news people rarely came there anymore. Nash knew he could drink at the Radio Grill without meeting anyone he knew, have two shots and two beers, and still have his carfare. If he wanted company and was ready to buy a round, he usually chose the Boul Mich, around the corner and up a flight of outdoor stairs, or the Billy Goat, oddly enough located about where the old Radio Grill had been.

Draining his first beer, Nash thought again how frustrating it had been to telephone so many Moricis and find no one who admitted to knowing Victoria. Consistent failure to get information made Nash angry. He decided he was going to discover something at Read before he gave up, whether or not it amounted to a story. He was stymied for the moment by the non-existence of Victoria Morici as a patient.

So what was he going to do next? Something was out there.

He picked up his money from the bar, just in case, stood up and removed his trenchcoat, leaving it on the barstool to save his seat. He stepped to a pay phone on the wall a few feet away, fished a piece of paper out of his pocket containing a phone number he had tracked down, and called Flannery's house. Flannery's wife said he was downtown "seeing his shrink. It's his regular appointment." When would he get home? Maybe 8:30. His appointment lasted until 8:00, she said.

"Tell him I called. Where's his doctor?"

She told him.

Nash sat down again and turned sideways to the bar. Three Mexicans with hair hanging in their eyes were playing pool near the front window and Nash watched, sipping his beer from the bottle. While he drank, he found himself wondering if he was going to have to think seriously about his marriage again. Pfff, his "marriage," he thought, what a word. His wife was what he meant. Perhaps he was obligated to think about her. It seemed as if it might be his duty. Sometimes, he knew, the thoughts could be very pleasant, relaxing, when he skipped the recent months and thought about the past, but such thoughts quickly provoked great anxiety. Then he always forced himself to confront the present, unpleasant mess and analyze it to death.

He finished his second shot, and the bartender came by.

"Want another?" said the man, placing his hand around the glass without touching it.

"No. Just one more beer." Nash did his serious thinking at home where it was cheaper.

Each time he began analyzing his relationship with Katerina, he began reasonably. What good would it do to start again, he thought? The problem had so far been insoluble and had no new elements. And he was afraid of it. Once in a while when he started to think about himself and Kate, he slipped down a dark well so deep and full of demons he could hardly climb back out. He was terrified that one time he wouldn't make it back, and he felt a small, involuntary shudder go through him.

Then he thought, "It's twenty to eight." If he left this tavern fairly soon, he could probably catch Flannery leaving the doctor's office. Maybe that way, mused Nash, he could do something useful.

22

"I'll never forget when I got your letter, Sam, saying you were going with one of the Greek girls, the stuck-up one. That was like the sun coming out at nighttime. It knocked me on my ass. You know how it was," said Flannery.

Nash shook his head. "Not like you." Nash had not seen any combat in Vietnam.

"Man...I know I've told you this before...but that was real compared to everything else. It changed my whole week. I thought, 'I know this guy, and I know this girl. I was there when they met. Nash is going with the Greek girl! There is *life* back in the states. Yeah, man! That's what it's all about.' My mind had shrunk before then. I was like an animal. Just like a rat."

Nash washed his hands, dried them on a paper towel and shook Flannery's hand again, this time more seriously. "How are you doing, Jack?"

"It's good to see you, too, Sam," said Flannery, giving Nash's hand a strong squeeze. With his left hand he squeezed Nash's upper arm. Flannery's face, which showed real pleasure, had filled out a little, and the black hair showed some gray. There was something else, Nash noticed. Flannery had a confidence in his manner and a serenity that Nash envied. Nash knew a person could fake this. He hoped Flannery wasn't. Let somebody be a success.

Nash had caught up with Flannery at 8:05 p.m. as Flannery got off an elevator in the lobby of the Garland Building, 111 N. Wabash Ave., right on time. Nash was 15 feet behind him, unseen. When Nash called his name, Flannery turned around and his jaw dropped. "Sam? Sam. What are you doing here? Hi. How are you?"

"I was looking for you. Your wife told me you'd be here."

"She did?"

"Is there a bathroom up there where you came from? Let's go back up. I need to use it."

Flannery was well turned out in a natural, camel's hair overcoat, a maroon satin scarf hanging loose, a gray suit, and Tote's rubbers that no doubt covered expensive shoes. Nash even liked his tie. When Nash told him what he wanted, Flannery was a little shocked.

"Wait until we get outside, Sam, geez. How long has it been?"

"I was thinking about that. I think we last saw each other four years ago."

"You should have two kids now, right?"

"Yep."

"And you're still married to Kate-the-Greek?"

Nash chuckled. "Yes." This was the term Herbie had made up to identify Nash's girlfriend many years earlier. Nash had not heard it in a long time.

Flannery had come back from Vietnam with two purple hearts and three cigarette cartons full of Southeast Asian marijuana. It was not a lot, but he had parlayed it into a brisk business in marijuana, pills, and LSD that became his sideline for several years. To Flannery, this was plain free enterprise. Lots of people wanted to buy. He sold. Flannery eventually told his friends he had quit that business and became very sensitive and embarrassed about any mention of it. Nash wondered what made people change.

When doing research, Nash always believed in going as straight as possible to a person who knew the field, even before reading books. Flannery was that person.

Returning to the ground floor, they walked onto Wabash, went south to Washington Street, turned left on Washington and walked past the old Central Library, renamed the Cultural Center. They talked along the way. Flannery asked Nash about his job. "You're still with the Chronicle, right? Have to be. I see your name once in a while."

"Yeah. What are you doing, Jack? Last time I saw you, you were buying and selling inventories from stores that went belly up. Now you look like you're buying and selling banks."

"Not quite. I'm selling business forms. I work for a big firm, Morrison, the top of the industry. It gives me company benefits and still lets me be on my own, selling. Let them carry some of the risk. My wife is now into producing plays."

"You *are* Jack Flannery from Quincy and Cicero?"

"Hey, who ever thought you'd be a newspaper reporter? I always thought of you as a guy who'd be a pitcher in 16-inch at this age with a beer belly. Sherri's still got her travel agency, which does very well, but her attention is divided."

Nash assumed that if Flannery had any children, he would have said so. Nash wanted to say, "You should have kids, Jack." Instead Nash paused, then said, "Isn't producing plays a little expensive?"

"Very. We hold parties and drag in other suckers. But they love it. And these are little plays. An audience of a hundred is standing room only."

From the number of play reviews published in Chicago papers, it seemed to Nash there were almost as many plays running as there were movie titles. Still, Flannery must have a lot of money, Nash thought.

When they crossed Michigan Avenue still going east and entered

Grant Park, Flannery said, "You'd better tell me what this is all about, Sam. I don't think I'm going to get anywhere near it."

The park was covered with snow. The asphalt sidewalk leading to the interior had been cleared by park district workers, leaving only the pigeon droppings on the walkway. By the light of the street lamps, tiny clouds of fine snow, like dust, were visible, blowing along the ground and swirling in small wind devils across the sidewalk.

"There's a good reason for my asking," said Nash. "To be honest with you—and this is going to sound a little crazy—I think somebody may have gotten murdered over a dope disagreement. I know about it, and the police don't. I have almost nothing to go on, but I want to chase it anyway just because I want to. I'm starting from scratch. I would like to see if there's dope traffic out of this hospital where I think the murder occurred. I thought I might sleaze around that neighborhood asking questions here and there and see what I can see. My knowledge of the dope business is very limited, so I need a little coaching."

They had passed a giant, concrete birdbath that loomed above them on a pedestal, and they climbed ten steps to an elevated portion of the park, running north and south along the right of way of the Illinois Central Gulf Railroad. The tracks were 20 feet below in a man-made gully that divided the park along its entire length. Flannery had left the sidewalk, continued across the snow covered grass, and was looking down in the dark gully. Nash came up behind him.

"Good place for a murder right here," said Flannery.

"Yep."

"Okay, Sam." Flannery turned to face him. "I don't do that anymore, and I don't like to talk about it. You're sort of presuming on our friendship. I was never a big dealer."

To Nash's limited knowledge, all dealers said this about themselves after they were arrested. But Nash felt bad about making his friend Flannery talk about it since he had quit.

"I'm sorry, Jack. I know it's a rotten thing to do."

190

"Where is this? A black neighborhood?"

"No. Northwest Side."

"Which institution?"

"You don't really want to know."

"Maybe I do. Maybe I want to avoid that hospital if the staff has its mind on other things."

"It's not a hospital you would ever patronize, Jack."

"A dump, huh?"

"It's an odd place."

"What do you mean, odd?"

"It's not the sort of hospital where auto accident victims are taken. It's a specialty hospital."

Flannery studied him. "Okay, forget it," he said. "How do you know somebody got murdered? Was this recently?"

"This week. A little bird told me. You don't want to be involved, Jack, and I don't want to involve you. I only want a little coaching in elementary dope trade."

"You must have a witness."

"Maybe I have a dead body," said Nash. "That would be a good indication."

Flannery's eyes widened. The look passed. "You'd tell the police if you had a body," he said, "and you wouldn't be investigating all by yourself." He turned away and looked in the gully again. "I think you're crazy to be doing this, Sam. The dope trade has gotten a lot rougher since we were young. You can't just ask, 'Excuse me, where do I find a dope dealer?' Once, you could almost do that. But you're the reporter. What do you want to know?"

Nash was buttoning the top button of his trench coat across his neck. He was already wearing his hat. Flannery's head was bare.

"Can we go indoors someplace, Jack? It's cold out here."

"Yeah, now that you mention it."

They started back toward the sidewalk. The view north on Michigan Avenue was like a post card, but you had to be warm to appreciate it.

191

In the northeast corner of the Chronicle Building on the fifth floor, next to the broom closet, was a small room, the size of a small bedroom, that contained a table surrounded by four, chrome metal chairs, lightly padded. Ordinary office chairs. Before they entered the room, Flannery gazed at a green plant in a pot at the very end of the hallway outside. "What's that?" he said. "I don't know," said Nash. "A plant." "No shit," said Flannery.

After Nash closed the door and they sat down on opposite sides of the table, Nash said, "I think the plant is there so when you get off the elevator and look down the length of the hallway, there's this nice green thing at the end." The small room had two windows, one looking on Michigan Avenue and one looking at the stone wall of the building to the north. With two exposures, the room was chilly. Nash told Flannery to leave his coat on.

"For starters, dope could be coming out of your hospital and going anywhere, Sam. It doesn't have to go to the local neighborhood."

"I know. Let's assume some of it is going into the local neighborhood even if it isn't supposed to. If it isn't, I wouldn't know where to start."

Flannery shrugged. "I don't understand what you're doing, Sam. Can you give me any particulars of what you know? Maybe it would help."

"I'd rather not, Jack. It's just my habit."

"Only for you, Sam. Do you use any form of dope?"

"No. I drink."

Flannery smiled. "If it is going to the local neighborhood, people make connections in the bars," he said.

"How long would it take to find the right person?"

"In Chicago, to find somebody that gets high? Oh, probably five minutes at the most. It will take longer to find somebody willing to deal. If there's anybody at all that can score, you can tell when you walk in the bar. Maybe there will be somebody with a little bit longer hair and a WMTL T-shirt or some other kind of insignia which means rock, hard rock. Maybe he'll have a marijuana patch on his shirt or a Van Halen T-shirt. Ozzie Osborne. There are guys who wear marijuana rings on their fingers. You want somebody obvious, of course. It's a little hard to describe, and I'm trying to look at it from your point of view. I could pick somebody out like that that gets high." He snapped his fingers. "I hope you're looking in a neighborhood where there's action, Sam, Lincoln Avenue, Rush Street, Division Street. It could be tougher at Addison and Narragansett where everybody knows everybody."

Flannery had inadvertently mentioned an intersection four blocks from the Read Mental Health Center which stood in the middle of a quiet, residential neighborhood.

"What next?"

"What next?" Flannery looked skeptical. "Boy. Okay. There's always a problem when you go into someplace new if somebody's gonna ease in with you or not. You gotta make friends first. You buy somebody a drink.

"You say, 'Hey, where you from?' The guy says, 'Oh, Portage Park.' 'Ooohhhyeahhhhhhh? I used to play ball there.' Keep it vague."

"I did play in a league there."

"Doesn't matter. You might say, 'Did you know so and so?' Give 'em a couple names, fictitious if you want. Then you might say, 'That O'Brien,' one of your fictitious friends at Portage Park, 'he was a real freak, high all the time. He said it was better for you than booze. But he gave me some real good stuff once.'

"If the guy seems interested," Flannery continued, "you say, 'Hey, you like to get high?' " Flannery said this very softly as if he were talking to someone next to him on a bar stool. Then he said louder, "Yeah? Me, too." Then very quietly again, " 'Say, anything good around here? Cause, you know, I'm a long way from home.' And you take your chances. Most guys won't go for this. They'll think you're a cop. You usually only deal with people you know. You'll have to have some excuse why you're not buying from your regular source. Maybe you just moved into the neighborhood or something. But if it's only pot, you'll score eventually, or get your head smashed."

"Maybe I should take you with me," said Nash.

"No way." Flannery took off his scarf and put it on the table. "I think I'm going to try and talk you out of this."

"Keep going, Jack. This is fine. I'll decide. How does it come?"

"How does what come?"

"Pot...or cocaine?"

"Bags, half bags, pounds, kilos, plane loads. You can buy anything if you're willing to take a chance. Pot, I mean."

"What's a half bag?"

Flannery's mouth dropped open. He started to lean back in his chair, then he leaned forward. "Sam, I'll bet there's 50 people here at this newspaper who could tell you. How can you be—you're the same age as me—39 years old and not know what a half bag of marijuana is? And you're in the news business?" Flannery laughed merrily then gave Nash a sidelong glance. "Sam, you don't want to do this. Forget it. You spent 13 months in Vietnam and you don't know anything about marijuana?"

"I tried it a couple times, a couple joints. Then I avoided it. I've always been afraid of losing my mind. It's my principal fear."

"Sam, you don't know what you're doing. That's probably for the best. Nobody would sell you an aspirin. Didn't you ever write anything about dope?"

"Just about dope raids, $100,000 and up. And I don't go to them. I only write a few paragraphs. So tell me what a half bag is."

"A half bag is half an ounce. It costs $20, or it used to, and it comes in a baggie, a sandwich bag."

"I know about the baggies."

"It's two fingers." Flannery held up the index and middle finger of his right hand, horizontally, staring at Nash. After a moment, Flannery shook his head and chuckled. "You know, we haven't even mentioned where this stuff is supposed to come from. All you're doing is trying to score a little reefer in a tavern."

Nash ignored that.

"Like two fingers of whiskey," said Nash. "But they could make it skinny in the bag, though, couldn't they, so two fingers wasn't much?"

"It's weighed on a scale. You can tell. I can tell by putting it in my hand. That's under. That's over." Flannery pretended he was holding a bag in his palm. "They will think you can, too. That will usually last you three days, four days at the most. An Oh Zee'll last seven. For a good smoker. An Oh Zee, also known as an ounce, a lid, or a 'bag,' used to be $40. That's four fingers." Flannery held the four fingers of his right hand horizontally. "I assume the price has gone up," he added.

"What's the usual buy, a half bag?"

"No. A bag."

"Why is it called a lid?"

"Just is. Why's a joint a joint?'

"All right. What about coke?"

"Are we talking about going into a strange bar again?"

"Yeah."

"Aaah, pshew. You gotta be crazy. You are crazy, I know. But it won't help. You're not ready for that. Nobody asks nobody for coke unless they know 'em. Nobody. Wouldn't you know somebody if you were buying coke? So why ask a stranger, see? Never. No chance."

Nash began to give in to the feeling that he was asking questions only for the hell of it. What, besides alcohol on the brain, had made him think he was a narcotics investigator?

"You never buy any powdered substance from strangers if you're sane. They could put it all PCP. You take a snort, enough to put a horse out. Bang, you're dead. Gone."

"How could this business operate if nobody ever bought from a stranger? You have to start someplace."

"Friends. Not close friends necessarily. People you know. Listen, Sam, I have only my own experience." Flannery leaned back in his chair and folded his hands in his lap. He asked, "How much were you guys willing to spend on this?"

Nash's eyes popped. "Holy shit!" he said. Then he laughed. The idea was so incongruous. And he hadn't even thought of it. You could not trace narcotics without buying, and the Chronicle never spent money. His personal narcotics probe had been shown up as an adolescent fantasy. Nash was briefly speechless. After a moment, he concluded that the story of a shooting at the Read Mental Health Center, as told by a crazy woman who disappeared, belonged strictly to Bryce at the State's Attorney's Office. If the story was too flimsy for Bryce to bother with, thought Nash, perhaps it was destined to be only a shadow by the side of the road at night or a voice carried by the wind over a long distance, making no sense.

He went home and drank too fast trying to find the place in inebriation where he was comfortable, and he threw up, alone in his basement apartment. He went to sleep thinking his stomach had done him a favor.

23

At 10:30 a.m. Saturday, Nash pulled up in his Chevy Nova in front of a two-story, red brick house on Normandy Avenue south of Foster Avenue, the house that was mortgaged in his name. The temperature was in the high 20's, and the bright sun was melting the snow on the edges of the grass nearest the sidewalk.

He rang the small, vertical bar doorbell he had installed himself when the old round one with the button stopped working, and his four-year-old opened the inside door. Her black hair was in pigtails, and she was wearing a red dress and white tights.

"Hello, Daddy, where are we going today?" she said through the window of the storm door.

"I think we'll go to the Sears Tower, Kimmy, because it's a clear day, and the Planetarium. Are you going to open the door?"

She rattled the handle on her side with the intense concentration of a small child, then she said, "I can't. Mommy did something to it."

Nash knew it was locked. He tried to look sideways through the glass to see the locking device and tell her how to undo it. At that moment, Katerina appeared with the breathless, harried look women get when the door bell rings while they're trying to dress their children. She quickly unlocked it, and Nash could see her examining him furtively to determine if he was annoyed. "I'll have to show you how to unlock that door, Kimmy. We can't leave your father standing out in the cold."

"Hello, Kate."

Nash was a bit surprised because his wife was fully dressed in a sweater that flattered her and blue jeans; her hair looked freshly washed and was held up on both sides in the back of her head with combs. She was even wearing a little makeup at 10:30 on Saturday morning. Many times when he had picked up his kids, Katerina looked a little worse for the wear, even allowing for her natural attributes.

At 34, she weighed not more than 10 or 12 pounds over what she had when they got married. It occurred to Nash that he liked the way she looked. She got to him.

"Hello, Sam." She tried to smile, but Nash could see her mind was on five different things.

"Kimmy, come here with your dad and sit on the couch," he said. "Let your mother do whatever she's doing." Nash sat on the couch, unbuttoning his coat. His daughter sat on the floor at his feet. The couch faced the rear of the house so they would both have a good view of any activity.

"How cold is it out, Sam? Bobby really shouldn't go. He's got a terrible cough. I still can't get him to spit up the phlegm. He just swallows it. But I kinda have to let him go anyway because he misses you, you know?"

"Are you giving him any cough medicine?" He could see the worry on her face.

"Yes, maybe a little too much, but I finally got him to stop coughing at 4 a.m. so he could sleep. He didn't get up until 10."

"We're going to the Sears Tower and the Planetarium," said

Kimmy. "If Bobby doesn't come, me and Daddy will go alone, won't we, Daddy?"

"Bobby's coming, Kim," said Nash. Then to his wife, "It's a nice day. Did you talk to the doctor? Bobby's always got something."

"I'm well aware of that, Sam. The doctor says it's another virus going around."

"Kate, I don't mean any criticism. I'm only asking. Do you think there's any more to his colds and fevers than another virus?"

"I don't know," she said, shaking her head. "Do you? He's eating a donut for breakfast. That's all he'll eat is one donut, and it takes him forever. Do you want anything, Sam?"

There it was again, thought Nash. Being nice all of a sudden.

"No," he lied. "I'm not hungry." Nash thought it best to avoid the family atmosphere. It would give the kids the wrong idea.

"Well, go say hello to your son, Sam. It will take him a while to finish his donut."

He could not very well refuse, so he walked through the house to the kitchen with his daughter alongside. She hid behind him when they entered the kitchen. Bobby was reading a cereal box and very slowly chewing. Nash saw that the boy's eyes were sunken and the skin dark underneath as if he had been awake for two days. Other than that, he looked okay.

"Good morning, champ. How's your health?"

Bobby looked up and made a gesture of resignation with his right hand holding part of a donut. "Same old stuff. Sick again," he said in his little boy's voice, seeming to accept his condition as the natural state. "I see you behind dad, Kimmy. You don't know how to hide."

"Oh yes I do. You can't see me now," she said, dropping down behind the table.

Nash sat down. "You want to go downtown with me and Kim today?"

"Yeah, sure, can we see a movie?"

"We're going to the Sears Tower and the Planetarium," said the voice of Kimmy under the table. "The movie is last."

"Shut up, Kim. We can see the movie first," said her brother. "Dad, how many times have we been to the Sears Tower?" Bobby took a new bite of his donut.

"Twice. I think it's fun, don't you, Kim?"

"Yeah, I like the elevator ride. It's so shaky," she said.

"Just once it was, Kim." Nash reached under the table and pulled his daughter away from her brother whose feet she was about to tickle. "Kimmy, sit down in a chair and tell me what's exciting in your life."

"I got a new coloring book. You want to see it?"

"Sure." Nash slipped off his coat, thought of having a cigarette, but decided against it. He thought it best to avoid smoking around Bobby. As Kim was running out of the kitchen, Katerina entered carrying two pairs of snow boots and two pairs of shoes in one arm. With the other arm she grabbed the sprinting four-year-old.

"Daddy wants to see my coloring book."

"Oh, he does, does he?" She let her go. Katerina dumped her burdens on the floor and took Bobby's shirt and pants off the chair next to Nash.

"Bobby, my little snail, can you eat that donut any faster?" Katerina said. Bobby was chewing slowly and staring off into space, thinking who knew what. He held up the last of the donut showing there was only one bite left.

"Where are you going today, Kate?" said Nash. She was standing next to him, but he didn't look at her.

"No place."

"Oh." There was silence as they watched Bobby chew. Nash suddenly felt a hand touch the back of his neck, a touch that was halfway between a brush and a squeeze, lasting only a second. Her nails barely brushed the top of his back as she withdrew her hand. He felt butterflies in his stomach and his loins stirred. He turned to find her. She was standing next to him and slightly behind him, cooly calm in a female way.

"This is the best coloring book I ever had," said Kimmy, bursting between her mother and father and pushing her mother aside. She started climbing onto Nash's lap, forcing Nash to push out from the table to give her room. Nash looked up at his wife's face. Not knowing what else to do, he just looked at her, all his armor down, wide open, willing to risk rejection or ridicule. His daughter grabbed his chin to make him look at the coloring book. He forced himself to study the pictures which were better than he expected. She stayed in the lines in some places and used more colors than Bobby had at her age.

"Who did all these, your mother?" he said.

"Hell no, Daddy, I did these all myself."

"Kimmy!" said Katerina and Sam together.

"Does your mother talk like that, Kimmy?" said Nash.

"Sometimes."

"Kimmy, I do not, and you shouldn't either."

"Well, Daddy does a lot."

"Yep, I do, Kimmy, but you don't." While saying this, Nash reached his right hand behind his daughter's back and touched his wife's very firm rump in blue jeans, resting his hand on the rise. He expected his wife to dart away, but she didn't. She moved away slowly. She gave him a gift for which he was very grateful, and for a second he closed his eyes.

Katerina put Bobby's clothes down; he was still chewing; and she began picking up dishes. Nash exclaimed over the pictures in the coloring book and every once in a while criticized one to make his daughter aware he could tell the difference.

"You sure you don't want anything to eat, Sam?" said Katerina from the opposite side of the table, picking up things and wiping the surface quickly with a dishcloth as was her style.

"I guess I'll have two donuts for my health," he said.

She had already turned her back to him preparing to put the milk and orange juice in the refrigerator. "Do you want anything else?" she said slowly without turning around.

Something in the way she said it made Nash's brain miss on a few cylinders. He was leery of letting his thoughts get ahead of reality or offending her.

"Yeah, uh, milk...if that's okay...Katerina." He saw she was standing still, listening to his answer with her back turned.

"Daddy, this is the best one," said Kimmy, pulling her father's cheek to get his attention.

"Oh, that really is," said Nash. Then he made himself look at it. "Yes it is, the best."

"What's new at work, Sam?" said his wife.

"Nothing. Same old stuff."

"Bobby," said his wife, "you get dressed now and brush your teeth. Your clothes are on the chair next to your father. Get dressed in the living room. Kimmy, go to your room and color until all of you are ready to leave."

"I'm talking to Daddy."

"I have to talk business to your father now so you go, thank you." Katerina smiled sweetly at her daughter. "Go on."

She set down a plate with donuts and a glass of milk.

"Did you see those pictures?" said Nash when his son and daughter had left. "They're really good."

She was sitting opposite him. "Kimmy takes coloring very seriously, Sam. It was good that you praised her like that. She's also a little toughie. She punched a little boy down the street the other day."

"Punched him?"

"Hit him in the face."

"My little girl.... You, ah, got some cough medicine for me to take along?"

"Could you buy some? I don't have much."

He nodded and started eating one of the donuts she had given him, making sure the crumbs fell on his plate. He held the glass of milk in his left hand without lifting it, feeling the coolness of the glass.

"Where are you going today?" He took his first drink of milk.

"True confessions. I'm going to the cleaners, grocery shopping, the telephone company to pay an overdue bill, and the library to return a book which fell down behind Bobby's bed and is three weeks overdue. Then I'm going to a male striptease joint to see if I can get off on just watching."

She had her arms folded on the table with her breasts touching her arms. Her expression was feisty with her dark eyebrows raised over sparkling black eyes.

"So what did you get all dressed up for?"

"I'm not all dressed up. This sweater is three years old, and these blue jeans are faded terribly. I need some new ones."

"I like faded blue jeans, especially on you, and that sweater is nearly illegal." The sweater had shrunk a little.

"It is not," she blushed and looked at herself. "Sam, do you ever go in Dominick's on Saturday and see what women are wearing to buy their groceries. Anyway, I'll have a coat on." She had just realized about the coat. "What are you talking about? Are you going to get nuts again?"

He knew she meant his attitude toward Verbecke.

He swallowed a bite of the second donut. "Did you get dressed up for me?"

"I got dressed up for myself. You know this is nothing special."

"I wouldn't mind if you got dressed up for me. I'd be touched."

"I didn't."

"...But I guess I was already touched. I'd be touched again."

She pursed her lips and shook her head slowly signifying denial, but he saw a glint in her eyes. Without any warning, Nash suddenly realized he had to make a big decision. He had thought about it often enough since the last time she had turned down his offer to return, but not in the present, always later. He had never allowed himself to decide because the negative possibilities were too painful to ponder. Now with no drum roll and no plan. . . . He wondered if big decisions were always like this.

"What do you think?" he said.

"About what?"

"You don't seem to hate me as much as you used to."

"I never hated you," she responded.

"Well, you didn't like me much for a while."

"You walked out."

"It was for the best."

"The best for whom? I still don't understand why you did it." She spoke in a low tone. "And it's not something I'm going to forget easily."

Nash knew he was almost completely in the wrong, but he did not think kneeling and begging forgiveness was the right move.

"Let me finish this." He ate the rest of his donut quickly and gulped down the milk, wondering if his wife would find something to do suddenly. She waited, which encouraged him. After he licked his lips to get the milk off, he thrust out his hand.

"What do you want me to do with that?" She pushed it away. He put it back in front of her.

"Can we shake?"

"I'm not one of your buddies."

"Let's make out and make up then."

"Hah."

"What do Greeks do to get their wives back? Hit 'em over the head?"

"You're not Greek."

First base was still 90 feet away. He stood up quickly, reached across the table and grabbed her hair near the scalp. She was taken by surprise, but she struggled which he had hoped she wouldn't do because he knew it hurt.

"You stupid idiot!" she said. "Ase me, vlaka!" (Leave me alone, you lowlife.)

"Kate, just walk around the table toward me. My arm's long

enough. If you don't fight, your hair won't be pulled. I'll just hold it."

"Sam Nash, you drunken dreamer," she grabbed his arm with both hands and dug her nails in. "If you ever want to see me or your children again, you'll let go—now!" She was growling.

He let go and she gave his arm a shove as hard as she could. The hair on the left side of her head was pulled out of its comb in back, and some of it fell across her face. She pushed it back angrily. "Don't ever!" She pushed back her chair so she was sitting sideways to the table and glared at him, her face flushed and her eyes flashing, leaving one arm on the table.

He sat down. "No promises. What do you want me to do?"

"Take your children to the Sears Tower."

"What else do you want me to do?"

"Quit drinking for a year."

"How about a month?"

"Six months. And if you can't control it after that, then forever."

"You want me to stay away from home for six more months? We can't afford it."

"One month, the first month, on your own." She lifted her eyebrows questioningly, a challenge. "If you can do that, maybe we'll make it. If you can't, Sam, there's no hope for us. And there's less hope for you."

"If I was drinking once in a while, how would you know?"

"You can't drink 'once in a while.' But okay, I don't know everything you do when you're here or not here. But YOU will KNOW."

He slumped back in his chair. This was like asking him to go out for the Olympics, he thought. A month seemed like a lifetime. Six months was infinity. He hung his head.

"You don't think you can do it, Sam. But you can. I know you. I'll help you."

He laughed at himself without looking up. "How can you help me, Kate?" There was nothing she could do.

"You can have me back, body and soul, if you make it through the first month." She dragged her chair noisily back to the table and leaned toward him. His head was still hanging. "I'll do anything you want...."

Nash looked up, mostly with his eyes.

"...over and over again."

He smiled and felt his throat tightening and a sting behind his eyes. He lifted his head. This was...his crazy, beautiful wife who, he realized, was just as sex starved as he was—so much so she didn't know what she was saying. He had taught her to enjoy making love in the daylight, and she certainly was passionate. But she considered climbing on top of him spontaneously to be the ultimate in unleashed sex. He longed for her to do it again.

"You want to look at me? That'll help you. We'll go upstairs, Sam."

"I'm all for that," he said, stunned, his head swimming, but desperate to get her alone.

She got up, went to the sink, opened a drawer next to it, and took out a long knife. Reconsidering, she put the knife back and took out a long, two-pronged, sharp fork used for barbecuing. She turned and looked at him with the fork in her right hand. He stood up.

"This is a pretty good offer," she said, looking him over, "but I know you, Sam. I'll use this." She bobbed her head toward the front of the house where the stairs were. She was wild, and he thought if he took her now, somehow avoiding that fork, together they'd make the house fall down, and he would teach her things.

"HEY! Kimmy! You stay out of here!" It was Bobby's voice from the front room followed by a deep chest cough, phlegmy, then another cough and another. Katerina whirled and threw the fork in the sink so hard it bounced out onto the floor. "Damn it," she said. "Damn," nearly running into the front room. Nash followed hearing the coughs one after another, each sound cutting through him like a barbed wire pulled across his stomach.

When Nash got into the living room, Bobby was seating himself on the couch, beet red in the face, coughing to the point that Nash wondered when he could breathe. Nash's erection, stirred up by his wife's actions, was gone.

He could hear his son's windpipe rattling like a hollow gourd with the phlegm trying to come up.

"Bobby, you've got to spit it up!" Katerina pleaded. "Get it in your mouth and keep it there. Then spit it in the toilet. Come on, let's go to the bathroom." She tried to pull him by the arm, but he resisted and continued to cough, big coughs that sounded as if his diaphragm would come up out of his throat alternating with lesser ones.

"Sam."

Nash picked up his son, holding the boy by his sides, and carried him to the bathroom in the middle of the house. He stood the boy in front of the toilet bowl and pushed his head down almost into the bowl.

"Don't swallow when you cough. Spit," said Nash. The coughing fit subsided quickly with the boy sobbing for air and sniffling. He had spit out only a few drops of saliva.

Bobby stood up. "I did it," he said breathlessly. "It's the best I can do."

"You didn't do it, Bobby. Phlegm is a lot. Big bunches. Not little drops like you did. Bend down and cough and when you feel that stuff again, gag it up and spit it in the toilet. Don't swallow it."

"I don't want to cough anymore, Dad."

"You have to." Nash pushed the boy's head down. Bobby coughed two weak coughs.

"That's all I can do."

"Okay, Bobby."

Nash let him straighten up, then put his right hand on the back of the boy's head and, without warning, put his left index finger and middle finger into Bobby's mouth, as gently as he could. Before Nash got his fingers in half as far as he expected to, Bobby began to gag and make choking sounds and bit the fingers. Nash withdrew his hand quickly and pushed Bobby's head almost into the toilet at the same time. The boy vomited, coughed, vomited, and coughed. He tried to straighten up, but Nash would not let him, and the process continued until Nash was satisfied.

Nash took a paper cup out of a dispenser on the bathroom wall, gave it to his son, and turned on the cold water in the sink. "Wash your mouth out." He looked in the toilet, then flushed it, picked up a brush from next to the bowl while the water swirled and ran the brush around the bowl.

Katerina was standing in the doorway, scared. "You think he'll be better?" she said.

"I don't know. He got up quite a bit. Had to get it out of there somehow."

"You shoulda told me, Dad. Don't do it by surprise," said Bobby sniffling.

"What started all that?" said Nash.

Bobby began to explain. "Kimmy tried to . . ." but his voice was chocked off by a new cough, a small one, like a man in a Western movie dying of gunshots. Nash filled up the paper cup again and made him drink it.

Meanwhile, Katerina said, "Bobby set up his Star Wars figures on the table next to the couch, and Kim threw a Frisbee at them from the stairs. One of them is always annoying the other. She was bored because she's ready to go and I made her color.

"Is she upstairs now?"

"Yes, but . . ."

"Bobby," Nash took him by the arm, "go sit on the couch and don't shout at anybody." Bobby was already breathing better, and his color was returning to normal. Nash shoved Bobby gently on his way as the boy sipped from the paper cup. Then Nash pulled Kate a step further into the bathroom and closed the door.

"You forgot your fork," he said, lifting the bottom of her sweater abruptly over her head and tensing for the fight, either scratches or a blow to the stomach. Instead, her arms slipped right out, slim and pretty, and she pulled the collar up over her head herself.

"Sam," she said as she dropped the sweater on the tile floor. His fingers felt the smoothness of the skin on her back; her breasts pressed into him; he covered her open mouth with his lips. He squeezed her so hard with his arms, and she him, and their legs were so entwined it was as if they were trying to mold together.

When they paused for breath, he loosened his bear hug a little so she could breathe, and he kissed her ear. "Kate, I wanted you every day," he whispered in her ear. This was a small lie, he knew. Every day he missed what they once had together, but he did not long for her on those days when she had been very sarcastic to him.

"I wanted you even when I hated you," she said.

He explored her ear with his tongue and breathed in it at the same time. She moaned and rubbed her body on him. Still licking her ear, he moved his hands to the back of her bra. She jumped back but hit the wall only an inch behind her, and she held up one hand in a desperate stop gesture.

She had pulled her head away, but Nash had kept hold of the bra, and he unhooked it. With the hand that had made the stop motion, Kate caressed his cheek and his ear, trying to disengage but arching towards him from the belly down.

"Sam, I love you."

He put his hand on her back, felt her woman's muscles, and pulled her. "Take it off," he said, then he started sucking on her neck.

"Ohhhh, oooooo." The sounds turned Nash on more. "Sam, please. No. No. No."

She pushed his shoulders with both hands which he ignored while he played with the skin on her back and kissed her throat. Then he slid his right hand around and held her naked breast under her loose bra, gently.

"Ahhhh! Sam!"

"Shhhhh," he said.

"Sam, my husband, please, please, please, ooooo, Sam, I love you, please, please, for me, ohhh, I want you, please don't, please, for me. Ohhh, Sam, pleeease don't."

She was rubbing against him ripe to bursting, but she kept up with the simultaneous pleading with him and begging him not to which he couldn't get out of his ears.

"Sammm!"

He didn't like it. He stood up straight.

"Kate, what the hell!" he whispered.

"Sam, don't do it, please." She leaned against the wall taking quick, shallow breaths. Her eyes were as wide as saucers and searching. "Don't be angry," they read. With her outstretched hand over his shoulder she was caressing the back of his head. "I want to help you. I thought about it a long time."

He closed his eyes in pain. "Stop thinking about it, Kate. Why don't we just have one roll in the hay, and then I'll go be a monk," he said with his eyes closed.

"Oh, Sam, I want to." He felt her nails dig into the back of his head. "Don't make it hard for me. This is important to us. This is important to you."

"Are you sure?" He felt her slip sideways away. He opened his eyes, staggered backward, dizzy, closed the lid on the toilet by reaching back and making it fall, then he sat down. He was weak, nearly dying. The hormones racing thither and yon had no outlet and were attacking him.

"Hey, Dad, are we going?" It was Bobby's voice outside the bathroom door.

"Yeah, son. Be right there. Go back in the living room. We're just cleaning up after you," he said weakly. Actually, there was nothing to clean up and almost no smell because Nash had handled it so efficiently.

"I killed you, right?" said his wife.

"You can see that."

"I'm sorry, Sam. I couldn't stay away from you."

Strangely, this admission was heard by his nerves and chemicals which began breaking off the attack on him. He took a deep breath and let it out slowly. The breath came out jaggedly because he was trembling. He turned to look at her. She was rehooking her bra. Just below the level of consciousness, his resources were regrouping.

"Do you know what this does to me?" said his wife.

"Is it anything like this?"

"Yes, my love."

"I'm sorry for you, too, Kate." He took another deep breath and exhaled. "What about the rest of the deal here?"

She gave him a look of wide-eyed disbelief. "That will just make things worse."

"When I'm into self-punishment, I like to do it in a big way."

"Sam, you're crazy, and I was crazy to say that. Why don't you please go, my love, and I'll be out in a minute." She pointed to the door.

"Gimme strength, beautiful, I got a long month ahead."

She had the scared look she sometimes got when she didn't understand him, but he knew his woman. Watching him warily, she unhooked her bra, took it off, and held it dangling from her right hand. She stood with one hip thrust out like a stripper. She always did like that fantasy, he thought.

"Hold your hands behind your back."

She surprised him and put both her hands behind her head, which wasn't what he'd asked for but was better. And she even had the hint of a smile.

"Utterly and completely fantastic." He sat back against the toilet tank in awe at the woman he had seen a thousand times. The title to an old rock and roll song came to him, "Venus in Blue Jeans."

"You could start or stop a war, baby. Are you sure we can't . . . ?"

"No. Now get out of here." She began putting her bra back on. Nash rose and in one step had his left arm around her naked waist. He thrust his knee between her legs to make her rub against his thigh, and he grabbed one breast with his right hand.

"No, damn you. Nooooo. Sam. I didn't do this right. Sammm."

She kept her face away from him so he could not kiss her mouth, so he licked her neck and throat. She kept playing with the bra, attempting to put it between them until Nash grabbed it in his right hand, tore it away from her and threw it on the floor. She hit him weakly. The pressure of his thigh between her legs almost lifting her began to arouse her again and he felt her move.

"Oh, Sam, you son of a bitch. Sam, I can't stop you, but I have to. Sam, I love you and I want you so much. Sam, nooooo."

The last "No," was a little strained, he thought, like a person falling off a cliff. He felt her body relaxing and joining him as he maneuvered her. He reached his left hand up and grabbed the back of her head to turn her face in his direction.

And he saw she was crying.

"Sam, I'll do anything you want." She looked in his eyes. Two lines of tears were running toward her upper lip. "But I don't want to."

"Relax, baby, it's gonna be great."

"Sam, I can't stop you anymore. You're tearing me apart. But I don't want to." She was sobbing now, and he could see her inhaling tears, and even hear the liquid sound as she breathed through her mouth. He lowered his head to kiss her, but she let out a long, shuddering sob that was pathetic. He didn't kiss her. He put her head on his shoulder, wrapped both his arms tightly around her, and looked up.

"Help," he said.

He held her close, rocked her like a baby, felt more shudders, and finally he said, "Okay, Katerina. It's over. You win. I give up. It's okay. I'm here."

When she was assembled and had washed her face, he opened the door. her hair was still askew despite a quick brushing, but she followed him out. The children were playing quietly together with Star Wars figures in the living room. Nash had difficulty walking he was so weak.

"Mommy, that happened to your hair?" said Kimmy.

"That hairdo was not meant for cleaning up the bathroom, Kimmy. It came apart."

"Were you crying, Mommy?"

"Yes, dear, I broke my nail and it hurt." She showed the broken nail to her daughter. Nash wondered how that had happened.

"You got your shoes on?" said Nash.

They both thrust out their feet to show they did. "I tied hers," said Bobby.

When they were all dressed, Nash pushed the kids out the storm door in front of him, then turned to his wife. He kissed her on the forehead and she rubbed his cheek with her hand.

"It has to be this way, Sam, because I could never stay away from you, and I could never throw you out," she said. "You have to do this."

"Mark it on the calendar, Kate." He could feel he was still sweating a little and his heart was pounding. "Remind me to pull your hair again, beautiful," he said with more self-assurance than he felt.

"I might."

On the way to the Kennedy Expressway, still dazed and afraid to think of the dry spell ahead, he stopped at a drug store and bought the earliest Sunday papers. All three were available at 11:30 on Saturday morning, the first editions. In the car in the parking lot while his children protested, he turned the pages and scanned headlines out of occupational curiosity and to take his mind off things. His animal story had made the Sunday paper in the middle.

On page three in the Post, there was a headline halfway down the page that said, "Alderman's aide arrested for dope." Nash's stomach dropped. He knew without reading it who the aide was, but he read anyway. More self-punishment.

Colucci's nephew had been arrested after a chase for going through red lights, speeding, and other traffic violations. Police said the nephew, who was driving the alderman's car, appeared to be under the influence of something. Marijuana was found in the car and a white, powdered substance that was being analyzed. Nash thought he had better call the office and tell them he had the nephew's entire sheet in his desk. But there was no hurry, he realized ruefully. The horse was out of the barn. He could not take over the Colucci story again and do it right at this late date. The new development would be somebody else's story, and the deadline for the final wasn't until 9 p.m. Nash's job for the moment was to take his kids downtown.

Nash fully expected to pick up the Post or the Ledger in a day or two and read about an amazing murder in the Read Mental Health Center. Why not? There were a lot of reporters in town, and many of them were smarter than he was and knew more people. He wondered what he lacked as a reporter. Ambition?

"Daaaad!"

He threw the papers on the floor on the passenger side. "We're going!" he said.

24

With the "new" Chronicle spread full open on his desk, Nash
pretended to be reading the columnists on the opinions page. He
had both his elbows on the desk, and his chin was resting in his
hands, but he wasn't reading at all. He was undressing his wife, pulling her panties down. She was willing. When she had shimmied her
panties down to the floor, she kicked them away and pulled him
against her . . . and Maureen Warmsley tapped him on the shoulder.

"Hi, Sam. You want to give me something for Sally Bernstein's
going away party?"

Nash turned in Warmsley's direction, still holding his head up
with his hands. She was at the side of his desk. He was not about to
move back from his desk at the moment.

"What's she wanna leave now for?" he said.

"What do you mean?"

"I mean the 'new' Chronicle is only a week old, and we have lim-
itless vistas here," said Nash. "This moment is pregnant with prom-

ise. Why just last week, I wrote a weather story about squirrels and it got on page one."

"What have you been smoking, Sam? Five bucks is the going rate."

Bernstein was the Chronicle's former national editor who had been forced out in a political shuffle a few weeks earlier, Nash knew. He heard she was going to the Ledger. Nash pleaded poverty and gave Warmsley $4. Then he resumed daydreaming. He was glad for the break, the first in a while.

Nash was in his 10th day on the wagon, and he was looking forward to a date with his wife after work. Unforseen crises had arisen during his abstinence from liquor, as usually happens. For instance, on the seventh night, a Friday night, as he recalled regularly, he discovered his wife was out having dinner with her young boss. Nash's mother-in-law had given him the information with apparent pleasure when he called the house on Normandy Avenue.

Nash panicked at the news and soon became enraged over the lack of character in females. Yet he resisted the temptation to have a drink. It became a matter of pride. He told himself that having forced himself to go on the wagon, he was not about to let his bitch (!) wife push him off.

The next day when he picked up his children, he was distant to Kate and maintained a cold resolve not to ask the obvious questions. He intended to continue being cool when he brought the children back Sunday, but, envisioning the rest of the week, he couldn't restrain himself any further. He took her aside and asked, "Where the fuck were you Friday night?"

Kate told him Sobieski the younger had taken her and Marlene, the legal secretary, out to dinner as a threesome.

Nash's body started to relax instantly, and he felt a weight lifting off his shoulders. "Damnit," he said, "could you have told me yourself without making me ask?"

"Okay," she said.

He wanted to grab her, but she parried his hands.

"Hell, Sam, I never go out at all. YOU never ask me out."

Nash's shoulders slumped and his head drooped momentarily, but it was a welcome sort of defeat. It had not occurred to Nash he was allowed to date his wife. He asked her out for Monday night. Then he managed to get hold of her, and they occupied five minutes saying goodnight, part of that time with the children watching.

On the job, Nash had run into a different form of crisis. For the first five days of the 'new' Chronicle era, his 3rd to 7th days on the wagon, Nash barely had time to go to the bathroom. The speed-up began with a lecture from Miller regarding the Colucci story.

"Did we forget something when we did that story on Alderman Colucci and his relatives, Sam? I read the original memo."

Nash explained why he had omitted Martin's police record and that Solomon had given his permission to leave the record out.

"Made us look a little silly, don't you think?" said Miller. "Maybe there's a lesson in this for us. If a guy's got a police record—and I'm talking about convictions—then he's got a police record, Sam. If we write about him and that fact is relevant, we mention it. We can't do it to some people because we don't give a shit about them and let others go because we feel generous that day. Solomon should never have allowed you to pull that stunt.... There's two bodies under the Ravenswood El tracks. Go with Lampkin." Lampkin was a photographer.

Thus began a string of assignments which made Nash feel as if he were the only reporter at the Chronicle. As soon as he finished one, and often before, he was given another by Miller or Wolfram. Press conferences, some of which he had to attend and others which he covered by phone. Small plane crashes and multiple fatality auto accidents, all of which he covered by phone. Weather features. Tracking down people from within the office or by going out who had stories the Chronicle wanted. And doing obits. By noon Tuesday, Nash knew something strange was going on and he queried Wolfram.

"Look around here," said Wolfram. "Everybody you see is working on some special, in depth story dreamed up by Solomon, Peterson, or Simonet or some big production for features to make the 'new' Chronicle different or unusual. But there's nobody to cover the news except you and Monica Platt, and the beat reporters. So Miller's going to run you into the ground."

Nash felt as if he were back at the City News Bureau where he started out. And the more stories he did, the more he needed a drink after work to wind down. Since he couldn't have one, he became a great walker at night. Once he skipped the El and walked back to his apartment from work, a trip of more than three hours, principally down Milwaukee Avenue. It was the most exercise by far he had had in a year and a half since he had fallen away from the habit of playing racquetball.

To reach Bryce to discuss Victoria and the Read Mental Health Center, Nash had to call him from a pay phone in a hotel while on assignment. Bryce sounded odd, but had apparently done nothing, Nash decided. Nash had also finally made contact with Dr. Medaven, the director of the Illinois Department of Mental Health, with predictable results. Dr. Medaven said he did not know what Nash was talking about, had heard nothing about any such incident, would look into it when he could, but considered the incident doubtful. For questions about Victoria or any other patient, or possible patient, Nash would have to write to or visit the individual institutions. That was the law, said Medaven. Nash was pretty confident he could locate Dr. Gerard Crawford on vacation somewhere in Hawaii with a barrage of phone calls, perhaps 20 or 30, but cityside reporters had to get permission from the desk for overseas calls. Nash had no intention of explaining this "story" to the desk.

Nash came to the conclusion that sometimes a reporter had to forget a dead end investigation for a while. Then when he came back to it later, the reporter would suddenly have new ideas, new interest, new hope.

This particular morning at his desk, Nash was feeling lackadaisical. Miller had induced Solomon to give him two other reporters to run ragged for a week, Abramowicz and DeCarlo. Nash had read what he cared to out of the newspaper, including an analysis of the gubernatorial primary which was neck and neck and turning into an exciting horse race, exciting to the spectators if not to all the participants. The Chronicle was printed in new typefaces with a new design which made Nash feel he was reading an out-of-town newspaper. Liberal use of color on the front page, even though poorly done because the Chronicle's printing plant was not up to it, seemed too loud to Nash. He thought such quick changes in the appearance of the paper gave off signals of desperation.

Nash's assignment was to put together an in-depth Sunday story on new houses being built in Chicago proper. Get 10 year, 20 year statistics and try to determine geographical patterns for a map. He read some clips and made six phone calls. He had to wait for the call backs.

By 11, Nash thought he had sat in the newsroom long enough to accomplish the impression of being there. He decided to journey to the morgue where he could read some magazines in peace. As he was walking out past the switchboard, feeling like a kid sneaking out of the classroom, the copy clerk on the switchboard said, "Nash, I got a call for you."

"Ahh, shit." He took the call at the switchboard.

"Nash, this is Mike Franzel. Remember me?"

"Uhhh, yeah. . . . The name's familiar. Remind me." He had no recollection of anyone with that name.

"The Wall case?"

"The Wall case? . . . Something's coming here. An 11-year-old girl kidnapped and murdered in the south suburbs."

"That's the one. I was one of the assistants on the case." Franzel meant he was an assistant state's attorney assigned to the south suburbs who had worked on the investigation.

As the memory came back, Nash felt a wave of irritation. Franzel was one of those young prosecutors whose answer to all questions was: "No comment." or "That's under investigation." In the one-week lifespan of the Wall case, Nash had been scooped twice. Small suburban police departments were notoriously cold to the press except for an occasional cop who knew a reporter personally. A reporter for the Post had such a friend on the Homewood Police Department. Franzel could have filled in the information gap for Nash and other reporters; assistant state's attorneys often did; but Franzel had refused. Now, thought Nash, here the guy was calling to ask for a favor. Maybe he wanted to get his name in the paper for some two-bit case, or he wanted to get some cops' names in the paper because he owed them.

"What are you doing now, Franzel?"

"I'm still with the State's Attorney's Office. I'm at 26th Street. But I'm not calling for myself. I didn't know who to call about this. Then I thought of you. You seemed pretty resourceful. (During the Wall case, Nash had caught up with the scoops as best he could by pestering Bryce.) Can you come out, Sam?"

Nash did not want to.

"Uhh, I don't know, Mike. I don't have wheels. You think you could just tell me what it is?"

"I'll tell you this much, but I'd prefer if you'd come out here for the rest and to see certain people. Bryce butted heads with the State's Attorney and Prince Charming over an investigation. They fired him."

25

Nash took the Douglas Park El to California Avenue and transferred to a bus. He thought he would freeze waiting for the bus which did not come for 15 minutes. Most reporters would have taken a cab from downtown. The company would pay for it later after an expense account was filed. But Nash did not have the money.

En route, Nash tried to imagine what he was getting into. Bryce had been acting preoccupied and overworked lately. Perhaps he was preoccupied because he already knew the chute was greased for him. Or, it could be that because he wasn't quite himself for whatever reason, the blows of life, he had stumbled and done something very dumb. Got one of the girls in the office pregnant? Franzel would never call a newspaper about that.

Nash recalled his last conversation with Bryce. Bryce had sounded as if he wanted Nash to understand something, but Nash could not get what it was. They had been talking about Victoria.

"I told you I spoke to somebody, Sam, the head of the Department of Mental Health. He wanted to see a police report. He and I went back and forth. No. There's nothing new.... I need that transcript tonight, Laurie.... I told you, Sam, that they were inscrutable and we were persistent. Is that why you called?"

"Yeah. It is. You see, Clarence, to you, I know if it's anything, it's just another murder." Nash intended to get his goat. "But I like this one. I have high hopes for it as a story. Do you think you could...?" Nash had been standing at a pay phone.

"Just another murder, eh? There's only one individual around here with that attitude, and he does not prosecute cases."

"Well, what am I to think, Clarence?"

"I can't push it any faster for you, Sam."

There was a moment of silence as Nash waited for Bryce to say something else. Bryce didn't.

"Uhh, can you give me an idea how long this will take, Clare?"

"I told you. A week or two. But it might be longer than that. There are various legal complications."

"Like what?"

"Just legal complications. I'm suddenly being held on a short leash here, Sam, so I can't wing this thing for old time's sake. This is also off the record."

Insisting that the conversation was off the record when nothing had been revealed was pure stress reflex, in Nash's opinion. Bryce was also pulling back into his official role like a turtle.

"Of course, Clarence," said Nash. "You haven't told me a damn thing anyway." Nash squeezed the pen he was holding in his right hand concentrating on how to phrase what he was about to say for best effect. He intended to push despite Bryce's resistance. "Uhh, I only told you my primary reason for calling, Clare, but I have a secondary reason."

"I'm all ears, Sam. Slow day."

"Heh. (Nash suppressed a retort.) What we have here, Clarence, is a situation where we have notified the Department of Mental Health that Victoria may be a witness to a crime in their institution, involving their employees, and she most likely remains in the custody and at the mercy of the Department of Mental Health. This is *exactly* what I was trying to avoid when I called you in the first place, and I feel responsible for it, if you get my drift."

"Do you have some new information to suggest she is endangered? I'm open to suggestions. Do you have anything to suggest anything, Sam?"

"Nope. Other than the fact that she is no longer where she was, and I don't know where she is."

"Can you tell me what you think the object of this conspiracy at the Read Mental Health Center is, Sam? That might be instructive."

"No. I don't know, Clarence. I once thought dope, but that was a wild guess. All I know is this woman reported an alleged shooting to me. I reported it to you. And you reported it to the people she was reporting it about."

Nash was going to add, "...and then you dropped her," but he restrained himself. Bryce knew.

"That's all I can do for now," said Bryce.

"Clarence, if there was no shooting, there's nothing to hide..." Nash's voice was pleading. It annoyed him to have to sink to this, but nothing else was working. "...unless Victoria knows some other secret I cannot even imagine. So why don't they let you see her? And if there was a shooting, why would the upper reaches of DMH risk being implicated by running interference and covering up for the lower reaches? And while we gab, perhaps some poor soul is in a jam over this. Then again, perhaps not, but...."

"Must be great to be a newspaper, Sam. When I'm reincarnated, I'm going to be an editor and tell the whole world what to do, but refrain from doing anything myself, of course. Newspapers don't care about legal complications, do they? The show must never stop."

"Oh, spare me, Clarence. What the fuck." Nash looked around to see if anyone in the lobby of the hotel was listening to his conversation. He had already put his notebook away since it was obviously

223

not going to be needed while he talked to Bryce. He fidgeted with his trenchcoat which he had draped over his arm. "Clarence, if you're going to say anything, say it fast. I've got another assignment right now. What's the problem? Who's stopping you?"

"I never said anyone was stopping me, Sam, although I may have given you a misimpression. I said there were legal complications.

"You've been part of the system long enough to understand what I'm talking about," Bryce continued. "I'm going to examine the alternatives again, and I may be very busy. I don't know. There's no point in discussing it further. I'll get back to you in a few days. Keep being yourself."

"That's easy."

"IS it, Sam?" said Bryce almost as if he were surprised. "Good for you.... That's very good, Sam."

"Are you okay?" asked Nash, but Bryce had hung up. Nash chewed on his pen and stared at the wall behind the phone, puzzled.

Whenever the heat was on in a public agency in Chicago, even if the heat came from nothing more than the boss's hemorrhoids, the employees always started whispering and talking cryptically to each other and to the members of the press they knew. Some spoke so cryptically, out of fear of being quoted, that reporters could not understand what they were talking about. These occasions sometimes turned out to be nothing when one got to the bottom. ("Joe's been transferred.") Bryce was the last person from whom Nash would have expected this melodramatic behavior. But Nash reminded himself that Bryce lived in a different world, and what was important to Bryce might be obscure to Nash. Bryce was, after all, a bureaucrat.

Nash had decided to give him his few days. He gave him five days and would have given him a couple more. Then Franzel called.

Nash got off the bus at 26th Street and California Avenue and thought he was stepping out of a time machine. The site of the Morris House, a traditional restaurant formerly on the northwest corner, had become a garish fast food stand. The antique, ponderous, six-story Criminal Courts building, built in a classical style that might be called "urban serious business" was still standing on the south-west corner, across the railroad tracks that ran along 26th Street, but the building seemed as if it weren't there. It had been dwarfed by an adjacent, 13-story high rise with rose colored windows—a modern, bright office building of the sort that a group of dentists might finance for investment purposes in Schaumburg. Next to the new Criminal Courts building, the old one, which was still in use, looked like an historic two-flat. Nash had seen the changes before, but had never adjusted to them and knew he never would. He walked up the steps toward the entrance to the high-rise courts building, crossed a plaza littered with wrappers from the fast food stand, went in and took the elevator to the 12th floor where Franzel had his office.

The office required another adjustment. Nash still thought of the assistant state's attorneys occupying tiny, dim rooms like the cells in flophouses. Franzel's spacious office, which he shared with two other assistants, had two enormous windows, modern chrome furniture, children's school drawings on the walls, and a raspberry carpet. One of the windows looked south past the newer jail buildings to the former Contagious Disease Hospital in the distance. The other looked west down into the jail yard and out across endless rows of old frame houses, the neighborhood.

When Nash greeted Franzel, he noticed Franzel still looked boyish but had acquired the confidence of a man of some accomplishments. Franzel closed the office door and cleared several fat case folders off a chair for Nash. Nash could read only two. Both were labeled "Murder" in large black letters written with a felt-tip pen. Nash and Franzel were alone.

"He's not at work today. I guess he's not coming back," said Franzel. "He spent the last few days of last week working with Laurie getting his files in order apparently for the next guy, and he wouldn't tell anybody what he was up to. Not even Laurie, his secretary. It was driving her nuts. She asked me to talk to him, but he wouldn't tell me anything either. He's had some problems lately. I knew about that."

"What kind of problems? Wife problems?"

"No. Here in the office. Or, I don't know, maybe that, too. He's been too aggressive in my opinion, pushing cases he shouldn't push. Sometimes you have to let things go if the evidence isn't there even if you know the asshole is guilty. He got rigid the last year or so. We didn't win any more cases, but it sure took us longer to lose 'em. But he didn't deserve to be fired, not by a country mile."

Nash sat alongside Franzel's desk, and Franzel sat in the desk chair, facing him, gesturing with an extra-long ballpoint pen that he bounced like a baton, lawyer-like. Nash was still wearing his trench-coat because he was warming up, and he had his hat in his lap. He could tell from Franzel's manner that Franzel did not smoke. Nash needed a cigarette.

"You got an ash tray in here?"

"Yeah, sure, Sam," said Franzel who opened a bottom drawer and pulled one out.

Nash flipped his hat onto another desk. He took off his scarf and threw it to the same location. Then he opened his coat and took his cigarette pack out of his shirt pocket and lit up, Franzel watching.

"The real problem is for more than a year now they've left him on his own with too much responsibility. I don't mean he can't handle the job. He can handle it better than anybody else here. But, you know, the first assistant and the state's attorney are supposed to share some of the burdens and some of the decisions. These birds think it's great that Bryce handles all this filthy criminal stuff, while the first assistant spends all his time politicking through the hiring and promotions process, dreaming up more and more reports for us to fill out so he can manipulate more and more statistics to make the boss look like Tom Dewey; and what the state's attorney does beats the hell out of me. Gives a lot of speeches."

"Bad situation there. He could only go wrong," said Nash, who understood.

"Exactly. Whenever we were successful in a big case, the credit was all theirs. Anything that went wrong was his fault because they never took part in any of the decisions."

"So why'd they fire him?" Nash turned his head again to avoid exhaling smoke in Franzel's direction.

"Okay, now this part I hope you can leave me out of. I'm going into private practice in two weeks so they can't hurt me too much. I'd just rather not be involved unless it's absolutely necessary. But if I have to, I have to."

"I don't know yet. I'll tell you when you're through."

"Apparently, he did something Thursday, issued a subpoena."

Nash bit his bottom lip on the inside. Somehow he had known it when Franzel first said Bryce had been fired.

"He did it all by himself, even typed it up himself. It was for the Department of Mental Health, a patient. On Friday, the Department came in with a motion to quash the subpoena, and Bryce was kept out of it. The first assistant went to court—for the first time, by the way—and said the office had no objection to quashing the subpoena. I got this from the assistant who works in the chief judge's courtroom. It's all in the record, so he's in no danger. Just say, 'according to court records' or 'court officials.' "

Nash nodded.

"Then I guess about 3 o'clock, Bryce was called in to see the state's attorney and the first assistant. He was in there about 15 minutes. When he returned, Laurie said he had the usual phone calls backed up, but he told her to have everybody call back Monday, today. He sat in his office for the rest of the afternoon seeing whoever came around as if nothing had happened. But everybody knew something very strange was underway...."

Franzel chuckled and leaned back, "because to anyone who asked for permission or advice, like to let somebody cop to a lesser charge, the usual stuff.... The answer Bryce gave to any question was, 'Do whatever you want. Fine. Fine. Whatever you prefer.' THAT is not the chief we know."

Nash got out his notebook and pen.

"Laurie asked me..."

"Let's go back to the subpoena, Mike. How do we know what it was for? Give me the name of the assistants in the chief judge's courtroom. I won't print them."

Nash made him repeat the subpoena episode. Then he asked, "How do we know he was fired or why? This is all pretty vague."

"He told me." Franzel leaned toward Nash and talked in a softer tone. "About 6:30 Friday night, I came back from Jean's." (This was a restaurant and bar a block and a half away, still in business, where the prosecutors and some public defenders drank after work.) "The office was pretty much cleared out, but Laurie was still here which is unusual. She got in my way. I had to move her bodily, and I walked in on Bryce. He said something about my being nosey, but he didn't try to hide the fact that he was packing books in boxes. His picture of JFK was already in the box.

"I asked him, 'Have you finally been fired, Clare?' I meant it as a joke. I wasn't thinking. He said, 'Since you ask, Yes.' I was shocked. Don't ask me what I thought he was doing or what else he could have been doing. I don't know. There's no explanation for it. So I just sat there and talked to him while he packed his things. He told me what had happened, and—this is the tough part because I'm violating my promise—he said, 'I wouldn't tell this to just anybody, Michael, but I know you never talk to the press and I hope you won't start now.' And I never have, in point of fact. You're the first, Sam. My father would kill me, but he's gone."

Nash remembered. Franzel's father had been a city plumbing inspector who once was named in a story about a grand jury probe but who was never indicted. Nash had seen the clip. The part about the elder Franzel was so small it seemed inconsequential, but the father felt it ruined his life. In the family's opinion, it sent him to an early grave. Nash had heard the story from Bryce who offered it as an explanation of why Franzel was so difficult.

"Can I have a cigarette?" said Franzel abruptly.

"I didn't think you smoked."

228

"I haven't since high school except every once in a blue moon when I'm drinking. People say they can't understand how I can have just one. I suppose they're like potato chips to most people."

"A lot worse than that," said Nash who stubbed out his own, crushing the ash, too, as he had done routinely since smoking became unacceptable to bystanders.

"Well?" said Franzel.

"What?...Oh, yeah, just take one." The pack was on the desk between them. Nash turned a page in his notebook and noticed that Franzel's hand shook when he took out a cigarette and lit it in an awkward way. Nash, too, was tense on the surface, but dead calm underneath, calm and concentrated, the calm that usually came over him when he interviewed someone. This was questions and answers, a jigsaw puzzle being assembled by his conscious mind with help from his unconscious, and with a clock running. There was always a clock running when you interviewed someone no matter what they said. And you had to be calm to leave the door open to your unconscious.

"I don't have a real good context for all of this, Sam. You'll have to check it out yourself. He doesn't want the press to know, but I think he's wrong about that and you're his buddy, right? He said—this is a quote as near as I can get it—'An inmate in a mental institution, and they don't want me to talk to her. I subpoenaed the mayor's budget chief, and all they said was, 'Do we have to?' I subpoenaed two aldermen and a state representative in one day, and the state's attorney says, 'You better know what you're doing.' "

"Where's the quote end?" said Nash.

" 'An inmate in a mental institution and they don't want me to talk to her,' is a quote. The rest is my paraphrase, but pretty close. You know what the reason is?"

"What mental institution?" said Nash.

"Read. Northwest Side."

"He said that?"

"Yes."

"And he said a female inmate, a 'her,' right?"

"Right. A 'her.' No name. I'll tell you the reason when you're ready." Franzel was watching Nash who was still writing, "st rep 2 ald 1 day – y b k w y d" which stood for "You better know what you're doing." Such notes made very good sense to Nash for at least a week and often much longer.

"Did he subpoena all those people he said he did?"

"If he said so. I don't keep track unless they're my cases. I don't think they're related to this. He was just citing them as a comparison."

"Okay. What's the reason?"

"The primary. The son-of-a-bitchin' primary election. They wanted to let the Read investigation slide because of the primary. Bryce refused. That's why he issued the subpoena Thursday, and they allowed it to be quashed on Friday."

"Wait a minute. That's a big bite here." Nash did not write it down. He wanted Bryce's words. "First, who benefits?"

"The governor and the two birds running this office."

"Who said, 'the governor,' and in what words?"

"Okay. I didn't realize this was going to be like a deposition. This is all hearsay, you know."

"Newspapers have a lot of hearsay, but we can try to get it right. So who said the governor's race was the reason they didn't want Bryce to subpoena this lady, or inmate?"

"I doubt they made it that explicit."

Instantly, Nash looked up and gave Franzel an ugly, nearly contemptuous glance. It was as if Nash had shouted, "Why the hell did you tell me such a story if you have nothing to base it on?" The look was reflex. Nash changed his face as soon as he felt the expression, and he did not say what he was thinking, which was: This is how a reporter steps in shit.

"Gee, I'm sorry. Don't hit me," said Franzel. "I think there was something...." He looked at his desk top, tapping his ballpoint pen. "Here.... According to Bryce, the state's attorney said, 'We don't feel it's proper to give aid or comfort to either candidate at this point when it's so close.' "

"Hold it." Nash wrote that down in full, spelling each word out. "Okay. That's word for word?"

"As best I can remember it. Bryce said they never explained which candidates they were talking about, but he assumed it was the governor and Havranek because the governor is in charge of the Department of Mental Health. It's an executive agency which reflects directly on him. And we know Havranek has been making hay out of any and all fuckups in state agencies."

"How the hell could they expect Bryce to ignore some crime.... What sort of crime was it?" Nash asked.

"A shooting, I believe. I think Bryce told me that. Somewhere I picked that up. Had to be Bryce, I'm pretty sure."

"A shooting?" Nash did not know why he was being so coy about his own role except that he didn't have time to think about it yet. "They expected Bryce to ignore a shooting? Seems very naive."

"Maybe nobody got shot, Sam. Maybe it was just an aggravated assault. (This was a charge that meant shooting at somebody and missing, Nash was aware.) Or maybe there's 10 dead. I don't know. But I agree that business about giving aid to the candidates was a stupid thing to say. Saddler, the first assistant, interrupted to say that what the state's attorney really meant to say was that the Department of Mental Health had conducted an investigation and was continuing to do so; and somebody in the state's attorney's office was assisting them; and there was no need for a subpoena at this time, that the matter was not indictable. That's what really ticked off Bryce. He didn't believe that part about somebody in the office 'assisting' the Department of Mental Health, probably because nobody had told him. 'Who is empowered to investigate shootings around here, Michael?' he asked me.... That's where I got the shooting part.... 'We are, and the police,' I said. 'That's right,' he said. 'Not the fucking Department of Mental Health or the Department of Aviation or the EPA or the state Tollway Authority.' "

Nash wrote it all down, then he said, "Yeah, but according to Saddler, somebody in the state's attorney's office was taking part in the investigation, right?"

"According to Bryce, according to Saddler. It's hearsay. But I think the word Bryce used; he was really pissed off; was 'monitoring' or 'kept informed of,' something like that, not actually investigating. Bryce was quoting Saddler but I can't remember the exact word."

Franzel suddenly laughed and threw his head back. "Hey, you gotta use this. This is the best part." Franzel held his hands up on either side of his head, index fingers extended and waggling. "Bryce said in the future we may have to keep a box of badges in the office in order to deputize people who want to investigate themselves and clear themselves."

Nash laughed, too, and wrote it. "Is that a quote?"

"Yep. That's a quote. 'We may have to. . . .' Did you get it?"

"I'm writing it down." After a pause, he said, "How do Saddler and the state's attorney benefit? You said they did."

"Well, that part is pretty hard to nail down. You know Peyser has been attorney general now for eight years. If he wins again this time, word is he intends to run for the U.S. Senate in mid term. Our state's attorney hopes to be appointed attorney general, but that can't happen if the governor gets voted out of office. Nice to have the governor for your chinaman, eh? Don't ask where I heard this. It's just talk in the office. Bryce had heard it frequently, too."

"Did he say that?"

"Yeah. He heard the same scenario I did. I'm about out of information for you, Sam. You'll have to investigate the rest yourself."

"Okay. The state's attorney and Saddler revealed all this to Bryce in that 15-minute conversation on Friday?"

"No. No. This was about a week ago or a week and a half ago, he said."

"Which?"

232

"A week and a half is my best recollection. BEFORE he issued the subpoena. They didn't want him to do it."

"What happened Friday?"

"Bryce didn't go into much detail on that. He said they fired him which was what he expected, and that his wife would be ecstatic."

"Yeah, I'll bet she is," said Nash smiling. "Tell me about this shooting."

"I told you. I don't know anything about it. I've told you everything, Sam, despite the fact that Bryce said he positively did not want the press involved. Now I'm having second thoughts. Bryce said he wanted to go away decently, not like a whining patronage worker who goes to federal court and claims he's a victim of politics. You know why I'm doing this?"

"No."

"I have devoted seven years of my life to this place, and Bryce a lot more than that, and these two are trying to tear down in a few days the reputation of the office that guys like Bryce built up over years and years. You hear about crooked judges all the time. You hear about crooked EX-prosecutors. But this place is for real. Very rarely do you hear about crooked prosecutors. We do not throw cases. That reputation is as important as the law books around here."

Nash liked Franzel's loyalty and admired his simplicity. It was Nash's opinion that a few assistant state's attorneys sometimes did throw cases, minor ones to be sure, for money. But in general, Franzel's high opinion of the reputation of the office was correct, Nash knew. Nash wondered what would happen to that reputation if he wrote this story. Franzel read his thoughts.

"These two are an aberration. Make sure you make that clear, and that's why I'm blowing the whistle on them."

Nash could not write fast enough to capture Franzel's speech about the character of the office. He let it pass for the moment and made Franzel go over the whole Bryce story a second time. Then he turned a page in his notebook just to get a clean page rather than from necessity, took a deep breath to relieve his surface tension and said:

"Here's the hard part, Mike. I can't leave you out unless you can tell me somebody else who will know all this."

"You can try Bryce. You and he are pals. And there's Laurie. Maybe somebody else I don't know of."

"If I can't find any such person, which is very likely, I have to use you."

"Damn. And I said you could do this, didn't I? Can I go back on it?"

"I'd rather you didn't."

"Try to find somebody else, okay?"

Nash nodded. "You'll have to repeat that little speech you gave about why you're doing this and how these two are an aberration. It was too fast for me to write the first time."

"Oh, geez." Franzel rested his forehead on one of his hands. "All right...."

When he finished, Nash asked, "By the way, who's the new chief of the criminal division?"

"Well, they haven't even officially announced Bryce is out yet, so they haven't named one, but scuttlebutt has it that it's Scott Campbell."

"Campbell? He was a baby here, a law clerk when I covered this place."

"He's almost 35 years old, Sam."

Nash picked up Franzel's phone and called Laurie Grzeskowiak, Bryce's secretary. As soon as he mentioned Bryce, she said, "Hey, you gotta be nuts, Nash. I love the guy, but he said not to talk to anybody, God bless him." And she hung up. Grzeskowiak, who was Italian despite her name, sounded like the West Side to Nash.

Next, Nash called Sineni, one of the assistants serving in the courtroom of the chief judge of Criminal Courts.

"Oh, yes, thanks for reminding me of that. I'll get back to you," said Sineni, who also hung up. Nash imagined Sineni was not alone at the moment. Nash phoned Bryce's home number, but got no answer.

"Now I'm going to have to make a scene," announced Nash. Franzel put his hands over the back of his head as he bowed his head over the desk, symbolically hiding. He peeked at Nash as Nash picked up his hat and scarf and walked out.

"Good luck," said Franzel.

Laurie Grzeskowiak's office, 11D38, was one floor below, adjacent to Bryce's office, 11D36. Nash appeared suddenly in her doorway and noticed that the huge window behind her looked east to a dusty horizon past what had once been an International Harvester factory complex as big as a college campus. The location had returned to bare ground. Laurie's eyes bugged out when she saw Nash.

"Get out of here, you asshole!" she said in a stage whisper, waving furiously for him to go away. They knew each other.

"I'll come in and sit down if you won't talk to me, " said Nash.

"Nash, you numbnuts, get out. I'm telling you, get out!" Her tone was threatening. Then she added, "I'm serious." Laurie's standard mode of speech consisted of abuse mixed with affection which made it necessary for her to add, "I'm serious," when she was. Nash saw that she could not suppress a nervous smile caused by the sight of him in the doorway holding his hat and scarf like a beggar. He stepped into the office.

"Sam, please," she said, still whispering. She tilted her head to mimic vulnerability. "I need this job. C'mon. C'mon. Be a nice guy.... You shit! Don't sit down! Nash, you jagoff, I'll get you for this." She dropped the whisper and spoke in the growl of a woman in her middle 30's who smokes and drinks. "Nash, you get the fuck out of here now. I'm not kidding."

Nash calmly took out his notebook and pen which he knew would drive her up the wall. The effect was as anticipated. Nash said, "I don't want to talk to you here, Laurie, and I'm not going to use your name. But I do have to talk to you. Where do you suggest?"

She was almost levitating in her chair and her eyes were watching the doorway, expecting doom any moment in the person of anyone who recognized Nash.

"Look, shithead," she looked at him; "I'll do anything I can to get rid of you. Where did you call me from? How did you get here so fast?"

"I called you from Franzel's office," said Nash.

"Oi vey." She hit herself in the head. "Go back there, and I'll see you there in five minutes. I have to get somebody to sit here and answer the phone. There better not be anybody around."

"You look nice today," said Nash, getting up.

"You give me boils, Nash."

When Laurie came to Franzel's office, Nash said, "I should speak to her alone, Mike," and Franzel stepped out. Most of the assistant's offices had a narrow, rectangular window, floor to ceiling, next to the doorway so that anybody could see in even if the door was closed. Nash and Grzeskowiak maneuvered out of the line of sight from the window as best they could, and Nash hoped nobody would walk in.

Speaking in low tones, Laurie corroborated Franzel's story about the previous week, at least the parts she was a witness to. The episode of the subpoena and the role played by first assistant Saddler she said she had heard from Sineni, but she had no direct knowledge of it. It was true that Franzel had been one of the last people to see Bryce; that she had tried to keep him out; and that Bryce and Franzel talked for a long time Friday night. Laurie contended she did not know what they talked about, and Nash imagined she was telling the truth on that point. But even if she had overheard anything, she wouldn't want to admit it. Secretaries didn't do that. Except for scuttlebutt, she said she had no idea why Saddler and the state's attorney made such an issue over the subpoena. Bryce had never discussed the subpoena controversy with her, even in passing, she said.

"I think Clare wanted to keep everybody out of it and just do it himself because of the heat, " she said.

Nash asked her what the scuttlebutt on the subpoena fight was, and she said, "The governor's race—going easy or covering up." The conversation took only two or three minutes, and Nash concentrated on asking every possible, useful question because he knew he would get to talk to her only once. Maintaining his mental acuity required a lot of effort. He knew she would bolt as soon as she could, and this knowledge made him want to ask all his questions at once, which would not have worked. There was another difficulty, but he did not even allow himself to think about it.

"Now that I have told you all this, do me a favor, Nash. Don't print any of it. I only told you to keep you out of my office."

"Why not print it?"

"Clare said he doesn't want any story. If he doesn't want one, he doesn't want one. You're supposed to be his friend. Maybe he wants to start the good life downtown without being known as 'the notorious' Clarence Bryce who was fired from the state's attorney's office.

"There's a little more involved, Laurie."

"You mean some hanky-panky in the mental health department? There's always some crap going on there, Sam. It's to be expected. Talk to people who work there. If your conscience is bothering you, do an exposé on them and leave Clare out."

"Who should I talk to in mental health? Got some names?"

"Oh, no. What kind of person would I be if I gave people's names to the newspapers?" She stood up and shook her hair. Nash felt nature's biggest distraction coming over him, which he had been trying to ignore. Laurie's chest filled out her blouse, and she had nice legs under her skirt.

"You see, Laurie, you don't want me to write about what I know, but you won't tell me how to get the part I don't know."

She bent down and kissed him on the forehead, her breasts quite near his face. Nash was nearly overwhelmed.

"You're the reporter, Sam. Now leave me out of this, you son of a bitch or I'll have my husband shoot you." Her husband was a police

237

officer with the Cook County Sheriff's Police. "See who's out there."

Nash went out and saw only a couple of assistants whom he did not recognize apparently going to lunch. When they were gone, Grzeskowiak left.

Nash found Sineni's office and concluded his business there briskly. Sineni and Nash were strangers, and Sineni was extremely suspicious. He refused to talk. Nash said, "Look, you know what happened to Bryce."

"No, I don't," said Sineni.

"Yes, you do. You know an important part of it. I'm not asking you to go on TV. Here's what I heard." Nash repeated the alleged events of Friday in the chief judge's courtroom.

"Hey, I never spoke to you; I don't even know you," said Sineni. "But that's right. You got it someplace else because I never spoke to you, okay?"

"That's what happened Friday?"

"Yes."

"I never met you," said Nash.

"Good," said Sineni.

The next stop was the office of first assistant Thomas Saddler. Saddler's office, also on the 11th floor, had an antechamber occupied by desks for two secretaries although only one secretary was at her desk. Nash could see this secretary thought he was a dubious person because Nash had no appointment and he did not look very presentable. For one thing, since Nash had come in from the cold and taken his hat off, he had not combed his hair. Nash saw her looking at it and tried to comb it with his hand.

"I think Mr. Saddler will be busy all day, Mr. Nash. Do you want to make an appointment?"

"Can't, ma'am. Have to talk to him today."

"He's in conference now, and I know he's got a busy day scheduled. You may be disappointed."

"I can see him in there. Who's he talking to?" Saddler's office

238

also had one of those narrow, floor to ceiling windows next to the door jam.

"Well, uh, one of the prosecutors."

"Okay, I'll wait." The only other chair was behind the second desk whose occupant was probably at lunch. Nash walked over and sat down.

"What are you doing?"

"I didn't bring a chair with me, so I'll just use this one."

The secretary, a classy lady in her middle 50's, wearing a yellow blouse with a bow and an open sweater for the drafts, raised her eyebrows in what appeared to Nash to be mock irritation.

"Oooo, my. You are . . . . a nuisance. What newspaper did you say you were with?"

"The Chronicle."

"You mean the NEW Chronicle?"

"Ahhh, thbbbbt to that," said Nash, delivering his opinion of the new Chronicle with a raspberry.

"I thought the changes were odd, too. I've always liked the Chronicle, especially Mary Parker, your gossip columnist. She writes about people I want to read about, like Frank Sinatra, not so much about these new wave people. Is Mary Parker her real name?"

"Yeah, as far as I know. Weird name, huh?"

The secretary chuckled then settled down to a happy smile, studying him. Nash knew he was doing well.

"What should I do here? Start a fire? You think that would get him out?" Nash fidgeted.

"I think if you choose to go that route, you should just say there's a fire rather than start one." She paused. "Do you want me to get him out? I'm sure he must be tired of whatever conversation he's having by now. They've been in there almost an hour. Wouldn't you think?" The secretary had a mischievous look on her face.

"If Saddler isn't bored, maybe whoever he's talking to is."

"Do you know him?"

"No."

"Oh, I thought you must."

Nash got out of his chair. "Madame, may I shake your hand and ask your name?"

"Why certainly. I'm Lois. Just a moment, Mr. Nash." She pushed a button on a plastic box that appeared to be an intercom. "Mr. Saddler?"

"Yes, Lois."

"Mr. Saddler, I'm so sorry to bother you. There's a newspaper reporter out here demanding to see you. He says he won't go away until you come out, and he's sitting at Molly's desk in Molly's chair. He's very persistent, sir, and I thought it would be better if I at least told you. He won't say what, exactly, he wants."

There was no answer. Nash stayed away from the narrow window so Saddler would have to come out if he wanted to see. Then the door opened and two men came out, one of medium height, hefty, with sandy hair, wearing a fairly ordinary sportcoat and slacks. The other man was thin with his clothes seeming to walk in front of him. He wore a dark vest, buttoned, a tailor-made white shirt with the sleeves rolled up just so in an imitation of a working attitude, an expensive tie and pinstripe pants. Nash was off to the side, sitting in Molly's chair again.

"Where is he, Lois?" said the pinstripe man.

She pointed, as if to a spider.

The pinstripe man turned on Nash. "How did you get in here? This is not a public part of the building, you know. The press is not allowed to wander around here."

"Sam Nash of the Chronicle, " said Nash, rising. "Thomas Saddler, I presume."

Saddler shook his hand reluctantly, saying, "You'll have to leave, Mr. Nash. You can make an appointment or talk to our press spokesman."

"Mr. Saddler, I've got some serious questions to ask you." Nash took out his notebook and pen. "And I have to ask them before I print this story." Saddler was pointing toward the hallway for Nash's benefit, ignoring what Nash had said. The other man stepped forward and thrust out his hand forthrightly.

"Scott Campbell, Sam. Haven't seen you in a long time."

They shook hands. Campbell had put on weight since he was a law clerk, but it had made him thick rather than fat. Nash liked the way he ignored Saddler's attitude and spoke for himself.

"Yeah, quite a while, Scott. You look like you're playing football."

"I wish this extra baggage constituted muscle." Campbell put his hand inside his sportcoat to feel his ribs.

"Scott, I've got to ask Saddler here some important questions. You can join in the answers if you like." Nash wondered if Campbell was innocent or if he had been promoted because he was part of the coverup. He feared the latter, but kept an open mind.

"Saddler, did you fire Clarence Bryce as chief of the criminal division?"

"What the hell . . . ?" said Saddler.

"I'd better go, Tom," said Campbell, who went. Campbell gave away nothing. Nash noticed he merely made a diplomatic withdrawal.

"Mr. Nash, you'll have to leave. Now," said Saddler.

"I asked you, did you fire Clarence Bryce? I plan to write a story saying you did, unless you say it's not true and demonstrate it."

"You know, Nash, it really bothers me to answer your questions because it rewards you for this kind of behavior." Saddler stood with his hands on his hips, relaxed and arrogant. He was more than expected, Nash thought suddenly. They stared at one another.

"Lois, call Pardee and tell him to come here right away, would you?" Saddler did not budge when he said it. He continued to stare at Nash.

"Yes, sir."

"I did not fire Bryce, Mr. Nash. I don't fire anyone. I'm not the state's attorney. Nevertheless, Clarence Bryce, who was a valued, highly experienced employe around here, quit. We wish he hadn't.

241

But he had worked a long time at a trying job, and he thought he'd had enough. You can ask him yourself, if you like."

"Did he leave Friday?" Nash intended to corroborate details bit by bit, hoping Saddler would continue to talk due to his supreme confidence.

"Yes," said Saddler.

"On Thursday, did Bryce issue a subpoena for a woman in the Read Mental Health Center named Victoria Morici?

"If he did or he didn't, that would be a grand jury matter and confidential by law. I have no comment."

"Court records show that the subpoena was issued and you, personally, allowed it to be quashed on Friday, stating that this office had no objection to the motion to quash."

Saddler calmly folded his hands behind his back and gazed at Nash. No flinching. No nervousness. "That has nothing to do with his resignation."

"Did you warn Bryce not to issue that subpoena before he did it?"

"Once again, you are infringing on the territory of the grand jury, Mr. Nash. That is not to be construed as any sort of answer. The subject is simply not your business." Saddler shifted his eyes to the hallway. "Fine then. Pardee, you're prompt. Mr. Nash is on his way out. I want you to take him down the elevator, across the lobby, and out the front door. Explain to the deputies by the metal detectors that he was in this office without authorization and we don't want him in the building the rest of the day."

"Uhhh...heh. Hmmm. Okay," said Pardee. "What's your name, buddy?"

"Hang on, Pardee. Mr. Saddler, this is going to look a little foolish in print, throwing me out of a public building, don't you think? Let me explain to you what I've been told—by several individuals— Clarence Bryce issued that subpoena to investigate a report of a shooting in the Read Mental Health Center. That's a rather serious report. You, sir, and the state's attorney, had warned him not to issue the subpoena. The state's attorney said such an investigation would give, quote 'aid and comfort,' unquote, to Havranek in the primary race against Gov. Beal, and you two wished to let the Mental Health Department handle the problem itself without notoriety." Nash knew he was embellishing things a tiny bit. In Franzel's account, the candidates were never named, but Nash thought a little extrapolation was necessary in this conversation. "After Bryce issued that subpoena, you personally allowed it to be quashed; then you fired him on Friday, either by yourself or with the state's attorney. Is that what happened, Mr. Saddler?"

"No." Saddler returned his hands to his waist. "That's totally erroneous, and if you print it, you will have egg all over your face, Mr. Nash. All over. From ear to ear. And I don't care if you say we threw you out. Nor would the public. Goodbye." He said "Goodbye" in a purposely cute tone. The guy was getting more relaxed, thought Nash. Carefree. Nash wrote rapidly, trying to get it all down. Pardee was tugging on his arm.

"I'm going, Pardee, relax. I have to write down what the man said, don't I? Now if we just get a comment from the state's attorney, Saddler, we'll be done, and you can shove me right out the door."

"The state's attorney would say what I've just said, Nash. Pardee, do it."

"Let's go this way, Pardee," said Nash, starting to leave. "The state's attorney's door is right here." Lois' and Molly's office was between the rooms occupied by the first assistant and the state's attorney. There was no sign on the door, but Nash knew which door it was. It was the only one without a window next to the door jam. He walked quickly to get ahead of Pardee and he thumped the door once with his right hand. "Mrs. Ryannn?" said Nash. He didn't expect much. State's Attorney Agnes Ryan was most likely in the downtown office.

"Don't be a jerk now," said Pardee, bringing his right arm up to pull Nash's arm down from behind. Nash wanted to hit him in the mouth with his elbow; Nash's adrenalin was up; but common sense told him Pardee was the man least likely to be enjoying himself in this affair. Cops always got stuck in the middle. The knowledge did not make Nash's control much easier.

"Okay, Pardee, okay." He shook himself out of Pardee's grasp. Surrendering and trying to be decent, he said, "Lead on, McDuff." They had gone only a few yards when Nash stopped short. "Did you hear that voice?"

"Yeah, I hear it. Don't get any ideas," said Pardee.

"Pardee, all I need is a 'no comment,' but if the lady has an explanation for this accusation I'm about to make, that would even be better, wouldn't it? She'd be glad you brought me back." For the 50th or 60th time in his career, Nash decided he had to make a fool of himself in the line of duty. Even as Pardee said, "No way," Nash turned and ran back.

"Mrs. Ryan, what good fortune," Nash said, trying not to appear overly rushed. "I'm inquiring into your firing of Clarence Bryce."

Mrs. Ryan had been talking to Saddler in a loud voice. She must have come out of the side door of her office where it connected to the secretaries' office, Nash figured. She was wearing a business suit, carrying papers in her hand and displaying a look of extreme displeasure on her face. Nash noticed Lois was gazing intently into the middle drawer of her desk.

"Nash, I told you . . . . !" said Saddler. Pardee already had caught up and had got a renewed grasp on Nash's upper left arm.

"The son of a bitch ran away, sir," said Pardee. "Pardon me, Mrs. Ryan."

"Mrs. Ryan, did you fire Bryce because he was pushing an investigation that embarassed the governor?"

"What?" She looked at Saddler, frowning angrily, then she turned her brown eyes on Nash and covered him in an irate glance. "Who is . . . ? Good heavens, what is this place? Is this the reporter? Pardee, how many other reporters do we have in the hallways, a dozen? You're a reporter, aren't you?"

244

"Sam Nash of the Chronicle. I think you heard my question, ma'am. Did you fire Clarence Bryce because of...."

"Be quiet, Mr. Nash, or whatever your name is. I'm sorry, Mr. Nash, I like the press, but this can't be tolerated. These are private premises. I have nothing to say to you. Please leave. Officer...." She waved her papers indicating dismissal.

"Madame, these are taxpayers' premises," Nash shouted as he left involuntarily, "and I asked you a very serious question." Dragging in the taxpayers was the lowest to which Nash normally sunk. Any fool could claim to represent the taxpayers, especially Mrs. Ryan who had been elected. Already Pardee had pushed Nash 10 yards down the hallway, and Nash allowed himself to be pushed the rest of the way to the elevators. There was no answer to his question.

On the elevator, Nash said, "Sorry. It's hard to explain, but I had to do that. It's my job. I hope I didn't get you in trouble."

"You're lucky. I'm a very easy going person," said Pardee, who watched the changing floor numbers.

"How come Bryce got fired?" asked Nash.

"Did Bryce get fired?" answered Pardee nonchalantly, still gazing over the elevator door.

"Yeah. What do you hear?"

"First I heard of it."

"C'mon."

The conversation produced nothing, and in a few moments Nash was out the door on the plaza. As he pulled his hat and scarf out of his pockets, Nash felt embarassed for the silly way he had been forced to behave in order to confront Mrs. Ryan and give her her chance to respond. Running down a hallway pursued by a long suffering state's attorney's investigator; Nash thought he was getting a little old for that sort of thing. Then he had the opposite thought. It was the old who were frozen into their dignity. He had done it, so maybe he was still young.

Young and still dumb. The two sort of went together. Standing still, watching the streams of people in and out of the building, he smiled while he buttoned his coat.

When he got on the California Avenue bus, and it was warm inside, Nash finally allowed himself to add up the situation. Did he have a story?

It was a one-on-one case, like most rape cases, Nash thought, falling into Criminal Courts logic; except this was one-on-two. The whole thing depended on Bryce. The fact that the subpoena was issued for the inmate at the Read Mental Health Center and quickly quashed was supportive but did not amount to much without a motive for the quash. Franzel's account of Bryce's words was entirely believable to Nash. Franzel was allowing his name to be used as the source, a very rare instance, and the story could easily be contradicted by Bryce if it was bullshit. In Nash's universe, no young lawyer with Franzel's earning potential would stage a hoax like this unless he'd gone 'round the bend.

Franzel was solid, and Franzel said he had never spoken to the press before, a strong element which Nash determined to work into the story. But there were a lot of negatives. Nash began listing them in his mind as the bus passed Harrison High School at California Avenue and 24th Boulevard.

—Nash himself was the source of the allegation about the Read Mental Health Center and was now ready to be the author of a story complaining that the allegation was not properly investigated. Almost seemed like a reporter's pet peeve, he thought.

—There was no proof that anything happened in the Read Mental Health Center, a minor problem unless it turned out that nothing did.

—There was no corroboration for Bryce's charges against Saddler and Mrs. Ryan. Maybe Scott Campbell could help. Have to call him, Nash thought.

—He had never talked to Bryce.

This lack of contact with the accuser was the biggest weakness. Searching for a reaction in himself, Nash found that paradoxically, it did not bother him as much as it might have. He slumped in his seat, feeling the bus hit the bumps in the street, thinking hard. He looked out the window, but the daylight was too distracting, so he stared straight ahead in the interior of the bus, seeing nothing. Nash knew he was going to continue to call Bryce's home number for the rest of the day; and, what the heck, he'd call his neighbors, too, to ask where he went. But Bryce was most likely hiding or out of town. Bryce understood that his co-workers, a couple politicians, and, most important, a few members of the press would start ringing his phone as soon as the word got out. When they couldn't reach him, life would go on; they would lose interest in a few days; and then he would come back. Reporters would give up quickly because the holder of the title of "chief of the criminal division" was unknown to the public, and the potential story, such as it was, would get old fast.

Even when Bryce surfaced, he would almost surely refuse to talk. As one of the few remaining protagonists of the old school in Chicago, Bryce would adhere to the unwritten code: When a man in a major governmental position quit or got fired, he kept his mouth shut as long as his superiors did, too. If they didn't attack you, you didn't attack them.

This silence was appreciated by certain serious people in town as the mark of a man who wished to continue to be on the inside and play the game, albeit from a different position. Many people would understand that.

Saddler's attitude seriously bothered Nash. Saddler lied too well. Saddler lied so well he seemed to think it was his God-given privilege. People like that were dangerous. Nash thought about what would happen if the Saddler types took over. What if Chicago reached the stage where you could ask, "What ever happened to Clarence Bryce?" and nobody would say. Imagine. NOBODY. That's how it was in many places in the world.

Even in Chicago, when a new administration took over in almost any office, a certain type of personality came to the fore in the beginning. "We're in charge here now. WE have moved in. Forget what came before; they were losers; how they conducted themselves does not apply to us. We will do what we think best, and you do not need to know most of what we do. When we decide it is necessary to make something public, we will summon you." This face was shown to the press when the television cameras were off.

Nash had seen this syndrome over and over, in the mayor's office, the police department, the school superintendent's office, the state capital, even the public library. It was the nature of taking power. (Sometimes the winning candidate or appointee displayed this attitude. More often, it was his staff.) Every time Nash saw the curtain come down in person and heard the lies start, he found it scary. He thought, How close we were and always would be.

Some people thought the system would last forever because it was older than they were. But to Nash, the system in which he lived was not like the earth. The moving parts of the system got up in the morning and went to bed at night, and if the system survived depended on the actions of the day. The system seemed to be a brief experiment. Nature might prefer force, or nature might not care.

But Nash felt he had become part of this system which he had been taught since his school days. He understood how it was designed and how it worked, and he understood the role of the press. What was the story that needed to be printed this time to maintain balance, he asked himself? And who knew it? He did. What if he didn't act? It was always risky to stick your neck out. Stories based on sources like this sometimes blew up due to unseen factors and buried the reporter.

After a few more moments of thought, Nash felt if he did not do this story, many other people would not do theirs, and the curtain might some day come down for good. Nash believed this. He was not thinking of a domino effect or imagining that he, personally, had tremendous influence. Rather, Nash considered himself to be the common denominator. The ordinary reporter. If he had lost the nerve, then for some reason, many people had lost it. So he couldn't lose it.

He went over it again in his head. The lynchpin was Clarence Bryce. If Bryce lied to Franzel, the whole thing was bullshit. Bryce could have had reason to lie. He'd been fired. In that circumstance, people frequently liked to justify themselves. But sooner or later, you had to believe somebody or have a good reason why you didn't. Clarence, Nash said to himself, I'm betting on you.

26

"Phelan."

The night city editor looked up from a story about a meeting of the Chicago Board of Education. He was glad to see it was written to correct length and had a nice lead.

"Yeah?"

"Two of the stories you sent us, 'Shoot' and 'County,' came over with no text, slugs only." Derrick Lepsius who was making this unpleasant announcement was the night slot man on the local copy desk, the man in charge of that desk. Lepsius had a way of describing electronic foulups which made them seem as if they were Phelan's fault.

"Well, can't you reconstitute them somehow, Derrick? We've got four or five stories out yet, and the computer is slow as molasses." Phelan was sitting in the city desk slot and Lepsius was standing outside the rim, leaning over, supporting himself with his hands on the horseshoe desk.

"We did all the searches, Phelan. We even had the boys and girls in the computer room look. They're gone. The computer ate them. And we can't get at the previous versions for reasons which are beyond me. This happened on the day shift, too. The computer is shooting sparks and will probably crash again. Meanwhile, what are you going to do about 'County' and 'Shoot?' "

"Killer," Phelan said loudly without looking at her. "Do you have printouts of 'County' and 'Shoot?' "

Anne Kemper, known as Killer because she was so small, was to Phelan's left, but when Phelan faced Lepsius, she was directly behind Phelan. She had written the last version of both stories.

"I've got 'Shoot' and the second to last version of 'County.' "

"Bad news, Killer," Phelan swiveled in his seat to look at her. "The computer swallowed them. Retype the second to last version of 'County' into the machine, but make it like the last version, your work of art. Gimme 'Shoot.' "

She handed over a printout and Phelan gave it to Lepsius. "I'll make you a deal, Derrick. This is the shorter of the two. If you have one of your people type that one, we'll do the other."

"You'll owe Keckley a beer."

Phelan nodded then looked at the clock. Eight-thirty, half an hour before deadline. "Kemper, before you type all of 'County,' try to reach the p/r man for the State's Attorney's Office again for their last chance."

"The computer's not responding anyway at the moment," she said.

"Tell him we want a comment from Madame Ryan, not from him or any other assistant."

Kemper gave the usual look of resignation she produced when she thought some directive was dumb. She pursed her lips and said in a lilting way, "We already have a denial by the first assistant; and we have Nash thrown out of the office; and we have Madame Ryan refusing to discuss it. We probably need more, huh? Whose idea is it to get everybody to deny things twice?"

"It's my idea, Kemper."

"Oh. Ahem."

"And Madame Ryan hasn't commented yet. In addition, go over to the copy desk and tell them to trim out the part about Nash being ejected from the office. I meant to do that before. It looks silly."

"Phelan, the system just went down." This was Youngman, who sat to Phelan's right.

"Call the computer room. Call. Call," said Phelan.

Nash's story was scheduled to be the line story on page one. Phelan did not approve, but part of him almost did. The story depended too much on Bryce whom Phelan did not know so how could Phelan trust him? All the editors had to trust Nash and Nash's opinion of Bryce. Phelan had no problem with Nash. Nash had even discussed the friendship issue, the friendship between Nash and the subject of the story, to Phelan's satisfaction. But if the Chronicle had to go to the wall for this guy Bryce, the night city editor thought, couldn't somebody at least talk to Bryce?

Nash had argued that he tried everything. Bryce was hiding, and if he were found, he probably wouldn't talk. If that were the case, and there was no other corroboration, Phelan would have killed the story.

Phelan did not say this in the doping session. Simonet was wild about the story. It was just the kind of exclusive story the new Chronicle should be printing to make people sit up and take notice, he said. Solomon had held his enthusiasm back a little. Solomon had appeared to be weighing his own contradictory opinions about the story.

"Bob, I told Nash that unless he got independent, credible verification that there was some sort of crime committed at Read, we were not going to use the story. He's working on that now."

"What else could it be?" Simonet had asked unhappily. It was not politic for Simonet to approve the story over the objections of the metropolitan editor. If the story turned bad, Simonet would be all alone with the blame.

Nash had come around near the end of the doping session and called Solomon out of the room. When Solomon returned, he told the doping session: "We have it from a very good source that there was definitely an assault at Read that is at the bottom of this, a physical attack. Unfortunately, we do not know who attacked whom, whether it was a patient on a patient, a member of the staff assaulting a patient, or even a husband and wife fighting in the lobby. And we don't know how serious it was."

"I thought Nash's friend told him somebody got shot and a doctor was involved?" said Simonet. Phelan had lowered his head and smiled to himself. Simonet apparently wanted to print the accusation of a mental patient.

"We have to ignore that part, Bob, for purposes of this story, IF we do a story," said Solomon. "That was the original tip, and it seems as if there's something to it, but I think it would be best if we did not mention where the tip came from and instead go with our other information. The assistant state's attorney, Franzel, calls it a shooting. For backup we can use Nash's other source saying it was an assault, or a physical attack. The second source is a very good one, but he does not want to say more. We're dealing with a very vague crime here."

"What do you recommend, Aaron?" asked Simonet.

"If it's true, it's a damn good story at election time. We have an assistant state's attorney on the record. We have independent verification that the subpoena was issued and quashed. We know this guy Bryce is definitely out of a job; they admitted that much. The question is, did he quit, or was he fired, and why? We know there was an incident which could justify the subpoena. It's all tied together with thread. I would prefer rope. If the story blows up, we could say all these people gave us bum information, but we'll still look like idiots. We could wait, but then we may lose the exclusive. It's a coin toss, Bob."

"I need a recommendation, Aaron. We're not going to have a coin toss."

"Under the circumstances, I say go with it. What do you think, Red?"

"I think it's too bad we can't talk to this guy Bryce," said Phelan. He said this in a mild, non-committal voice. Phelan said no more and did not try to kill the story.

In addition to all the rules of journalism Phelan had absorbed over the years, there was an extra one that said none of the other rules applied if you didn't have a newspaper any more. It was that rule that Simonet and Solomon were thinking of, Phelan understood. Phelan was not sure what he would do if he held one of their positions. A picture came to his mind of one of the Chronicle's legendary reporters, a Pulitzer prize winner, who was at the top of his game when Phelan was a beginner. Whenever anyone complimented this great man on his latest big story, his standard line had been, "Thank you. I only hope it's true."

Nash's lead, which had gone through many hands, said:

> *"State's Attorney Agnes Ryan has fired her chief prosecutor for pursuing an investigation that could prove embarrassing to a political candidate in the upcoming primary election, the Chronicle learned Monday."*

The story did not say directly that the governor's race was involved. The evidence for that was circumstantial. But the circumstantial evidence was presented high up so the story left little doubt what the Chronicle's opinion was. The key quote: "We do not feel it's proper to give aid or comfort to either candidate at this point when it's so close." was in the fifth paragraph. It was attributed to Agnes Ryan, but it was clear it had come through Bryce and then through Franzel.

The story was approved and edited and was sitting at the local copy desk, waiting for some real comment from Ryan.

After the computer crashed, the computer room called in less than three minutes to say it was back up.

"All right, we're in business," said Phelan. "Georgia, don't play with that 'Taxes' story any more. Let me have it." Phelan put the "School" story in the copy desk file and ended it.

"I can't do a damn thing," said Krolikowski. "The machine says, 'Please sign on,' but it won't let me sign on."

"Me, neither," said Kemper.

"What did you sign off for?"

"We didn't," they said in unison.

"Aw, fuck. What does it say, Killer?" Phelan looked at the clock. Eight-forty.

"It says, 'See terminal 12 A.' That means it thinks I'm working on 12 A, and it doesn't like you to be in two places at once."

"All right. Find 12 A."

Kemper simply smiled.

"Hers *is* 12A," said Krolikowski. "Mine is 13 A, and it says, 'See 13 A.' "

"Youngman, are you working?" asked Phelan.

"See 15 A," said Youngman. "A for buttfucked."

"AAARRggh." Phelan put his pen between his teeth sideways. "Please bring back typewriters," he said through his teeth. "Why is mine working?"

"You're on the B system," said Krolikowski.

"All right, Youngman you work over here. Let me read your stuff before you move it." Phelan gave his spot to Youngman and walked outside the rim. "Georgia, call the computer room and get this straightened out. Killer, who are you talking to?"

Kemper waved him away.

"It won't work, Red," said Krolikowski. "Last time this happened over the weekend it took an hour to get our terminals back."

"I want it straightened out in 30 seconds." He looked at the clock again. Eight-forty-three. "This is fucking crazy. What if I kick in a screen? Would that help? We're gonna blow the deadline."

"Let me call somebody and get their password and sign on as somebody else," said Krolikowski.

"Yeah. That's good, Georgia. Call Cannon and Burke. They're roommates, aren't they? Get one for Killer, too."

"I don't know them very well. They may be afraid we'll peek in their personal files."

"C'mon, Georgia. You can do it. Be sweet with 'em. Promise 'em you'll...." Phelan stopped.

With her head cocked to one side, Krolikowski said, "Promise them what, Red?"

Phelan snorted, then smiled. "Promise them you'll give them a big kiss on the cheek, Georgia. You and Killer, too. Cannon is always sniffing around her, ain't he? See what a nice guy I am. Keeping up morale. Now let's GO!"

"Phelan, do you want to read this?" asked Youngman.

"No. Yes. I have to read that. Gimme the chair, Paul."

Phelan skimmed Youngman's story about a contribution the Chronicle was making to the charity bank account for an infant with a rare, but possibly curable, disease.

"Phelan."

"Yes, Killer. What is it? Did you get signed on?" He did not look away from his screen.

"No. But I will. You have to talk to this guy from the State's Attorney's Office. He's on six."

"Can't you do it?" He looked at the clock. Eight-forty-eight. "Did you type that 'County' story yet?"

"How could I? Do you want me to put him on hold? He wants the editor."

Phelan felt a body next to him and looked up to see a copy editor standing there, appearing apologetic. "Put him on hold and get typing. Yeah, what?"

"Lepsius says the Ming Dynasty was from 1368 to 1644. The 'Theft' story talks about a Ming Dynasty statue from the 13th Century. That would put it in a different dynasty, I suppose."

"Can't you make it Ming Dynasty and forget the century? Or just make it . . . . Let me see, the 13's are called the 14th; somebody just made a mistake. Call it the 14th. Just do that."

"You should have done that to begin with. Lepsius won't believe it now. Anyway, there's one name spelled three different ways in here." He held out a printout of the story. "It's either Hung dash Wu, Hung without-a-dash Wu, or Hung Wo, no dash. I circled the names."

"Leave it." Phelan meant the printout. He picked up the phone and punched six. "City desk."

"Are you the editor?" said the voice at the other end.

"Yes. Who are you?"

"I'm Thomas Sadder, the first assistant state's attorney of Cook County."

"We already quote you in our story about the state's attorney's office, Mr. Saddler. We're looking for your boss."

"Mrs. Ryan asked me to call you to prevent you from making a mistake. You had a reporter at the Criminal Courts Building today, a man named Nash, who is not your usual reporter for that building, I don't think. Nash came up with a story of which he was very proud concerning how we had fired Clarence Bryce, our chief of the criminal division, for reasons which Nash considered to be newsworthy. Unfortunately for you, his information is quite faulty and the story is foolish."

Phelan had a pad of paper in front of him and a pen poised to write, and he was waiting.

"Mr. Saddler, it's late here. We're right on deadline. If you have something to say, say it. You haven't said anything yet."

"I thought I had. That's as far as I'm prepared to go on the record. Anything I say from now on is off the record and not to be printed, you understand?"

"Yes, Mr. Saddler." Phelan sighed with impatience.

"Mr. Bryce resigned at our request. So in that sense, one might say he was fired, although we allowed him to resign. He was asked to resign because it came to our attention that he had recently severely overstepped his authority and acted outside the law in ordering illegal searches; and he also allowed or ordered wiretaps without judicial authorization. You are aware that legally approved wiretaps for anyone except the federal authorities are rare in Illinois."

"Yes." Phelan was intimately acquainted with the subject.

"Mr. Bryce's activities, which he had kept to himself and a few investigators, came to our attention only after we lost an important decision regarding the admissibility of evidence in the murder of two police officers. That evidence, which may be absolutely vital, was thrown out because it was obtained in an illegal search. We are prepared to explain all this to you or to a reporter you designate tomorrow. But we do not wish to see this information published. Bryce has been a fine prosecutor for many years. Perhaps too many years. We would prefer to let him go quietly."

"Just a second." Phelan cupped the phone. "Georgia, call this guy whose statue was stolen and find out what century it belongs to again and when the Ming Dynasty was." He threw her the printout. "Also ask him if the circled name is Hung dash Wu or Hung Wo, no dash."

"Forrest is on two," she said.

"Find out what he wants. You take care of it, Georgia."

"Mr. Saddler," Phelan said into the phone again, "wouldn't it have been a lot easier for everyone if you had told Nash this stuff this afternoon?"

"He did not appear to be a person we could trust with this information," said Saddler. "He also was too personally involved. I believe Mr. Nash was trying to pursue his own investigation of the Department of Mental Health—based on the report of a mental patient, no less—and he had apparently enlisted Bryce in his wild goose chase. You are familiar with this, I assume."

"I just found out about it today. Mr. Saddler, this is all very interesting five minutes before deadline. What if we had never called you tonight? What the hell were you thinking about there?"

"I've reached you in sufficient time. I've made it a point to know the newspapers' deadlines."

This guy really thought he was clever, thought Phelan. "Okay, why'd you quash this subpoena?"

"There's no need to discuss that. I told you it was a wild goose chase. I didn't get your name."

"Phelan. P-H- E-L-A-N."

"Phelan, the issue here is why we let Clarence Bryce go. I've told you that, and we're prepared to back it up to your satisfaction. I'm not going to get into a wide-ranging discussion of all our cases."

"I didn't ask you about all your cases. I asked you about one. What happened at the Read Mental Health Center?"

"Once again, the crime, as reported by Mr. Nash, did not occur, as any sensible person might have suspected."

"Okay, I've got more questions, but it's too late, Saddler. I'm going to recommend that we hold this story back, and someone will definitely be out to see you tomorrow. It will probably be Nash, so be prepared for that. He's a good reporter."

"I was looking for more than a recommendation from you, Mr. Phelan. I want your assurance that the irresponsible charges Nash made in this office today will not be printed. I've been very open with you."

"This is just about an assurance. The owner and publisher aren't here right now, but I think we can hold this for one day. I've got to go. Thank you for calling."

"Phelan?"

"What?"

"You understand it is Bryce's public reputation that is at stake here. We are trying to do this decently, but we will defend ourselves."

"I understand. Goodbye."

Phelan hung up. "Whew! Okay, guys, where do we stand?" He looked at the clock. Nine p.m. The deadline.

"You've got 'Taxes' and that little item about the missing woman," said Krolikowski.

"Open them up, give them one more careful look and move them to the copy desk yourself, Georgia."

"The Chinese statue mystery is straightened out," she continued. "I relayed it all to the copy desk. And I told Forrest to go to lunch. The mayor didn't show up."

"Good. Killer?"

"I gave you half. I'm on the second half." She was intently typing and did not look up.

"Georgia, you look at Killer's story and move that, too. Sit over here and read all this stuff," he lifted his 'in' basket, full to the brim with City News, AP, and UPI copy about the city and the state, "and answer any calls for the desk, Georgia. I'm going to be busy for a few minutes."

Phelan knew what he was going to say would throw the news desk into a tizzy. It wasn't that they didn't have time to make the change. If a great story broke at this moment, and they had enough information to make it the lead story on page one, they'd be glad to make the change. But they did not like to simply subtract things at the last moment.

By now, the number one news editor had drawn a front page design that he considered a potential prize-winner. The content of the front page had been approved by a variety of higher editors who had since gone home. All the technical orders had been given for story lengths and widths, picture sizes, headline sizes, as well as styles of type. The jump pages were also planned where the page one stories were continued on the inside. Phelan did not relish trying to stop this freight train, but he was confident he could do it.

Frank Coleman was the number one news editor. Manny Rodriguez was the number two, doing the inside pages. Don Karpis came on for the next edition.

"Frank, I've got a headache for you, but it can't be helped," said Phelan.

"Oh oh," said Rodriguez, smiling and pointing to his watch.

"What is it?" said Coleman.

"Our line story, 'Ryan,' has to be pulled back for a day. Some new information just came up as to why the central character got fired. We may not have been told the whole story. On the other hand, we may, but we have to check out this latest stuff to be absolutely sure." Phelan protected the reporters as much as possible in such discussions, and Nash was also his friend.

"It's awful fucking late to be bringing that kind of news, Phelan. Don't you think it would be better to check these things out thoroughly before you dope them for page one?"

Coleman flicked his ballpoint pen to retract the point, wheeled around so that his legs came out from under the desk, and leaned back to stare at Phelan. "I didn't like this story in the first place," Coleman added.

"Frank, some guy we interviewed before suddenly called the desk and decided he had a different story, partly contradicting what he told us earlier. It can't be helped. I want to hold 'Ryan.' "

"What's this new information?"

"The first assistant state's attorney originally told us their chief of the criminal division, Clarence Bryce, resigned on his own. Now they admit they forced him to resign, but not for the reasons in our story. The rest is off the record and not to be repeated."

Coleman waved nonchalantly to indicate that he agreed to the terms.

"They now say Bryce has been ordering his investigators to do wire tapping and illegal searches, without, of course, the knowledge of the top bananas. Supposedly this got them into trouble in at least one important case, the murder of the two cops last summer, and cost them major evidence. So they canned Bryce. We can check out this version tomorrow."

"That's a better story than this one," said Coleman, making a little sarcastic face, holding up a printout of Nash's story.

"To you, maybe. If it's true, and somebody will put it on the record, it might be a decent story. I realize you have to redraw page one, Frank. I wouldn't suggest it if it wasn't necessary. Can we consider the 'Ryan' story on hold for now?"

Coleman swiveled back under his desk. "I'm going to call Simonet at home. You people sold this to him originally. Now you'll have to unsell him, Phelan."

"If it's true, sounds like we better hold it," said Rodriguez.

"We'll let the editor decide," Coleman responded, punching the buttons on his phone.

"Bob, this is Frank. Sorry to bother you. The city desk has decided to pull back their lead story—at five minutes after nine. I'll let Phelan explain it to you." He handed Phelan the phone.

Phelan spoke into the phone loud enough so that Coleman and Rodriguez could easily hear him. He described the situation with appropriate apologies, but was consciously firm so that no one would think there was any chance of talking him out of his position.

"How do we know this guy Saddler is telling the truth, Phelan? First he tells us one thing and then another," said Simonet.

"We can't tell. Until tomorrow, sir. I'm not killing the story. I just want to hold it, Mr. Simonet."

"By that time I suppose everybody in town will be onto this. The way I understand it, this man Bryce holds a position of major responsibility in the state's attorney's office. They can't keep the fact that he's been replaced a secret."

"You've got a good point there, Mr. Simonet. But the allegations Saddler made are not the sort that can be proved or disproved tonight. A few hours inquiry tomorrow will clear up the questions and we'll still be way ahead of the competition if there's a story. Either way, we've still got to hold this story out tonight, sir."

"Why?"

"If it's a phony story, it will make us look bad, sir."

"But we don't know it's phony, Phelan."

"It's a good possibility, sir. If what Saddler says now is true, it contradicts our story completely leaving us in an untenable position."

"What did he say about the alleged shooting in the Department of Mental Health and the subpoena that was withdrawn?"

Phelan felt antsy. The longer they jacked around with this conversation, the more difficult it became to change the front page. Pretty soon, somebody would claim it was too late to do anything.

"He didn't want to discuss it, sir, which is not unusual when a guy claims the entire story is wrong and something else actually happened. He did say the shooting did not occur, or words to that effect."

"What do you mean, 'words to that effect?' "

"He said the crime, as described by Nash, did not occur."

"You mean, maybe it happened, but not exactly as we think."

"Sir, the shooting isn't our real problem here. Our problem is did Bryce commit these alleged misdeeds Saddler accused him of, and are they grounds to fire him?

"If that part is true," Phelan continued, "then our story saying he was fired for a different reason involving the governor falls apart. At best, we would have a 50/50 proposition with their side sounding a lot more believable than ours. That's why I advise that we hold the story."

"But everything he said was off the record, Phelan."

"It may not be tomorrow, sir. They say they are trying to protect this man Bryce's reputation. He's a revered employee, I guess. They didn't broadcast the fact that he was fired, sir. We dug it up."

"What does the reporter say about this? Nash, is it?"

"Nash doesn't know yet, sir. Saddler called right on top of our city desk deadline, so there was no time to involve Nash."

"Don't you think Nash should have something to say about it, Phelan? You call Nash. And call Solomon. If Solomon wants to pull the story back, then we'll do it."

"Sir, it's going on nine-fifteen. What if we can't get a hold of Solomon and Nash? Then what?"

"Then we'll go with the story, Phelan. It's a good exclusive. Well researched by Nash, I'm sure. It sounds to me like Mr. Saddler is just trying to get out from under. But if Saddler wants to put his excuses on the record tomorrow, then maybe we'll have another good story."

What a stupid fucking thing to say! thought Phelan. The guy thought he was being a hard-nosed newsman.

"Mr. Simonet." Phelan's voice was dropping lower and he could feel the bile in his throat.Phelan was paid to know his business. He'd been playing with hard news for longer than any of the people he was dealing with. He knew how stories came about from years of daily repetition, so he knew how the process could go wrong occasionally. He also knew the "sounds" of a good story and the "sounds" of a story coming unravelled. Coleman and Simonet had no idea how stories were made, especially Simonet. They were supposed to take Phelan's word. But Simonet didn't even know THAT.

"I don't believe we can put the reporter in that position, Mr. Simonet," said Phelan very distinctly, trying to control himself. "The man he talked to, Saddler, has changed his story completely, and the reporter is not aware of the change. If he were aware, I assure you he would recommend exactly what I'm recommending. It would *not be wise* to print this story tonight, Mr. Simonet. I tell you that from *long experience.*"

There was a silence on the other end. Phelan suspected the man had caught the significance of Phelan's tone of voice and didn't like it because it was insubordinate. "Just a second, Mr. Simonet, Coleman wants to talk to you again."

Coleman was not so cool anymore, Phelan noticed. Coleman's problems were worsening as time sped by. Phelan handed him the phone in response to his gestures.

"Bob, I'm sorry. This is Frank. We're really up against it. We have to have a go or no go. Whatever you say is fine with me, Bob. . . ." Coleman listened for a moment then passed the phone back to Phelan. "He wants to talk to you some more." Coleman made a nervous, circular movement with his right hand, indicating, "Speed it up!" Phelan glared at him.

"Mr. Phelan, why haven't you consulted with Aaron Solomon on this?"

"Sir, I told you. There was no time."

"Well, you get hold of Solomon and Nash right now. I'm surprised you didn't do it before calling me. Your city desk approved of this story, Mr. Phelan, and I didn't hear you saying, 'Kill it,' at the doping. If the metropolitan editor and the reporter say to hold it, we will. But I'm not holding it on your say so. Is that clear?"

It was clear to Phelan that Simonet had lined up his scapegoats, should they become necessary, but was sticking with the story because he liked it.

"Yes, sir," said Phelan.

"Give me back to Coleman."

Phelan handed Coleman the phone and walked away. Half way back to the city desk, he shouted, "Georgia!" Krolikowski jumped.

"Call Nash right now. Call his home. Call his wife's home. Call the Radio Grill, the Billy Goat, the Boul Mich, Riccardo's, the Corona, O'Rourke's, any place you can think of. I want him, and I want you to get him."

"Sure. Sure," she said, moving in three different directions trying to remember where to start. "Trouble?"

"Just do it."

Phelan called Solomon's home. There was no answer.

27

Nash leaned on his left elbow and stared at the form of the girl playing the juke box. She was bent over, reading the titles. He felt approximately like a starving man staring at a Christmas turkey. He sensed his blood vessels dilating and some chemical entering them, and he took a deep breath, savoring the feeling.

Then he sipped some water, his fourth or fifth glass. He noticed this was the first time he had been able to sit still at night for a long period without getting up and moving around. He was usually very restless, but he wasn't worried about it. It was part of being on the wagon.

Katerina turned away from the juke box and came toward him wearing the same jeans and sweater she had worn the day he pulled her hair. He boldly studied her breasts as she walked, then he looked at her belly and the way her hips moved. As she came closer, he gazed at the zipper on her jeans and imagined pulling it and unsnapping the snap. Nash felt like a fine animal that was called upon—

and ready—to be what it was. He was in harmony with the universe.

"You are disgusting, Sam," she said as she slid into the booth.

"I know. It's great, isn't it?" He looked at her face.

She grinned and her eyes were wide. "Yes."

She must have played four or five songs, so they were going to stay for a few minutes, it appeared. Nash had picked the restaurant because it was near home; the food was good; and it was one of the few remaining restaurants that had a juke box. He sat up straight. "You know, Kate, I don't believe I ever had lasagna and Coke before. Not even when I was a kid. We never heard of lasagna."

"How was it?"

"The lasagna was fine. I drank a lot of pop when I was a kid so I suppose I can get used to it again, or I'll take up drinking tonic water."

"Have you had enough, Sam? You want another salad or a bowl of soup?"

"I think I'll have dessert. It comes with the dinner. I think I will have apple pie, and I'm going to have ice cream on top even though it's extra."

"Whaaat?" She chuckled. "Since when do you eat dessert?"

"It's my new vice. It's the nearest thing I can find to sex."

"Shhhhh! Keep your voice down," she said. But the reference left her all atwitter.

"Why don't you have a few beers or half a carafe of wine, Kate? It won't bother me." He gestured grandly with his fork.

"No. When you don't drink, I don't drink. That wouldn't be fair."

"Then how am I going to get you into bed?" he said softly, leaning across the table.

"I don't know," she whispered, leaning across toward him. She lifted her eyebrows.

Encouraged, he asked, "You wanna go park after this? Where could we go?"

"Park? And make out in the car?"

"No. I was thinking of doing our income tax. But if you would prefer making out, that's okay."

"Sam, it's winter. It's cold out."

"As I recall," he said, sitting back up, "there was about a foot of snow on the ground, and the temperature was quite cold—I don't remember exactly what—and it was pitch dark when that police officer shined a flashlight in our window on the road near the lagoon in Columbus Park."

"I don't remember that."

"Maybe it was somebody else," said Nash, looking into the distance.

"Okay, I kind of remember. That cop must have been a pervert or something."

"That's what I thought at the time. But you, I believe, thought he was paid to enforce the morals of the community. You were afraid we would be arrested for public petting." Nash laughed cheerfully. "And your parents would find out!" And he laughed some more.

"Sammm."

"I'm sorry. Hoo." He was trying to stop laughing. "It was so funny."

"That would not have been funny."

"No. I wouldn't be here today." He beamed. "I have since learned that every year a few kids die outdoors in the city making out in old cars on cold nights. They keep the engine running; the exhaust leaks into the car and puts them to sleep, permanently. The cop was just making sure everybody parked there was awake and trying to move us along—and getting in his peeks occasionally."

"Oh, wonderful. And you want to go fool around in your Nova, Sam?" she said softly. Then in a normal tone, she said, "Here's the waitress. Do you really want pie and ice cream?"

After the waitress took his order, a song came on the juke box that Katerina had picked, a song with a driving, spinning beat that set up sympathetic vibrations in their chests and stirred their adrenalin since they were both rock and roll children, even Katerina. They looked in each other's eyes and let the loud, juke box sound roll over and through them. After a while, Nash turned sideways in the booth, put his feet up, took his wife's hand and pretended to be listening to the song.

At the end of a day such as he had had, Nash would normally have proceeded to get drunk, going over the story again and again in his head while sitting and brooding and drinking. The intense concentration involved in reporting and writing such a story for a daily deadline was almost impossible to turn off. The story kept repeating itself in his mind. Sometimes he discovered errors this way, and he called the office late at night, half soused, and corrected the errors for later editions.

But he was determined not to let the story win out this time. He wanted to concentrate on seducing his wife. With that in mind, he decided he would allow 30 seconds to go over the images that kept forcing their way into his thoughts, hoping the incidents would file themselves and go away.

"Scott, I have to know. Did anything happen at the Read Mental Health Center or did Clarence get fired for nothing?" Nash had gotten through to Scott Campbell near the end of the normal work day by identifying himself only as "an old friend."

"Who is this? Is this who I think it is?"

"Yes. It's Nash. I have to know because I'm the person who reported the alleged crime at Read to Bryce. If I got him fired for nothing, it's all my fault." They went around the mulberry bush for a while. At length, Nash said, "Scott, I'm not interested in what your role in this is, if you have any. I'm not asking about that." (I should be interested, Nash thought, but I can't afford it. I need this guy.) "I just wanna know, was all this about nothing?" Finally, Nash said, "Did somebody get shot?"

"I can't answer that, Sam," said Campbell smoothly. "That is not to be construed as a 'yes' or a 'no'."

"Was there any sort of crime?"

"That's a matter of interpretation. And I should not have said even that. I believe this matter is between you and the state's attorney."

"Scott, did anybody attack anybody there? Bryce got fired for this."

"You said that. I never did. There was an assault, colloquially speaking."

"Are we talking about loud shouting or a physical attack?" Nash had to ask this because a simple assault in the language of the Illinois statute books was generally a threat.

"The second thing."

"A physical attack?"

"Yes."

"Was this attack a shooting? Did someone die?"

"Forget it. I can't discuss this anymore with you. The only reason I talked to you at all is because we knew each other a long time ago. I hope I'm not going to have to pay for it."

He should have simply said "No," Nash thought.

"You won't be involved. Your name will not be mentioned. I'm doing a story."

"I wouldn't . . ."

"Why?"

"Sorry, I have to go."

So Campbell was in on this somehow, but he was still willing to talk to Nash a little. Playing both sides? Nash wondered.

That took care of Solomon's objection. Phelan had expressed his own privately while Nash was typing the story on his computer terminal.

"Sam, do you think you can see straight to write a story like this on behalf of your buddy? I don't know if the others are aware, but I think this guy, Bryce, is your close friend, right?"

Nash leaned back and looked at him. "I thought about that a lot, Red. You know, years ago when I worked with Hughes, and once after that, I wrote stories attacking a couple of my friends. It happened twice. It's very crummy. But nobody said, 'Are you sure you can be unbiased here?' Nobody said that. These were friends I made in the course of this business, you know, they used me; I used them. Convenient relationships, but friendly. And one day the wheel turned; and I got assignments to look into some things; and they were on the other end. But I did it. I got out of investigative reporting after the second time—or I thought I did. But I did those stories. I also stopped making such friends. So what should I say, Red? In this business we only attack our friends? We never defend them?"

Phelan had laughed. He apparently had not expected so intense an answer. "I'm just mentioning it, Sam. This is between you and Solomon anyway. I'm playing the devil's advocate."

The waitress brought Nash his dessert. He put his legs under the table again, picked up his fork and dug in. "Mmmmm," he said.

"Is that what you wanted?" asked Katerina demurely when he had eaten a third of it.

"Sure is, baby. Just what I wanted." He looked up at her and grinned. She grinned, too, apparently realizing how silly they were. "Do you want some?" he said.

"No."

"You sure?"

"No thanks, honey."

"Kate," he whispered, "I wanna squeeze your body and run by hands over you and in you and take your clothes off and make love to you. That's what I want. Let's forget the car and go to my place."

He saw his words had the effect as if he did touch her. She moved a little, low down, just right, which made him almost jump out of his seat. He saw she almost forgot to look around to see if anyone was listening to their whispers.

"I can't go to your place, Sam," she whispered. "I feel funny about that."

"Sure you can. Put out of your mind whatever is bothering you and look on the lust side."

"No. I can't," she said.

Nash was pretty confident he could persuade her. His month without drinking still had three weeks to go, and, according to the terms, he was not allowed to take her to bed until it was over. But since he had picked her up, Nash had sensed that maybe they could reach a brief, humane compromise without changing the goal of the agreement if he handled it just right. He told himself to slow down and go easy.

"All right. I understand." Nash adopted a morose expression. "Look, Kate, we can't go home because your mother is there."

"Definitely not." They continued to converse in whispers.

"And if you hadn't canceled the Master Charge card, we could have gotten a motel room. I realize it was my fault for foolishly running up the bill." (He did not even mention the Visa card, and his wife looked slyly innocent.) "And you won't go to my place. Soooo ...we try it in the car, Kate."

"Don't get carried away, Elvis. I'm not going to undress in the car."

"Of course not. Just a little, though."

"Sam, be serious. I have two children. I'm not going to make love in your Nova in Chicago in the wintertime."

"Okay, we'll go home and get your car," he whispered. "Then we'll have to drive around a bit to find a spot. Maybe over by the cemetery."

She frowned.

"It'll be all right."

"I don't know, Sam," she said softly.

He decided this was the moment. "My dear Katerina, that is why we have to go to my place. We can just pretend it's a warm spot out of the wind where the cops will not peek with their flashlights."

With a look that begged for forgiveness, his wife said, "I won't go there, Sam." She was shaking her head.

"Kate!" Nash grabbed the front of his head with his open right hand, then dragged his hand down, pulling his face in frustration.

Damn, he thought. What happened? Somehow he'd got off course. He was going to have to start all over.

"Kate...," he began. She had been fiddling with her purse off and on while they whispered, but now he saw she put one hand on the table and moved it across to him. She wanted to hold hands. He took her hand. There was something in it. His jaw dropped in disbelief from the feel and then the sight of it, and his joints became weak from sudden happiness.

He looked at her and was surprised to find she was cautiously waiting to see his reaction. He said, as a declaration, "You love me, don't you, baby!" This was the right thing to say. She liked it.

"Yes, you idiot."

He took it out of her hand. "Kate, when did we get another credit card?"

. . . .

Katerina had told her mother she would call home at 10 o'clock exactly, when the news was starting on TV. Otherwise, her mother kept the phone off the hook. People still called the Nash home at night occasionally asking for Racine Airways, as they had for years, and Mrs. Demopoulous contended this woke up the children. Also, few of Nash and Katerina's friends spoke Greek. Mrs. Demopoulous found it simpler to take the phone off the hook than try to talk to them.

While his wife was on the phone, Nash finished his dessert, using his coffee spoon to scoop up the melted ice cream at the end, then leaned back, stretched and listened to the juke box, thinking there was somebody in heaven.

He was staring at nothing when his wife returned, sat down, and reached for her purse.

"There's the bill. There's the money," he said lightly, indicating with his head the place on the table. "Let's go."

Katerina stayed seated, not looking at him. Then she put her right hand in her hair and raised her eyes. Nash's heart sank. Her expression was fearful, which meant she was afraid of him, which meant bad news.

"Bobby's awake, and he's crying," she said, making it almost a plea for kindheartedness on his part as well as a statement.

"I don't want to hear it, Kate."

"My mother thinks he's got a high fever."

"Did you tell the old gypsy to give him an aspirin?"

"He probably should have a bath to make his temperature go down, Sam, and I might have to get his antibiotics refilled. What do you want to do?"

"What do *I* want to do? Apparently I've been too...unclear, ambiguous. I oughta take speech lessons or something so people can understand me. What the fuck? Son of a bitch!" He picked up a piece of Italian bread from the basket in the middle of the table and squeezed it into a mess. Then he turned over the whole basket, dumping out crackers and bread sticks, and crushed a handful in his left hand until the cellophane wrappers broke and crumbs leaked out between his fingers.

"I said, let's go, Kate," he repeated, looking at her.

In the parking lot, Nash suddenly kicked the driver's side door of his car with his heel and put a dent in it. It did not change the overall appearance of the car much, but it was loud.

"Sam."

"Be glad it's not your mother."

Nash held the wheel tightly and stared straight ahead as he drove. His wife sat near the passenger door and neither spoke. When they were about two blocks from home, and it was clear where they were going, Katerina said, "Do you want to park for a while?"

Nash knew, to his regret, that this was a female tightrope act, an effort to placate him, rather than an expression of sexual desire.

"Yes, I do, Kate. Why don't we check out the situation, then maybe we'll do just that? Or something better." He reached his hand out for her and she slid over to him.

When they parked near the house, she gave him a big, long kiss and rubbed her whole body over him in a way that made Nash relax, then surrender completely with an empty mind and start to feel her with his hands. When he kissed her a second time, he noticed she was not concentrating as much. Well, she was a good mommy, he thought.

"Kate." He squeezed her against him as hard as he could, and she fit into his bones.

"Yes?"

"What do you want me to do?"

"Get his medicine. And move back home tomorrow."

28

Going downtown on the El Tuesday morning, Nash felt bouncy for the first time in a long time. He was glad to see his story was the line. The story no longer consumed him, but he knew it was a good story, and it was going to take off, he was sure, as pressure forced more disclosures. Under ideal circumstances, Nash knew it would have been better if he had most of the incident in the Read Mental Health Center in hand—who was shot? why? (the name of the culprit was maybe asking too much)—before he printed the story. But once Bryce was fired, it was only a matter of a day or two before other reporters got involved. The Chronicle had to make its move. Because he had not wrapped up the story substantially in advance, Nash knew his chances for a journalism prize were lessened. Other reporters would probably make some independent discoveries of facts and dilute the credit. But it had to be that way; and he still had a chance depending on how things worked out.

He was also glad he had done what he could to support Bryce, and maybe even to help Victoria, although Victoria seemed very remote at the moment, like one of the starving people in Bangladesh. Then, he thought again of the one person who really needed him. Katerina. She needs me, he said carefully to himself, feeling healthier and more significant as he thought about it. She is why I was born. He slid down in his seat basking in the idea. He was going back. All this mess was over, this terrible period. Kate wanted to consume him and smother him. That was great. That was super. And he would be with his kids again. An extraneous thought came to mind. He could still use a bank loan. The first bank had turned him down. So what? he thought. Sooooooo what. Consider the lilies, as his mother used to say in tight times. (They neither toil nor spin.)

It was not in Nash's nature to moon for long. After a few minutes, he took a deep breath, slid up straight, shifted his shoulders under his coat and rolled his head rearward to get the morning kinks out of his back and neck. Then he looked at the papers in his lap and tried to concentrate. His story in the Chronicle was almost exactly as he'd written it in his final version with only minor changes made by the copy desk. He paged through the Ledger and the Post to see if they'd done any recovery on the story. He knew they'd tried. That's how all the newspapers operated in Chicago.

Neither paper had recovered the story. They could get it only two ways, from Bryce or from Franzel. Most likely, nobody had Franzel's home number, and Bryce, whose home number they should have, was either hiding or still not answering his phone. An unscrupulous reporter could have merely copied the story and pretended he had spoken to Bryce or Franzel. One or two reporters in town still stole stories that way, although the rest of the reporters thought such behavior was the lowest. And even the guys who did it would be ashamed to admit it. That was funny, thought Nash. Plain old lifting without attribution had once been common; but things changed.

So it was a clean scoop through all three editions of the morning

277

papers. Theoretically, this was what he worked and hoped for. In practice, Nash did not always mind seeing a rival forced to chase and corroborate his story. It was flattering and reassuring with certain types of stories.

Nash started working on a followup in his mind. It was an incontrovertible rule with Chicago newspaper editors that if a reporter had a big exclusive one day, he had to have a big follow for the next day. This sometimes led to contrived or exaggerated followups when there was nothing else to say. Or sometimes reporters held part of the story back just to have a story for the second day. But Nash knew he had no choice. This particular story demanded a followup. An interview with Bryce was the best of the realistic options. The perfect follow story would be to reveal the exact details of the incident at Read and the coverup. But Nash didn't know the details, and he felt the Department of Mental Health would never say anything outside the grand jury. From the Department's history, it was clear they were impossible to embarrass in the press. They were impervious to criticism and proud of it. The simplest story, Nash knew, would be to get a reaction from somebody. "This situation is an outrage!" Havranek would most likely jump in. A response from the governor would arrive without any solicitation. And Nash knew he would have to give Madame Ryan an opportunity to say something again.

Possibly, Madame Ryan would decide to defuse the situation by offering a few, honest facts and presenting them in her own, self-justified way. That was very handy because it usually amounted to an admission. He found he was nodding his head several times, slightly, agreeing with his own assessment. Boy, some day you're going to do it, he thought, talk to yourself right out loud on the El.

Nash was pretty sure other angles would occur to him once he hit his desk and picked up a pen.

"Solomon wants to see you," said day city editor Miller when Nash stepped up to the city desk horseshoe. Miller spoke before Nash could even say, "Good morning." Miller pointed with an outstretched right arm to Solomon's office. Solomon was in it. Nash did not like the tone of Miller's voice, but he knew Miller fancied himself an animal trainer and liked to intimidate people at odd moments just for the heck of it. Miller thought this was good for the staff.

Nash stood at the doorway to Solomon's office and waited to be noticed. "Ahh, hello, Sam," said Solomon, looking up. "Come on in and close the door."

Nash did. Solomon ostentatiously put his hands on his desk and sat back; then he put his hands in his lap.

"Phelan tried to reach you and me last night. They gave up looking for you around midnight. It's none of my business, but if you'd like to tell me, I'm curious as to where you were. I'm just devilishly curious. It's not really why I called you in here."

"I was out with my wife."

"You were? You're separated, you two, aren't you?"

"We're getting back together."

"Son of a gun! That's nice. . . . I'm glad for you, Sam." Solomon shook his head with a rueful smile.

"You look overjoyed."

"No. No. It's not that. Maybe. . . well, it's just one of those things, I guess. It really is. I was out, too. Read this."

Nash had to read Phelan's memo twice before it sunk in. When he absorbed it, his first reaction was annoyance because the day was not going to be as straightforward or as lighthearted as he had planned. He realized he was going to have to work very hard, which meant to him cajoling, begging, persuading like the day before, maybe doing a little threatening; making phone call after phone call rapidly; possibly working through lunch; possibly working late. The prospect was distasteful because all he really wanted to do was go home as soon as possible. Saddler and Ryan were going to hit him with stuff on Bryce he hadn't known about; and Nash knew he was going to hit back. . .with something; he didn't know what; that's what the day was for.

He hadn't thought it all out. His mind was not completely engaged in his work and didn't want to be. But Nash assumed the fight was going to be even.

"This is the first I've heard of this eavesdropping, illegal search stuff, Aaron."

"Of course. I don't like the feel of this," said Solomon slowly. "I have a feeling we're in for a real mess before the day is out. The first thing I want you to do is get a hold of Bryce, on the phone, go to his house, whatever. Get him on the record supporting our story."

"I planned to. I'll do my best. But I told you yesterday, he's old-fashioned. He's an inside guy. He would rather take a little beating in the press and wait for it to blow over than to be a public whiner."

"Then it's up to you to explain the facts of life to him, Sam. We're not talking about one negative editorial here or a couple stories complaining about excessive plea bargaining. Bryce blew the whistle when he talked to this Franzel and told him what he told him. That's done. I think he's going to be publicly drawn and quartered by the state's attorney for sure, in all the media, and maybe even by people that Beal's campaign will push into the act. It's election time. If Saddler and Ryan go public with the charges in that memo, it will become open season. People will start popping out of the woodwork with alleged information proving Bryce is a liar, an incompetent, a carrier of diseases. His job is to stand up for himself, Sam. He has to."

Nash was reluctantly being drawn into seeing the seriousness of the situation, although Solomon was still ahead of him. How could anyone get Bryce? he thought. Among people that knew Bryce, his reputation for honesty was rock solid. I wish Saddler had simply told me this alternate version of Bryce's firing yesterday, he said to himself. I'll bet I would have found the holes in it, and I could have checked it out leisurely. Then aloud he said, "Aaron, this is my story; it's got my name on it. I'll handle it. But I do have to ask, if Saddler told us all this *before* the deadline, why didn't we just hold the story for a day until I could check out the new stuff?"

Solomon looked more rueful. "Phelan tried to hold the story. Simonet insisted we go. An honest disagreement. It's all in the note, Sam."

Nash knew he was supposed to swallow this politely like a good fellow. He declined. "I read that. I didn't understand it. Where the hell does Simonet get off telling Phelan he's wrong in such a thing. Simonet never covered much local news. Phelan KNOWS."

Solomon reached over his shoulder with his right hand and scratched his back, frowning. "It was late. The news desk told him they couldn't change the page, and...."

"Late? Aaron, 9 o'clock's not so late."

Solomon abruptly stopped scratching his back and sliced the air with his hand in an irritated way. "Sam, it's over. It's an editor's privilege to make a wrong decision—if he did. Simonet has been trying to make the paper more interesting every day, keep it alive. We've got all flags flying with our version of why Bryce got fired. Nobody recovered it. So what is everybody going to do around town if they can't get your story?"

"Knock it down, I imagine."

"And Saddler will be passing out the ammunition. So we've got to make the story stand up. We need more on this incident at the Read Mental Health Center. Why did it happen? Who did it? How did they cover it up? Check with the cops, the Department of Mental Health. We *need* Bryce. He should start talking at least as loud as Saddler and Ryan are going to. Get a hold of Franzel and see what else he remembers. I'm going to have Cannon check with some cops on this, too. And I'm going to have Anderson check out all this eavesdropping business, talk to Saddler, get it all on the record, then check out the details as well as he can. They're all going to report to you. I want to know by 10:30 where we stand."

Solomon was checking things off on his fingers. "What's the chance of bringing your other source into the open? The guy who verified the incident at the Read Mental Health Center. What's his name again?"

"Scott Campbell. He's the new chief of the criminal division. There is no chance. He'd have to go against the people who just promoted him."

"See if he's interested in telling the truth. I also told Miller to have somebody call the governor and Havranek for a reaction. I suggested Gentile."

Geez, what a production, thought Nash. He did not like all these other reporters doing what he should be doing. It wasn't their story, and they wouldn't be very interested or very sharp about it. They would get whatever was easiest. But he could see with the pressure of time. . . .

Nash was getting nervous. This whole thing could blow up. And if all the media turned on his story, he would be massacred.

"What are you going to do first, Sam?" Solomon leaned toward him, and Nash could see he was pretty nervous, too, feeling the time move.

"Call Bryce. And if I can't reach him, go to his house."

"Okay, good. Go." The metropolitan editor hadn't even asked where Bryce lived or how long it took to get there. Nash knew when he left the office, all these reporters would have to report to somebody else.

"Aaron, it might be better if we have somebody on rewrite as the collecting point. I can't collect from other reporters and make phone calls, too. How about Stern?"

"Good suggestion. I'll tell Miller to clear the decks for her. Get busy. Remember: ten-thirty." It was 9:15. The deadline was 11:30, but Nash understood that Solomon needed to inform the managing editor, the executive editor, and the news editor early so plans could be discussed.

Nash now had a very queasy feeling himself. There were about a half-dozen things he could try, but each one required a certain amount of time, so they all had to be rejected in favor of the best alternative: Call Bryce. He thought, "Clarence, don't chicken out on me now." When he called the number, nobody answered. Nash looked at his watch and let the phone ring for fully one minute, probably a waste of time. But the next step required that he be sure the phone route was useless.

He stepped in the doorway of Solomon's office again. "Bryce is not answering his phone. I'm going out to his house. He lives in Oak Park." Solomon repeated all the reasons why Bryce should talk, and Nash listened politely and impatiently. He then walked over to the photo desk and persuaded the photo assignment editor the Chronicle might need a good, up-to-date picture of Clarence Bryce. Thus Nash acquired a ride. All photographers had car allowances.

Bryce lived on Cuyler Avenue south of Augusta. Nash and Kate had been to his house twice, once for dinner, and once for a surprise 40th birthday party a few years earlier. And Nash had been there one other time himself, on the day he and Bryce had arranged on a whim to play golf, although neither was a golfer and they both had to rent clubs. As the photog turned south on Cuyler, Nash thought absent mindedly that this was not a good day for golf. The temperature was in the teens. The most recent snow, partially thawed and refrozen, looked stony where it was piled up in ridges alongside the sidewalks and driveways. And the light was dull. The sun had never come out. He noticed that the surviving, lofty elms on Cuyler, remnants of what had once been a cathedral of trees before the Dutch elm disease, looked thin and embattled with many limbs amputated. The dead elms had been replaced by some kind of saplings that were leafless and scrawny in the winter.

Nash pointed to the house. They parked in front, and the photographer, Richard Balukas, asked how Nash wanted to do it.

"Come right along with me, but wait until we get inside the house. This is the guy we're defending. He's the hero. No grab shots, Rich. I need him to talk to me or I'm up shit creek. Tell me when you're ready."

"Yeah. Give me a second." Balukas had a tremor in his voice. He had already pulled the strap of one camera over his head, and with the camera resting on his right thigh, he fidgeted nervously with the lens setting, then put his left hand over the lens and shot blank pictures to test the shutter and the automatic film advance. The camera sound was kachew, kachew, kachew.

To an unaccustomed observer, it might have appeared that Balukas had lost confidence. This behavior was routine to Nash. Many news photographers were habitually fearful and fidgety. It meant nothing. Balukas was his ordinary self.

The two-story frame house was set back 30 or more feet from the sidewalk. It was an outsized, exaggerated old house as were most of the homes in north Oak Park, difficult to heat and impossible to air condition. But the rooms inside were impressive and solid. Shades and lace curtains covered the front windows. Joanne liked an antiquey look. Bryce's two big elms were bent over precariously to the south as if they had been in a hurricane.

Nash rang the doorbell five or six times, then knocked on the front window adjacent to the door. No answer. He looked out at the street past Balukas, who insisted on staying at the bottom of the stairs. The only car parked for 40 yards on either side of the street was Balukas' car. Oak Park probably still banned street parking at night, Nash thought, so most people used the garage. He lifted his trenchcoat, pulled his wallet out of his back pocket, and extracted his press card. Then he walked out to the village sidewalk, over to the next house to the north, and up the front walk to ring the neighbor's doorbell. The neighbor's house was an outsized stucco with a full width front porch and a porch swing on chains, left out in the winter.

The woman who answered was in her late 20's to early 30's with light brown hair tied back in a scarf. She peered through the small square window on the inside door, and Nash held his press card against the window of the storm door. He said loudly, "I'm a reporter for the Chronicle. Can I talk to you a minute?" She opened the inside door warily and stepped into view, but kept the storm door closed.

"Yes." Her voice sounded muffled from behind the door.

"I'm Sam Nash of the Chronicle." She looked at his card through the glass and compared his face to the photograph. "I might have talked to you yesterday, ma'am. I'm looking for Clarence Bryce, your next door neighbor, or his wife, Joanne."

"Somebody called me from the Chronicle yesterday," she said. The window of the storm door rattled a bit when the wind blew. "What do you want them for? They're very nice people. What's the matter? I thought maybe you were a bill collector yesterday. That's why I wouldn't talk to you."

Nash laughed. "I'm not a bill collector although I'm acquainted with a few, but that's a different story. I'm looking for Bryce because he's an important official of the Cook County State's Attorney's Office, and he got fired in a way we consider outrageous. We're defending him in the paper, but we need to talk to him." Nash was talking quite loudly.

"Oh, boy, is that it?" she said. A child about three appeared next to her in pajamas and she put her left hand on the child's head. "He got fired?" She opened the storm door a crack to be polite, and Nash moved sideways to talk through the opening.

"Yeah. It might not be his fault, though. Politics."

She pushed the child toward the interior, saying, "Go back in the living room, Sean, you'll get a draft. See what your brother's doing." Then she turned back to Nash and said, in a matter-of-fact way, "Really," indicating she was not overly surprised by such things. "I suppose this will be on television."

"Yep."

"Well, they took off very early this morning; loaded up the Blazer. Joanne called me and asked me to pick up her newspapers so the burglars don't see them. I figured they were going to Florida on an impulse to escape the weather, but it was rather sudden. You never know when you hold a city job, do you?"

"It pays to have a sense of humor." It was actually a county job. "They didn't leave you a number or anything, did they, ma'am?"

"No. She didn't say where they were going; just said they'd be away for a few days. Sorry. Is this in the paper today?"

"Yes." Nash reached into his inside coat pocket and took out his notebook. "It's in the Chronicle."

"Oh, I'll read it. I have their papers in the kitchen."

Nash wrote his name and work and home numbers down on an empty page, tore it off and offered it to her. She opened the storm door wider and took it.

"If you hear from the Bryces, tell them I was here and I need to talk to Clarence as soon as possible. Or if you hear where they are, call me. Could you do that?"

"I'll have to read your story and see what you're up to."

"Good. Do that. Could I ask your name and phone number, ma'am?"

"If you called us yesterday, you can call here the same way again. I truly don't know where they are, though."

As he walked back down the sidewalk to Balukas' car, Nash checked his watch. It was 10:15. He had so far consciously avoided full consideration of the consequences if Saddler and Ryan went public with their accusations against Bryce and if the Chronicle had nothing to hit back with. But the consideration was creeping up on him.

"Let's find a phone," said Nash as he opened the passenger side door. He sank into the front seat in a slouch and looked at the sky through the top of the windshield. He decided to do some cold thinking. He had a good story, but he could not back it up any further. He had shot his wad. The guy he was trying to defend in this story was skipping town. Ouch. The best Nash could hope for in the way of something new, he thought, would be a statement by Havranek calling for an outside investigation. Any sophisticated person would recognize that was a weak followup, but what the heck.

On the other hand, did Bryce do the stuff Saddler said he did, wiretaps and illegal searches? Maybe he did, thought Nash. Every law enforcement official was severely tempted sooner or later. Nash remembered from his days in Criminal Courts the evasive testimony police officers sometimes gave, supported by the prosecutors, in hearings over the validity of search warrants, or the validity of street stops and street searches.

Nash sometimes thought God would have to make an exception for a few police officers when judging the conduct of people under oath. He remembered thinking in those days that it didn't seem fair to put the police officer on the spot all the time. After all, the judge was getting paid more than the cop was. The prosecutor and the defense lawyer—if they weren't already—would soon be making much more than the police officer. Yet the guy who had to lie under oath, the guy everybody waited for expectantly and even relied on to do the dirty deed so that some psycho could be removed from society (or at least the trial could proceed) was the cop. Would a judge respect a detective who told the literal, absolute truth on the witness stand about every investigation and didn't care who went free? Would a prosecutor respect such a cop?

The result of this system was that the prosecutors were drawn, as if by magnets, to join in with the occasional deceptions of the police. Nash had seen some young prosecutors, who did not have a well-defined sense of themselves, get drawn in early, actually take part in the deceptions, and become worse than the police. The best prosecutors, who were also the most arrogant, tried to stay aloof from it all. They expected police officers to do their jobs intelligently and to *describe* their investigations intelligently. If the procedural details seemed a bit contrived once in a while (to mesh with the encyclopedic court rulings on investigations), or not entirely credible to a practiced ear, this was not the prosecutor's problem as long as the descriptions would stand up in court.

If a police officer was dumb and going to tell dumb lies, well, that was different, and the prosecutor was not going to be identified with such testimony. Young lawyers joined the state's attorney's office, before moving on to more lucrative work, to gain trial experience and to build good reputations.

But a career prosecutor, like Bryce, was an unusual animal in Cook County. Except for Bryce, Nash had never known one well. And Nash had to admit he did not know how Bryce thought anymore. Bryce was very hard to know that way. It was as if after a man knew a certain amount of secrets, major and minor, he could no longer be completely open and palsy-walsy as he had been when younger. He had to constantly weigh what he said. Bryce had been under extra pressure since Madame Ryan took office. Add to that the killing of two cops which had threatened to go unsolved (a situation Nash knew was not allowable or even thinkable to anyone in law enforcement). Maybe Bryce tried to cope; cracked some eggs; got caught.

What was it Bryce had said when the evidence was suppressed in the cop killing case? "Technical problems with the search warrant." Ahhh, you son of a gun, Clarence. Look what you did here. Chubby, you're supposed to let me know about these things.

The highly respected chief of the criminal division had tried to cover it all up by walking away from the office when he was asked to take a walk. And it almost worked. Clarence, did Victoria really have anything to do with your getting fired? Or did you just say that to Franzel? Are you feeling so much pressure, Clarence, that you need to concoct phony excuses? This analysis did not entirely satisfy Nash.

Bryce did issue the subpoena, Nash reminded himself, and it was quashed. Balukas was driving south on Ridgeland Avenue. Was it possible, Nash thought, that Bryce had already been partially replaced when Victoria's allegation came up? What if Bryce was supposed to occupy himself with routine decisions and getting ready to leave and was supposed to turn over all new business to somebody else? In that instance, when they found out he was talking to the head of the Department of Mental Health and trying to get permission to interview a patient, Saddler, Ryan, and maybe Campbell would have taken the case away from him. Bryce could have refused to give in (Nash could picture him getting ornery at the end), and gone ahead and issued the subpoena without their knowledge. Laurie did say he typed up the subpoena himself. That was kind of strange behavior. What if somebody else in the office had already interviewed Victoria and checked out her story and discovered her ravings were exactly that? Nash had to create this alternate scenario because he had to face what could be, and he had to figure out for himself what might have gone on. His brain would not allow him to accept peacefully anyone's version at the moment, not even his own version from the day before.

"Wanna use that phone there?" said Balukas, pointing to a phone outside a gas station on the southwest corner of Ridgeland and Chicago Avenue. Balukas had already radioed the message to the photo desk that Bryce was gone, "taken off somewhere."

"No thanks, Rich. Try Lake Street. Let's find an indoor phone." In a manner similar to Phelan's, Nash had learned through years of practice to become outwardly calm when pressed. In rare panic situations, this did not really achieve anything since he was still just as panicked inside, but it looked nicer.

Nash had realized when he wrote the story that he did not have it all nailed down. Solomon and Phelan had realized it, too, although Simonet did not know the difference. Together, the three of them, Nash, Solomon, and Phelan had agreed without saying it out loud to take a chance. They'd done this before. Nash felt they understood each other. If they took a day or two to get statements from every conceivable person so that nothing could go wrong, by that time everybody in town would have the same story, and the exclusive would be lost. It was the sort of story that you based on the quality of the witnesses and the reasonableness of what they said. Nash considered Franzel to be a highly reliable witness, and Bryce (through Franzel) to be even better. As for further corroboration and detail, you got it in the havoc that followed the first story when people started making excuses, thus admitting things in order to defend themselves. And more people often came forward voluntarily to bolster the original charge. ("I loved your story, but that's not the half of it, guys. Let me tell you. . . .")

It was a touchy game, but Phelan and Solomon, and a few of Solomon's predecessors, usually trusted Nash to get his information straight and to make his best judgement in the field. Nash trusted them to stop him if it looked like he was going too far, because it wasn't always easy for a reporter to be objective when he got excited, and he especially trusted them to be flexible and ready for changes right up to the deadline. Everybody had done his part. When the story changed drastically at the last minute, Phelan had pulled it just as he was supposed to.

Then Simonet had stepped in, the amateur.

Now Nash knew he was stuck with the situation, and he had to make the best of it.

"It looks like if he wasn't hiding before, he's definitely in hiding now, Aaron." In a drug store on the northwest corner of Austin and Lake, Nash stood at a bank of pay phones. He heard the sounds of a nearby electronic cash register, chick-chick-a-chig, store employees asking each other questions, and the scraping of customers' feet on the tile floor. The sounds were so ordinary and almost reassuring, it seemed odd to Nash that he might be in danger of a serious career and personal crash as he stood at the phone.

"Bryce is acting like they're really got something on him," said Solomon.

"I know." Nash did not wish to dwell on it. He had decided to suppress his fears, assume his story was correct, and start turning over rocks to prove it. This was not a decision representing actual belief, because he wasn't sure anymore. It was a procedural decision. It was his responsibility to support the story. If he couldn't, with his own reputation on the line, surely nobody else could. And if Saddler and Ryan were putting up a smoke screen, they shouldn't be allowed to get away with it. "When I get back, I'm going to call Franzel and see if he remembers anything useful. I'll try Bryce's secretary and see if she can give me a lead on him. What do you hear from the rest of the people?"

"The governor has issued a blanket denial of being involved. Says it's entirely news to him," said Solomon.

"We never said he was personally involved."

"So, he's denied it anyway. Havranek is studying the matter and will have a response later."

Shit, thought Nash.

"Saddler refused to talk to Anderson," Solomon continued, "until after their press conference." (Oh, boy, here it comes, thought Nash.) "Mrs. Ryan has called a press conference at the Daley Center for 11 a.m. Do you want to cover it? I'm sending Anderson there all the way from 26th Street because I want him to go back afterwards and check everything they say." Hayes was the Chronicle's regular Daley Center reporter.

"I want to spend my time getting something for our end," answered Nash. "We already know what Mrs. Ryan is going to say."

"Yes, we do," Solomon continued. "For the 11:30 deadline, I was thinking of using a lead saying the governor denies being personally involved, then sliding into our original story, then following up with whatever Saddler and Ryan say at the press conference.

The lead in the afternoon paper had to be different from the morning lead, but Solomon did not have to ask for Nash's opinion of what it should be. Nash guessed the metropolitan editor was vainly hoping to hear a better idea.

"That's all we can do for now, I think," said Nash. It was obvious Solomon was trying to prevent Saddler and Ryan from taking over and dominating the story with their version. But Nash doubted Solomon's lead would fly. When some of the other editors got wind of the charges against Bryce, they would argue to put that on top because it was new and interesting. Managing editor Peterson had no stake in the original story because he had not been around the previous night. Peterson probably considered Solomon his rival and wouldn't mind seeing him stumble, Nash imagined.

"I'm on the way in, Aaron," said Nash.

. . . .

"An already hot primary campaign for governor got a lot hotter Tuesday with the publication of a newspaper story saying that a serious crime has been covered up in one of our state mental hospitals. The story in the Chicago Chronicle said the coverup was orchestrated to protect Gov. Beal who is in the race of his life to hold onto his job.

"However, in some dramatic developments this morning, Gov. Beal has completely denied the allegation. And the Cook County State's Attorney's Office says the story is a fraud concocted to protect a former top county prosecutor who had to be fired for serious misdeeds of his own.

"Marci Lester has the details. . . . "

Nash had told himself he was not going to watch the noon news because it was a waste of time. But he couldn't help himself, and, in fact he had already made all the phone calls he could think of. He sat with Solomon in Solomon's office, both of them staring at a cheap, black and white television on an end table next to Solomon's couch. The TV relied on an indoor antenna in a building that contained a lot of metal so the picture was crummy, but the images were decipherable and the sound was good. Nash was chewing gum. He had overdosed on cigarettes.

"State's Attorney Agnes Ryan says she asked the man who was the chief of her criminal division to resign last week. In effect, she fired him. She said she learned he had been allowing police and state's attorney's investigators to use wiretaps without court approval and he also had been condoning some illegal searches."

Lester was speaking in television cadence from what Nash recognized was a hallway in the Daley Center. She was on live.

"One of the illegal searches apparently was conducted during the investigation of the murders of Chicago police officers John Kruss and Albert DiRienzo last summer. Evidence that was confiscated in this search was expected to be used in the upcoming trial of Roland Hawkins, the accused killer, but Mrs. Ryan said that evidence has been thrown out of court.

"Mrs. Ryan surprisingly admitted that she had not intended to make all this public. But she said her hand was forced by what she called an erroneous story this morning in the Chicago Chronicle. That story accused her of firing the chief of the criminal division because he was pursuing an investigation that would embarrass Gov. Beal. Charges and countercharges may be unravelling for days. But for now, Mrs. Ryan says one of her top prosecutors went wild and damaged important cases, so she fired him. She denies any other motive. And she admits a county grand jury may be asked to consider criminal charges against her own former prosecutor.

"This is Marci Lester."

"Uhh, Marci, could you tell us what this investigation was, this alleged, apparently separate investigation that was supposed to embarrass the governor?" (It was the anchor man asking the question.)

"According to the Chronicle, Doug, there was a shooting in the Read Mental Health Center, a state hospital on the Northwest Side, that has been covered up. But the Chronicle story is very vague. It doesn't say who was shot or who did the shooting. The Chronicle suggests it was covered up because the mental hospital is under Gov. Beal's authority. The story also does not name any wit-

nesses, so I guess we'll just have to wait to see if the Chronicle has any more to tell."

"Meanwhile, we'll be looking into it ourselves, Marci."

"That's right, Doug. But I should point out that whatever the results of that investigation—and Agnes Ryan says that story is a hoax—we know for certain this morning that State's Attorney Ryan has fired one of her top prosecutors. And she hinted, without saying it directly, that because of errors by this prosecutor, the accused killer of two police officers may go free."

With his hands on his thighs, Nash chewed his gum and continued to stare at the screen. After several moments of silence, Solomon said, "A hoax, eh? Well, Mrs. Ryan and Saddler got what they wanted. They substituted one scandal for another."

Nash's thoughts were so intense, it seemed as if Solomon was speaking from far away and that he was talking about something very trivial. What earthly significance could there be, Nash thought, in what Saddler and Ryan wanted? The problem, in Nash's mind, was what was happening to Bryce. All this could have been avoided; it was unnecessary. Nash knew scandals were continuous in government, the professions, and business, and many of them were never going to be revealed, including scandals in the news business. What was exposed was a matter of chance. With no outside interference from Nash, Bryce's alleged problems at the end of his public service career, the sort of temporary weaknesses that happened to anybody who made too many decisions, could have gone into the city's closet and stayed there. Bryce could have started a private law practice with a well-earned reputation subject to nothing more than the usual rumors that follow every successful person like pilot fish.

If I had known, I would never have started this, Nash told himself. It was just a story. Then he remembered something. He had assumed somebody was dead. The inner debate became confused and caused him to frown. Too many variables. He dropped that line of thought and switched to other considerations.

Solomon was sitting in his chair again after getting up to turn off the television. There was another pause. Finally, Nash raised his right hand off his knee and was about to say something. Solomon spoke first.

"They must have wanted to suppress your story pretty strongly to go this far, Sam. They've really hurt themselves with these accusations against Bryce."

"It might be true both ways." Nash had turned in his chair to face Solomon. "Their story might be true; and our story might be true, too."

"You think he did all they said he did." This was a statement rather than a question. Solomon was hunched over his desk playing with a letter opener.

Nash waggled his hand in the air, could-be-could-be. He said, "It's awfully dangerous and complicated to make up."

"That's what I think. Did you have any knowledge of this, Sam?"

"Nope. It's out of character for Bryce to launch a personal, anti-crime crusade outside the rules. I think he could be reasonably flexible, but he never gets carried away. Or he didn't used to. He took excessive pride in imagining he could operate in any system. I figured he had things on his mind lately. For the last few weeks, he was sounding a little off: righteous, stiff, too serious. You've seen prosecutors get that way when the pressure is really severe, chins up, rigid. But obviously there was a lot more on his mind these days than I thought. Ryan's going to have to flesh all these illegal acts out. But she should know that." Nash's eyes were squinched up and he was staring at a corner of Solomon's desk. Specifically, he was staring at the molding where it curved around from the long side to the short side of the desk. He sucked on the inside of his cheek.

"You can never really be in somebody else's shoes, can you?" Nash continued. "Franzel said Bryce was pushing too hard. Maybe he's just been going up to bat too long, and he got tired of seeing the strikes go by, so he cheated. Anyway—I'm just thinking out loud here—if he's weak in the head, this could be a tricky situation."

Solomon made an irritated face and fell all the way back in his chair. "Go on," he said. Nash recognized the attitude from several previous occupants of the chair. It said: "All right, I'm the city editor/metropolitan editor of the Chicago Chronicle, and when you say something like that I am compelled to hear you out so nobody can say I ignored this vital information. But this is a waste of my time."

"Even if I can make our story stand up here, Aaron, that won't get Bryce out of this other jam."

"It would tone it down."

"Yeah, but in reality, you know we're all about to do a tap dance on Bryce." Nash meant all the news media.

"What are you worried about?"

"Well, you know, sometimes people..."

"Crack up."

"Or worse."

Solomon's eyes looked at the ceiling for an instant, disbelieving. "Sam, I think you're getting way, way ahead of yourself. In my entire career in Chicago, I never heard of a public official jumping out the window when he was under attack. They have too much pride. They go to jail instead."

Solomon sat up and placed his forearms on the desk. "I managed to keep Madame Ryan's version on the bottom for the first afternoon edition the way we discussed. But I'm going to have to bring it up and lead with it for the afternoon final. For the morning paper, I want to support our version of why he got fired. I want new evidence, a strong new witness. Use every source you have. Pull in all your IOU's. Find Bryce. I'm wondering where the fuck he is. His reputation is going to be ground into mudpies if he doesn't surface, and maybe if he does—but we won't tell him that. He should fight back. Meanwhile, we're checking out Mrs. Ryan's allegations about him, are we not?"

"Anderson's working on it."

"So, we have no choice. I want you to go all out on your story and help out on the charges against Bryce, too."

Nash felt enough superfluous advice was enough. "Aaron, I

296

would have done all that if you had stayed home. But remember a moment ago when you acted like you had an obligation to listen to me about Bryce's unusual behavior?"

"Yes." Solomon's eyes were narrowed.

"Well, I felt I had an obligation to say it."

Back at his desk, Nash tried to reach Franzel again, but Franzel was avoiding him. That was annoying. The story was Franzel's idea. Nash had doubts about Franzel, not about his truthfulness, but about his perseverance. Deep down Nash did not completely trust the character of people who routinely refused to talk to the news media, as Franzel had done for so many years. This was Nash's occupational prejudice.

Laurie Grzeskowiak, whom Nash trusted, was refusing to talk to him, but Nash understood that. Dr. Crawford was still allegedly on vacation, and there was no Gerard Crawford listed in Chicago or suburbs. Nash had found two messages on his desk. When he returned the calls, he discovered the messages were from people who wanted to complain about the treatment their relatives had received in state mental hospitals. Nash's story had activated the callers, but their complaints were unrelated to his needs. He recalled Solomon's instruction, ". . . every source you have." Nash liked the ring of it, as if people all over town were waiting to spring into action when he gave the word. Aaah, to be an editor. He put his feet up on his desk and tried to let his mind roam seeking some unusual way to get information. Instead of reaching a form of calmness that allowed his mind to wander, he had to suppress panic. He put his feet back down. Things to do, Sam, he told himself. One at a time, and you might get lucky.

He made a phone call to Scott Campbell and left a message that he did not expect to be answered, the second of the day. He considered it axiomatic to always call the people who possessed the needed information—even when you knew from the start they wouldn't talk. You call them because it's common sense, and it costs little.

Then he phoned Area 2 homicide on east 111th Street, almost as far away from the Read Mental Health Center as a police station could be in Chicago, and a Sgt. Curran answered. Nash closed his eyes with relief and tension and delivered a flat out, personal plea into the receiver, without a hint of advance warning, to a man he had never seen. The plea hung on blood.

"This is Sam Nash. I need help, Sarge."

"Okay, Nash. You got my interest."

Nash and Curran were distant cousins. Nash had discovered the relationship years earlier in a rambling conversation at a wedding reception with a relative who knew both parts of the family. The Curran family was South Side Irish, and the Nashes were West Side—as they said, "when there was a West Side." Nash had never tried to make anything out of the relationship. But one time while questioning the sergeant about a routine murder, Nash had explained who he was, and the sergeant had agreed, yes, it seemed they were cousins. Since that time, their few, similarly routine conversations about murders contained an overtone of curiosity and something akin to friendship, but different, a sense of wishing the other well, as if each man thought to himself, "This is my invisible cousin." From his voice, Nash judged Curran to be over 50, around retirement age for most police officers.

Curran listened to the whole story, interrupting twice to answer another phone and shout ("Hansen, pick up 3"). When Nash finished, Curran suggested creating an inside source with plausible, new information for the time being "if you really think this happened." Curran remembered the resourcefulness of police reporters in his youth who were under daily, hourly pressure to turn in new developments about investigations that actually were stuck. They created.

"I wouldn't know how to do that and get away with it, Sarge. It's a lost art. I need information, even rumors. I'll take rumors. But it's got to be. . . ."

"True rumors, I suppose."

"Yeah, like that. I need something to go on. I know this is way out of your geographic area, but I'm hoping you can call around and tell me what you hear. Just between you and me."

"That's a state institution, Sam. Chicago police may not have been called there in a long time. It's a gray area. It could have been the Illinois Department of Law Enforcement."

"Whatever you can do, Sarge."

"Whatever I can do, Sam, I will do. I wish I could promise it will help you, but I don't know."

Nash realized when he hung up that calling Sgt. Curran represented true desperation. But he had more unlikely calls to make. He called the Read Mental Health Center looking for Leon Murphy who was the head of the union local representing Read employees. It took 15 minutes and five phone calls for Nash to track him down.

Nash had spoken to Murphy the day before and had gotten a runaround for which he had little patience. This time he intended to work harder.

"I've got nothing to say to you, Mr. Nash," said Murphy in a molasses smooth voice. Murphy was a little too careful in his diction and ended up sounding insincere for it. "I spoke to you yesterday and told you that to my knowledge there had been no shooting here and no assaults on the day that you mentioned. But I am not a criminal investigator. I noticed that the persons charged with that responsibility in this, um, area of legal jurisdiction stated today that your accusations were erroneous. So perhaps you should address that issue in your newspaper."

"Murphy, you didn't tell me that nothing happened at Read when I called you yesterday. What you said was that you were not a detective and neither was I and that such things were out of your 'purview.' If you are saying now that there was no such assault or there has been no shooting, I want to get it straight. If there was a shooting, and we prove it, there's a lot of people who are going to end up being charged with complicity in the coverup just like Watergate, Murphy. I will put your name up high in my story so the authorities will get the idea." This was baloney. Unless Murphy was personally involved in the coverup—as opposed to just "forgetting" things he might have heard—Nash knew Murphy would not be charged with anything.

"Mr. Nash, your attitude does not appear conducive to me. I think you attitude is hostile and lacks intelligent professionalism. If you are trying to intimidate me, Mr. Nash, I stand behind what I said yesterday and today."

Nash switched tactics and tried to convince Murphy that uncovering the alleged shooting would be good for the members of Murphy's union. If a killer was running around at Read, he should be caught.

"Be that as it may, Mr. Nash, you are the only one who seems to be concerned that this danger exists. If you wish to do a story about some improper promotions and other questionable personnel actions on the part of the Mental Health Department, I would be glad to help you."

The trouble with Murphy, Nash thought, was that once he got into his lofty denial mode, a bureaucratic habit, the act just carried forward from its own weight. It was a variation on a routine. So Nash could not detect if he was denying something that DID occur or something that did NOT occur.

The Illinois Department of Law Enforcement was no help either. The agency (with the unfortunate acronym of IDLE) was run by a former federal prosecutor, Guy Ross, who would not take a dive, in Nash's opinion, even for the governor who appointed him. Ross was friendly and open and said he had told one of his agents to look into it at 9 a.m.

Mrs. Ryan had assured his agent that the incident was an altercation between a patient and a staff member at Read and was not fit for prosecution. A state mental institution in Chicago was indeed an area of overlap as far as determining investigative jurisdiction, Ross said. But the state's attorney's office would be the agency to prosecute no matter who investigated. If the state's attorney's office conducted the initial investigation, too, that was probably legitimate if a little out of the ordinary.

"She said that: a patient fought with a staff member?"

"That's her description, Sam. Her word was altercation. You understand that patients at Read are not good candidates for prosecution right from the start."

"Yeah, I understand. What if it went the other way around?"

"A staff member attacking an inmate? That could be— theoretically. But we can't go in and investigate their investigation without an official request from somebody or reasonable grounds."

"And she said her office did investigate?"

"Contradicts your story a little, doesn't it? That's what she told my agent, Sam. Off the record, we may question Clarence Bryce when he turns up just to keep the books straight. But that really has to be off the record. We have no way of prosecuting our cases in Cook County on our own. We have to work with Mrs. Ryan."

Next, Nash phoned the headquarters of the Department of Mental Health in Springfield and asked for Dr. Charles Medaven who was unavailable as usual. The department's p/r man said Medaven was unable to talk to all the media callers personally, but he had left a statement.

"We are satisfied with the announcement made by Cook County State's Attorney Ryan this morning. The Read Mental Health Center is one of the finest institutions of its kind in the nation, and we regret that its employees and all the employees of this department have been tarred with unjust innuendo."

"What does that mean?" said Nash.

"It means what it says, Mr. Nash. We are not going to feed this thing you started by getting into a quarrel with you."

"Let me talk to Medaven."

"He's going to St. Louis to give a speech. He'll be back tomorrow."

"Where in St. Louis?"

"You are free to search for him, Mr. Nash. I don't know. I hope your story tomorrow will reflect what Mrs. Ryan said at her press conference."

"It will, partly. Are you in on this?"

"Am I? Am I 'in on this?' You mean like some kind of conspiracy?" The p/r man laughed.

"Yep."

"Nash, can I go off the record for your benefit?"

"Sure."

"Good. Minor confrontations between patients in state institutions or between patients and staff members are not unusual. They are expected and come with the territory. A shooting I consider extreeeemly unlikely. I don't personally know what happened at Read to get you all fired up, but I know from experience it doesn't take much with the press sometimes."

"Why don't you know? Shouldn't a p/r man take it upon himself to inquire after an accusation comes out like this?"

"You've got a point there, Nash. One for your side. Now let me ask you a question that is more apropos. . . . Shouldn't you know before you write it?"

Nash was not in a mood to let this argument bother him. He felt he had followed his usual procedures before going with the story. After a few more questions, it was apparent the p/r man either did not have the information Nash wanted or was keeping it to himself. So Nash hung up. He had Medaven's statement in his notebook. Although he refused to go back and worry over the way he had put together the story, Nash's doubt about the story was growing rapidly. It was becoming harder and harder for him to think straight. He knew he had to keep going until he had nothing left to stand on.

At 2:45, Nash's phone rang. It was Anderson.

"The desk tells me you're gonna write this, Sam."

"Write what, exactly?" said Nash in a sharp tone. He was preoccupied.

"This stuff about Bryce, the searches, the bugging."

"Oh, shit." Nash had put that half of the story, which threatened to become the whole story, out of his mind. He was tempted to ask the desk to give Anderson to somebody else, but he quickly decided against it. "I forgot. What do you have that wasn't in the afternoon edition?"

"A lot, Sam."

"Lemme get a headset on."

A sense of futility, of uselessness came over Nash. At the same time, he thought, What if my information is out there, and I miss my chance to get it while I'm fooling around with Anderson on the phone? This was a real fear, but his mind told him probably an unnecessary one because...there might not be anything to miss. He took a headset from his bottom, left hand drawer, plugged it into a jack on his phone, and signed on to his computer terminal to type Anderson's notes, moving slowly. He felt very heavy, especially his arms, and also felt an urge to act out and throw his headset across the room, but he allowed his body to be pulled along by a deep, habitual process, almost like the process of getting dressed in the morning.

The process was the thing that was stable. It was the work. It was almost salvation. According to this process, information came in, or you went and got it, then you wrote it, and it went out. When all the stories and cataclysms were added up, and almost all forgotten, the process remained. Sometimes the process represented the only order in one's life. Whatever was going on in the world, if you were covering it, at a certain point you stopped time. You wrote the story; ended it; and sent it along. The event or problem may have kept on madly running, but from the process you learned that everything ended, first in phases, then altogether, and other things started in the meanwhile, and they also would end. The process survived. It was always waiting for you to put margins on things, the length of the story and the deadline by which it had to be done. And after the process was completed, you found yourself in the calm eye of the hurricane for a few minutes, both the hurricanes of events and the hurricanes of the self.

Nash settled in his chair. He said, "All right, Tommy, what have you got?"

29

"Boy, you really started something, Sam. I heard you were out here, but I didn't know what you were up to until I read your story this morning." Nash adjusted the receiver on his left ear so he could hear better and moved the whole headset around to get the tension on his head just right.

"How many cases do they allege have been affected by bugging or illegal searches, Tommy?"

"Mrs. Ryan didn't say at the press conference how many cases were supposed to be affected, but she gave the impression it was a big deal, of course." Anderson's voice was higher pitched than normal because he was tense from working fast, and Nash understood he was also dealing with a general uneasiness. "You'll see that in the afternoon story, Sam. Saddler is telling everyone, quote 'as many as 20' unquote and insisting we attribute that to sources. I checked with a guy I trust with the state's attorney's investigators who swore that the number was four, maybe five."

"That's a quote, too?" Nash was typing on his computer terminal.

"Yeah, four maybe five is a quote. I got a lot of this from Judge Clifford, but not that part."

"Did anybody say what these cases were, Tommy, other than the cop murders? I never heard of any of this."

"Hey, me neither," responded Anderson, reaching a particularly high note. "Clifford said the other judges talked about it at lunch. I'm embarrassed to tell you some of this, Sam. Try to cover for me a little bit." Anderson was being completely honest because Nash was just another reporter.

"I will tell everyone who asks that it all got by more experienced Criminal Courts reporters than you—including me."

"Thanks. The judge said, 'It may come as a surprise to you, son-n-n, but not everything gets in the papers.' It started leaking out about a month ago, he said, which would be the week after I was assigned here. It seems there was a motion to suppress evidence in a dope case. . . . Clifford said we should really get corroboration for this someplace else. . . . The defense put a certain witness on the stand, and the state immediately asked for a recess."

"Slow down a little."

"Okay. The defendant was then allowed to plead guilty to a lesser charge. (pause) The surprise witness was a former investigator for the state's attorney's office who got fired recently, and apparently he knew about cases in which electronic eavesdropping was used, including that one. (He paused again.) So the prosecution didn't want him to testify. The judge made the assistant state's attorneys fess up in chambers before he'd go along with the plea bargain. This slow enough?"

"That's better. Who was this judge?"

"I don't know. One of the Narcotics Court judges. Clifford said I'd have to find that out on my own. Absolutely none of this can be attributed to Clifford, you know."

"I know."

"According to Clifford, within 10 days, this guy turned up in pre-trial motions in two other cases with stories of some kind of eavesdropping without court order. . . . Not all of the cases have been settled yet as far as Clifford knew, but the cases are pretty well shot. . . . Off the record, Clifford said most of the judges feel Bryce must have known about this. Each one of these cases is big in its own way, but more of interest to the cops than the public, I would say. Certain guys they were anxious to get."

"Ahhh, did anybody say that? 'Certain guys they were anxious to get'? That would at least be an explanation."

"That's what my friend in the states attorney's police said."

"In those words?"

"In those words, yeah."

"Where do you know this guy from?"

"We went to school together. He's not an old hand here, but he's been here longer than me. He's been here about a year. Don't mention that to anybody, Sam."

"I won't. I need the name of this state's attorney's investigator who turns up in all these cases and when and why he got fired."

Anderson gave Nash a name. "The rest I don't know. This is like pulling teeth, you know, getting this stuff."

"I understand. Gimme some description of the cases."

"I don't have details on the cases."

"We have to have it, so you'll have to get it. Try Scott Campbell after we hang up. Names, dates, charges, the whole schmeer. Dispositions."

"Boy, I don't know, Sam."

"We need it. Now tell me about the Hawkins case."

"A real big deal. I get the impression that the Hawkins case is in a different dimension. Everybody is touchy, and a lot of the assistants are mad at Ryan and Saddler for dragging that one in. Clifford is the judge. He said they had an extended hearing on a motion to suppress evidence, and he was forced to throw out the murder weapon and Hawkins' sweatshirt because he said the search warrant was invalid."

Nash finished typing that information, then asked, "Why was it invalid?"

"This is tricky, Sam, and I'm not even sure I get it myself, so I'll just tell you what he said. The cops raided this apartment five days after the murders. The raid was on a Monday. They already had Hawkins in custody, but he wasn't charged yet. They only had him for a couple hours. Then they raid a certain apartment and they get the gun which ballistics shows to be the murder weapon. It also has Hawkins' fingerprint on it. And they get the sweatshirt which the two eyewitnesses described the killer as wearing—faded blue with the arms cut off. Hawkins isn't talking, but they charged him with the murders."

"Take a breath and let me catch up," said Nash. Nash typed what Anderson said in a crude form of shorthand. "Okay."

"Clifford said the search warrant that led to these items was based on an informant whom police and prosecutors could not produce later. He said there were serious contradictions in the search warrant, and in his opinion, the informant does not exist—a phantom, but not exactly. Clifford said the defense charged that Hawkins was the subject of illegal, electronic surveillance and that the search warrant was based on either a bug in the place where he was staying or in the car he was driving or wiretapping. The cops overheard Hawkins or somebody tell where he stashed the gun and his clothes. He said the defense never produced any evidence of this, but off the record, he said it was a pretty good theory and he wouldn't be surprised if it was correct."

"Wait a minute." Nash typed it all, even the off the record stuff which could not be used. The judge meant for the paper to have the information for purposes of understanding. "All right."

"I don't understand why Hawkins didn't throw the stuff away," said Anderson.

"You'll see that again. Be glad for it. If all the criminals start doing sensible things, the world is in big trouble. Who was doing the bugging?"

"I don't know. But everybody says this one was not related to the other three. It seems to me like Chicago police must have done it."

"How'd they get tripped up? Police use anonymous informants all the time to justify search warrants. That's legit."

"I'm gonna tell you. This is the tricky part. Clifford pulled his written ruling out of his files for me and let me copy it. You can use it like it was from court records."

"Nice work. Go slow."

While Anderson paused, Nash looked over at his friendly, white pillar which prevented the city desk from seeing him, and he studied some irregularities in the plaster. He looked at his sportcoat hanging on its hook in the pillar and wondered how long the hook would hold. He turned and looked down his side of the room, seeing the heads of men and women talking on the phone, typing at their terminals, or bent over reading. He could hear in his left ear Anderson mumbling to himself while he sought the proper spot in his notebook. Anderson found it, and Nash returned his attention to his fingers.

Judge Clifford's ruling quoted the complaint for the search warrant, which said, in effect, that an informant who had been known to be reliable in the past had visited with the occupants of an apartment near 43d Street and Indiana Avenue on the weekend following the murders. The informant had seen a faded blue sweatshirt with the arms cut off and a handgun which could have been a .38 both behind a couch. Two of the occupants were friends of Hawkins who was under investigation for the murder of the police officers. Police had reason to believe Hawkins was the owner of the sweatshirt and the gun.

Nash thought somebody might wonder how a casual visitor could look behind a couch and tell that a rolled up sweatshirt had no arms. But he knew search warrant complaints frequently sounded just like that and took a little getting used to. This one seemed normal.

Clifford summarized the testimony given much later by the three occupants of the apartment, Claudell and Wardell Merritt and their mother, plus a neighbor, and a clerk from the County Jail. What it amounted to was that the brothers had been in the Wentworth Area lockup and the jail from Friday night to Monday morning prior to the search, on charges unrelated to the cop murders. Their mother had been in County Hospital that weekend and for several days before and after and had papers to prove it. The neighbor said the apartment had been locked and various people who tried to get in over the weekend could not.

Nash shook his head as he heard this. It was so human. He wondered how the detectives felt after working out this scheme in advance thinking everything was going to be fine. It was a little too close to home for Nash.

"Okay, I get it, Tommy. If the apartment had been locked and nobody was home, how did the informant visit the occupants or even visit the apartment? Was he a burglar, or what? That was obviously why the judge wanted him brought in."

"The judge said that in the absence of further evidence, the police version was quote 'not credible' unquote and he had no choice but to dismiss the search warrant. The evidence went out, too. He upheld the arrest because he said the witnesses were sufficient for that, although I hear they may have trouble with them."

"He wouldn't throw out the arrest. Clifford's tough, but he's not dumb."

"You know, Sam, I've been thinking about this ever since I talked to Judge Clifford. I don't get why everybody jumps to the conclusion that electronic surveillance occurred here."

"Maybe because of the gossip. Three prior cases."

"I think the tip could have come from one of the Merritt brothers trying to make a deal, and the cops just covered up for them."

Nash took a break, leaned back, folded his hands in his lap, then spoke into the transmitter hanging in front of his mouth. "I'm thinking about that, too. If the tip came from one of the brothers, the detectives on the case would have known where the brothers were and would most likely have known nobody was home at the Merritt estate. Then they would not have composed a completely bullshit search warrant. They would have picked a reasonable day to have the phantom informant make his visit. See? . . . But even if it was the brothers or the mother, I think there must be ways for the state to explain that to the judge and introduce the parties to each other in chambers. The state didn't have ANYbody, it looks like. They got caught with their pants down. And the story was too fucked up to be saved by an actor, so they cut their losses."

An old Hughes legend was filtering into Nash's consciousness from a corner of his brain, but he didn't quite have it yet. It was somehow related.

"Anyhow, let's continue into this swamp, Tommy. Who ties Bryce into this? On the record."

"Saddler and Ryan. That's what their press conference was all about. They didn't say how they knew it was eavesdropping or how they knew Bryce was involved; they just stated it. If you try to pin Saddler down, he says the information will be presented to a grand jury after their internal investigation is completed. But Clifford used to be an assistant state's attorney a long time ago. He said in a case of this magnitude, the assistants on the case knew everything about that search warrant before they asked the judge to sign it. And if they knew, Bryce knew, Clifford says. Even if they didn't know, Clifford says, Bryce knew."

"Who were the assistants on the case?"

"Forget it, Sam. They aren't saying a thing. They just walk away from me."

Nash felt very weary. "All right . . ."

"I hate to say it, but where does this leave your story, Sam?"

"I wish I knew. We're not doing real good on this end."

"Sorry. You know, if I had found all this out when Clifford originally made his ruling, maybe we wouldn't have got into this situation. But it's taking me a while to understand this place."

Nash rolled his eyes while listening to the apology. Bryce had slipped this episode past him, too, and past City News, and reporters from the other two papers who were assigned to Criminal Courts. Reporters tended to give pre-trial hearings only cursory attention and to rely on prosecutors for most of their information. Bryce was so straightforward about most things that a rare piece of bullshit from him was able to waltz right by. Nash detected panic trying to rise inside him again like vomit.

"Don't worry about that. Go get that stuff I told you about, thumbnail descriptions of the three other cases and dispositions, and why the former state's attorney's investigator was fired. You're doing fine."

Nash took off his headset and laid it on the desk. He pushed his chair back and found a cigarette he had lit lying on the rug where it had fallen from his ash tray after burning down to a butt. He retrieved it, blew the ashes to disperse them on the rug, and dropped the butt in his ashtray. The rug was impervious to cigarette burns.

He put his hand on his phone and gritted his teeth. The wrong story was coming together just fine. Anderson would keep at it. He seemed to be aware of what he knew and what he didn't know, an ability to distinguish that some people never acquired, and he didn't try to fool the rewrite man. Nash became aware that his hand was on the receiver as if he was about to call someone, but he couldn't think of who it was he was going to call. The motion had been reflex. He stared into space thinking about this and saw the copy clerks bringing in the oppositions' afternoon editions. Then he averted his eyes and called Scott Campbell for the third time.

Nash's relationship to Campbell for the moment was that of a beggar. Campbell, whom Nash years ago had treated as a puppy dog, possessed information that Nash desperately needed. Campbell probably knew exactly what happened at Read, Nash thought, although the new chief of the criminal division would probably not reveal it. It was irritating to Nash to be at the mercy of the younger man. When key public officials were his juniors, he thought once again, he was getting too old for this line of work.

He couldn't get through to Campbell and left another message. Then he walked to the city desk and grabbed copies of the Post and the Ledger. Although there were only enough copies to serve the editors, nobody stopped him. He walked slowly back to his own desk, slapped the papers down, and dropped into his chair. He arranged the newspapers and looked at the headlines.

The headline in the Ledger, across all six columns of the front page, said, "State's Attorney fires chief prosecutor." This was followed by a two-column readout just above the story which said, "Illegal searches in probe // of 2 cop killings is cited." The Post led with the story, too, with a screamer across the top of page one: "Top county prosecutor dumped." The Post also had a two column readout about the story: "Ryan says 'bugging' // caused his downfall."

The headlines were so powerful, they were frightening. Nash had never been on the other end, and he had never realized what they could do to a person. He could feel his blood race and his hair stand up a little on his scalp. He tried to imagine how Bryce was going to cope with headlines like this and the stories that went with them as the outcome of his career. Bryce thought very highly of himself. He always knew his career would not be acknowledged by the general public. The state's attorney, the elected official, got the attention. But as far as Nash was concerned and many other people around town, Bryce could rightly pride himself as being one of the principal men who kept the barbarians and maniacs, white, black, and brown, from overrunning the city in his time. (Bryce would say, "And preserved the law, Nash, and preserved the law.") In unguarded moments, Bryce was even resignedly proud of being underpaid for all these years. It was part of public service.

So how was he going to cope with this?

Every one of Bryce's relatives was going to ask him in a veiled or not-so-veiled way, "What did you do?" Friends from his childhood would be sympathetic; and they would also wonder if Bryce had become a crook or only tragically incompetent. That noise in the media was probably exaggerated, they would say, but they would believe he must have done something that was dishonest or stupid. Lawyers who had gone up against him and lost, or who had never liked his style, would gladly spread rumors about him. The big man was down.

Nash read the stories and hoped for some call backs. The first call came from Sgt. Curran, who said, "Sorry, Nash, no Chicago police. Anyway, it's too political now. Who knows what happened? The rumors ain't worth a shit. People are making them up."

"Give me one."

"Give you one. Well, one's as good as another; they're all the same. Mrs. Ryan's husband had a tootsie who wound up at Read, and Mrs. Ryan had her murdered."

"Aaaahh." Nash was disgusted.

"See what I mean? People are just jagging themselves off. Sorry, pal. No help this time. I tried, though."

"Thanks, Sarge."

At 4:05 p.m., Nash's phone rang and he was startled to hear the voice of Scott Campbell.

"Sam, I'm sorry it took me so long to get back to you," said Campbell. "I've been tied up meeting with a lot of people and trying to get up to date on some of our cases. I'm beginning to appreciate Bryce's talent for administration even more than I did before." Campbell sounded like a cheerful bureaucrat, just promoted, as if nothing had happened but a smooth transition from one boss to another, Nash thought.

"Scott, I'm going to ask you point blank. What happened at the Read Mental Health Center?"

"The question of the day, huh? Or one of them?" His voice adopted a more serious tone. "I can't go into all the details for you, Sam. You know my hands are tied on some things, especially regarding the Department of Mental Health. The privacy laws governing the patients are pretty all-encompassing. I did tell you there was an

313

assault, colloquially speaking, an altercation. And I advised you not to print it."

"Scott, the privacy laws are designed to protect the patients' identities and reputations. Let's say we omit the identities of the patients and just talk about what happened."

"Yesterday," Campbell continued, "I also encouraged Tom Saddler to be more frank with your paper concerning the circumstances of Bryce's resignation. I understand he finally was. Somebody there chose to ignore what he said. That was foolish. These people are not dumb, Sam."

"My editor is, unfortunately. I'm asking you again, Scott. What happened out at Read?"

"You have a one-track mind. Believe me, I'd like to help you, but we have to talk completely off the record."

"Okay." Nash had no choice.

"Let's go to the beginning. As best I can reconstruct this affair, you called Bryce; he called Dr. Medaven; Dr. Medaven called Mrs. Ryan; and Mrs. Ryan asked me to look into your original report. So I did."

"You did?"

"Yes, I did—as much as I was asked to do."

"Did you tell Bryce?"

"Off the record again, the answer is no."

"Why not?"

Campbell didn't miss a beat. "There were several investigations I didn't tell him about."

"Whose idea was that, Scott?"

"Come on, Sam. I just work here. I have bosses just like you do. I don't mean to be cryptic."

"Okay. Okay. I understand. But Saddler and Ryan told Bryce the Department of Mental Health was conducting the only investigation and your office was simply being kept informed. On top of that, Mrs. Ryan let it drop that she had decided to keep the lid on it because of the election."

"I don't think that's exactly what you said in the paper, Sam. I believe you had her saying it wasn't fair to help either candidate, period. Let me point out a couple things to you. We're still off the record?"

"If we have to be."

"We do. Ryan, and to some extent, Tom Saddler, too, had an inordinate fear of Bryce because of his reputation and his standing in the office. When Mrs. Ryan got elected, they wanted to put in their own guy right off, a lawyer in private practice, to replace Bryce, but their guy wasn't qualified. They took advice from several quarters and went against their instincts to let Bryce stay on. We have to give them credit for that, Sam, because Ryan and Bryce are from opposite political parties. Ryan and her aide, Saddler, are totally political animals. They see everything in that context. But they are learning, slowly, that this is not the mayor's office or the city council. This office is different. They're trying."

"So what?" said Nash.

"Hey...now, hold on. They felt they got screwed when this eavesdropping started to surface because Bryce wasn't even Mrs. Ryan's choice, and all of a sudden she feared she would be blamed for his—what are alleged to be—his mistakes. If you're wondering, Sam, I had no connection with that press conference this morning. That was a travesty, but I'm not the state's attorney. Your reporter, Anderson, came around here for some information a little while ago, and I helped him out as best I could because he mentioned your name."

"You were explaining why you went around Bryce."

"I think the proper point of view would be why the state's attorney went around Bryce, Sam." Campbell was being defensive. That was fine with Nash. It was natural behavior. "I'm just guessing. I'm not privy to all their political discussions. So if you ever print this, I'll strangle you myself."

"No danger."

"She wanted to get rid of Clare because of the threat of a public

315

bugging scandal, but she was afraid if she moved against him in the wrong way, he would do something nasty to damage her. So she told him he had to resign but to take his time and if possible everything would be kept quiet for the good of everybody. But she *didn't* tell him I had apparently been his replacement for some time in her mind, and that I had already been handling some sensitive things without his knowledge. I think she and Saddler felt that might really set Bryce off. Their biggest fear seemed to be that he was going to do something overt and political at the end to embarrass her. A lot of hostility had grown up that could not have been predicted."

"You're trying to tell me they thought Bryce would stir up an incident at the Read Mental Health Center into a scandal just to make the governor angry at Mrs. Ryan?"

"There was that possibility or any of several other things that could have been used here, things not related to DMH. Perhaps they were afraid of what a prosecutor can do with an allegation, leak it to the media, stretch it out, keep it going for a week or more, raise suspicions, when the original incident may not be entirely what it first appeared to be."

"Scott, let's get real. We're talking about Clarence Bryce here, not some political jamoke like Saddler who I'm sure would do anything."

"They don't know Bryce the way we do, Sam. But maybe now you see why Saddler quashed the subpoena that formed the centerpiece of your story."

"Run that by me again."

"We already talked to that girl. I did."

"YOU did? You actually did investigate this? You talked to Victoria Morici?" She was the crux. When Nash had begun this quest, all he had wanted was for somebody in law enforcement to talk to her and check out what she said.

"Yes, I did, Sam."

"Where?"

"At Read. She is still there, as far as I know."

316

"Scott, you gotta tell me this. What did she say?"

"Now you be real, Sam. I talked to other people, too, and, as Mrs. Ryan said, this incident was not a matter for the courts. But you know what will happen to me if I start passing along information from mental patients directly to the news media? I'll tell you this much without going into the content. What Victoria Morici said would have been more interesting to a psychiatrist than it was to me."

"Scott, don't play around here. Did she tell you that somebody got shot? Did she say she saw people dragging a body away? Did she say a guy named Dr. Crawford was involved?" Nash could hear that his voice was much too intense. He had lost his cool. He was desperate, and it showed. Any hint of this usually made news sources clam up. No one trusted a guy who was desperate.

"Uhhhhmm. Hmmm. Let me ask you a couple questions, Sam, then I have to go. I've given you a lot of time here, but you are one of my favorite reporters."

"Scott, seriously!" Nash was speaking through clenched teeth, "I don't need questions. Did she tell you that and did you check it out? I need answers. Even if you have to answer me completely and totally off the record. I don't care."

"I guess you don't. Here's one question, Sam. In fact, one question is enough. How often do you think about the relationship between intercontinental ballistic missiles, portable radios, and the late Nelson Rockefeller?"

"Scott, damnit!"

"Not very often, I'll bet, Sam. But some people think about that relationship a lot. Some people could talk your ear off about it. I'm sorry I didn't realize completely what your intentions were yesterday, or maybe this mess wouldn't have happened. I didn't know all that Franzel had told you. I gotta go, Sam. By the way, call me in a couple weeks when I get organized and this affair blows over, and I think I'll have a couple cases of interest to you and your editors. Also, I think Mrs. Ryan exaggerated the damage to the Hawkins case. We're not abandoning ship. We're going to hang in there. I think your story should reflect that. Okay?"

Nash did not respond.

"You still there?" said Campbell.

"Yes."

"Bryce is finally going to make the kind of money he deserves downtown, Sam, and he'll survive this. Good to talk to you. Bye."

Nash couldn't think straight to weigh all the angles. A wind filled his mind. Everything was blowing around. It was supposed to have been a murder or something very serious. Mrs. Ryan's attitude did not matter. She was a politician. But there was no way Campbell or anyone else who came up through the State's Attorney's office would cover up a serious crime that others knew about (think of all the people who would have to know) and blandly state that, yes, he was the principal investigator. It was absurd.

Nash feared few things more than to be shown up as a spreader of false tales after he had made a serious allegation in print. He had a choice of reactions from his peers: laughter, pity, or contempt. But deeper than that, to report the wrong information, as he concluded he had, to be completely and totally wrong in print was shattering. All the demeaning things he had endured or made himself do over the years; all the efforts to stay unbiased despite his own beliefs; all the times he had sat on his own sensibilities, denied his own feelings (including feelings of revulsion or sorrow for some of the things he had to write about) to keep his feelings from interfering: all this had achieved him what?

When it counted, he was wrong.

Nash opened his notebook to a clean page and began to doodle rapidly, making rigid, angular doodles with heavy lines while he tried to think. He doodled for five minutes and hoped nobody was watching him. Anderson called. Nash was annoyed at first, but then he was grateful. He put on his headset and turned to the computer terminal. Motion. The process. Anderson had almost everything

Nash could have asked for—everything about the misdeeds of Clarence Bryce. And Anderson had one request:

"Sam, if you're really going to nail Bryce in this story, and I don't see what else you could do, leave my name off it, would you?"

"Almost all the new information is your's, Tom."

"I can live without this byline. A lot of the assistants like Bryce a lot and don't care for some other people. I want to get in good around here so I don't miss things. I'll say I was responsible for keeping the number of eavesdropping cases down to four or five. You're using that, aren't you?"

"I haven't thought about it." Nash was in a fog. "We'll probably use both estimates."

"You know best. The way I see it, this is still your story, Sam."

30

Solomon was grim but philosophical when Nash explained he had found nothing further to support his story of the shooting at Read or the coverup. To save face for Solomon as well as himself, and because part of him refused to accept his own inner verdict, Nash added that he still believed his original story was correct, but that all the information was running the other way, and he had no choice but to write it the way it led. Nash felt the desire to escape of a naked man in the middle of a crowd, so he had to fake composure again. With his hands on his hips, he delivered the report slowly as if he were describing the death of a mutual acquaintance.

"All right, dope the story with Georgia, too," said Solomon. "Red's not here today." Nash assumed Phelan was taking a day off in protest over the printing of the story against his advice, or maybe he had gotten drunk. "Write whatever it takes," Solomon added, "but be reasonable." This meant to Nash about 30 inches.

The effort and concentration required for writing gradually reduced Nash's emotions to a more manageable level. For a little while, he slipped into the alternative dimension known as the newspaper story where his longtime friend, Clarence Bryce, was just another guy in public office who had fouled up and earned notoriety. The writing went more smoothly than Nash expected. Didn't make any difference if Clarence was his friend or not, it seemed.

Illegal investigative activities linked to a former top prosecutor have seriously damaged at least four major criminal cases and perhaps as many as 20 cases, officials in the Cook County State's Attorney's Office said Tuesday.

As a result of the illegal activities, several street gang leaders and a man reputed to be one of the city's major narcotics dealers have escaped prosecution for felonies. Moreover, key evidence against the accused murderer of two Chicago police officers has been thrown out of court, according to a variety of sources.

The former prosecutor, Clarence Bryce, 44, who was chief of the criminal division for the State's Attorney's Office was forced to resign by State's Attorney Agnes Ryan last Friday.

Ryan announced her action Tuesday. She said an internal probe is underway in her office to determine the scope of the alleged illegal activities, and that findings could be presented to a grand jury in the future for possible indictment of "whoever was involved."

Ryan said that Bryce had condoned the use of illegal electronic eavesdropping by investigators and unjustified search warrants without her knowledge.

Bugs, phone taps, and other forms of electronic eavesdropping, which are widely used by the FBI, are illegal in many instances for state and local police forces in Illinois because of strict state laws.

Ryan said Bryce became "overzealous" as a prosecutor and he "lost control of himself."

Sources close to Ryan contended the number of cases damaged by Bryce's alleged actions was "as many as 20." Mrs. Ryan herself gave no number.

Other sources in the office more directly involved with day to day criminal investigations said the number was four or five. But one source said Bryce's alleged actions constituted "one of the worst screwups seen around here in a long while."

(This was Saddler. Nash used the quote because it was true.)

Ryan said the State's Attorney's Office voluntarily withdrew evidence in some cases after a defense lawyer brought forth information showing the evidence had been improperly procured.

The Chronicle learned that two cases in which the State's Attorney's Office voluntarily withdrew evidence were a street gang murder and a major, street gang narcotics case. The Chronicle also learned that evidence in another major narcotics case involving Digby Wells, a reputed South Side narcotics kingpin, may be withdrawn shortly.

Sources said that the information brought forward by the defense lawyer was, in fact, a witness, a former state's attorney's investigator who had recently been fired.

The former investigator was prepared to testify that electronic eavesdropping had been used in the three cases, sources said.

Authorities had hoped to send to prison several prominent street gang leaders and Wells as the result of the three cases. But the sources added that only one man went to prison—on a probation violation for carrying a gun—in the street gang cases, and the rest of the defend-

ants received probation after pleading guilty to various minor charges. Wells may also go free, these sources said.

(This was all from Campbell to Anderson.)

The most notorious case has yet to go to trial, the double murder of Chicago police officers John Kruss and Albert DiRienzo last summer.

State's Attorney Ryan labeled as a "hoax" and a "smear" a Chronicle story in the Tuesday morning editions saying she had fired Bryce for political reasons.

The Tuesday morning Chronicle story said Ryan fired Bryce to prevent him from investigating an alleged shooting in a state mental hospital that could have an impact on the primary race for governor.

Ryan said that a report of "an alleged shooting" at the Read Mental Health Center was investigated by her office and state mental health authorities and found to be a "non-indictable matter." She said, "There was no crime to prosecute. The incident, as it was reported to us, did not happen."

Ryan declined to answer a question about whether anyone had been shot at Read, even if, for some reason, it was not a crime. One of her aides said later her words were "intended to deny the whole thing."

(Saddler again.)

Of the four known cases affected by the charges of illegal eavesdropping, the only one identified by Ryan was the murders of Officers Kruss and DiRienzo. Ironically, sources said this is the only one of the four cases in which eavesdropping is strongly suspected rather than admitted by a participant. (Campbell to Anderson.)

A source close to the internal problem in the State's Attorney's Office said, "We are pretty certain it was done. And we are pretty certain Clarence Bryce either knew of a Chicago police-operated wiretap or he condoned it after the fact."

(Saddler to Anderson on Anderson's second interview.)

Criminal Court Judge Arthur Clifford, who is presiding over the case, ruled recently that the Chicago police story of a secret informant who led them to key evidence was "not credible." Clifford said. . . . "

The story went on for a total of 30 inches. When he had finished writing it, reading it through once again, and making his final changes, Nash sat back. From this relaxed position, he reached his left hand well forward and hit the "kill" button on the top row of the keyboard. Then he absently watched the entire screen blink off and on, off and on, warning the user that the story was in danger of being erased.

Nash needed information from prosecutors, and Bryce liked to see that things in the newspaper were correct, and sometimes, that they also included a mention of his own name. It had begun 12 years earlier when Nash was assigned to Criminal Courts and Bryce was trying cases in one courtroom. Out of a regular routine of questions and answers, gossip, bizarre humor common to both their occupations, and drinking to celebrate the day of the week, a well-earned guilty verdict, or a death sentence, they had come to trust one another as far as that was possible in their jobs.

(When glasses were lifted in Jean's restaurant on California Avenue and 25th Place to toast a death sentence, Nash had discreetly held his. He considered this the prosecutors' family ritual for the emotional support of the two assistant state's attorneys who had to ask for the latest death sentence. Unexpectedly, the criminals sentenced to death in those days were never executed.)

Both Nash and Bryce had always been amused by the society around them. Yet, early on, each had been glad to see the other committed to this society as something for which they both assumed responsibility—even while they joked.

Bryce had wound up with substantial status and influence in his line of work; yet, Nash was sometimes surprised to hear Bryce wish for Nash's influence. They talked to each other regularly, mostly about business, long after Nash left Criminal Courts, and saw each other once or twice a year. The two men had, in a mature sense, grown up together for 12 years. On the few occasions when both the Nashes and the Bryces were together, their wives got along and respected one another. Nash had wanted to invite Bryce to his children's christening parties. In fact, he had fleetingly considered making Bryce the godfather to one of his children. But Nash drew the line there.

One never knew.

The "kill" button required two hits to erase a story. After sitting a while watching the screen flash, Nash reached forward and hit a different button which negated the "kill" message. The screen became steady again; the story waited unchanged. He rolled the story back to the top and typed his name on it. It needed a byline. The he hit the "end" button and sent the story to the city desk.

31

On the way to the elevators after the last of the editors' questions and the compulsory rearrangement of paragraphs (the editors highlighted the inconsistencies in Mrs. Ryan's statements), Nash felt empty and almost pathologically detached.

He had called Kate just before leaving and had wondered if he should tell her to buy a big bottle of whiskey before he got home. That would not do, he decided. Maybe he should buy flowers, he thought. The Sheraton, which was renamed the Hotel Continental, and the Marriott, both of which were just north of the river, had little flower shops, and he considered that there was a chance one of the shops would still be open.

In the hallway to the elevators, he noticed he was walking alongside Bob Wolfram which struck him for an instant as strange because Wolfram started at 7:30 a.m. and should have been long gone. Nash had no desire for small talk, and Wolfram was fortunately, and uncharacteristically silent, so they ignored one another. When they got on the elevator, they could not help looking at each other, and the silence became strained.

"Have a nice day?" said Wolfram with a slightly sarcastic smile.

"No," said Nash, thinking Wolfram worked the damn desk and had to know what was going on. Nash hoped Wolfram would say something like, "I know what you mean," and the discussion would fade away.

"Aren't you going to ask me if I had a nice day?" said Wolfram.

"No," said Nash quietly. The doors closed. No one else was on the elevator. Nash shrugged his shoulders as if he had something on his mind. He thought he knew what Wolfram was trying to do. Wolfram was going to make some complaint about something rotten that had happened to him; and he would make it in a funny way so they would both share a laugh; and he'd kid Nash out of his funk. You'll have to carry it off yourself, Bob. I cannot play right now, was the way Nash felt.

"They finally made me feel like a nigger," asserted Wolfram.

Nash was watching the floor numbers descend to 1. He slid his eyes down and to the left to see Wolfram without looking directly at him. He didn't want to look directly at him. Get me out of here, thought Nash. He said, "Oh," tonelessly.

"They treat me like a nigger so I guess I should feel like a nigger, right?"

"I don't know, Bob," said Nash, shrugging again, shaking his head. The doors opened. Nash was fairly confident Wolfram would just drop the subject. A black man couldn't talk to a white man about being a nigger. The white man could not be expected to understand it. Nash was waiting for Wolfram to say something like, "Yeah, you *don't* know. Well, I'll see you." They had both stepped out of the elevator. The door to the street was a little to the left, and Nash was waiting for Wolfram to lead.

"You want to have a drink?" said Wolfram.

Nash closed his eyes and grimaced. He opened his eyes because he knew he was not being polite. "I can't, Bob."

The look on Wolfram's face was hurt, but it appeared to stem from something earlier and more consequential. There was something about Wolfram's eyes that Nash recognized from interviewing black men who had been laid off, and black men who were looking for work, if they were vulnerable, not hostile. It was a combination of fear and pain and the question, "Do you see me?"

Or maybe it was that combination plus the fact that the whites of his eyes were a little tan.

"Hey, forget it, Sam," said Wolfram. "You got your own problems. It was a poor idea to talk to. . .somebody like you. But if you change your mind, I'll buy the first round. I could really use somebody to complain to, and you're about it right now."

Nash guessed Wolfram meant the lobby was empty except for the two of them. Nash was well known to be easy to persuade in the matter of drinking. Nash and Wolfram were not bosom pals, more like good office friends, but they had drank together quite a few times over the years.

"Bob, I apologize. Let me have a rain check. I'm not all here."

"I told you not to worry about it," said Wolfram. Wolfram turned away and walked toward the revolving doors.

Nash took a deep breath, felt better for having refused, and watched Wolfram's back. That's best. Let him leave, he thought.

After Nash stepped out the door onto Michigan Avenue, he noticed Wolfram had turned north which was where Nash was going anyway. Wolfram had obviously reached out. Moreover, Nash felt he could not just dog Wolfram's footsteps like a gumshoe.

"Wolfram. . .WOLFRAM. Where are you going?"

"The Goat's," said Wolfram, turning only half around and continuing to walk.

"Well, wait up. I'll walk with you."

Wolfram did not stop, but Nash caught up with him in front of a Chinese carry out place. Nash said, "I'm going this way. So now, if we could avoid all talk of 'niggers'. . ."

Wolfram gave him a funny look and said with suspicion, "I'll keep it to myself."

"Save it for somebody who can relate to it." Nash did not know if he was being terminally insensitive or simply making conversation. He knew it was one or the other, but he was too tired to analyze it. "So, what - in - the - hell happened to you?" A strong north wind was going down Nash's neck, and he adjusted his scarf. Wolfram had his hands in his coat pockets and his collar up. They walked rapidly and talked intermittently.

"I have worked nights. I have worked days. I've worked general assignment and two of the beats," said Wolfram. "I've been here 10 years, right? At the paper?"

"If you say so. I don't know." They walked for a time.

"That Polish chick has been here maybe four years," said Wolfram after a while.

"Polish chick?" asked Nash.

"Polish chick. Krolikowski."

"Oh. Okay. Six years. I can swear to that. She started when she was 23. Now she's 29. And she's one of the best reporters we've got." Nash had to talk loudly because the wind pushed his voice behind him almost before he could hear it himself.

"Sure. I'll give her that. But so what? She had never worked the desk. A couple weekends, maybe." They walked along. Nash had not the faintest idea where this conversation was going, and he began to get distracted with his own thoughts. Wolfram was speaking again. "I have put in four years on that desk, all in the same spot, the same chair, assistant to Miller."

"Why were you in the office this late?" asked Nash who wanted to get to the point.

"Solomon made me wait," said Wolfram over the wind and the traffic. "It was demeaning."

"Solomon asked you to stay, and then he made you sit around?"

"No. Staying was my idea. I wanted to see him. But he made me wait two and a half hours . . . as if I was some guy off the street looking for a job. The motherfucker!"

Wolfram rarely swore, so Nash knew this was significant and tried to stir himself. "Two and a half hours? That's against the law. You got a good gripe, Bob." They were on the bridge over the river where the wind was always the worst. Nash knew the time from 3:30 or 4 p.m. when Wolfram got off, until 6 or 7 p.m., was the busiest time for the day shift editors. They had all their meetings, pondered the future of the world, and made all their decisions, some of which were blessedly ignored or changed by the night shift editors. This time crunch was partly why Solomon had done what he had done, Nash imagined, but still, Nash considered this behavior uncalled for. They passed the midpoint of the bridge. "What did you want to see him about?"

"Do we work at the same place?"

Nash thought he must have missed something. He was having difficulty concentrating. "I don't know. Just talk."

"I wanted an explanation of why Krolikowski was named the new night city editor instead of me. And he made me wait two and a half hours!"

The bridge railing was very cold. He should have put on his gloves, he thought. Then Nash realized he had touched the railing to help support himself while walking, because he felt he needed to, for the first time that he could remember. He took a long step to cover up the fault in his gait. He continued to walk, but his mind had come to a stop, and his inner atmosphere was motionless and watchful the way nature is during certain hours in the spring, waiting to see if there is going to be a tornado.

"Tell me about that, Bob," he said evenly.

"Let's continue this downstairs at the bar. It's too damn cold," said Wolfram. Wolfram began walking very rapidly and Nash kept up with him. They didn't say much. When they were half way to the stairs leading to lower Michigan Avenue, Wolfram said, "Man, it will be good to see the warm weather come, won't it?"

330

"Yeah, it will," said Nash absently. By the time they started down the stairs, Nash had pretty much decided what had happened. But he had to hear Wolfram say it. The Billy Goat was a newsman's tavern just off lower Michigan Avenue. The underground level is close to the natural level of the downtown area which the city fathers lifted up over the former swamp.

Wolfram ordered draft beer in a stein and a shot of Wild Turkey "for heat." Nash ordered a glass of ginger ale.

"Ginger ale?" asked Wolfram.

"I can't stay long."

"You could at least have a beer."

"I don't want one. Do we really have a new night city editor?"

"Yeah. The story is that Phelan got in a fight with Simonet over your story last night and gave Simonet a lecture on how to be newsman. So Simonet pulled the rug out. I understand it's not the first time they've had disagreements. This time Simonet really stepped on his own dick by printing your story over Phelan's objections. Sorry."

"That's okay." Nash had lit a cigarette and was staring at the glowing tip.

"So I guess Simonet figured somebody had to pay, and it wasn't going to be him. Phelan may be given a job with the Sunday editors." (Sunday editors worked Monday to Friday putting together the Sunday paper.) Wolfram had downed his shot and ordered another one. "I'm really asking for trouble here. You want a shot?"

"No. I'll just stick with this." Nash indicated his ginger ale. Wild Turkey was 100 proof, and the thought of it made Nash's mouth water. "I'll get this one, Bob."

Wolfram pushed Nash's money away with the palm of his hand, but Nash insisted, a little too forcefully. John the bartender, a dark haired Greek who openly liked some customers and disliked others, and who was liked even by many of those he disliked, was a little younger than Nash. He gave Nash a sideways glance and said, "Now Wolfram, you bought him a fuckin' ginger ale when he walked in. And Nash wants to buy you a shot of 100 proof Wild

Turkey in exchange. That's a fair trade. I think you better let him."
John sounded as if he were talking out the side of his mouth even
when he wasn't. Nash had accused him of cultivating this talent.

"He's bought me a lot more drinks than I've bought him," said
Nash, referring to Wolfram.

"This is true," said the bartender, nodding. Nash and the bartender and Wolfram had known each other for years, and the bartender had a pretty good idea of the overall score.

Nash pushed forward his money again with his right hand, restraining Wolfram with his left, and the bartender took it. This
small disturbance brought attention to them. A man to Nash's right,
where the bar curved into an L shape near the front door, said,
"Nash, that was a hell of a story you had this morning. I wanted it
to stand up, and I wanted that bitch, Ryan, to take a fall. What happened?"

Nash looked at him. He knew the man, and he knew he worked
for the Post, but he could not remember his name. For no good reason, Nash wanted to pick the man up and bang his head on the
floor to see what sound it made. Nash gazed at him, pondering this,
savoring the real possibility. Finally, speaking only as loud as was
necessary for this individual to hear him, Nash said, "Takes time."

The bartender's ears had perked up. He read all the papers every
day; he watched the news on television; and he listened to it across
the bar. He understood it. Nash saw him walk over to the man from
the Post and say, "Have another beer, Rich, you're slowin' down."
He took Rich's beer mug, which was half full, and Rich grabbed it
back.

"I'm not done, John."

John grabbed an empty mug from under the bar and put it under
a tap. "I'll fill you up another one, asshole. I really like you, Rich. I
call everybody asshole, don't I, all you assholes?" He looked at six
or seven people sitting and standing at the bar who nodded in agreement.

"Yeah, you asshole, you do," said somebody.

"So have another one, Rich," said John, setting down the over-flowing mug. "Whaddya owe me now, about five bucks?" He toyed with Rich's money on the bar.

"I don't owe you anything, John. I didn't even order this," said Rich.

"Yeah? How's your midlife crisis, Rich?"

Rich laughed. "Funny you should bring that up," he said, and he began to tell an anecdote.

I have to get out of here and go home, thought Nash, fully aware that the bartender had saved him. Nash was boiling inside, but he intended to keep the lid on that. He decided to ask Wolfram one more question to let him talk.

"So, you gonna quit, Bob?" Nash said, looking at the surface of the bar.

"I don't know. Solomon's story was they had to appoint a woman because Sally Bernstein got dumped. But if that's the excuse, they should have appointed a woman to Bernstein's job. Sam, I never felt this way before, but I feel like a case study, the token...minority person...who gets appointed to the lowest rung of management and is left there. And I don't want to think that way. It doesn't appeal to me. I resent being made to think that. I want to be judged on what I do or don't do, and let's have it on the table. Explanations. White people get that consideration.... Then, of course, there's Phelan. Man, did he get the shaft, from what I've heard."

Nash was still staring at the bar, rigid. Despite trying not to, he was thinking about Simonet's demotion of Phelan rather than simply listening. He said, "This guy has got to be a fucking pervert! Simonet wears little girls' dresses, Wolfram. I know it! The cocksucker. The stupid, manicured, evil motherfucker." Nash turned his head to look past Wolfram at the television high up behind the bar, looking for some outlet for his steam. The television was off.

"Take it easy," said Wolfram. "If you could see yourself right now, you're overdoing the idea of being white. How's your scary old lady with the cute voice? Or shouldn't I bring that up, either?"

Nash was about to answer the question and switch to a better topic when someone said, "Hey, Nash! How you gonna handle Mrs. Ryan?" This was a voice from the other side of Wolfram. Nash did not recognize it, but the man got off his stool and stood on the bar step so Nash could see him. It was a thin man with beard stubble and yellow teeth who either was or used to be with the Ledger.

"You had what I thought was one of the great phony-fucking stories this morning, Nash. But Ryan came up with an even greater and phonier-fucking story than you did. Everybody wiretaps everybody. And she's pretending she just discovered it. She makes Bryce out to be Dick Nixon. You gonna go her one better?"

Nash turned away and stared at the liquor bottles on the wall, not really seeing them, simply trying to ignore his questioner.

"You're not gonna let her get away with it, are you?" said the standing man. "I think you could come up with a whole string of crimes in state mental hospitals. It's been done before."

"Shadup and sit down. I don't allow people to stand on that step," said John the bartender. "They fall off and sue somebody."

"I really think Bryce is gonna be Chicago's Dick Nixon," said the same man whom Nash continued to ignore. Nash's jaw muscles were working although his mouth was tightly closed. "The lady makes it out to be a big deal that he tapped a cop killer's phone, and every reporter in town picks it up like this is a real scandal."

"Wait until they lose the case," said someone else in a sober voice. It sounded to Nash like Julian Petrocelli of the Post, but Nash did not look around.

"They're not going to lose the case," said another voice with confidence, a low, easily identifiable voice. It was Larry Epstein, a television reporter. "Nobody is going to let Hawkins go no matter what happens," Epstein continued. "I guarantee you. They may have to run him over with a Sheriff's bus by accident, but they're not going to let him go."

The conversation swirled briefly around the same topic until the man who brought up the Nixon comparison apparently stood up again, as Nash judged by the direction from which his voice came.

"Nash, you did the public a great favor. First we had your charges. Then we had Madame Ryan's charges. Now if Bryce will just go on TV and make *his* charges, this could be one of those great weeks in Chicago journalism. Everybody accusing everybody. Journalism lives! I'll drink to your health, Nash."

Nash looked up and to the left and stared at the man while feeling a sort of dangerous pleasure within, an anticipation.

Wolfram, who was watching Nash closely, used a wrist movement and his thumb to point to the man to his left two stools down. He said, "John, who is this asshole?"

"You're right, Wolfram," said the bartender loudly as he filled a clean stein. Gazing at the loudmouth, the bartender said, "You are an asshole, buddy. I mean that in the pejorative sense. I told you not to stand on that step. You violated that rule twice. Now sit down and shut up for good, or I'll toss your ass outta here."

"Sam, what are you going to do from your end? What are we going to read in the morning Chronicle?" It was Laura Berndock asking. A relative silence ensued around Nash. The rest of the Billy Goat, a medium sized restaurant and bar serving principally hamburgers and beer, was filled with people eating, drinking, and talking at tables.

From the silence, Nash knew he had to speak. He imagined himself pushing back from the bar and simply walking away and out the door, but it would be so dramatic, he couldn't bring himself to do it. And he wasn't sure he could walk easily. His muscles were stretched so tight, they were vibrating like guitar strings. He could leap, but could he walk?

He said nothing. But where he had been leaning forward, he sat up straight with his head erect and his chin up and he rested his forearms lightly on the rim of the bar, waiting. Then he felt at ease, in a way, and his inner atmosphere became still again.

"I got a great TV shot to end this thing," said the obnoxious man. "A helicopter lands on Bryce's front lawn, and he and his wife and kids board it—with bags over their heads—and leave town forever."

Nash visualized Bryce's kids against his will. The oldest boy was fat and smart, but spoiled. The daughter was a skinny girl with glasses who could run very fast, according to her parents. The little boy was the little boy. The daughter always shook Nash's hand as if she were an adult.

Nash got what he was waiting for. He let the stool slide out between his legs and started turning to the left as soon as his feet touched the floor, all in one motion. Wolfram grabbed him in a hug around the shoulders. At the same time, someone pushed Nash back into the bar, throwing him off balance because the stool was in front of him. Nash struggled to find his feet, not in the least disuaded. He got himself to the right of his stool and knocked it over with his left hip so he had a place to stand. A big person kept insistently pushing him from behind trying to pin him to the bar. With his left arm, Nash cleared Wolfram off his barstool, which was easy because Wolfram was leaning over to hold Nash. As Wolfram fell, he maintained his hug, the weight threatening to pull Nash over backwards, but Nash leaned forward and started toward the obnoxious man, pulling along Wolfram and whoever had been behind who grabbed Nash around the midsection.

These small hindrances were to be expected. Nash's mind was quite clear. It was white in its clarity, and the hindrances were low level, background static. Nash shoved Wolfram's barstool out of the way which fell over accidentally. On the next stool was another drinker who had swiveled sideways to see what the commotion was. Confronting Nash, the anonymous drinker was momentarily paralyzed. Then he jumped off his stool and scampered into the table section. Nash knocked over that stool, the last obstacle, and pulling his entourage advanced toward the obnoxious man. Nash felt bodily memories of having done this before. (It was teenage football, but

Nash was not conscious of that.) The obnoxious man looked to Nash as if he were pleased with the developments. He was getting attention. Nash seized the man's throat in his right hand and tried to bring up his left to grasp the body, but somebody was holding his left arm, so Nash squeezed with his right hand to keep hold of his object. The obnoxious man's eyes showed shock, and by heaving himself away, he fell off his barstool. At the same time, Nash felt a new arm around his own head and neck, the forearm bone like a pipe against his chin, pulling his head well backwards. They're going to hurt me, Nash realized, or his body did, and blood flow and adrenalin rose to a maximum.

"Not his head, damnit! You'll break his neck!"

It was Wolfram's voice, the first sounds that had registered on Nash since he stood up. The forearm that had pulled Nash's head back was released, but suddenly the arms around his chest and stomach gave a mighty heave and Nash felt himself falling backward, with his right hand still extended to grip the throat that had got away. Nash knew he would land on top, and he was even more angry than before.

As soon as he landed, hearing shouts of pain and exertion, banging of bodies, and a woman's scream, Nash felt the grips loosen and he prepared to get up, throwing his elbows back hard.

"Geez!"

"What the fuck!"

He tried to rise from the waist, his blood pumping, his mind still cleanly, clearly seeking the obnoxious man, and somebody seized his shirt collar from behind, choking him. "Sam, he's too old!" This was Wolfram's voice. Nash threw himself to his left to turn over and face whoever was choking him, but somebody had seized his right arm. So he threw himself the other way with more success and found no one except the retreating feet of someone who had been on the floor with him. The person who was choking him and holding his right arm had been under him on the left. Nash had eluded the hand in his collar, but somebody knelt on his back, and somebody else clamped his right arm again. His left arm was jammed against the bar with nothing to hit. He could hear Wolfram's voice saying, "Go easy. Go easy." Nash felt this was not directed at him. Nash started to rise, lifting the person on his back; then someone grabbed his feet, and this annoyed Nash because he knew if he started kicking and searching for this person's head, he could kick the guy's face in. He did not know who it was, so he had to control himself, although his blood and adrenalin continued to pump.

"Get off! Get off!" growled Nash.

"Let him cool down first."

"Get off or I'm gonna throw you off. And get that guy outta here."

"Let him up—slowly." That was Wolfram. "They're escorting him out, Sam."

As Nash stood up, Laura Berndock was screaming, "You shit heads! You big jerks!" She was brushing her clothes, so Nash assumed she had got knocked down. Three barstools had fallen over, and a beer had been spilled on a table near the struggle causing a young couple, who had to leave their chairs, to look indignant.

"That's it, folks," said John the bartender loudly. "It's all just fun. Next show is at 9 o'clock. We call it improvisational violence."

Nash was in no mood for the humor. His mind had lost its clean edge. His anger had become disorganized and pointed in several directions; and the adrenalin was eating him up because he couldn't use it. Seeing his eyes, Epstein said, "You sure he's all right? Give him a drink."

"Gimme a shot," said Nash, visibly trembling all over. He felt fear, too, because his heart was banging too hard, and he knew he was way out of shape.

"Sam, don't you think you should stick to ginger ale, seriously?" said the bartender. No one present knew Nash was on the wagon.

"Gimme a shot, John!"

"Give him a double," said Wolfram.

"And gimme a roll of Certs," Nash added. These words were

hardly audible because Nash was losing his voice with the effort to control his emotions.

. . . .

At 10 p.m., Georgia Krolikowski was busily rewriting a story about the City Council that she had considered poorly written earlier but had been forced to send along due to deadline pressure. The version she disliked would be in the main, home delivery edition, but the new, improved version on which she was working would run in the 4-star and 5-star which accounted for some home delivery and all street sales. She had skipped her lunch, and she was very hungry, but she also felt pride and determination. Solomon had told her that her lofty promotion was provisional, but he added that it could become permanent if she showed an aptitude.

"Some very good reporters make terrible editors, Georgia. And some mediocre reporters make pretty good editors," Solomon had said, adding, "The only way to tell is to try it."

Krolikowski had vaguely considered becoming an editor on the few weekends that she had worked the desk to cover someone's vacation. The idea grew dim as soon as she got away from the desk. But her ambition to be a success and be promoted to something, anything, was even stronger than her desire to get off nights. When Solomon offered, she jumped. She felt bad for Phelan, but she knew that was entirely separate from her.

An hour earlier, the copy desk had howled because she had held almost all the new, 3-star stories until the last minute, and she now realized that was a big mistake. She had wanted to carefully read and rewrite almost everything, but she spent too much time on a few stories, and the rest simply sat in the city desk file in the computer while nervous copy editors a few yards away prayed for the return of Phelan, sometimes aloud.

The copy clerk on the switchboard announced a call for the desk, and she grabbed the phone. The next deadline was an hour and a half away.

"City desk."

"This is Sgt. Mitchell of the 18th District," said the caller, who, Krolikowski noted, was black. "Do you have a reporter named Nash, Samuel Nash."

"Yes, sergeant."

"Do you happen to know where is now?"

"No, sergeant. I could take a message. He left a long time ago."

"I will tell you where he is. He is in this district on a charge of disorderly conduct, and perhaps a few other things if he doesn't calm down. I am telling you this as a courtesy."

She was caught by surprise, and Krolikowski had mixed emotions about Nash which made her initial response confused.

She had known Nash for a long time, and she joked and flirted with him regularly. (Flirting was as natural as walking to Krolikowski.) She respected his abilities, and he hers, and as reporters, they were capable of working well together. Their shifts dovetailed; and sometimes Nash worked late or Krolikowski came in early and they were assigned to the same story. She occasionally caught herself studying him intently while they conferred. When Nash noticed her doing it, he would sparkle but nevertheless carry on almost as if nothing had happened—until Krolikowski wondered if anything had. Once in a while, more rarely, she caught him looking at her. At such times she would either ignore him, or, do the reverse, catch him with an all-knowing glance of her own (which said, "I beg your pardon, buster?"). Or she might plop down on his desk and show some leg or flounce her hair outrageously until Nash retreated, laughing and shaking his head. But Nash never followed up on his study of her or her own study of him. And, since Nash was 10 years older and must be more wise than she was, she decided this was Nash's way of kidding around on the square. Because it seemed best, and because she did not want any more inner complications, she avoided touching him which was made easier by the fact that Nash avoided touching her.

Immediately upon hearing that he was under arrest, Krolikowski understood he was drunk and why. She thought, Sam, you jerk. And she also thought, You're going to mess me up here.

Calmly, she said, "Gee, we're very sorry, sergeant. Is he all right?"

"If he was all right, I wouldn't be calling you."

Wrong way to start. She detected her thinking was inefficient because of her feelings about Nash which interfered with her normal practicality. She had seen Phelan help Chronicle employees in trouble. She decided she had to do this right. Otherwise, people would say, "If Phelan had been on the desk. . . ."

"Sorry again, sergeant. What did he do and how can we take him off your hands?"

"He was crossing Rush Street on Illinois Street, and he erroneously thought a car had gone through the stop sign endangering his person. He got in a dispute with the occupants of the vehicle, and the occupants, three young men, got out to remove his head. Fortunately, one of our squads was in the vicinity. The officers restrained all the parties. The officers were prepared to release Mr. Nash, but he became abusive. He also could not explain exactly where he was going. He was either looking for his car or walking to the subway. He also said something about a flower shop. He has become a pain in the butt here; and the arresting officers have performed beyond the call of duty."

"I apologize for the newspaper and for Mr. Nash, sergeant. He is normally a good man. I don't know how this could have happened. He's drunk, I take it, and we apologize for that, too. What is his bond?"

"Oh, yes, ma'am. He's drunk. Right now it's fifty dollars on the disorderly. One of the young men here is attempting to press charges of criminal damage to property. Something about denting the side of the auto. If we decide to allow this charge, that will be another hundred. Mr. Nash, of course, has only the change in his pockets, as near as we can determine, so we will have to lock him up. He has earned it, Miss, and he is earning it more every minute. I'm inclined to allow the further charge."

"I see." Krolikowski felt this was a challenge to her ability. She had to say something right away to divert him. Speaking "man to man," she said, "Sergeant, Nash's behavior is unforgiveable. He had a very tough day here, but still, this kind of behavior is always hard to understand. I'm sure nothing like this ever happened to you."

A little too strong, she thought.

"That's not the point, Miss. Aww, shit. All right. Just get him out of here, Miss. I want him *out*."

"I'm sending someone immediately. Thank you very much, sergeant."

"Think nothing of it."

"Sarge...take care of him for me, wouldja?"

"Miss, you have a bit of a problem. But I will, as best I can."

When she hung up the phone, Krolikowski figured she would have to send over $150 just to be sure. She had only $30 herself. She could get the whole amount out of the safe. She had the combination now. But that would require a written explanation. Do it the way Phelan did. Where did he start? She got out of her chair. Phelan started with the local copy desk, she remembered. As soon as she thought of it, she knew this was right. She knew the copy editors would respond. Why was that?

She approached the local copy desk and stood between two people on the rim, a man and a woman, but spoke to all of them. Some were eating lunch at their posts.

"Ummmm, excuse me, one of our troops..."

This got their attention.

"...has been stricken, and is now at the 18th District. I need $150 to bail this party out. I can put up twenty-five. I'd rather not say who it is."

"No, you shouldn't, dear," said a gray haired man on the rim.

The older ones reached for their wallets immediately, and the younger ones followed.

32

"Well, how have you been, Victoria?"

"I don't know, doctor. I still get sick. I think somebody has planted something in my brain, an electrode, you know? They want to make me do things. Somebody's listening to my thoughts. Right now, they know I'm here, and they know what I'm saying, and they know what you're saying. And they're watching me to see how I act. A couple of the patients are part of this, I think. They're not really patients. You tell me this is my illness. Everybody says that. But I don't know. Are you in the Secret Service?"

"Have you stopped taking your medicine?"

"I did. I get tired of it, doctor. I want to take cocaine just to fool them. They didn't know I stopped, except some of them did. I just started taking it again, but I pretend I don't. Even the ones who are watching me are not sure. I don't want them to know. But now that I've told you, they know. I may stop. Or I may not stop. How was your vacation?"

"It was fine. Restful, a little. I want you to take your medicine. You have to be responsible about that. Don't you find you feel better when you take your medicine?"

"I hate it. Did you see the President? I knew John Lennon, and my 22½ per cent of a pizza; if he didn't tell me, how could I know they wanted me to swing the swing too high? She killed my big brother; and somehow the truth is the mind's equation with my dog, many things. A hundred thousand dollar contract on my life by the President...."

"I'm not in the Secret Service, Victoria. You're getting nervous. Take it easy. I don't know the President. He doesn't know me, or you. He doesn't think about us at all. He's not doing anything to you."

"I know."

"I want you to take your medicine."

"It's no good. They've done something to it. They've spiked it. Senator O'Brien took my baby. He's not the father, but my dog is my baby in the New Right, and so they want to stop me, make me altruistically Orangemen, lest any man should think, turn on their data fuse...."

"Why do you say something is wrong with your medicine? Stop that other talk for the moment. I need to know about why you stopped taking your medicine. Your medicine is very helpful. It works well for many people. You think there is something wrong with it? Is that why you quit taking your medicine?"

"There's a man at Northwestern who knows Rockefeller and the nuclear environment and the radios. Not the dead Rockefeller..., or maybe him...."

"Victoria, tell me about your medicine. Relax. It's okay. Tell me about your medicine."

"It made me sick, too. You shot somebody. I saw the gun. I saw you dragging him. But I'm sick. They operated on my brain."

"Your brain has never been operated on, Victoria. I promise. Now listen to me. If you think I shot somebody, you're wrong.

Okay? But being wrong is not the same as having delusions. You just made a simple mistake. You saw something and heard something that made you think that. Your perceptions were...probably working all right. But you came to the wrong conclusion. People do that all the time. It's normal. *I* did not shoot anybody, Victoria. At the same time, bad things do happen. I won't deny that. Your medicine is good for you. You need it. It does NOT give you delusions. Do you understand?"

"Did you shoot somebody?"

"No, I told you. Get it out of your head that I did that. I'm a doctor. I'm sorry if events have hurt you and made you confused. I truly am."

"Nelson Rockefeller began the myth of empire, and 20,000 Olympics went up in a suggestion, whereas...."

"Victoria. Stop a second. I think you've been drinking coffee, honey. You shouldn't drink coffee. Now remember when you told me your father cheated on your mother? If he really did, your father never told your mother because that was his secret. Well, I have secrets, too. We all do. It's natural."

"I used to play with myself in second grade. Masturbate."

"Maybe you did. I don't know. I don't always know when you're telling me the truth, Victoria. But you understand that I can have a few secrets, too."

"Yeah."

"What happened that day in the hallway, I'm not at liberty to discuss. That's the way it is. But I don't want my silence to hurt you, Victoria. Maybe we can go over what you saw and how you feel about it. Remember your medicine is not spiked. It helps you think about things clearly. Have you talked to other people about this?"

"I told my friend, two of my friends."

"Are your friends here?"

"No. I called them on the phone."

"You did? Oh boy, oh boy. That explains it. Well..., you're a free person. I hope you didn't tell them that I shot anybody."

"I don't remember exactly. Can I talk to my friends again? They keep taking the phone away from me."

"I'll bet. I'll look into that, Victoria. Let's say it's probably best that you should talk about this with me. But, uh . . . you are a free person. Tell me what bothered you about it. I'm sure it was very upsetting."

33

"Hey! Hey, stay awake, you dummy. Sit up. Sit up, Sam!"

Nash felt a hand pulling on the back of his head, trying to lift him up, but he could not understand what the emergency was, and he slipped his head off the hand, and pushed the hand away roughly when it pulled his head again.

"Oh. Sam! Damnit! SAM, YOU GET UP or I'm going to dump something on you!"

"What is the matter?" said Nash. "Geez." He opened his eyes and saw his wife standing over him, looking severe, not at all nice, disgusted. He wasn't even sure where he was.

In a sudden crash of fear, he knew he had done something terribly wrong, irretrievably wrong, foul, perhaps killed someone, run over a child with his car. He was terrified because he didn't know what he had done, but something inside said it was worse than ever.

He sat up abruptly and swung his legs to the floor; his head began banging; the organs of his body were shifted hard and they shouted; he was temporarily blinded. There was pain, but that was not the problem. What was it?

He had done something. He had his hands on his knees, his head was down, and his equilibrium was reeling.

"What did I do?" he said.

"You got drunk and got arrested."

"No." He shook his head.

"No!? You are still drunk! You smell like beer. You can't even wake up."

"That's not it."

"That *is* it. Have you lost your mind?"

"No. Shut up!" He waved at her to be quiet, and he strained his mind to think. "Oh. Aaahhhh." He put his hand in front of his face. His sight had returned. He realized he was sitting on the couch in the living room of his house. But he didn't want to see. He knew now. "Oh, shit. Awwww, gee. Awww, fuck! I can't believe it." As bad as his mistakes were and their effects on others, Nash's perceptions of them were also magnified several times over by alcohol-induced depression. He started as if to pound the couch with his hand in a fist, but he stopped and was paralyzed with emotional pain and clenched his fist so tight he hurt his hand in the squeezing. His body compressed into itself and became as small as it could from the weight of the thing pushing down on him, and his mind told him he should never go out again, he should be dead.

He had done in his friend.

He had done in two of his friends, Bryce and Phelan.

The media barrage against Bryce would go on four or five days, Nash knew, without even thinking about it. In such times of great stress, politicians leaned on their supporters to hear that they were still wonderful and the newspapers sucked. But Nash knew nobody cheered a slightly known bureaucrat under attack. Bryce would be alone. And I started this, Nash said to himself. Out of a desire to win a Pulitzer Prize, or some big prize. Of all the childish....And when the story turned on Bryce, I turned on him, too. Well, we both knew that might happen some day. That was business. . . .

But rights and wrongs were much clearer in the office than they were at home. Sitting on his couch, he could not be sure which took precedence, his job or friendship. He felt he might have decided wrong.

Nash also had a picture of what was in store for Phelan, self-doubt on Phelan's face and in his bearing, fear of being old. Nash had seen it before when middle-aged guys got demoted. The reasons didn't matter.

Kate, too, he had hurt very deeply. But she was part of him, and she had agreed to pay for his mistakes while other people got caught by surprise.

"Hey, I'm sorry, baby," he said.

"Sorry?" Her tone was incredulous. "I'm sorry, too, Sam. You should see yourself. I'm sorry for a lot of things. Very sorry."

"What do you want?" he said.

"What do you mean, 'What do I want?'?"

"Right here! Right now! You're standing there with your coat on prepared to tell me something. Tell me. That's all I mean." He wanted to go back to sleep. Then Nash remembered his behavior as a drunken jerk in the police station the night before, like all the drunken jerks wearing suits and ties he had seen in police stations over the years who wanted the world to know they were too important to be arrested. Suddenly, Nash was one of them.

He tried to expand his memory to take in all the things he had done in one day to see if there was a limit to them, an end, so that he had it all. Meanwhile, Kate began to explain in a hostile voice about taking Bobby to the doctor; and the babysitter's husband's car wouldn't start so she had to drive her husband to work; and Kim couldn't sit still in the doctor's office so it would be best if she stayed home; and was Nash in any condition. . . ?

Nash felt growing dismay and confusion caused by too much going on inside and outside simultaneously. What the hell was she talking about?

He became enraged, partly from a chemical reaction almost beyond his control. He suppressed it with great effort. As part of this forceful suppression, he agreed to everything, whatever, and he laid back down and fell asleep.

. . . .

Forty-five minutes later.

"Daddy. Daddy. Daddy." He heard that word over and over in his dream. Then he realized a small hand on his temple was pushing his head back and forth and he wasn't dreaming. His daughter was saying his name cautiously but with childish determination.

"What do you want, dear?" he said without opening his eyes.

"Mrs. Gant is here."

The babysitter, he thought. Wrong name, but things were complicated, and he hadn't paid any attention. He was relieved to realize he was covered with a blanket. That was new. Was he dressed? He felt his trousers with his hand. Yes. But he was embarassed to face the sitter. Couldn't she simply take Kim? Say, "Let's go, dear."? Things had to stop happening. Nothing should be going on. He opened his eyes.

"Excuse me, ma'am. Have you come for Kim?" He was looking at an old lady with white hair in a black babushka, a black cloth coat and black slacks. She had a pale, wrinkled face. He had seen her in the neighborhood.

"No, I have not, mister. Why should I? What's wrong with you?" she said in a thin, hostile voice.

"Aren't you the sitter?"

"No. I live at the end of this block." She pointed to the south end. "I can't stay in all day. I may be an old lady, but I need to walk. Your sidewalk is terrible. I have to walk here to get to the bus. Your walk is all cracked up, and I could fall, Mr. . . . . . Nash, isn't it? And you don't shovel your snow, you. Why don't you shovel your snow

350

and get your sidewalk fixed? Can't you have some consideration for other people?"

"Madame, why are you here? You're in my house." He was clutching his blanket at his chin, and it occurred to him, painfully, that he might be telling a falsehood.

"I thought your wife was here," she said in a crackly voice. He could see she was as surprised by this confrontation as he was, but she was going to say her piece. "I have asked her over and over," she began sideling away toward the front door, "to fix your sidewalk. It's your responsibility, you know."

"It's the city. . . ."

She was near the front door which was only a few feet from the couch, but she turned to face him directly. "Are you the newspaper reporter? Somebody in one of these houses is a newspaper reporter. It's you, isn't it?" She pointed at him like a very old grade school teacher. "Why do you people print all those awful things? That family of that poor girl in Lombard who was murdered. You people torture them. It's all over your front page. And I saw you people on television last night pestering her mother, making her cry. It's terrible. Have you people no decency?"

He had only wanted to sleep. Instead, as if from an injection of an overpowering drug, Nash's rage flooded back. He jumped up, blood hot in his head, eyes wild, and tripped over the blanket but ignored this. For an instant, the old lady shrank back into the alcove for the front door as he covered the distance in three steps; then the old lady stood up to him which was what Nash wanted.

"Lady, youuuu. . . !" He didn't know what obscenity to use. "I have called up a father after his son was killed in a Little League game, and I asked him what the score was and who was on base at the time!" He could feel his steam popping, and it was good. He was only six inches from her face. The old lady's eyes widened.

"That's disgusting!" she screamed back, curling her lip. "Why would you do such a thing?"

"Why? Because it's BASEball, lady. Get it? It's base-ball!!!" He had begun screaming, completely berserk.

"I called up a mother in Nebraska after her son was murdered here. I told her the kid was dead. She didn't know it. Then I asked her what his major was in college and if he played any musical instruments!" He began waving his arms in the air. "I called up a woman 15 minutes after her husband shot himself in the basement, before they'd carried him away. And I asked, 'Had he been feeling bad?' " He said the last dripping with contempt.

"She said he WAS! You euhh...." He still could not think of what to call an old lady, cunt? bitch?

"You're one of those people!" she said.

"Yes, ma'am. I am!"

He yanked open the door and said, "Out! Out! Let's go, lady. Out. Out the door." He let her open the storm door herself. With effort he prevented himself from helping her along with a shove when she gave him one last, revolted look.

When she was gone, he closed the inside door and felt the reaction. He leaned on the door knob, experiencing all over the full weight of a tremendous, overpowering sickness from excess of drink. The effect had been brought to life partly by his emotional exertions, but mostly by his physical exertions in leaping off the couch, confronting Mrs. Gant, and driving her out the door. During his days on the wagon, Nash's body had lost its acquired tolerance for liquor, it's self-defense mechanism. So this time he could feel he had literally poisoned himself. The poison had been absorbed. And every cell and organ and muscle in his body was poisoned, all of them now screaming this fact in their various styles.

On top of this, he was suffering from the after effects of his rage, and a continuing mental depression so heavy it threatened to make him fall to his knees or become unbalanced.

"Kim, don't let anybody else in except your mother or the baby-sitter, okay?"

"Yes, Daddy. Daddy, did you want to scare Mrs. Gant?"

"I scared myself, Kim."

He tried to sleep again, couldn't, and went upstairs and took a shower with his eyes closed, attempting not to think. While drying himself off, he saw a brand new toothbrush still in its box on the sink, and he winced at the thought of Kate standing in the store buying it for him. He used it anyway to get the pastiness out of his mouth. He never even considered shaving or combing his hair. He couldn't remember if he had any clean clothes here and didn't want to look, so he put on the same clothes and started downstairs only to discover the babysitter waiting to take Kim.

"How do you do?" he said.

. . . .

Nash awakened again and heard a voice or voices. He got off the couch, walked to the kitchen doorway, and found his wife talking in Greek on the kitchen wall phone. She hung up as soon as she saw him. On the kitchen clock it was 12:05.

"Who were you talking to?"

"Soula."

Katerina was wearing the same white blouse and blue slacks she had put on to go to the doctor's office. She looked at him, he thought, as if he were an escaped convict.

"Good morning," he said. "You want me to leave?"

He waited. She didn't answer, just looked at him. He padded up to the kitchen table in his bare feet and peered into a grocery bag there.

"Would you like something to eat?" she said in a low voice, slowly, with what he thought was a touch of sarcasm. Her attitude annoyed him. She understood nothing, he said to himself. She was simple minded. A true innocent who thought she was superior but in fact had no idea what was going on in the world. "Do you have any cigarettes?" he said.

"Yes. In the bag."

He rooted around, found the cigarettes, opened them, took one out, walked over to the stove, and lit it using a burner on the stove.

353

The fact that she had bought cigarettes seemed good and mellowed him. She didn't smoke any more—except once. Buying cigarettes for him was friendly.

"Where's Bobby?" he said, turning towards her quickly.

"I took him to school. He seemed much better."

"Good." This meant to Nash that he could smoke, in addition to the fact that his son was better. "Did you call in sick for me?"

"Yes. I called in sick for myself, too."

"Oh, yeah. I forgot."

"No doubt. What happened last night, Sam." She folded her arms.

"What's with Bobby? What did the doctor say?"

"He needs his tonsils out."

"Oh, yeah? That's it? Is that going to cure all this?"

"We hope so. What happened last night, Sam?"

He sat down at the kitchen table and looked at his wife still standing near the phone wearing a severe expression.

"I owe you that, Kate. No question about it. No matter what happens, I owe you that. But it's too fresh. Don't make me stir it up. Seriously. I apologize. I didn't mean for this to happen. It has nothing to do with us." The cigarette was making him feel terrible.

"Oh, I think it does. But tell me what happened when Mrs. Gant was here. She came back again all upset."

He rose from the table, put the tip of the cigarette under the faucet and ran water on it, then threw it in the garbage bag in the cabinet under the sink. He took his time and sat down again.

"It was nothing. She came in here and started to harangue me, and I threw her out."

"She's afraid of what Kim might have heard. Did you call up some woman and tell her her son had been murdered and ask her some ridiculous question?"

"Kate," Nash made a face. "You know what I do. You know how often I used to call up the next of kin at City News. I still do it once

354

in a while. I'm in the same business, and I'm always very nice. That has nothing to do with anything. Forget it."

"You don't inform people of the deaths, Sam. Police do that, or hospitals, before they release the names."

"Nobody's perfect, dear. They screw up once in a blue moon."

"So when did this happen? You never told me about this."

"A few months ago. A year ago. I can't remember." He waved a hand in the air. "The mother decided there was no God, but I convinced her, for the moment, that there was. Took a little while. 'Your son had 20 years of life. I think only God can give that, ma'am.' Not bad, eh?" he asked Kate. Nash immediately felt guilty. "Excuse my attitude," he said to his wife. Then, looking up to the ceiling to ward off lightning, he said, "Excuse my attitude! I really meant it when I said it." He brought his head back down, rested his chin on his hand, noticed he hadn't shaved in a while, and ran his hand over his face finding it interesting.

"What about a boy killed at Little League?"

"Hmmm. She remembered all that?" He was surprised and becoming uncomfortable, and decided he wasn't going to talk about any of this.

"When was it?"

"Within the last two, three years." He wiggled the fingers of one hand indicating uncertainty about the number. "What's the difference?"

"What about the other one? A woman whose husband killed himself?"

He thought for a moment. "Fifteen years ago."

"Fifteen years ago! Why are you bringing that up today?"

"Because the old lady pissed me off." Nash was becoming even more determined not to fish in these waters.

His wife walked to the table and sat down opposite him. It appeared to Nash that she was getting ready to do serious talking and listening. "Tell me about it," she said.

"Kate," he put his hand on his forehead, exasperated. "No. Not now."

Death was an unusual category. People couldn't deal with it unless they dealt with it: death, and the relatives of the dead, and the circumstances of the dead, the descriptions of the dead, the stories of the dead, the pictures of the dead. ("Umm, ma'am, would you have a picture we could borrow?") One day, doing his usual obituary for Wolfram who had trouble getting people to do them, Nash turned to Gentile and said, "Jose, did you ever stop to think how many people are dead? I mean, almost everybody is dead."

"Just how do you intend that, Nash?"

"I mean deceased, passed on."

"Yes..., I suppose that's true."

"That's a lot of people. And here's another one. There's no end to 'em! You and I are truly out of the ordinary, Jose."

Putting together a description of how a person died, from the fire department or the police and others, if the deceased was someone a reporter could identify with and the death had been terrible, was very disquieting at first. During his early period at the City News Bureau, Nash did this so frequently each day for accidents and homicides (to ask the right questions, it was necessary to mentally put himself in the scene and picture it vividly to see if the pieces were accurate) that Nash felt it left a film on him when he was through work, as if he were covered in something. He sometimes looked at his hands. And he wondered how homicide detectives managed who did more than picture things mentally.

Part of the difficulty at City News was being continually notified of the grotesque terror, grief, and misery his fellow citizens inflicted on one another at all hours without letup, in his own town. ("You can imagine what part they cut off first.") The unavoidable message pounded home was that not only were the victims something of himself, but the murderers and maimers, too.

Contacting the relatives of the fresh and potentially newsworthy dead, usually from violence or accidents, was always painful. Reporters, including Nash, rarely volunteered. Nevertheless, Nash once calculated he'd done this task 400 to 600 times.

When he was good, Nash talked to parents as if he were a son or a boy from down the block (much later as another parent); to brothers and sisters, he spoke as someone who also had brothers and sisters; to spouses, he spoke as a friend or a fellow married person. When he was bad, he just asked questions until they hung up. And sometimes he called them back.

When Nash asked the wife of the man who committed suicide if her husband had been feeling bad, he did it to cut the interview short. He offered her an all-purpose motive so she could give it back to him and avoid his delving. "He's been depressed lately," Nash told his editor, taking a miniscule risk there was no real story. He did not often slough the job, but sometimes he did.

When he asked the father of the boy killed in the Little League game what the score was and who was on base at the time, the father had first stated, "He was trying to win the game." Once that was said, as far as Nash was concerned, man to man the father understood what Nash wanted to know, and Nash guessed why the father wanted to tell him. It explained how the boy died, the father's son.

On the night shift at City News, always, and at the Chronicle, periodically, there was so much death and

*deadness and wallowing in it, because no responsible
news organization could ignore it, that Nash adjusted to
most of it as natural and walled up anything indigestible.
Discussions of routine murders between reporters and rewritemen were frequently funny. One Chronicle reporter's favorite line when the knife was still in the body
or the body was shot and in a trunk, was, "Police suspect
foul play." (Murders of children were sometimes exempt
from jokes.) If an outsider seriously challenged this humor, reporters could become hostile. The unspoken response was a suggestion, "You do it."*

*None of this went through Nash's head as he looked at
his wife. As soon as he chose not to discuss the subject or
ruminate about it, it was not there and left no conscious
trace.*

Her right arm was crooked over the top corner of her chair; her
hands were clasped on her hip; and she was staring at him sideways,
threatening him.

"Sam, I think I deserve an explanation. After all...after everything....Whyyyy didn't you come home last night? Don't you *like
it* around here?" The last was more a threat than a question, he
thought, but that was understandable.

He exhaled through his nose. After bouts with the state's attorney,
with himself, with his friends in the Billy Goat, with the 18th District, and with Mrs. Gant, losing four and tying one, and facing a
bout with his wife, Nash was getting punchy. He sank down in his
chair, trying to think. He let his muscles go, hung his head over the
back of the chair, and said, "You're right....I mean no disre-
spect....I don't want to...or I do want...I want something....I
can't. That's it. I can't. If you want better explanations, you'll have
to get a different guy. Most likely you could. Get somebody who has
good explanations, if you can. I mean, if you like. I don't even know

where to begin. By the time I finished, I'd be dead anyway." (He meant this only theoretically.)

"You jerk."

"Hmm?"

"You ass."

"Yes?" His head was still hanging backwards over his chair looking into space.

"Don't you think I could do better than YOU?"

In his depression, Nash considered himself lower than he'd ever been, lower by ten fathoms than when he thought Kate was losing respect for him because he drank and had failed to amount to much. He felt that in the previous 24 hours he had become as big a fool as he was likely to be in his lifetime, in her eyes and in the eyes of others. In this context, she was asking a comical question.

Against logic (he assumed it was the result of being punched silly), a smile welled up; he felt it coming; and when it arrived on his face, it was a grin, and his eyebrows raised up over suddenly twinkling eyes. He would never have believed he was capable of it until it happened. Nash's chair was sideways to the table, and Kate could see the expression on his backward-hanging head.

"What are you laughing at? I could do it today!" She stood up to get away from him.

With his smile growing broader, he said, "I know." He sat up and nodded vigorously in agreement.

"So what's so *damn* funny?" she said in a nasal tone, swinging her hips for emphasis, with her hands on her hips.

His smile started coming from several different sources as he got adjusted in his chair and watched her. It wasn't often Katerina adopted the twang and mannerisms of a tough, teenage girl on the West Side. He knew she had been exposed to that style, when she was relatively new in the U.S., but he could never discover if she had used it herself. By the time he met her, she was a mature 19, the age by which almost all the girls had dropped the hard mouths and the swagger and acted as if they had been young women all along.

359

"I was wondering how much I could get for you," he said.

"Youooo would get jack shit," she said with her hands still on her hips, wagging her head. "I'll make my own deal on my own terms, and I'll collect." She pointed to her chest. (Yep, she would, he said to himself.) "You, Nash, will be the first and last mistake."

"Wouldn't I get any consideration for services rendered all these years?" He was making eyes at her.

"You've been paid in full. That was even-steven."

"Oh, was it?" His eyes became a little teasing, but the smile remained. Katerina had required a lot of patient bringing out, years of it. With the help of nature, he had been pretty successful, and he had enjoyed every second—well, almost, he thought. He had gotten frustrated only sometimes.

"You were very privileged to get what you got."

He nodded. He agreed with that, too. She didn't see this nod because he noticed she could not look at him directly. Then she did, with a satisfied smirk.

"You could have your car," she said.

"My car? That's a piece of junk."

She turned her back and shrugged. Nash studied her down and up. Wow, he thought, did he want to fuck her. "So who's going to be your second husband? That up-and-coming politician?"

When her head turned, her face showed amazement and disgust. "Please." Then she turned away again. "He'd be okay for having an affair with. But marry that guy? Come off it. Never. He's as poor as you are. Come to think of it, I don't even think he'd be fun to have an affair with."

"How about that nice lawyer who took you out to dinner, Kate?"

She turned full and squinted at him, obviously astonished, viewing his two suggestions with contempt. She was quite serious, he realized. Okay, he thought. He was willing to be serious about it. He was enjoying it.

"Sam, you will always be second rate. Third rate. It's the way you think. You have some idea that this is desireable."

He nodded again. She struck the truth in what she said, not the truth she imagined, but she was onto something.

"You think there are things you would not do," she said, reading his mind. "Well, I-I-I-I might." She pointed to herself again. She was probably as sexy as he had ever seen her, he thought. Her face was flushed; she was sending out subliminal waves. She knew what she was; and she wasn't a child on the West Side anymore. She was a prime piece of ass, smart as a whip, educated, a highly suitable decoration, an expensive, worthwhile acquisition. She could be all that.

"You think because I'm an immigrant, I don't know anything. I suppose you think I'm trapped here in this little house on this little street, and I'm just pleased as heck to be here, couldn't possibly ask for anything more, and if you get run over by a car, I'll be desolate."

"Not exactly."

"Sam, what kind of men are you talking about? You're not even in the ballpark in this. I'd start by going down to the Board of Trade."

"Not bad," said Nash, nodding his approval.

"That's just to meet people with dough and get invited to parties. I wouldn't settle for some fancy gambler in commodities who's going to lose all his money the day after tomorrow. But those guys would be fast. They'd pick me up, take me to the right events. Then I'd check things out. And once I met who I wanted to meet, I'd dump the guy that brought me."

"Whommm do you want to meet?"

"The president of a major corporation or a very big lawyer or a very big banker—although bankers, lately, I don't know. They're shaky. And whoever it is has to be greedy and have it all socked away; in what, I'm not sure yet. I'm studying that situation."

"You've got all this figured out." Nash was tempted to feel insecure but found that for some reason, he didn't. Her nipples were erect under her white blouse. She was aroused. She was thinking about this. Her hair was behind her ears the way he liked it. What a face. What a body. Nash was aware this talk was an interlude, unexpected, surprising, and there was plenty for him to pay for as a result of his recent screwups. He wasn't even sure yet how grim it was going to get. He had an idea of his limits. If he lost his job and couldn't get another one, or a decent one, his personality might be destroyed. If she tossed him out, he could sink further. Yet he was old enough to know some things had to be appreciated when they came, whenever they came, however strange the moment.

"I've been thinking about it," Katerina said defiantly.

"I can see that. And what if this guy didn't turn you on?"

In a suddenly raspy voice, she said, "His money would turn me on, Sam." She clearly meant it. "I could DO things for money."

"Like what?"

She sat down for only a moment and leaned toward him. "Like what do you want? Think about it. I have."

"You?"

Standing up again, she laughed and threw her head. She seemed as if she were drunk. "And Sam," she said, when she was through posing, "if I wanted to, I would make it part of the deal that I could satisfy my own desires for men in the way I saw fit as long as I was discreet."

"Maybe that's where I would fit in," he said, his grin returning and his twinkling eyes.

Air exploded out of her nose and mouth and she turned away, laughing again, this time with more humor. Nash watched her, enjoying her laughter as much as she did. He wanted her to be able to laugh, to be happy. He almost wanted her to get what she thought she wanted. But he figured he would fit in exactly where he said. She was almost close enough to reach, and looking at her, he knew how to touch her. He knew how to move her. He knew how to make her forget everything and exist only in her body, squirming and moaning and naked, outside time, outside place, all feel, and come, and wanting.

He knew. For some mysterious, unfathomable reason, she was crazy about him. And he could touch her now without touching her.

362

He was doing it. With his eyes. With this conversation. He was drawing her out, letting her go, asking her questions to make it real. Soar, baby. Feel it. Want it. Never doubt who you are. He was not calculating in this. He simply liked her. He thought he had a string on her, but at the moment he was willing to take a chance. And even if they broke up, he thought she would be crazy about him. Despite his failures, this seemed, surprisingly, like the knowledge of his own name, and he realized it was the reason for his original smile when she said, "Don't you think I could do better than you?" Down where something was still intact, he knew.

She turned back toward him. "You *really* think you would fit in there, don't you?" She noticed the way he was looking at her. She was feeling his eyes.

"Yep."

"You haven't even been *around* here lately."

"Nope."

She moved away two steps to evade him and looked up at a corner of the room. "You know where I think I belong? Those houses on the hills along Sheridan Road where the ravines lead down to the lake, where is that?"

"Winnetka."

"What about Lake Forest?" she said.

"We drove through there. They have some nice mansions, sort of like manor houses, with wrought iron gates down by the street, and long, long driveways leading to the house. Lots of grass to cut, though."

"Who cares about the grass? I think I would enjoy a place like that. I'd have to have an apartment in the city, too." She had a dreamy look in her eyes. He began to feel sympathy for her and regret. She deserved such a place, and after 14 years with him, what did she have? He did not feel sorry for himself any more.

"That's right. You should keep an apartment in the city in case you need to go shopping."

"Obviously. I'm not sure Lake Forest is it, either. It's sort of old fashioned. Do they have horses in Lake Forest?"

"I think Lake Forest probably has all different types of things, including lots of horses."

"Maybe I'll move to Barrington Hills," she said, her eyes lighting up. "That's where you said the children ride horses from one house to another to see their friends."

"I don't really know, Kate. That's just what I heard. The minimum lot is five acres and many are bigger. But maybe they really ride dirt bikes or mini bikes..." (He caught himself. Hey, come on.) "...no, but I'm pretty sure it's horses. The children ride horses around to see their friends, and the wives do, too."

"My father would not understand why people would want to ride horses."

"Different point of view."

"And you think..." Katerina began studying him studying her and drinking it in, soaking it in, with her head and one shoulder cocked. "...that just because I want to take my clothes off for you, that I'll give everything, the whole world up, for that?" She made it a harsh question at the end.

"I hope so." He nodded.

"That's ridiculous."

"I know."

"It doesn't make any sense."

"If it's any consolation, I don't understand it either."

"I should get away from you."

"For your own good, you probably should."

She looked away.

He knew this was hard for her to accept, the knowledge of what she would always be because of what he was. But his bones told him he could make her joyous in it, make her glow and burn, make this her own mountain to look down from.

"Kat-e-ri-na."

He said it very carefully, as if it were the first time.

She took a deep breath. "Don't....Why didn't you come home?"

He hesitated. This was like being asked to confess to a crime of which he was very ashamed. But he found he had accepted it. He said, slowly:

"I got upset at work about a bad story I did that hurt some people, and I lost my head."

"I'll have to hear the whole thing before I decide."

"I'll tell you. Are you prepared to be married to a foolish man?"

She whirled on him. "Are you kidding?" Her eyes bugged out beautifully.

"Come here."

"Forget it." She made a contemptuous face, but she was rooted in one spot.

"All right. Take your clothes off."

"No."

"I didn't think you would."

He rose, walked over wondering how he was going to accomplish this, and stood next to her. Part of him, the irrational part, which was not completely stupid but was often misguided, told him he owned her completely and she couldn't live without him. The rational part of him told him those ideas were dangerous—but made the world go 'round; and he had to be willing to lose.

As she looked up at him in a disdainful way, he reached out his right hand, followed it with his eyes, and touched her blouse on her soft flank just above her waist—as an allegedly friendly gesture—with only enough pressure to contact the skin underneath.

She pushed his hand away.

"Hey, I'm not going to do anything violent," he said. "I like you."

He put his hand back in such a way that three fingertips moved over her skin, covered by her thin blouse, for maybe an inch, then stopped and stayed, touching her side. It was a challenge for her to disdain that, too, he knew. Since this was the only point of contact between them, and barely held, it was hard for either one of them to be sure his fingertips were actually touching her skin without both of them thinking about it; and it required mutual tension between them not to make the touch more or less. He could feel the energy in his fingers running up his arm from her side, changing his breathing, and he hoped it was going the other way, too.

"You were just kidding, right?" he said.

"About what?" They were looking at one another.

"About wanting . . ." He was getting dizzy, getting palpitations, looking into her eyes, standing directly in front of her, touching her. ". . . to take your clothes off for me."

"Yes." She was looking into his eyes. Was she dizzy? Her face was starting to move in his field of vision just a little. Or he was moving. Something was moving. He grasped her side as if for balance, and she accepted it as if she were trying to balance, but it wasn't enough.

"Were you . . . ?" Nash couldn't think of what he wanted to say.

"I . . . ," she said.

They were going to fall over. He moved his hand around her back to hold them both up. "Honey, I . . ." He pulled her and she fell into him, and he was still dizzy, feeling her all through him, and he wasn't sure what was happening except he had her, and his head was fuzzy, and he put his other hand behind her head, and held her against him, and he squeezed her into him, and she came, and her breasts pressed into his ribs. He turned her head up and kissed her mouth, and he felt something going out of him into her, and she wanted it, whatever it was, she was straining upward.

"Sam? . . . Mmmmmm . . . What are you doing, honey?"

He rested his cheek on her head and held her against him, and smelled her hair, breathing it. She put her arms around his waist. "I don't know," he said. "Do you?"

"No." She squeezed him and buried her face in him.

Strange experiences they had had went out of each into the other, especially recent painful ones, and fears, wishes, hellos. The passage of these things was like a conversation.

For a long time, they held each other and rocked. Gradually, they entered a rhythm.

After a while, he put his arms under hers, and she knew what he was going to do, and she clasped her arms around his neck to help him even as she said, "Sam, no! Aaaah!"

He kissed her when their faces were even and she was up in the air.

"I don't believe this," she said.

"Yes, you do. You know, don't you?" He was smiling.

"I don't..." She wrapped her legs around him. "...know anything. Yes. Yes. I know. I don't want to. I mean, we're supposed to talk about this."

"We will," he said.

She grabbed his hair with her hands and put her tongue in his mouth and explored it, squeezing him with her legs. She said, "I just..." There was a small hollow sound when she spoke into his mouth. She moved her lips all over his mouth in different ways, holding tightly onto his hair. Then she said, breathing hard, "Whatever..." She kissed him. "...you..." She kissed him. "...want."

They got down to the floor in a couple moves that might have been difficult if they were not so crazy, and she clung to him ferociously as if she were drowning. She was, in a different way. She surrendered so much and admitted so much by this, he felt he had to make her whole, to assure her the terrible risk paid off; and he wanted to because he had to; it was true. He said, "I love you, baby."

"Oh, you, Sam, I love you, I want you, I need you, I love you, I love you..."

34

Nash walked across the green rug that covered the raised floor of the city room that covered the cables for the computer terminals that looked a little incongruous in the dated building. He kept his eyes straight ahead as he walked, hoping no one would accidentally get in his way or say hello until he reached the city desk. He did not know what to expect as a result of the story that fell apart so spectacularly, and he preferred to avoid people until that was resolved. For another reason, he also walked more deliberately and with better posture than usual.

He stepped into the slot, stopping just behind and to one side of Miller and announced himself. Uncharacteristically, the day city editor put down his pen, took both his hands away from the desk, and swiveled around. Miller was wearing his usual, long sleeved, white shirt with the cuffs rolled up twice and a neat tie. "Look who's here." Miller was smiling, appearing somewhere between friendly and fatherly. "I thought you hung yourself."

368

"Hanged, Al," said Nash. "Hanged myself." Nash had the feeling that at least half the people in the city room were looking at him and talking about him even though he knew intellectually they probably had other things to think about so early. There wasn't any doubt about Wolfram or the two rewrite people, including Mary Stern. They were looking at him. He wondered what to do with his hands so he put them in his pockets.

Miller chuckled. "I always did get that wrong." Then Miller began to study Nash which Nash expected. Nash imagined Miller wanted to know if Nash was fractured or still mostly whole and useful. But Nash was guessing.

"A story like that happens to everybody, Sam," said Miller. "You know that as well as I do."

"Yeah." Nash pretended to agree, then said, "I hope you've got something for me to do."

"Maybe later. If you've got a feature you want to work on, go ahead. It's slow today." Miller seemed to concentrate on trying to read Nash's face. "I hear you felt responsible for what happened to Red. Don't. You know how many night city editors the Ledger has had in the past 15 years?"

"I never counted."

"Nine. They have had nine night city editors in 15 years. Red had the job twice for altogether eight years. That's a good run. Sooner or later, somebody wants your scalp." Miller paused. "I'm always ready. I just go day by day."

Miller had come from a small newspaper in southern Illinois where he had been the city editor and the news editor as well as reporter at different times. He had also sold ads. He had joined the Chronicle as an assistant photo editor before Nash arrived.

"It wasn't just this week or the fight over your story that got him," Miller continued. "He had one of those strings of bad luck that happen. Red's gonna be all right. Trust me." Miller looked directly into Nash's eyes for a moment, then he said off-handedly, "I suppose Bob would be happy if you'd do an obit."

Nash turned partly to Wolfram, smiled, and took the piece of paper Wolfram held out. The paper had the name of a dead person on it and the phone number of a funeral home that had called. Transferring the first piece of paper to his opposite hand, Nash said, "Gimme another one." Wolfram handed him a second one.

"Gentile is handling the latest in the state's attorney's office," said Miller. "Do you want to get back in that?"

"Nope," Nash answered.

"That's a good decision. Bryce was your friend, I'm told. We screw our friends enough here."

"Never trust a reporter. Can I borrow Bob a minute?"

Miller waved assent, and Wolfram got up as if he had been waiting. Miller, turning back to his desk, said, "We used to take care of our friends when I started in this business. Now we crap on everybody objectively, and we wonder why people don't like us."

Nash grunted and nodded.

Nash and Wolfram walked over to the sports section. Nash was glad to sit down, but he let himself down slowly, leaning with his right hand on the rim of the sports copy desk in what he hoped was an unobtrusive manner.

"How'd your old lady take it?" said Wolfram.

"Hmm?" Nash was concentrating on his lower back.

"How'd your old lady take it?"

Nash was finally in the chair and exhaled. "We're back together," he said.

"No kidding!" Wolfram hit him in the shoulder. "That's all you needed was proximity."

Nash winced, then smiled sheepishly.

"How'd you two split up? She throw you out?" asked Wolfram.

Nash shrugged and showed the palms of his hands in a gesture which meant literally, "Who can say?" or "Life's like that." He had never told Wolfram or anyone else the reasons for the breakup, figuring this was the best way to handle a personal problem. But cooped up in the dark, the relatively ordinary reasons had taken on the aura of fearful monsters. He was grateful to be rid of them.

Nash whispered, "How did I get home, Bob?"

"Didn't she tell you? Me and my old buddy, Youngman, brought you home." Wolfram paused to let that sink in. Nash knew that in Wolfram's opinion, Youngman had sabotaged Wolfram's vacation tryout at night city editor. "We had to sort of carry you in there," Wolfram continued. "I wanted to take you to your own place, but Youngman said you shouldn't be by yourself, so we took you to the address on your driver's license. For better or for worse, right?"

Nash felt his face getting red with embarassment as he imagined the scene. He said, "Tell me what happened—briefly."

"I went to the john, and I came back out, and you were gone. I switched to beer after your little disturbance because you were acting very strange. I tried to get you out of there a couple times, and you kept saying, 'Just let me finish this drink,' and then you'd order another one. John refused to serve you after a while. Then you disappeared. I walked around the neighborhood looking for you—I was a little buzzed myself—and finally I called the office and found out you were at the 18th District."

Nash shut his eyes very tightly.

"I went there and tried to appease the cops. Youngman came a little after to bail you out. Where the hell did you think you were going?"

"I was supposed to go home; you know, really home. So that's where I was going. How much do I owe and who gets it?"

"You got off easy. Fifty dollars. I wrote down your court date in case you lost it." Nash had no idea where his arrest papers were. Wolfram brought out his wallet and gave Nash a note telling him where and when to appear in court. "The money goes to Georgia. She collected it, and she didn't tell anybody who was in the shithouse, except me and Youngman, of course. Nobody else knows."

Nash was relieved. "Sorry, pal."

"Forget it. I didn't know you were supposed to be on the wagon."

"How do you know now?"

"Your wife told me. I tried to tell her what happened, but she didn't want to hear it. She was a little miffed at you. I told her it was my fault, and she told me to shut up." Nash could well imagine that.

"So I figured I'd call her after I talked to you."

"Just let it pass. She knows everything, and she's giving me a break. Thanks, Bob." Nash reached out and shook his hand sincerely. "It's amazing the stuff a person can survive, isn't it?"

"If you got a good wife. I think I'm going to get me one again."

"Anybody I know?"

"You'll meet her, if I can talk her into moving to Chicago. What's the matter with you?"

"I woke up with a bad back this morning. First time. I thought it just happened to other people."

Wolfram laughed uproariously while at the same time trying not to be too loud. The effort at restraint made him laugh longer.

"It's not what you think, exactly," said Nash, waving his hand from side to side gingerly so as not to aggravate his muscles. He figured it wasn't lifting Kate that did it, but lowering her. He was glad the back problem hadn't shown up until morning. Thoughts about the previous day with Kate invaded his mind as if from ambush, so that even while he sat talking to Wolfram, part of him was going back and getting aroused again. But he kept an eye on Wolfram.

"You were taking out the garbage. I know," said Wolfram, who laughed more at Nash's attempted denial and his relative immobility. He started as if to punch Nash in the shoulder, and Nash knew he could not escape. But Wolfram slowed up and just touched Nash on the shoulder and said, "I'm happy for you."

Back at his desk after he bought a cup of coffee from the machine, Nash lit a cigarette and noticed somebody had stolen his ash tray. This was a troublesome theft. There seemed to be hardly any ash trays left in the office because very few people smoked anymore. (When he had started at the Chronicle, every desk had an ash tray.)

372

He flicked the ashes on the rug, sipped his coffee, and gradually worked up the nerve to collect the morning papers and read them.

Gentile's story was primarily an interview with the new chief of the criminal division, Scott Campbell, who tiptoed around the scandal. The appointment, under the circumstances, was news all by itself, whereas prior to the hullaballoo, Campbell's appointment would have been a line in a larger story or an item in a gossip column or perhaps ignored. Gentile's story repeated the charges against Bryce, adding demands by the ACLU and several defense lawyers for a grand jury investigation. Gentile also reported a proposal from a state legislator for appointment of a special, independent prosecutor and a special grand jury. Nash skimmed the article.

The story in the rival Ledger was a "think piece" on electronic eavesdropping. It took the literary approach that Bryce was an unfortunate bureaucrat, a victim of the times, who was overpowered by the temptation of electronic eavesdropping because it had become so easy, so promising, and because the feds used it every day. Reading the quotes from various experts who had never met or spoken to Bryce, Nash could visualize their image of him as a little man who wiped his brow a lot and whined, "What to do? Oh, what to do?" The story started out by quoting a defense lawyer who said he thought the extent of the eavesdropping admitted by the state's attorney's office was really the tip of the iceberg and that many more cases would probably be affected. Somebody always said this, thought Nash. It was predictable.

The Post story was a different animal altogether. Written by reporter John Schuty, who was one of the more successful reporters in town, the story was a hatchet job on Bryce. Schuty revealed to readers of the Post that Bryce was a career incompetent whose rise had been inexplicable. The story then hinted that Bryce's apparent incompetence was a coverup for something worse.

Schuty listed the crime syndicate murders committed in Cook County during Bryce's tenure as chief of the criminal division and pointed out that not only had Bryce not convicted anyone, he had indicted almost no one.

(The headline said: "Bryce was soft on city crooks".)

The story went on to compare the number of high public officials in Chicago and Cook County who had been convicted of taking bribes and similar acts of corruption by the U.S. Attorney's Office in recent years ("not counting ordinary police officers and clerks") to the number of such officials convicted by the state's attorney's office while Bryce was at the helm of the criminal division. The feds had convicted around 20, and the state's attorney's office under Bryce, zero.

The implication was clear. Bryce was a hack political appointee, a Chicago archetype, who played footsie with the crime syndicate and who would never harm any other hack politicians because Bryce was one of them; they were in cahoots.

To the uninformed and to the forgetful, as well as to intelligent readers whose minds were only superficially engaged in the story, the evidence would convey a strong, negative picture of Clarence Bryce. Even people in the news business whose interests did not run to crime and punishment would say, "Look at the facts. He's a bum," thought Nash.

It would not occur to many people that a reporter could write a completely falacious story by citing facts and figures that were correct, but meant nothing once the context was supplied. Nor would it occur to many people that a reporter would set out to write such a falacious story.

Crime syndicate murders in the Chicago area, as Nash and Schuty knew well, had routinely gone unsolved for decades prior to Bryce's tenure. During Bryce's tenure, local police departments, the primary investigators on all murders, had arrested almost no suspects in gangland hits for Bryce to prosecute. Moreover, the FBI, with wider resources, had investigated every one of the gangland murders listed and had also failed to solve them. Schuty omitted the background. That part of the story was crude, but effective. (If you said someone was to blame for something, the charge often stuck unless there was a vigorous response. This was particularly true when the charge involved civil servants.)

But Schuty's real gall, as far as Nash was concerned, showed in the comparison of public corruption cases. Here the story went beyond crude balderdash, such as a political candidate might use, into more subtle, intellectual deceit. The entire story was written as if Schuty were a college professor from Vermont who looked at some facts about crime and punishment in Chicago, but without knowledge of the city, and arrived at his own, remarkable interpretation.

In reality, Schuty had been covering news in Chicago for as long as Nash and knew the city just as well as Nash. But Schuty had chosen to use pretend ignorance, fake simplicity. This was a common journalistic device. Schuty, you phony bastard, thought Nash.

Both men knew of half a dozen cases that Bryce and his staff had investigated and sent to the U.S. attorney's office for trial because they were easier to try in federal court or to avoid certain judges. Federal prosecutors had the advantage of being able to request a jury trial while state prosecutors did not. Only the defense could request a jury in state courts. Thus, if a criminal defendant in state courts had money and influence and was lucky enough to be assigned to a judge who could be fixed, the defense would request a bench trial and win automatically.

Nash felt the irony of being forced to face this issue. In conversation, he generally took the position that the corruption of the Cook County judiciary was exaggerated, at least in Criminal Courts, by people who had no knowledge. Nash knew judges who were crooked and half-crooked. Some of them ran excellent courtrooms when there was no money involved. Usually there wasn't because the defendant didn't have any. But for Schuty to ignore the effect of the crooked judges, a doubt and a despair among prosecutors and police which spread far wider than the number of such judges, was highly calculated deceit.

Nash and Schuty were well aware of other advantages enjoyed by federal prosecutors, such as federal immunity.* Nash lifted the page containing Schuty's story a few inches off the desk and punched a hole in it using a ballpoint pen. Then he punched another hole.

To himself, Nash said, How about the four magic words in federal court, Schuty boy? Nash was thinking of "mail fraud" and "wire fraud." He recalled that an envious Clarence Bryce had once defined these federal charges as "using the mails or the telephone to further a profitable scheme that might be offensive to the public." The state had no such catch-all laws.

Finally, as Nash and Schuty knew well, the U.S. attorney's office selectively prosecuted only about 850 criminal cases a year. Bryce's state's attorney's office had to prosecute each year nearly 20,000 felonies and half a million misdemeanors. So what's the bottom line? thought Nash bitterly. Who is holding the line against the chaos?

The story made Nash grit his teeth. But Schuty's story did not surprise Nash. He expected it, and he imagined Bryce did, too.

Bryce had never trusted John Schuty because of Schuty's habit of manipulating facts and trying to manipulate people. For years, Bryce had refused to give Schuty anything exclusive or sensitive because Bryce did not trust Schuty to print it correctly. Schuty's long-awaited payback was inevitable. This hatchet job on Bryce would solidify Schuty's relationship with State's Attorney Ryan whom Schuty portrayed as a hero. Schuty's story also served the function of warning other public officials of the cost of crossing John Schuty. No matter how many readers and members of the media were fooled, public officials would know Schuty's attack on Bryce went well beyond a supposed news story. This was personal.

Schuty threw in a filip which caused Nash to give him grudging credit for covering the ground. Schuty had located Mike Franzel,

---

*When the federal government grants a person immunity from prosecution in order to compel that person to testify in a criminal case, the immunity guarantees only that the witness' words cannot be used against him. If the federal prosecutors can prove a case against a witness without using his own words, for any crime he reveals, prosecutors can still send the witness to prison. In Illinois state courts, a person granted immunity from prosecution is immune from punishment for any crime he reveals while testifying, no matter how unrelated or heinous the crime. Thus state prosecutors use immunity very sparingly.

Nash's source for the original story on the coverup of a crime at the Read Mental Health Center. Whatever Franzel might have told Schuty, Schuty used only one quote: the Chronicle, meaning Nash, "blew the thing out of proportion."

Most people would interpret this quote to mean that the principal source for the story was no longer willing to vouch for the story, or for Bryce.

Nash found himself in the unaccustomed position of being an angry reader with no way to rebut Schuty's article. The Chronicle had been forced to switch in mid-stream from portraying Bryce as the hero to portraying Bryce as the goat. No Chronicle editor would be interested in a story defending Bryce again. It would look schizo. The Chronicle especially would not print any defense of Bryce written by Nash who had fouled up the situation in the first place. There was no way for Nash to respond except writing a letter to the editor of the Post. Reporters did not do that.

Nash rose out of his chair and walked to a large trash can on wheels. He threw Schuty's newspaper in so hard it thumped the bottom.

35

For the next few weeks, Nash's workload at the Chronicle was eminently manageable. It seemed the editors had pretty much forgotten him. Younger reporters were carrying the ball. Nash did what he was told to do and was thankful for his job.

Every reporter is periodically forgotten or ignored, and it had happened to Nash before, but he suspected this time was different. He felt he had fallen into the category of older reporter. A good way to become an older reporter, certainly not the only way, was to screw up at age 39 as Nash had done. Suddenly, he imagined, views of him had changed in various quarters.

Reporting for the city desk was generally for the young unless a reporter had a good specialty and was capable of churning out copy in that field despite the threat of personal boredom. Some editors had difficulty understanding, in an unspoken way, why older general assignment reporters hung around. Why didn't the older ones go someplace? Move on. Go into politics. Go into public relations.

Go to another paper. For the most part, older reporters made too much money, crimping the city desk budget. And they were likely to question an editor's judgement. There was no set policy, however, and the editors kept changing, so older reporters who persevered sometimes made comebacks on the same paper.

Nash felt he could redeem himself if he proved that the incident at the Read Mental Health Center was real and substantial, and that the state's attorney did cover it up for political reasons. But he could no longer convince himself the story was out there. And if it was, he couldn't figure out how to get it. The two mental conditions complemented each other. He also was concerned about renewing the whole bugging controversy that had hit Bryce. After six straight days of negative stories, the controversy had been pushed out of sight by other news, and the promised grand jury investigation remained a promise, nothing more. Nash wondered if he owed it to Bryce to leave him in peace.

Nash had encountered many stories and rumors of stories that were great, but just—could—not—be—seized, no matter how far one stretched. He thought he knew the solutions to several famous, unsolved murders. (These were the detectives' private solutions.) Nobody had ever been able to get enough evidence that would stand up in court, not even in a preliminary hearing. The solutions, once learned, were in some cases obvious, and in other cases plausible and believeable, but none of that mattered because everything had been done that could be done.

And there were other things on Nash's mind in those weeks.

With little to do, he became detached from the team spirit arising from day-to-day competition with other papers, and he looked around in a new way. He had to admit to himself that the Chronicle had committed malicious hatchet jobs on people just like the one Schuty had done on Bryce. The Ledger had done this, too, and the TV stations. Nash was surprised to remember an incident which he had never expected to forget, that he had taken part in such a hatchet job himself when he was a young reporter. He had written it. Hughes had supplied the information. (Hughes had been unable to write a sensible newspaper story. He was purely a reporter.) This particular story had seemed unusual to Nash from the first. There were allegations that were not really backed up, and other allegations that did not amount to much or probably could have been explained away. Nash assumed Hughes was trying to bring down a well known, dangerous character who could not be touched with solid facts because this character was too devious. Nash made the story read better than Hughes expected.

A while after this story was printed, Nash had discovered from another reporter that the attack was most likely a personal, political favor Hughes had done at the request of one of his long-time, highly placed sources. It was a hatchet job to order. This revelation had angered Nash, not so much because of the effect of the story on the subject, who survived. Nash was angered because he had been conned into violating his own, just forming principles for no damn reason.

Nash recalled that he later sabotaged another, one-sided exposé by Hughes by pretending to be wooden headed and writing the story straight, even putting in responses and explanations where Hughes did not want any.

Nash was amazed in the present to realize he had forgotten how his relationship with Hughes had turned sour. It was so long ago. And Nash began to wonder who had ultimately been right. He began to see there were styles of living and codes of conduct that contradicted what he had believed for so many years but made sense in a way. One day alone at lunch, apropos of nothing, Nash suddenly appreciated John Schuty. Nash was in a hot dog emporium on Dearborn Street, and when he had the inspiration, he put down his hot dog and stared at the white wall directly behind the narrow counter where he sat.

Schuty wanted to control the sources of information. If some news source did not want to cooperate, or worse, was hostile to Schuty, well, life was a fight. Schuty fought in his usual way by manipulating facts or language in the newspaper to embarass that person. This was highly effective. Public officials wanted to avoid public embarassment. Once the threat was common knowledge, it was not necessary for Schuty to do this every day. Thus, much of the time Schuty had marvelous stories from marvelous sources.

Nash had always understood Schuty's method. But Nash had clung to the belief that a better, long-range style was to present things each and every time as close as possible to the way they occurred. He had considered Hughes a leftover from an earlier era and Schuty a fraud who would soon get his comeuppance. That never happened.

Staring at the white wall in the hot dog eatery, Nash suddenly had to ask himself how many legitimate, serious scoops he had conveyed to the public in his career compared to Hughes and Schuty? Who had really served the public with more and better information, even allowing for the occasional excrement from those two. There was no doubt about the answer. And Hughes and Schuty seemed to have a good idea: control something, control anything, or one was a leaf on the wind, like Nash.

. . . .

"Hey, Dad, Ma says to warm up the arni yiahni (lamb stew). It's good. We ate early."

Nash could tell by the wildness in his son's eyes and the condition of the house that the children had been on their own for a while. Nash was beginning to adjust to Bobby's new voice.

"Where's your mother?"

"She's upstairs lying down."

The radio was on and Bobby was dancing in his stocking feet on the kitchen floor using outlandish moves and gestures as if he were a rock star. One particular twirl was so good Nash had to stop to watch.

"Do that again, Bobby."

Bobby did. Nash felt deep surprise like the first time he had seen the Mississippi River. He had never shown Bobby how to dance, nor, he was sure, had Kate. The boy was an independent entity who existed apart from Nash and what that entity would do, no one knew. "So what's happening, Dad?" said Bobby, breathing hard.

"I don't know, guy. Not too much. That was good."

"Thanks."

Kim was sitting cross legged on the floor in the dining room watching television. Most of the 10 by 11 foot dining room was covered with tiny scraps of paper. She had obviously been cutting things with her scissors for some reason until she got bored with it.

Nash had the feeling, for a moment, that he rented these children, or, more likely, that they were assigned to him to look after for a while. They were not entirely understandable, the way animals were not, but his job was to keep them in good order and teach them a very few things, and zip, they would go. Nash did not feel the invisible umbilical that his wife felt connecting her to the children at most moments. The children did not hang on Nash, and to him they always seemed partly independent.

Then Nash wondered about their futures. Would Bobby and Kim be rich and famous? He hoped his children would rise above him.

The supper dishes were still on the kitchen table, and the milk was out.

"Dad, I can't hear," whined Kim. The radio was loud.

"Turn off the radio, Bobby."

"Why? Tell her to turn off the television."

This made annoying sense. It was 50–50.

"Bobby, turn off the radio. Kim, turn off the television!"

"What?" said Kim, who began to whine like a cat in the nighttime.

"Kim got in trouble at the babysitter's today. She knocked over a bunch of plants and all the dirt came out."

"Bobby, you're gonna die when you go in the Little League," said his sister.

"Kim, stop that," said Nash. "Pick up all those pieces of paper.

Every one of them. I don't care if you throw them away or save them, but pick them all up now."

Nash was going back and forth in the doorway between the kitchen and the dining room. He turned back to the kitchen, and Bobby said, "She thinks some kid got killed in the Little League, Dad. She's been bugging me about it."

"That's right. That happened." Nash picked up the milk carton off the table and walked to refrigerator. "It won't happen to you or anybody you know. It's more unusual or rare than getting struck by lightning. A lot rarer, in fact." He moved things around on the top shelf of the refrigerator and jammed the milk in.

"Did you know him?" asked Bobby.

"No. I just wrote about it."

"How come you wrote about it?"

Nash sighed and began to pick up the dishes, then decided to take off his trenchcoat which he threw over a chair. "So people would know the boy wasn't killed by a werewolf or kidnapped by Rumplestilskin."

"Daad."

"That's part of the reason. It was a scary thing and scary things have to be explained. The boy might have had a weakness that nobody knew about. That's my guess. Do you want me to bring the story home so you can read it?" Nash guessed this was the wrong approach as soon as he said it.

Bobby squinched up his face and shook his head. "Ehh, no."

Nash changed his tone of voice. "We don't need the story. We'll talk about it in a little while. Don't you have any homework?"

"I did it."

"Then read something." Nash meant a book, but then he had a different idea. He opened the cabinet under the sink, found a newspaper in the garbage bag, took it out, shook the newspaper over the sink, and gave it to his son. "Here. Read any story you want. It has to be at least six inches long. When I come back, you can tell me about it."

Bobby accepted the newspaper with an expression of distaste because it was from the garbage.

"You're weird, Dad."

Entering the dining room, Nash said, "Kim, I want you to draw me a picture when you're done picking up there. Draw me, uhh... some person. Draw me a friend of yours, or your brother." She could draw stick figures.

"I don't do that anymore."

"Why not?"

"I'm just not interested."

"Do it anyway."

"I do it when I want to do it."

Nash judged this disagreement to be a tar baby intended to hold him to the spot. He left it unresolved and went up stairs.

He found his wife in bed, curled under a blanket, her face haggard and pale, her hair a mess. By the light from the hallway, she looked at a minimum 35 years old, which she would be in the summer.

"What's this? No supper?" he said as he closed the door. This was one of her days off from the office. Kate had gone back to working only three days a week because it made life simpler for the whole family.

"It's down there," she said weakly. He had expected a more creative response.

"What's the matter?" Nash was standing by the closed door letting his eyes adjust to the darkness.

"I've been having abdominal pains all day."

"Something to do with your period?"

"No. And I'm not pregnant, either."

Nash took off his shoes, sat on the bed, rubbed her back, and aroused her ire by doing what came natural to him. He asked a lot of prying, personal questions.

"I don't know! I don't know!" she said repeatedly. Eventually, she added, "Why don't you just see what the children are doing."

384

He began focusing his questions in a certain direction, based on a guess, and Kate began giving him short, sharp answers intermixed with more suggestions that he find something else to do. After 20 minutes of questions and answers, he could feel her loosen a bit. Nash announced that Katerina was having a delayed, physical reaction to the entire trauma of their separation and the shock of the way he had been brought home drunk. Moreover, he said, she probably mistrusted him and was afraid he was going to walk out again.

"Let's just say I view you in a new light," Katerina responded in her best sarcastic tone.

With her back to him, talking to the wall, Katerina went on to contradict Nash's interpretation of events, saying she had handled the separation and all that came with it.

"You are basically unnecessary around here," she said.

"That's why I'm so useful," he answered.

Bobby's operation had been one thing too many, she said, and now that Bobby was better, she was collapsing.

Nash saw how the two explanations dovetailed. She had held out until the last crisis was past. Admirably female behavior.

"Ekanes kala (You did well)," he said.

"Never again!"

Nash's hand paused an instant in its back rubbing; then he made it resume. He decided to overlook the fact that the declaration she sought was not meant to be made on demand, and he said, "Never again."

He owed her. He fully realized this time, as opposed to when he got married, what an extraordinary promise he was making. Because she demanded it, he made the promise voluntarily, a paradox. They talked about their different versions of why he left and his attempts to come back.

Nash was struck inwardly by the will of his commitment and the weakness of himself. He meant what he promised; could he do it? The problem was Nash did not feel the power of the universe behind him as he once did. And he didn't know himself any more. In fact, he knew himself less and less each day.

The editors wouldn't give him anything substantial to do at work, and stories he submitted on his own did not get in the paper. He felt he was losing touch with his mates, losing touch with the ground. Was he really a reporter? Why did they pay him? How long would they keep him? Like many reporters, Nash needed to perform. He needed to report and write and see his words in print or he began losing his professional confidence, then his self-image, then his confidence in other spheres, and, if he wasn't careful, he started to look different.

At home, he tried to keep his image up and play the strong, silent type—until he started having skyrocket attacks of anger with the kids. Then he had found it necessary to tell his wife some of what was bothering him.

As he began to disintegrate, or the mold began to disintegrate that he thought was himself, he began to have, for Nash, unusual ideas. He discovered he wanted money. He really wanted it. Just as Kate had always wanted him to, he wanted it. He wanted money hungrily, and lots of it. But for starters, he mused aloud to Kate that people often got a couple thousand dollars in Chicago by robbing a bank in daylight, enough to pay off the Nashes' most pressing debts. In considerable detail, they talked about how to do it, knowing they were kidding.

Nash felt a yearning for power and position. He realized he had taken the wrong path to be a U.S. Senator or president of General Motors, and he wondered why he had been so stupid. *How* could he have been so stupid?

He didn't tell Kate, but he occasionally wanted to kill someone. He had no target in mind, but he wanted to kill someone as a form of animal declaration, a statement of boundaries, putting people on notice that he could and would. And he wanted to enjoy it. As an excuse, this homicide would preferably (but not necessarily) be for a good cause.

These urges, and others to be described, washed over him in the form of waves of emotion, mystifying him, scaring him, and alerting him that he had to continually watch himself. He did not know the source of the feelings and ideas, and he learned quickly that they were generally not subject to his summons or dismissal. He was subject to them. Sometimes he savored them, embracing his own amoral capacity for mayhem. Other times, he prayed for relief from the inner tumbling. The only aspect he consistently controlled was action. That led to a daily test of his will.

He thought that some day he might tell Kate about his homicidal notions. But one thing he knew he would not tell her was this: Women were driving him nuts.

The hunger to consume women had started earlier, at the end of his separation, and he had blamed it on his separation. But since his work had become less demanding and less fulfilling, it had occurred to him that the pursuit of women might hold the promise of interest, challenge, and satisfaction. Sitting idle in the office one day, he had counted on his fingers the number of women with whom he had been intimate, a small number, and it dawned on him that he had foolishly inhibited his body's natural quest until suddenly his only body, only partially used, was about to turn to dust!

He was going to be dead!

Seen in this blinding light, Nash decided that in regard to the females of the planet, he had been shamefully, immorally negligent. The thought of dying before he had screwed his quota of women— 25 to 50 women; some days a hundred—panicked him. Not yet! I didn't understand!

Part of Nash was aware that his craving for sundry women, and a few in particular, after he had reunited with his wife, was disgusting and embarassing, in theory. But the impulse was so strong and so much himself that Nash could not disown it. He would not. He had to deal with the impulse, and he was doing it, but he wouldn't disown it. It was him.

While he still had his hand on Kate's back, she rolled over and looked at him in the dark. Nash looked at her with a half smile, if she could see it, to cover up his preoccupation.

"I think you're going to be pretty dependable," she said.

"I'm glad you think that, Kate."

Later that night, they sat reading in the living room after the children were in bed and the house was quiet. The very tiny hum of an electric clock was audible. Nash was distracted by the silence, perked up his ears, and looked at his wife. She looked at him. When he had returned to his book, Kate asked, "Would you mind if I went back to work for Verbecke?"

Nash twitched visibly. Then he felt a rush of annoyance. Why did she have to do that? He was supposed to be the one with existential difficulties. But instead of understanding him, she wanted him to understand her. The field was crowded.

"If I had my druthers, I'd rather you didn't. I'd just like it better."

He tried to read another paragraph and failed. "Why... This is ...Why do you want to go back to work for Verbecke?"

"I don't like to start something I don't finish."

He told her what had bothered him when she worked for Verbecke the previous time. She said she was sorry, and if he didn't want her to do it, she wouldn't. He knew this was true. He could decide.

A few minutes later, he broke the silence by proposing—if hypothetically she did go back to work for Verbecke—how she would have to conduct herself. He was serious; plus this was a test to see if she would fight his wishes.

She teased him.

He teased her in return.

The conversation became very funny. When his wit was running pretty well, she came over behind his chair and leaned down pressing her breasts into his shoulders. She said into his ear, "Emai diko sou, hazouli." ("I am yours, you sweet idiot.") She licked his ear. Nash slid down in his chair and was losing the thread of the conversation. (Yet he knew.)

She did go back to work for Verbecke, two nights a week if Nash was home, and Saturdays, and Nash hated it. But he couldn't tie her up. He wanted to, but she was more alluring to him when she flew around and came back to him and clung to him because she couldn't help herself. Still, he hated her working for Verbecke, and felt it was risky. She was too good looking. It wasn't much of a sacrifice, was it? Yes it was. He didn't trust that guy. Nash could never make up his mind whether he was doing the right thing.

She also had him chasing her again. He was grateful to her for that. It was a small antidote for a giant dose of lust. There were so many women in the world! But once in a while, she took the edge off it.

36

Verbecke lost the primary race, but came close, and Nash judged from experience that Verbecke would be back and eventually win something. Gov. Beal won by about 45,000 votes, close, but not a photo finish. His problem would be repairing the damage from the primary before the general election.

By election day, the Clarence Bryce scandal was just another historic flash fire to the press. It had never been tied up very well to the governor, and it only appeared in lengthy, wrap-up stories which summarized the incidents and issues that marked the campaign.

Bryce never said one word in the newspapers or on television throughout the days of the controversy or afterward.

Weeks earlier, as the scandal was dying out, the Chronicle's oldest columnist, Harold Gruninger, had written a belated defense of Bryce that pointed out the distortions and near lies that had been published "in some segments of the press." Nash had asked Gruninger to write something, only to discover that Gruninger had already decided to and had done his research. The defense included a list of Bryce's accomplishments, the major criminal cases he won as a courtroom prosecutor, and glowing testaments to him from the U.S. attorney, a former state's attorney, and two of the city's better detectives who were by then members of the police department brass. The column was well done, but it could not change the direction of the coverage since it came at the tail end. The columnist himself was out of fashion, so the effect of the praise was even more muted. Nevertheless, it was in print, and it would be in the library for history, Nash told himself.

Two days after the election, one of the city's radio stations, an "all news" station, broadcast a sketchy report that the Chronicle was going to fold. Management denied it. The television stations picked up the report on the 10 p.m. news and added that the Chronicle had just cancelled a series of radio and TV ads promoting the paper, the "new" Chronicle. The fearful rumor had been around the Chronicle office and on the street for five days before the cancelling of the ads.

In the last hours of the campaign, politicians and their aides frequently asked Chronicle reporters if it was true the paper was going under. The reporters felt strange being on the receiving end of the questions. And they had to admit they didn't know.

After the first public report appeared on television, Nash got a call at home from a friend who told him about it. Nash immediately called the office and asked for Krolikowski.

"If it's about the future of this great institution, Krolikowski says to tell everybody who calls, 'Je ne sais pas.' You are roughly the 50th caller, Nash."

"Who is this?"

"Shirley."

Shirley was a smart ass copy girl, the kind who took the job for the alleged romance of it. They didn't last long. They grew up. But the attitude was refreshing.

The next Monday, Nash was gratefully engrossed in trying to put together a small story on an incident of carbon monoxide poisoning in a South Side two flat where the chimney backed up. Four or five families lived in the two flat, and no one knew how many people had been taken to hospitals because the Fire Department had taken some, the police had taken some, and neighbors had taken some. By close to 1 p.m., it was apparent no one was going to die, and Nash thought he had figured out how many hospitals were involved. He expected to be told to write five paragraphs at the most. He looked up and noticed strangers standing in the newsroom and more filtering in.

"What's the latest, Jose?" he said to Gentile behind him.

"All hands have been summoned on deck for a 1 p.m. announcement. Very shortly, the band will strike up, 'Nearer My God to Thee.' "

An unusual group was assembling, ad takers, salesmen and saleswomen, printers in their aprons, a smattering of pressmen in inky overalls and square paper hats, secretaries, guards, nattily dressed executives from the business side, conscious of their aura of authority but at the same time ill at ease, some nervously smiling, seeming to wish people in the newsroom understood them for once. Nash thought he saw two men across the room who could have been delivery truck drivers who were probably in the newsroom for the first time in their lives. A few of the girls were teasing the drivers who seemed to enjoy it.

When Mike Schuman walked into the newsroom at 1 p.m., Gentile said softly behind Nash, "Don't get on the desk. Just tell everybody to go back to work and keep on walking."

"Jose," said Nash, "I believe he's getting on the desk."

Then Nash and Gentile had to stand up to see because everyone was.

"We have let your colleagues into the lobby," said Schuman. This was greeted by nervous laughter from the people nearest Mike Schuman and a shout of "Can't hear," from the back.

"We have let your colleagues into the lobby!" Schuman was referring to the contingent from the other media who had obviously been tipped and had gathered outside the building. "They claimed they were freezing to death!"

Someone yelled, "Let 'em." And off to the side of Nash, someone else said in a normal voice, "So what? Let's get on with it," amidst a general, meaningless murmur.

Schuman raised a hand and waited. Then he said to silence, "This will be an announcement none of us ever wanted to hear...."

That was it. Nash didn't need to listen to the rest. He couldn't believe his own ineptness, except that he had to admit it fit his recent style. He had pushed his luck too far for years and waited too long to leave; and what he had known would happen, could see was happening, what everything had predicted would happen, had come to pass. And he was standing here on the very day when he had told himself he would be long gone. Instead of all the smart things he had intended to do for years, such as bringing in one paycheck while he leisurely searched for a new and better job, the best position he could get, dealing from a position of strength, acting on his own instead of as part of a herd; instead of that, he was about to be one of scores of reporters, writers and editors dumped into a poor hiring market on the same day. And he would be broke.

The opportunities for revising his self-image were becoming increasingly unwelcome, turning Nash bitter. He came out of the mood to look around the crowded room, and he wondered, Is everybody thinking, "Why me?"

Schuman was carrying on about the losses per month. Nash turned his head to speak to Gentile who was standing behind him. "What did he say was the last day?"

"Thursday," said Gentile. "The Friday paper."

. . . .

Thursday morning when Nash arrived in the office, the place looked strange. It was filled with boxes. Most were medium sized boxes from supermarkets and liquor stores, but in one case a reporter had next to his desk a tall stack of 10 shoeboxes carefully tied together with rope. A few of the male employees were wearing jeans and flannel shirts. Some of the women had dressed up a bit and applied a little more makeup in anticipation of being caught by the television cameras. But the appearance of the office cast a gloom over the staff. Things were gone from the walls, like calendars, posters, some of the clocks, and large photographs of the newsroom as it had been 40 and 50 years earlier. These left only the outlines of their shapes, and sometimes not even that. The panoramic view of the newsroom, which had once looked exactly the way a newsroom should, revealed a crummy, old dead hall, filled with boxes of junk and the too-free daylight that came with stripping and abandonment. Scattered throughout, of course, were the computer terminals.

Before going to the city desk, Nash went to his own desk and draped his trenchcoat over the chair. The employees had been required to turn in their locker keys, and the lockers were now all locked.

Gentile was wearing a tuxedo. Nash noticed two other reporters were wearing tuxedoes. Nash had passed up this idea.

As he approached the city desk, one of the copy clerks on the switchboard—there were four to handle the extra calls—handed Nash a note. "Ald. Colucci called for you about 15 minutes ago. He said he'd call back," said the youngster, his face showing bright eyed liveliness. This was a memorable day for him.

Nash took the message form which had X's in the boxes labeled "Please call" and "Will call back." He guessed the demise of the paper had put it in Colucci's mind to render formal thanks for Nash's semi good deed of a few weeks earlier and perhaps to offer a free bushel of apples from South Water Market. Nash decided he'd take the apples. He might need them. He pictured himself loading the bushel into his trunk with Colucci looking on, smiling. Then Nash knew he wouldn't take the apples. Trying to think of a philosophical principle that applied, he settled for: Better to keep people uncomfortable than to let them think they'd evened up.

He waited for his turn to talk to Miller and looked over the room, filing away the sensations. Then his mind surprised him with a higher voltage notion. Colucci—a job?

When the reports of the Chronicle's demise rose from the gossip level to the level of stories in the media, most staffers, including Nash, immediately sent letters and placed phone calls to the Ledger or the Post, or both, to all the television stations, to government agencies, to colleges, to any place that might need someone with a newspaper background. About eight people had been snapped up without hesitation. Georgia Krolikowski was going to be a reporter at the Post. She was staying with the Chronicle until the last day. Bob Wolfram had been hired as an assistant city editor at the Ledger and promised a shot soon at night city editor. Solomon was rumored to be negotiating to become political editor of the Post, which meant, despite the title, that he would be a reporter again. Phelan had resigned earlier to become city editor of the television station whose news show was third in the ratings.

Phelan's job was actually a step up, and he had told Nash in a telephone conversation that he received a significant increase in salary. This surprised and pleased Nash because it seemed such an odd outcome. Phelan's reputation was apparently high around town, and the television station had been pleased to get him. Phelan had sounded confident and a little amused about his new environment. He sounded, Nash thought, younger. Phelan was not sure the job would last past his two-year contract, television jobs being notoriously unreliable. Neither Phelan nor Nash had ever heard of a city editor of a TV station. Nash had been greatly relieved to realize that Phelan took care of Phelan, and did it well.

Nash noticed most Chronicle employees were trying extremely hard to stay in the Chicago area. The pull of the coasts had ebbed. But Nash knew many of these employees would have to move to survive, and he thought this might include himself.

A few employees were too depressed to do anything; and the employees near retirement age, whose pensions were safe but smaller than expected because they were not yet 65, were working their math, talking to their spouses, estimating the lengths of their lives.

"What are you planning today?" asked Miller as Nash moved into the slot.

"Getting a byline," said Nash. Nash had silently decided he would call Colucci as soon as possible, discarding the just-devised philosophical principle on never letting people even up.

"Good luck. The house stories are all assigned." This meant stories on the history of the paper and features on its failure. "They're taking ads up to the last possible moment, so there might be some extra space to fill. See if you can slap together something on this, 15 inches, trimmable to 7 or 8." Miller handed Nash a press release on the Illinois Department of Public Aid's program to track down deadbeat fathers. Nash was expected to expand it with explanations, statistics, and an anecdote or two. It was obvious the story had little chance of making the paper.

Nash nodded, shifting his lips to one side of his face and sucking on the inside of his mouth.

"Yeah, I know," said Miller. "It wasn't my idea to let you sink roots over there." He looked at the pillar that hid Nash's desk.

Nash wanted to ask, "Whose idea was it?" Something, he guessed pride, stopped him. "Where are you going now?" he asked Miller.

"Tennessee for a couple weeks, fishing. Then we'll see," said Miller.

"Little early for fishing, isn't it?"

"Seems just right to me."

Back at his desk, Nash called Colucci's neighborhood office and got profuse apologies from some woman who said the alderman was out but would certainly call Nash again very soon. The woman sounded very new.

By 12:30, after three lengthy phone calls, Nash had written his story complete with one superb anecdote, and he thought it would be a shame if it never got in the paper. He went to lunch at the IBM cafeteria with Gentile in the tux, and three other male reporters who soon commenced the drinking formalities due the occasion, so Nash excused himself and drifted back to the office.

Colucci had called again. The message was on top of Nash's empty desk. Nash had already cleaned out the drawers and taken most of the useful things home. An editorial writer, Larry Zack, was walking down the aisle playing a blues tune on a flute. Nash called Colucci again and this time got him.

"Sorry to hear about your newspaper, Nash."

"Not as sorry as I am. You called earlier, alderman. What can I do for you?" Nash sat down in his chair, put his feet on the desk, and fantasized that Colucci was saying something like, "I know where there's a job open at $40,000 to $50,000 a year if you'd be interested."

Colucci was actually saying, "I really am a fan of the news media. I'm working at understanding it. How come you didn't write up my nephew a while back?"

"Uhh, somebody here did. It was my day off when he got busted."

"You know what I mean; when you did the nepotism story about my office staff. You left out his drug history."

"I knew what you meant. I guess it was a social experiment." After he said that, Nash had to force himself to go back and remember. What was the reason at the time? Thinking out loud, he said, "It struck me that he was more stupid and weak than dangerous. And from a personal standpoint, I didn't want to be the one to finish him off."

"You think he's finished now, I guess."

"Who knows about druggies, alderman? That's aahh beyond me."

"Me, too, Nash. I assume my nephew never called you, and I know I never called you to express our appreciation even though that story on the whole caused me a lot of trouble. It's hard to figure you guys out. I don't know what you want."

"Right now I'm looking for a job." Nash felt the boldness of necessity.

"I haven't got any jobs that would satisfy you, Nash. I'll keep you in mind if I hear of something that fits you. You can believe me on that. By the way, what ever happened to your story about the Read Mental Health Center? I follow your bylines."

Nash laughed out loud, felt his body shake, and relaxed inside again. This apparently was just small talk after all with some blatant flattery thrown in just in case Nash turned up on another Chicago paper. Wrong subject nevertheless. "Hold on a second, alderman." Nash lit a cigarette, took a deep drag, and blew out the smoke, then said, "What happened was exactly what it looked like. It was in all the newspapers and on TV."

"I noticed you never pursued it after that. Did you lose interest, or what?" Colucci's voice was the same as before.

Nash squinted, becoming half alert like a dog raising his ears while dozing; and he tried to hear Colucci's question a second time in his mind. He took his feet off the desk to help himself think, but was still leaning back in his chair. "Well, let's put it this way...," he said, stalling. What was Colucci up to? Colucci should have more sense than to continue asking about a subject that was clearly embarassing to Nash. Nash rolled to his right to lessen the effort required by his back, then sat up straight. He had the phone in his left hand. He knew that with certain types of politicians, the shift from pleasantries to confidences came quickly; and they spoke indirectly out of habit, allowing the other party to collaborate or walk away. Nash guessed if anything was going on here, Colucci wanted to know if the fix was put in. It was a charming idea that brought a fleeting smile to Nash's face. Everybody thought everything was fixed. Maybe Colucci wanted to see if the editors had put the kabosh on the story, or if Nash himself had done it, he thought.

"To tell you the truth, alderman, Clarence Bryce, the prosecutor, is a long time friend of mine. I wrote the original story to help him out, and because I thought it was true. When the story backfired, I didn't give a shit about it any more." Nash phrased it in a way Colucci would appreciate, but it was pretty much the truth anyway.

"That's what happened, huh? Why didn't somebody else pick it up?"

"Who would want to dredge up a turkey like that? But now that you mention it, maybe somebody would under different circumstances. I might myself if I had something new to go on. But before elections, for most of the press, there's not much free time. Maybe's somebody's got it in his back pocket and is going to chase it now."

"I thought I heard somebody else was making inquiries. Things get quiet after the election. I see. Do you know John Schuty?"

Oh, fuck, thought Nash. "I've met him. I don't know him personally. I know him through his work."

"What do you think of him?"

"He's...uhh...not my type. He's a little too heavy handed."

"Heavy handed?"

"It's hard to describe." Then Nash thought, Why am I letting Colucci pump me for information? Let him learn about Schuty from somebody else. "Alderman, you didn't call me to discuss John Schuty."

"How do you know?" Colucci paused. "But you're right, Nash. I really called to say thanks for what you did for my nephew even though he wasted the opportunity we both gave him. I'm sorry I don't know of any jobs in your line." Colucci hesitated for a long moment of silence, then said, "Your paper's through, I suppose."

"No. No. Not exactly. Tomorrow we're through. Today we're still putting out a paper. We'll be writing until 1 or 2 in the morning." Come on, Nash thought.

"Well, I wish you luck..."

"Alderman, what do you want?"

"Just checking. Some people I know wanted some advice."

"What kind of advice?"

"General advice. How long to you expect to be at this number?"

"How long do you want me to be?"

"A few minutes. A half hour at most, if it won't inconvenience you."

"Can you tell me what we're talking about?"

"Some people I know wanted to talk to a reporter. They wanted me to contact Penny Warnecke. They like what she does on TV and thought Warnecke would listen to an alderman. But I don't know her. I've had some experience with you."

"What's the subject?" Nash dropped his burning cigarette in his ash tray to keep from dropping it accidentally somewhere else. He was starting to tremble.

"You can discuss that with them, if they agree to call you. A business acquaintance of mine tells me her son has found himself in an uncomfortable situation, quite innocently. Or that's what his mother says. She's got a good lawyer. It isn't the legal side that concerns her principally. They're worried about what this will look like when it comes out, especially with this guy Schuty involved. She wonders if there is a way the truth could be presented, um, sympathetically, so that her son would not be 'chewed up by a pack of mad dogs.' Those are her words, not mine."

Despite his tension, Nash had to smile. "I understand. I'm sympathetic as hell, alderman. But you realize the truth and sympathy might be two, separate things."

"I'm aware of that, Nash." Colucci sounded insulted, as if Nash had doubted his intelligence. Nash often found it necessary to risk that reaction to make things clear. Colucci continued, "They would want you to agree to certain terms beforehand. Do you want it?"

Nash closed his eyes tightly and took a deep breath through his nose. "If this is about the Read Mental Health Center, absolutely. Otherwise, you gotta tell me what it is."

Colucci sighed. "I would call you up to give you a pig in a poke, Nash. This is something you're interested in. And you may leave me out of it."

"Okay, okay. Have the son call me. I'll take care of the terms. You're out of it."

"Don't go away. I don't want to spend all day on this."

As Nash waited for the call, he leaned back in his chair, folded his hands in his lap and meditated. The trouble with Schuty, he thought, chewing the inside of his lower lip, was that Schuty periodically did things that were completely unacceptable, like the hatchet job on Bryce. So you finally decided the issue of what was right, and you gave yourself an award for not being Schuty, and you reclined on your virtue. Meanwhile, Schuty was still burrowing away, pulling his levers, distorting his distortions, threatening his threats, saying whatever he had to say, apparently standing for nothing, and before you knew it, you were scooped by another Schuty story.

When the phone rang, Nash sat up to grab the receiver and felt physically afraid. He hadn't done anything demanding for a while, and the last time, he had fallen.

Perhaps to fool himself out of his fear, he told himself this was probably just another tease, more unverifiable information.

"Nash," he announced.

"Nash, you called me quite a few times, but I never returned any of your calls. I'm Dr. Gerard Crawford."

37

The asphalt parking lot in front of the Read Mental Health Center was full of holes, something Nash noticed for the first time as he drove around and parked 50 yards from the main entrance, the nearest parking space he could find. Leaving the asphalt and stepping onto the concrete sidewalk that ran along the front of the building, he saw scoopfuls of unmelted rock salt dotting the way, like urban cow pies. Rock salt ate through concrete and asphalt and killed grass and shrubs, but it conveniently melted small snowfalls (that still came down in March) saving the the bother of shoveling. No owner existed here to worry about the property.

Walking through the doors of the glass-front building, Nash hoped Dr. Crawford would be where he was supposed to be. Something registered. Somebody had washed the windows! Promote that man, thought Nash. No. Don't promote him. He won't wash the windows anymore. The lobby was smaller than Nash remembered. The floor of red, ceramic tile was filthy with hundreds of white, salty footprints. At the far end of the lobby, a man was standing by the scale model of the hospital which rested on a table. Had to be Crawford. The man had his hands clasped behind his back and appeared to be waiting for something.

As Nash approached, the man said, "Mr. Nash?"

"Yes. Dr. Crawford?" They shook hands.

"Let's go this way." Crawford pointed to Nash's left down a corridor. Nash felt anxious to get out of the lobby, and apparently the doctor did, too. Crawford was in his early 30's, about the same height as Nash, and prematurely bald across the top of his head in a way that seemed to suggest he was athletic, perhaps because he looked like a thin version of former football player Terry Bradshaw. The hair on the sides of his head was light brown, and his eyes were blue and steady. Nash had expected a momma's boy, but he didn't look the part. The doctor was wearing a tan, pullover sweater and neat, brown, corduroy slacks. A white shirt collar stuck up out of the sweater. He had the young, competent appearance on an intern in an emergency room on a Sunday afternoon. Crawford asked, "Have you ever been here before?"

"Yeah, once," said Nash.

They were walking side by side, with Dr. Crawford a little ahead, down the corridor off the lobby. The floor had changed from red ceramic to light tan, linoleum floor tile.

"Was it a professional visit or a personal visit?" From the intonation and the doctor's nod, Nash guessed this might be meant as a small joke, which didn't come off very well. He decided Dr. Crawford was more nervous than he looked. "Pardon that," said the doctor.

"Let's say I was crazy enough to come here looking for you," said Nash.

Crawford laughed, then turned and looked at Nash's face, sizing him up again. They soon made a right turn and were out of sight and earshot of the lobby. Walking along another corridor, Crawford said in a softer voice, "Do you know John Schuty?"

Nash stepped up to be even with the doctor and responded in his own muted voice, "Yes. I understand he's taken an interest in Read."

"In the hospital and in me." Crawford was looking straight ahead as he spoke. Nash could see a scowl from the side. "This is an original experience for me, Nash." Crawford had switched to a whisper. "I've never had anything to do with reporters, or investigators, or even lawyers. You know what I find?"

"No."

"The best lawyer in the world can't protect you from the news media."

Nash nodded. "That's true. Thank goodness."

Nash saw a head and neck motion preparatory to a response, but the doctor held his answer. They were strangers feeling each other out. Then, after a few moments, Crawford turned partly and said, "Do these things have entertainment value for you people?" Curiousity seemed to be mixed with high indignation, a well-acted doctor's manner.

What things? We haven't discussed any, thought Nash. Nash decided it was not yet time to quarrel. "No offense, doc. I was just looking at it from my point of view."

They turned a corner and Nash knew he was about to be lost. He hadn't kept track of where they were going. Crawford stopped. They were near a door leading outside, and the corridor was empty.

"Your colleague, Schuty, has called up my friends and asked them about me, what sort of person I am. He never says anything I can sue him for." Crawford looked down the corridor past Nash, and Nash looked in the other direction. "But he leaves the slimy impression that I have done something. How does he know who my friends are?"

"Probably found out where you went to medical school," said Nash without hesitation. "He wants you to talk to him, and that's his way of putting pressure on you." Nash could see the cleverness of the tactic, but he did not approve of character assassination done in advance just to fish. That could be turned on one's self or one's mother.

"If I have anything to say about it, Schuty won't get anything in connection with this story. You people are dangerous, Nash. And when this is over, I'm going to call his editor—or would that help him more than hurt him?"

"You do whatever you want, doctor," said Nash, shaking his head.

"Do you need a quick tour before we sit down to talk?"

"No, thanks." Nash was going to say the place gave him the creeps, but he didn't want to offend the doctor. "Maybe after we talk. How do you know Colucci?"

They went out the door into the air; the temperature was in the 40's; and they crossed a courtyard with patches of snow here and there on brown grass. The courtyard was decorated with crab apple trees with multiple trunks.

"My mother manages a restaurant. I won't say which one. They buy from Colucci's company on South Water Market. You know, vegetables and..."

"I understand."

"This is a shortcut," said Dr. Crawford. "When we enter the unit, just walk through like you're with me, and don't say who you are. I think the nursing staff will assume you're a relative or friend of a patient. When the time comes, I'll tell them."

Nash nodded. He thought: The time is today. I'm going to interview them. But he said nothing. Disagreements were unnecessary at this point. People who were dealing with a reporter for the first time often said, "Now you do this, and you do this, and I think this is very important for you." The suggestions were usually harmless. But once in a while, if you paid attention, such people had good advice.

They came to a one-story building on the other side of the courtyard, and Dr. Crawford knocked on the glass door. Someone inside recognized him and buzzed the door open. As they entered, Nash could see what he assumed were two nurses, one of them wearing a white uniform, behind a counter on the opposite side of a large room. Scattered about the room on chairs and couches or moving about were approximately 15 men and women Nash assumed were the patients. He avoided looking at them with the exception of one young man with a slack face and bags under his eyes who approached Nash and the doctor and said, "Hi, I'm Bruno," with his eyes wide and a stupid look on his face.

"How are you this afternoon, Bruno?" said Dr. Crawford.

"Hello, Bruno," said Nash.

Bruno did not respond, just stood there. "This is the day room," said Dr. Crawford. Nash took it in from left to right and noticed a bank of three pay phones on the wall behind him to his left. A day room in the old County Jail was a circular room surrounded by tall bars, like a lion tamer's cage in the circus. This day room was roughly rectangular. The front wall where they had entered was about 60 per cent glass. The other, real walls were beige, the floor tiles were brown, and the boundaries of the room were partly imaginary because the room blended into succeeding rooms or wide hallways. The architecture gave off no hint of jail. It suggested a meeting room in a park district field house built in the 1960's, pleasant but institutional. Crawford pointed with his finger off to the right and led Nash into a corridor off the day room and then into a small office, one of three or four in a row along one side of the corridor.

"Who's Bruno?" said Nash while he took his coat off. He laid his coat over the back of an office swivel chair on wheels and put his hat on top of his coat. Then he sat down in a matching chair.

"Specifically, I can't tell you because of the privacy guarantees. In general, many of the people here, in addition to their other problems, have difficulty socializing and are starved for relationships." The doctor had sat down behind a desk and was moving his waste basket out of the way of his feet. Nash was sitting where he assumed a patient sat. The office had plain, prefabricated concrete walls painted white with not even a clock disturbing the surfaces. The well-used office furniture seemed to have been bought at an auction, although Nash guessed it was brought here haphazardly from some other public building. All three chairs were black steel and chrome as was Dr. Crawford's desk, but the top of his desk was brown wood grain, some sort of glued on contact paper which covered the original surface and which clashed wondrously with the black metal sides. On the desk were two lamps, a small, bedroom lamp with a shade and an old-fashioned flourescent reading lamp, neither plugged in. A flourescent light in the ceiling lit the room brightly. Next to Nash was a banged up, gray metal filing cabinet, much older than the building and out of place. Only a state institution would have an office like this, thought Nash.

Back in the newsroom, the people on the city desk had lit up with amusement when Nash said he had to go out on a possible story and didn't want to say what it was. Such an announcement was to be expected from a reporter once in a while. But no one had remotely expected to hear it on the last day. Nash could have said he was going to a movie, but he felt a need to abide by the newsroom routine until it ended.

He knew he should have taken a photographer along, but he would have had to explain what he was up to, and this story had made a fool of him once before. He borrowed Gentile's gas guzzler car.

In the small office at Read, Dr. Crawford was sitting sideways to his desk, leaning on the desk with one arm, still playing with his feet a little, trying to get comfortable, or hesitating. Nash had a view of Dr. Crawford's right profile and of the window behind the doctor that looked out onto the courtyard. Crawford abruptly put his head back, compressed his lips, and appeared to be examining the ceiling.

"When I was reckless and raunchy, Nash...," Crawford breathed in and out once through his mouth with a slight tremor and looked at a different part of the ceiling. Nash had opened his notebook to an empty spot without rustling the pages. He took the top off his pen. "...I used to sometimes describe this place to girls as the end of the world."

The doctor smiled, obviously laughing at himself, and switched his gaze to the side wall. "It was a good line," Crawford continued, nodding to himself. "And it's a useful image, properly understood. It's not entirely a negative thing. Like all analogies, it lacks here and there." The doctor demonstrated "here and there" by waving his hand, then turned to Nash. "I'm just trying to figure out how to get started. You're not writing this down, are you?"

"About your love life? Actually, so far I've written 'end of the world,' but you should assume I'll write down what you say from here on out." Nash wondered all of a sudden: Was this guy a killer who was also a psychopath? Psychopaths could act normal and charming. Maybe, Nash realized, he should have brought along an off-duty cop with a gun. Then again, maybe there never was a killing here. Nash's face remained at ease during this distraction.

"My understanding was that you would present this the way I want it presented, in context that I will give you," said Crawford, "and in return you get it exclusively. That's clear. That's settled, isn't it?"

"Did Colucci tell you I agreed?"

"That was the deal from the beginning."

"Let me explain how we work, doctor." Nash let his notebook and pen rest in one hand. "As far as the terms go, you may be able to be a source rather than a name. I doubt it at this stage because things have gone too far. But it's a possibility. You can go off the record once in a while. That means what you say off the record won't be printed. You have to say in advance when you're going to do that. I don't advise doing it too much."

"My line for young ladies is off the record."

"Fine. But after this, you have to say in advance. And I will write the story, based on whatever the information is. The first time you'll read it is in the paper. I'm pretty fair. I'm sure Colucci told you." The doctor could clam up here, but Nash decided he had handled this situation before, and he could do it again. Besides, the doctor was driven to talk.

"I want to examine the story before you print it, at least get to read it."

"Won't happen. We don't do that. You're not going to get any other deal from any serious reporter in Chicago. I may indeed end up writing a story you like. You might hang it on the wall. And I will probably include some of your 'context,' whatever it is, but only if it seems proper to me and my editors."

"You mean I'm at your mercy."

"You can take out an ad instead and say anything you want, as long as it's decent. The stories written as a result of your ad will be better read than the ad. You can pass out your statement on the street. But I think what you want is a story in a general circulation newspaper."

"Somebody is going to write a story in the newspapers whether I want it or not, it seems!" Dr. Crawford sat up straight. "And with my name in it. Schuty's been dropping hints about this Sunday or next Sunday. That means to me somebody here must be talking—other than one harmless individual we may both know."

Nash guessed Schuty was dropping all kinds of phony hints and threats to scare Crawford into opening up.

"I don't wish to be a scapegoat in this affair," the doctor continued. "And I would like to see a story told right in the newspapers for once without a lot of mindless accusations and misleading information."

Nash smiled. Same old shit. "Okay, doc, let's jump in the water. Did somebody get killed here? That's what I think."

"Yes."

Nash sighed and took his pen out of his notebook hand. The confusion had lifted a tiny bit. He thought, Bryce, maybe we'll make this right yet. He wrote, "Dr. Crawford Read Thurs 3 pm Killing? Yes."

"Shot?"

"I'm going to tell this my way, Nash. And I'm going to ask you to write it all down. I guess I can't control what you do afterwards. But I can ask that you write it all down."

"I accept. Let's get moving."

Dr. Crawford lolled his head back in his chair with his mouth open again, then straightened up slowly as he began to speak. "As I said, this hospital. . . . This part is off the record, just the beginning. It's for your understanding. This hospital can be viewed as the end of the world. Not in the temporal sense, but in the geographic sense. If you think of the world as being flat, people could fall off. They do, in fact, and they always have. Mankind knows this and centuries ago created devices to catch those who fall off. Perhaps they made these devices to keep order, or out of compassion, or perhaps out of fear that the makers might need to be saved themselves some day, or some combination."

"You don't want me to use this?" Nash was writing anyway.

"In a way I do, but I don't want that phrase, 'end of the world'— even though it's mine. You know, that's not . . ."

"Why don't I just start with thinking of the world as flat, etc.?"

"Okay. If you could do that."

"Also, slow down, doc. In general, pause once in a while and watch me write. When I stop, you start."

The doctor waited for only a moment, turned and glanced out the window behind him at a crab apple tree (or what Nash guessed was a crab apple tree) and the brown grass, then started again. "At first these devices were simply human pens for people who couldn't keep their balance enough to stay on the flat. Occasionally such people spontaneously got better and returned to the world on their own. There were great reforms and gradual improvement over the ages, but even until the middle of this century, there was little anyone could do medically for a person who was acutely psychotic, acutely off balance."

Nash was way behind. He was willing to pass up what he had just heard, but he didn't want to continue this way. "Have you got a tape recorder, doc, or does somebody here?"

The doctor quickly opened his middle drawer and pulled one out. "Be my guest. I had plans for using this with the patients, but I ha-

410

ven't had much time in my two-and-a-half years here. I spend most of my time doing the mandatory medical workups on the patients."

"Just set it up and tape yourself." Nash remained ready with his notebook and pen. Crawford ran the tape for a while, presumably rewinding.

"Maybe I should ask what you know about this place, Nash?"

"Nothing. I thought it was over there," said Nash, pointing to the east, "at Irving and Narragansett."

"The old Chicago State Hospital." Crawford stopped the tape and started it again, this time presumably recording.

"Or Dunning."

"That was another name. Chicago State was a very interesting place. In the late 50's and early 60's they had almost 5,000 people over there. They had their own fire house, church, laundry, a big auditorium, a school for children. It was a regular little city. That's what I want to explain."

"Five-thousand," repeated Nash, writing it down, amazed but preoccupied. He resigned himself to getting his education in one part of his mind while keeping another part alert for incidental homicide details, watching the time, and composing questions on the story for which he came.

He was accustomed to the burning need of people who worked in "misunderstood" institutions to provide history and background before they would finally get around to the news. As often as Nash had found the background useful, it had never ceased to be nerve wracking to listen to.

"I was over there recently," Nash said, "and I didn't see any place for 5,000 people." From his youth Nash remembered once seeing three or four people far off, swinging on swings. But 5,000?

"Dunning, or Chicago State, had rows of wards, like dormitories or barracks. Almost all the old wards have been torn down. A couple at the far north end, a good hike, have been bought for a private school," said Crawford.

"How many people do you have here now, at this place?"

411

"Residents, I assume you mean, not the staff. I was talking about residents over there, too. About 320."

Nash kept writing and said off-handedly, "The rest are roaming the streets."

"Some of them, perhaps. Not all the street people are crazy. But the issue of where all the patients went is vital here. That's partly what this is all about."

"Good."

"In the 1950's and before..." The doctor looked at the tape recorder to see if it was operating and seemed to be satisfied. "...when people came to Chicago State in an acute, psychotic condition, that is, delusional, agitated, and confused, they would often stay that way. We had in those days what we now call warehousing of the mentally ill. Once in a while, you would see spontaneous remissions, but the warehouse usually remained full. Many commitments were for a lifetime.

"Then along came psychotropic drugs or major tranquilizers. With these, you could bring the patients down, calm their agitation and confusion, clear up their delusional systems enough to enable them not to have to remain in a hospital setting. In my opinion, this was as big a development as Freudian theory, but not as well known. Of course, these drugs have side effects. If you keep giving patients too much of these drugs over many years, they'll lose control of their muscles, start to drool, shake, have trouble walking. It's like anything else, you can take too much. It took a while to learn that. But the drugs were definitely a boon. Partly as a result of their discovery, a whole new commitment to human rights for mental patients began in the Kennedy era."

Nash decided it was impossible to keep up. He wriggled the fingers of his writing hand to relieve the muscles, then rested his chin on that hand and stared at the doctor, giving up all attempts at note taking. He knew he could come back to some of this later, if necessary, and it was supposed to be on the tape.

"The crusade began to clean out all these state mental hospitals, 'snakepits,' people called them."

"Were they?" said Nash, to show he was listening.

The doctor shrugged. "I wasn't around. But if you put 5,000 crazy people together in one place before the advent of drugs, I think you might have a pretty difficult situation, maybe trouble getting staff as well. In my opinion, the patients wouldn't all have been troublesome, or even crazy. Some were probably retarded. Some were eccentric and unlucky. Some were psychotic but not aggressive. But even 10 per cent aggressive would have a ripple effect."

Crawford waved a hand cutting himself off.

"That's the past. With the discovery of tranquilizing medicine came the idea of getting patients out of the state hospitals back to some form of independent living, maybe in halfway houses, maybe back home. And we were going to build community mental health facilities where..."

Nash flicked a piece of lint off his knee and noted mentally that the doctor had used the term "crazy" several times just as a layman would. That was interesting, Nash thought.

"...Only a fraction of these community, mental health facilities were ever built, and they don't do everything they were supposed to do, such as the short term admissions or day treatment, like day care. But..." Crawford knocked on the desk with the knuckles of one hand, "the state hospitals WERE emptied out as planned. And the push for patients' rights DID go forward as planned. It's a whole different ballgame now."

"Do you approve of this?" asked Nash. "Or are you complaining about it?" Nash glanced surreptitiously at his watch. He decided to let the doctor go on for five more minutes.

"Do I approve of it?"

"Yes."

Dr. Crawford glanced at Nash's wrist but tried to pretend he didn't see Nash checking the time. "That's the situation, Nash, whether I or anybody else around here approves of it or not. It's a

413

given. It's the work setup. But, do I approve of it?" Crawford tilted his head. "Yes, for the most part, I do. I think the idea has to be to treat people and put them back in the community. There is some discussion, strictly conversation, that perhaps we do need some permanent institutions again for people who will never cope. A friend of mine, a psychiatrist in private practice, said he thought we were really doing a disservice to some people, dumping them over and over into the community stresses they can't handle, only to have them be readmitted again and again.

"He said someday we're going to have to find a stable place for such people. In his words, 'Let them walk on the grounds, talk to the grass, talk to the birds. Let them live out their lives in a humane environment.' "

Nash tried to look pleasant and attentive, but he thought, Where the hell is this guy going? Then Nash had the fantasy that he was the shrink, and Dr. Crawford was the patient. Crawford was taking a roundabout way to get to the hard part because he was afraid of it, Nash decided.

"You got me off the subject, Nash." The doctor rose and looked out his window. "Or maybe you didn't. I'm sorry. I'm wandering. This is hard for me."

"I'm sorry, too, doc. But I think you'll have to sit down at your desk because that's where the recorder is."

The doctor flinched. "I forgot." He sat down. "The subject I was on was patients' rights." He opened the right hand drawer of his desk, pulled out a piece of paper, and handed it to Nash. It was labeled at the top, "Summary of Rights—Read aloud to recipient." Nash started to fold it up, intending to put it in his pocket.

"Take a look at it. Read it."

Nash opened it and skimmed it. The first sentence said: "1. You have a right to maintain all of your legal rights." Another, down the page, said, "You have a right to unimpeded and uncensored communication." And another said, "You have a qualified right to refuse services." There were 12 such items.

"This is two or three times longer than the Miranda warnings, doc."

Crawford ignored the remark. "We read that to each patient at the point of admitting him to the hospital. Sometimes this can be a little surreal if the patient is really freaking out. He's in Oz, and I'm reading this, but we do it. And we give it to them to keep. I believe in all those things, Nash, including the right to refuse medication unless the patient is a danger to himself or others. That's what 'qualified right' means."

The doctor leaned forward and started to speak a little more slowly. Nash recognized this as the "you-must-understand" phase of the interview. "The point is that these are great advances. This is not a warehouse; the average stay here is about a month. There are some patients who are here for six or eight months, and others who leave after three days, but the average is about a month. And this is not a prison. You see all those rights." Crawford pointed to the piece of paper Nash held, "Here's another version." Crawford straighted up abruptly, opened his right hand drawer and pulled out another printed paper which he thrust at Nash.

"This is a longer version which we summarized in the first one for the sake of efficiency. But I have it memorized. It starts out, 'As a general rule you lose none of your rights, benefits, or privileges."

"That's what it says." Nash folded it in half and put it in his notebook, saying at the same time. "Stop a minute and let me put down what you said." Nash wrote in his notebook, "The point is that these are great advances. This is not a warehouse. The average stay here is about a month. And this is not a prison. You see all those rights." If Crawford said this was the point, Nash wasn't going to argue with him. And he finally had a suspicion of where Crawford was going.

"Who did you kill?" said Nash, guessing the time was right. After he said it, he realized he should have said, "Whom."

"I didn't kill anyone."

"Who got killed?"

415

"A patient."

"Why?"

"The patient who was...killed had killed before and was trying to do it again. It was a life saving effort by a member of the staff."

Nash came to life, scribbling, reminding himself to keep it legible, and suddenly sensing the purpose for all that background. He couldn't see exactly how it all fit, but he could feel that whole batch of information was going to be very useful. He wanted it now as part of the story and was grateful for the tape recorder.

"What was his name?"

"His name was Billy March, M-A-R-C-H, March. I'm crossing the Rubicon to unemployment here. I should not be discussing individual patients with a reporter."

Nash was writing everything Crawford said verbatim, and when Nash spoke, he spoke to his notebook. "This is a special situation, doc."

"Yes. I would say so," answered Crawford.

"How old was he?"

"Twenty-eight." Nash heard a desk drawer open again and looked up to see Crawford pulling a manilla folder out of the middle drawer.

"Where did he live?"

"In Uptown, mostly. His parents live in Schiller Park."

"Give me their names and phone numbers."

"I can't, Nash."

"Doctor, think about it. You have to. You want this done right, don't you? You want me to check this out?"

Crawford hesitated with an expression of pain on his face, then relented. When Nash had that information in his notebook, he asked, "Who killed him?"

"That I really won't say."

Nash sighed. "Once this comes out, there's no way to keep that confidential. It is generally not allowed in our society to kill people confidentially."

"Nevertheless, I'm not going to say."

"Are you sure it wasn't you?"

"It was not me!" Crawford perked up at that. "There is somebody here, our little friend, who seems to think it was me, and somebody in your profession who seems to have that idea, but it was not me. Is that what you think? Is that why you left all those messages?"

"So you got them."

"Yes."

"Doctor, I really don't care who did it. I just want to know for purposes of this story you wish me to write."

"It was a technician, a member of the nursing staff."

"What sort of technician?"

"A mental health technician. That's the job title. It's like an aide or an orderly in a regular hospital. I feel that the homicide was justifiable in the law, so I'm not going to name the person."

The last sentence was an excellent quote, Nash recognized, and he made pains to get it exactly right. The doctor might never say it so clearly again even if they came back to the issue.

"How was March killed?"

"A gunshot wound to the head. I believe the gun was a .25 caliber automatic. Somebody from the State's Attorney's Office took it, but I don't know the caliber for a fact. Death was instantaneous. He was shot in the temple. Bang. I hope I never see anything like that again."

This was terrific stuff, Nash realized. "Stop a second, doc. Let me catch up."

"He was very dead. I'm a doctor, and I'm confident of my abilities in that regard. Now I'll wait for you."

When Nash had scribbled the last sentences also, thinking, I hope I have room for that line, he took a deep breath and looked up. "Uhh, why were you dragging him by the leg?" It occurred to him immediately he should not have given the doctor a leading question, but it was out.

417

Crawford laughed nervously. "He was...he was on the floor in front of the ladies shower room! There was a patient in the shower room who wanted to come out, and she was becoming upset, so we had to move him. We couldn't let her see him. Who told you? Was it...?" The doctor did not finish.

Nash was writing as fast as he could, concentrating to remember until his pen could catch up with the words. When he finished, he answered, "It's my turn to say I can't say, doc." He was getting random material, and pretty soon he was going to have to make the doctor go way back to the history of Billy March, then walk through the whole affair slowly to the present. But first, "Tell me briefly what happened."

The doctor leaned back in his chair holding March's folder in his right hand. "I was working intake because one of the other doctors called in sick. I'm normally assigned to the A unit in the daytime, but we have a backup roster as in any hospital. March had come here from Chester about a week earlier. Our mandate is to keep patients in the least restrictive environment that is feasible; and this usually means giving them more and more freedom as they improve. He was to spend some time here while we monitored his medication and his behavior to see if he was ready to be released. Reed is less restrictive than Chester which is maximum security."

"Released to the world."

"To the world."

"Time out." Nash had got a sudden, belated warning from his mind. "Stop the tape recorder. Rewind it a little and play it back." The doctor followed Nash's instructions, and the tape was perfect. When the machine replayed Crawford's last words, Nash said, "All right. Put it on 'record' and go."

"The staff did not trust March, the nursing staff. One of them wanted him sent back to Chester. Perhaps I should have listened to them more. They're with the patients much more than I am. He got in at least one fight. There was some disagreement over who started it. He also refused to take his medicine a couple times claiming there were germs in it. Then one time he did ask to be medicated because he felt an episode coming on. He was monitoring his own behavior, and this is a sign of some improvement. Apparently, this particular technician was afraid of March and brought a gun to work. This is strictly forbidden, of course. It's just...totally beyond the bounds. We have no guns or weapons here. It was a small gun and fit in his pocket. Nobody knew. March is incredibly strong. The man he killed, he broke his neck on the sidewalk on the North Side while two people were trying to stop him. Not guilty by reason of insanity. That's why this department had him.

"I was in intake at about 8:45 when I got a call from a nurse asking me to authorize medication and restraints for March against his will. A doctor has to do this, and March was starting to become agitated, yelling, throwing furniture around. But it was sporadic. It wasn't an all out riot, he would be quiet for a while, and they were talking to him.

"When I arrived and he saw me, he jumped behind the nurse, grabbed her—he had her by the head and neck—and they both fell to the floor. March was on the bottom, but he was turning her head. Before I knew what was happening, this technician put a gun to March's temple and shot him. I didn't see the gun until afterward. I only saw his hand. But I heard the noise. I said, 'What did you do?' He said, 'Him or her, doc. Him or her.'" Crawford looked at the ceiling. "If only I had been sick that evening or the other doctor hadn't been sick or the roster had been different or I had done something about March. I was going to leave this place in a few months anyway and join a private clinic in Evanston. It's all arranged, but now I don't know what will happen."

You might be indicted for concealing a homicide, thought Nash. But he didn't say it. He said, "Who saw this?"

Crawford lowered his face to level and looked at Nash. He held up his right index finger. "One, me. Two, the technician." He raised a second finger. "The department will fire him now. I don't see any

419

way around it. Maybe he'll be prosecuted. Not the homicide, but the gun. I imagine it was unregistered. Most of them are, aren't they?"

"I don't know." Nash took the question seriously, and did not know the percentages. From his years in the news business, he firmly believed in banning all handguns except for the use of police and soldiers. This incident did not change his opinion, but he felt in a story, as in court, every incident had to be considered in and of itself.

"Three, the nurse March attacked, who has quit."

"You're lucky she hasn't sued the state."

"Maybe she will. That doesn't affect me personally." Crawford pointed to his chest. "Or will it?" He looked away. "Malpractice!"

"Who else?"

"Ohhhh. This really pisses me off, Nash. I haven't been able to analyze this thing logically. Damn." Nash considered this excuseable emoting, a voicing of ordinary reactions that were better kept to oneself. Nash knew that by playing up these self-interested remarks in the story, he could make Crawford look like an idiot, but Nash did not need such material, and besides, Crawford was helping Nash.

"Four, another nurse." Crawford plowed ahead. "And four-and-a-half, a patient who had a glimpse of the aftermath. The rest of the patients were in the day room or their bedrooms at the opposite end of the unit, except for the one in the shower room who saw nothing and is, um, not real aware. We calmed her down and told her everything was all right."

"Who is four-and-a-half?"

"Do you ever get phone calls from here? I think you know. She was new to this unit. She had been on our twin unit and was doing very well. She was transferred here to even out the patient load. Afterwards, we sent her back to remove her from the scene of the trauma. She's regressed, though. It's..." Crawford threw up his hands.

"What day did this shooting take place and what time?"

The doctor gave the same date Nash had been relying on since the beginning. Victoria had said it happened the day before she called. The time, 9 p.m. seemed about right. Victoria had not given a clock time.

"All right, doctor, we still have to go through what happened after the shooting, the State's Attorney's investigation, the coverup. But I want to go back to before the beginning. Give me Billy March's history, whatever you have in that folder there, not too technical, just the major events, to sort of explain how he got here and how he got shot."

"Don't you have enough?"

"I remember what happened the last time I wrote this story, doc. I'm not going to allow it this time. By the way, where's the body?"

"I wasn't involved in that, but I understand he received an ordinary burial at state expense through a funeral home chosen by the parents. The parents were probably happy to keep it quiet, too."

"Start with the history." Nash got his pen ready.

Forty-five minutes later, a fast forty-five minutes during which both expended much energy, one in memory straining, the other in understanding, and both in supressing emotions and communicating, Nash was getting tired. If a brain could overheat, Nash's would have been whistling with the escape of steam. But he was high. "Okay. Is the aide, the technician who did the shooting here today or expected to be here today?"

"I'm sorry. I'm not going to say, Nash." Crawford was sitting up straight rubbing the sides of his head with his hands.

Nash was not positive this technician existed. It was the most likely explanation. Nash believed he existed, and believed everything Crawford said. He doubted he could be fooled in this situation. But in terms of mathematical chance, it was possible Crawford's whole story was a lie. For instance, Crawford did not remember the name of the assistant state's attorney he talked to. This seemed surprising to Nash, but possible. Nash had to proceed, for the moment, as if the story was beyond doubt, and it was near time to leave Crawford's office.

"Doctor, I don't know if this is a personal question or one for the paper." To let himself down a bit from his nervous plateau, Nash decided to ask a question out of personal curiosity, one he did not expect to be of business use. "You seem like a reasonable guy, and I'm sure a few other people in the Department of Mental Health are reasonable. So whyyyyyy, just between you and me, don't you guys hold onto these killers? Keep them! I can name you two that you let go who went out and killed again. Stop doing that. Keep them in Chester until they're old. Nobody wants 'em. Nobody's interested in them—except in the negative sense that they hope they'll never come back."

"I don't lose interest in them, Nash," said Dr. Crawford, leaning forward again as if to impart a secret. "But I do distrust them. I'm not sure they belong in the Department of Mental Health where we are mandated by law to see that the patients keep most of their rights. Since they are sent here, we are required to treat them. Aside from lobotomy, which is willfully inflicted, major brain damage, there is no 'treatment' you can give a person to absolutely guarantee that he'll never kill again. If we ever found such a treatment, it would probably be outlawed. That sort of permanent manipulation of a human being could be used and abused for many reasons. The newest techniques being worked on still require the willpower of the patient."

The interview was taking too long. Nash had a lot to do yet, but this was good stuff. "You mind if I use the last part?" He continued to take notes out of habit and distrust of tape recorders.

"Go ahead. I don't even know what I said. You can put this down. We can't hold people without legal grounds to hold them, including people you call killers who have been found not guilty by reason of insanity. Not guilty is not guilty. Nor can we hold newspaper reporters who get on our nerves or threaten us. We do have to continue to work with violent people somewhere and improve our treatment because even if these, um, killers, go to prison, they will eventually be released. There's a new law under which a few of these individuals are being found "guilty but mentally ill" and are being sent to prison. But just as many, if not more, are still coming our way as innocent due to insanity. I don't know what the public wants. But if they want killers to go away for 10 years or more, the Department of Mental Health is not the place to send them. We're not a prison."

Nash asked for both tapes, and Dr. Crawford handed them over. The interview required two tapes because Nash wanted recording on one side only. "You may notice I'm getting antsy here, doc." Nash's movements were becoming agitated. "Time is short for me. But I want to see the scene and have you explain it there."

Dr. Crawford agreed. They left the office and walked a few yards down the corridor until the doctor stopped. "I have to do something," he said. "Let's go up front." They reversed course and walked to the day room, up to the counter at the rear of the day room, the nurse's station.

"Mrs. Smith, I don't want you to think this is underhanded, or I'm trying to harm the staff." Crawford was speaking to the nurse in the white uniform who was standing up, writing something on a form on the desk below her. While Crawford talked, she resumed writing, letting it be known she would not drop everything to listen to the young doctor. She had a dominant air about her, and Nash guessed that Mrs. Smith was really in charge of the unit. "This is Mr. Nash of the Chicago Chronicle," Crawford continued. Mrs. Smith's eyes came up, and she examined both Nash and the doctor as two burdens, as trouble, but she still had her pen to the page. "You can guess why he's here. I invited him. He's my responsibility. You may object if you like."

Mrs. Smith raised herself erect, placing down the pen, taking over the area. She said coldly, "This place is off limits to the press. Only legitimate visitors can come here visiting specific patients."

"Yes, we know that, Mrs. Smith," said Dr. Crawford.

A tall, strong woman—the mother of football players, Nash guessed—Mrs. Smith placed one hand on her hip and stood still, holding the stage. Her attitude seemed to suggest that men were repeatedly, inexplicably childish, incapable of forseeing damage or of dealing with reality. Nash watched her and enjoyed the dilemma. He wondered how she was going to sort out the conflicting responsibilities to her workers, to the patients, to the larger world to which she belonged, to the hospital, and lastly, to whatever her relationship was with Dr. Crawford. What a mess, he thought.

She raised the hand from her hip and looked at her nails, then turned the hand over and studied her palm. She dropped the hand and looked at Nash and Crawford. "You have to leave, Mr. Nash," she said, finally.

"He's just about to," said Crawford. "We only have a few more things to do." Another woman whom Nash assumed was a nurse was lounging in a chair, her arm stretched out full length on a desk behind her, watching the show. A third woman who acted like an employee had come up to the counter from the outside and was also watching. "It's settled that you ordered him to leave, Mrs. Smith. I brought him here, and I'll be responsible for getting him out of here soon." Crawford turned and walked back down the corridor. Nash followed.

When they had advanced out of earshot, Nash said, "Were you giving them an out?"

"Most of these women are supporting families," said Crawford, walking rapidly. "This is my way of doing things reasonably."

When they reached the end of the corridor, they turned left and were outside the ladies shower room. The doctor began to lay out the action without prodding, seeming to feel his own need for hurry, but Nash forced him to be tediously precise. Nash even drew a picture with stick people in his notebook.

"There's another nurse here who can corroborate what I've told you," said Crawford, "if you agree to keep her out of it. She's already here for the night shift." Nash looked at his watch. It was 4:20. Crawford started back to the day room down the left hand corridor, the corridor down which they had come, but Nash re-

424

trieved him and insisted they take the right hand corridor. The whole meandering 'A' unit was roughly rectangular with the ladies shower room on one of the short ends, and the day room at the opposite short end. Going down the corridor that they had not yet traveled, they passed what Crawford called the dining room, the visitors lounge, game room, and some bedrooms where Nash could see a few patients staring at the walls or out windows. Nash and the doctor came to the nurse's station from behind instead of from the front. Mrs. Smith was apparently instructing two night shift workers, but all three stopped and gazed at Nash and Crawford with suspicious expressions. The whole day room seemed to Nash more subdued.

"Lucille, may I speak to you a minute?" said Crawford. All the women were in their 40's. "Let me speak to her a minute," said Crawford to Nash.

"Sure," said Nash. "I'll stand right next to you." Nash wanted Lucille to be unprepared.

"Don't get involved, honey," said Mrs. Smith.

Lucille turned out to be the woman who had been lounging with her arm on the desk. She listened blandly, showing no expression at all, while Dr. Crawford spoke. The other two women listened also, pretending to be aloof. Crawford kept talking, waiting for some expression to appear in Lucille's face, until Nash began to feel that she was getting too much pressure. He could almost feel how difficult it was for her to hold that expressionless face.

"Miss, it's completely up to you," said Nash, interrupting. "If you choose to help, I won't use your name or title. I'll describe you as a source in the hospital or something like that. I'm going to write about this incident in a couple hours, and the newspaper will be on the street tomorrow. It's just a question of whether, when you read the story, you'll be satisfied it was told fairly. It's up to you." Nash shrugged.

"Lucille...," said Dr. Crawford. Nash touched him, and he stopped. They waited.

"How do I know you'll write in the newspaper what I say?" asked Lucille slowly, suspiciously.

"You don't," said Nash, smiling. He opened his eyes wide. "How do I know you're telling the truth?"

Lucille turned her head and looked elsewhere as if she were being jived, but Nash saw a trace of humor in her eye.

Nash guessed something had started here through the staff's observation of himself and Dr. Crawford, that a natural momentum had begun which everyone present could feel. It was the human urge to tell the darn story which lived side by side with the urge to cover it up. The telling urge, once indulged, had its own force and satisfaction. Even those who were silent would get off on the telling. But if somebody dropped a cup or a clipboard, that could break the spell.

Lucille turned her head again and considered Nash, then said, "Come here, Mr. Reporter," and led him back down the corridor.

38

Nash sat on a chair made of hard plastic with metal legs and waited for Dr. Crawford. Lucille had described what seemed to Nash to be the same incident, with some discrepancies, down by the ladies shower room. Upon returning to the day room, Nash found that Dr. Crawford had gone off, but was supposed to return quickly, so Nash decided to wait. He wasn't through.

He looked around the day room, keeping his line of vision high, purposely seeing little. Out of the corners of his eyes, he noticed that two or three patients regarded him curiously. Nash was afraid of all of them. He thought of them, together, as a great drop, as the view just across the edge that was dangerous to look at.

Eventually, he forced himself to look. Two young men in ordinary street clothes were playing Ping Pong at a table near the front windows, an activity Nash thought suspicious. Directly in front of him, in the middle of the room, a chubby young woman in a lime green dress was collapsed across a couch, looking like a boneless, muscleless child, utterly flacid, breathing like a fish through her mouth made crooked by the weight of her head on the couch. She appeared to be catatonic or escaping rather than asleep. Two more men in their 20's paced around the fringe of the room, one white, one Hispanic, their jaws set, eyes determined, something driving each man within. An old black woman with kinky gray hair, wearing a winter coat and hat indoors, sat in a chair with her head bowed, shaking her hands endlessly in front of her chest. Other patients sat calmly, looking dull, like people passing the time.

Twenty feet to the right, two men in white t-shirts and dark pants stared hard at Nash and smoked. Both had unkempt, black hair, sunken eyes, and needed shaves. One was hunched over, his elbows on his knees. They looked to Nash to be normal, or recently normal. Deteriorating Southern boys, he thought, the kind one might meet in a bar in Uptown.

He took a deep breath. He probably wasn't going to catch anything. Nobody was going to do anything. It was even fairly peaceful in the room. The nurses were doing whatever they did behind him, getting ready for supper or the evening. He began to feel impolite for his staring.

Well..., what are we all doing here, guys and girls? said Nash in his mind. I'm from a yellow apartment building on Adams Street near Moore Playground. (He could see it, and this seemed like a suitable introduction. Everybody was from somewhere. Patients at Read were sorted by neighborhoods. He thought this introduction in images rather than words.) That's basically what I am, he said, in words meant for himself and for the patients, speaking only in his mind, referring to the image from his childhood. Somehow, he thought further, I am also this newspaper reporter you all see sitting here, and I am about to write a story that will create a great sensation in the state of Illinois for about a week. I tried this before, but this time I think it will stick, and the air will be full of accusations and wonderful noise. That's kind of strange that I should be doing that, huh? Yes, I think so, too. (He actually nodded and caught himself.)

428

So what happened to you guys? You're all jes' folks, I'll bet. Eh, maybe not. Not the frozen girl there. You two are boozers, I think. (He stared at the two serious smokers who stared at him, and he rearranged his coat where it was bunched under his leg.) What do you two see in me? You see a boozer like I see in you? You ever get violent? Sure you do. That's why you're here. Ever spin your wife across the room like crack the whip on ice, then go to sleep? But nothing stops you, huh? I stop drinking once in a while because I've still got that wife. What do you got? No, don't tell me.

The doc here thinks there's hope for you guys and girls, some hope. (Nash scanned the room again.) He thinks most of you have something to say about how things turn out. That's more than I'd give you—unless I was in here myself. Seventy per cent of you are schizophrenic, he says. That must be freaky. You can get better if you take your medicine. Then you go out; you're cool and you're well, but the medicine makes you feel slow. So maybe you quit taking your medicine. Then you get weird again. Impossible to accept, right? But, hey, what do I know? I saw a lady leave here once. (He could see the classy young blond again.) She was quite a chick. She seemed okay. She left on her own, I think. I suppose you'll all be leaving soon. Gotta make room.

Nash's mind then stumbled over the question of why they were all here in the Read Mental Health Center and he was not. He did not verbalize this question, although he almost did. Some things he refused to ponder, and he would not allow the question to be phrased. He interfered with his own, spontaneous thoughts, and they became jumbled. He approved of himself in a non-verbal fashion and felt the natural superiority of the well over the sick. He saw the kinship and let it go at that.

He put his hands under his thighs and sat on them, watching. And in a moment, he wondered who, looking at this room from the side or above, would be able to distinguish him from the others. He felt himself smile slightly, and he knew his face had been showing various expressions accompanying his inner monologue all along, and he knew he had nodded at least once in answer to his own question. What WAS the difference? Something in his head, the top half of his head? He allowed himself to think it, and his eyes darted from one to another of the patients. Two or three of the patients sitting along the wall looked normal, relatively clear eyed, but nervous, as if waiting for something bad to happen.

"Mr. Nash?"

He jumped a bit and thought he must look like a little kid here, sitting on his hands. He turned and saw Dr. Crawford and at the same time, Nash automatically reached inside his sportcoat for his notebook.

As he arose, leaving his coat on the chair, he saw that Dr. Crawford was escorting a young woman with a round, pretty face framed by short, wavy, brown hair. She was wearing a sweater and an old skirt that did not go together, bobby socks, and girls' flats. Although she was a little plump, it was a youthful plumpness. Nash found himself wondering if she would be a good lay. He immediately kicked himself hard internally and put on a polite smile.

"Umm, doctor, would this by any chance be Victoria Morici?" Nash took a guess.

"Yes. She has to get back quickly, but I thought it would be nice for her to meet you. Perhaps if you spoke to her, it would help clear up some things. Victoria, this is Sam Nash."

Victoria's face became agitated, and she stepped back, and rubbed the fingers of one hand on her sweater, starting at her breast and moving toward her side. At the same time, she looked him up and down in a glance and looked around as if wondering where to hide. Nash sensed that he was the guest who comes to the party on the wrong day. Pretending he did not notice her discomfort, he said, "Hi, Victoria. I guess I did come to see you after all." He extended his right hand.

She leaned forward from the waist and shook his hand awkwardly and quickly, but did not come closer, and she continued to look at him as if he were the last person she wanted to see. "Hi. How are...?" she said, biting off the words. She didn't finish.

"Victoria, I didn't know you would be so pretty," said Nash.

"I'm not dressed," she said, to Dr. Crawford instead of to Nash.

"It's okay," said the doctor.

"Victoria, I ain't the Pope. I'll bet when you get dressed up you are really very pretty because you're pretty now. How's the doctor treating you here?"

"Senator O'Brien took my baby. My dog is my baby. I knew John Lennon and his mother. She owes me. Twenty-two-and-a-half per cent."

Victoria said these things with conviction. Nash frowned and tried to go over what she said quickly in his mind to see what the meaning might be.

"Victoria, this is Nash..." The doctor lowered his voice to a whisper and leaned toward her ear. "...a reporter at the Chicago Chronicle. I think you might know him. Did you speak to him on the phone?"

"There's a hundred thousand dollar contract on my life in the New Right. They killed my brother, and I went to Skid Row to see my dog." She continued in this vein, and Nash gave a puzzled look to Dr. Crawford.

"Just talk to her normally and ignore the senseless things," said the doctor. "I've upset her by springing you on her so suddenly, and she hasn't been taking her medicine regularly." Then to Victoria, he said, "Mr. Nash came here because I think he believed you when you called him on the phone. He wants to ask you some questions." Then to Nash again, "I'd rather have her speak to you than Schuty. But I don't know what you're going to get."

Nash was determined to pry out whatever she knew. She had been right so far, and she was probably an unbiased witness. Fleetingly, it occurred to him that perhaps he should leave her alone because of her condition. But he rationalized that there was more dignity in exploiting her as real than in ignoring her as nothing. "Now, Victoria," he said, "let's walk a little way." He took her arm, but she pulled it back, so he put his hand in the small of her back and pointed her toward the near hallway leading to the ladies shower room. "Victoria, when I talk to a pretty woman, I like to think she's going to talk to me, too," he said. "We were friends. Are you gonna?"

"I'm not dressed," she said, obviously embarassed.

Nash was encouraged. "I know. Hey, forget it. I should have let you know I was coming. It's my fault. C'mon, can we walk down here?"

"Do you believe me? Can you get my baby back?" She started walking where Nash led.

Nash felt he should try to figure out what this meant. In his limited study of psychology, he thought he had learned that all things crazy people said meant something if you could figure out the symbolism. But Dr. Crawford told him to ignore some of it. Did she have a baby?

"Do you have a baby, Victoria?" At least they were walking; then she stopped.

"I did. I lost it, the way Daniel Ellsberg projects his vision of dollars. Missiles and dollars together, Nash. The truth is photocopied by men with asphalt brains."

Nash frowned and thought for a moment, then rejected her utterance as not his business. She was holding him off with this baloney, he decided, whatever it meant. It was using her, but partly she was using it. She was probably afraid of him.

He shook his head. Then he said, "Hey, remember when I called you...I mean, when you called me? Remember that?" They were standing near Dr. Crawford's office.

"I heard a bang, and I called you the next day."

"Yeah, that's right. Good. Good. When you heard that bang, what did you see?"

"Dr. Crawford. Wait, Nash..."

"What was he doing? Yes, I'm Nash."

"Dragging the man's leg. I have the evidence that if all the people in the New Right were aware . . . " Her face became more animated. ". . .the Democrats and the Republicans are all the same. It's all based on missiles. They want to kill. There's a murder wish. I had a therapist once who talked about a death wish. He had it on his wall."

"He had a death wish on his wall?"

"I'm speaking figuratively. It was cocaine, or my dog, or a license to kill. His license to practice medicine. That's a license to kill secretly, you see. Some of us know. But if you don't give them what they want; they want me to take my medicine. Senator O'Brien took my baby."

"What do you mean, he took your baby?"

"My parents took my dog. They put it to sleep. They are the devil."

"What does that have to do with Senator O'Brien?"

"He told them to, over the radio."

Nash closed his eyes and shook his head to clear it. Then he said, "Victoria, that's ridiculous. Senator O'Brien did not take your dog or your baby, and he did not speak to your parents about it over the radio."

"Yes he did. I heard him."

"No. That didn't happen." Nash thought he could understand this one. Senator O'Brien must have been on the radio in some political announcement or interview during a struggle at home over her dog. Lunacy. "Now, come on. I need your help. I'm going to repeat that. I need your help. I need you to tell me exactly where you were sitting or standing when you heard the bang."

"I was lying on the floor." She had turned abruptly around and pointed to a spot back in the day room somewhere. A pacer was walking across the near side of the day room looking intense.

"You were lying on the floor? Let's go back there." Nash realized he should have started from the day room in the first place, but he did not believe she was lying on the floor. The attendants would

433

have shouted at her to get up or moved her. He walked quickly feeling the pressure of time, and she kept up with him."

"Show me where you were lying."

"I was sitting in a chair...here." They were along the near side of the day room between the Ping Pong table and the nurse's station with the hallway behind them.

"Which chair?"

"I don't know." She waved her hand back and forth limply indicating any one of several. Some of the chairs were moveable, and there was no chair at her designated spot at the moment.

"Why did you say you were lying down?"

She shrugged.

"What did you see when you heard the bang?"

"A killer." She said it matter-of-factly and looked at Nash for his reaction. He had the feeling she was searching him, tolerating him, trying to hold his attention, just as he was doing to her.

"Who was it?" Nash noticed Dr. Crawford watching them from across the room.

Victoria turned toward Nash, turning the side of her face to almost everyone so no one could see her mouth directly. Then she spoke softly out of the side of her mouth away from the room. "He's my friend. You're my friend, too. You're the only ones. You and Schuty. You should run for President. I could be in the Secret Service."

"Who is the killer?" said Nash, bending down, speaking out of the side of his own mouth.

"I think Dr. Crawford's a killer, but he's my friend. Many things are more in the strategic-political..."

"Wait. This is real important, what I'm going to ask you." Nash thought they hadn't got there yet, but they were making progress. "No bullshit now. The instant you heard the bang..." He snapped his fingers. "...what did you see?"

"Nash, could you get me out of here?" she whispered. "I'm okay. They're disturbed here. It's bad for my mind."

He stiffened and narrowed his eyes. Was she acting? He suddenly remembered he had told her to act, and to talk gibberish a long time earlier. "I don't know. Let's do *this* now. This is why you called me. What . . . did . . . you . . . see . . . when . . . you . . . heard . . . the . . . bang?" He snapped his fingers again.

"Him." She pointed across the room without looking.

"Who is him? There are 9 or 10 people over there."

"He'll come around. He used to watch me. He's not really a patient. He's a Frenchman or a Dutchman."

Nash stood up straight. He was getting lost.

"He was trying to make me move my chair," Victoria added. "I like to bug him, make him trip."

"Are you talking about one of those guys that walks in a circle?"

She nodded.

"When you heard the bang, he was trying to make you move your chair? Which way does he go?"

With a horizontal movement of her index finger, she indicated from left to right. Then she fixed her eyes on Nash, pleading. "You have to understand, Nash. The Democrats and the Republicans got us into this, but you're going to get me out of it. Take me with you. Tell them you're my husband. They won't follow you. Not you. There were people shouting somewhere. He was shouting. They were shouting. I was shouting. If I had my baby, Senator O'Brien would never get it. I've got a box in my room for my baby."

"People were shouting. Which way were you facing when you heard the bang?"

She turned and faced the center of the room, acting put upon, but humoring him. The doctor and the nurse said the shooting was in the hallway behind her 20 or 30 yards away and around a corner. Victoria's original story suggested that, too. Even if the shooting was in the open in the hallway, she could not have seen it facing this way. She turned back to him.

"Nash, get me out of here or get me some beer. I really need something. A little smack. They've planted something in my brain. Take me with you. I need some help."

"What happened after the bang?"

"I let that French spy suck his duck."

"What does that mean?"

"I was going to move the chair to another part of his route just to bug him. He's sick. But I wanted to see. The hell with him."

"What did you see?"

"The other side of the mountain. No." She laughed. "What did I see? The truth is my mind, the devil, mybrotherLouiscanmultiply-you. Johnson told us all to go back. I went down here..." She pointed down the near hallway where Nash had taken her. "...then he did. I went around there." She pointed to the side of the nurse's station where the other hallway led off, the same one Nash and Crawford had traveled at Nash's specific request. That hallway, too, led to the ladies shower room.

"Let's walk around there," said Nash, taking her by the arm. She resisted.

"No, no. I know this." She was shaking her head.

"What do you mean you know this?"

"I know. I don't need to. I saw Dr. Crawford down there dragging the man's leg. He's a killer. But he's my friend." She whispered the last two sentences. "That is not important. I know it is to you. Okay. But there's more. A front page story." Her eyes were imploring him to listen to her, follow her reasoning, but showed doubt that he would.

"The missiles, Nash. They're decoys. The missiles are impotent. The bombs are in the radios! Do you get it? Ghetto blasters! They laugh at us because they don't think we see it."

Nash closed his eyes. When he opened them, he sighed and asked, "Who had the gun?"

"One of the aides had it. Do you see? Ghetto blasters."

"Did you tell John Schuty you saw Dr. Crawford shoot somebody?"

"Schuty's my friend, too. You never came to see me. Neither did he. Maybe he did it. Or you, Nash. No, you'd kill 'em with your bare hands, wouldn't you? I'm speaking figuratively. I know." She seemed to be apologizing.

"Did you tell John Schuty . . ."

"I don't know what I told Schuty. They gave me him when I called." She made a violent slice in the air with her hand, dismissing the subject, then she continued, "Maybe. He's nice. I'm marked now like Janis Joplin and Daniel Ellsberg."

Nash was getting a headache with the effort to listen to her. He had long ago put his notebook away, and he had taken no notes of what Victoria said. Just listening required all his concentration and made his knees weak. He told himself Victoria deserved to be trusted, and she deserved to be listened to, and he had done it.

"Thank you, honey," he said. He reached out to put his arm around her shoulders. Her eyes opened wide and followed his arm, and he wondered if he was doing the right thing. He changed the course of his hand, gripped her near shoulder, and squeezed it. "I think you tried hard because I asked you to. You're okay. You really helped me. Thank you." He wished he had placed his arm around her shoulders.

"If you put that story in the paper about ghetto blasters, you don't have to say I told you. I don't mind."

"Victoria, I'm talking about what happened here down the hall. What you called me about two months ago. You know I don't care about the missiles and the ghetto blasters."

She withdrew some of her familiarity and looked away, as if she had been chided, or as if she feared he considered her to be crazy, but she quickly perked up. Looking across the room, she said, "You and I could make the Democrats and the Republicans invisible."

"No. That's not real, honey. You helped me with what I needed. About the bang. Thank you."

"Can you get my baby?" she said.

He stepped in front of her. "No, I can't. What do *you* think?" He put his hand on her shoulder again and looked in her eyes. "I'm asking you to take your medicine and do whatever Dr. Crawford tells you to do. Remember that. Sam Nash was here, and that's what he said. Take your medicine." Then he wondered if that was right, but he decided he had to trust the doctors.

. . . .

Nash took the leisure to look at the parking lot on his way out which he had not done on his way in. Twilight had come. Last year's weeds were still sitting in lines following the cracks in the asphalt. Some day they'll have to mow the parking lot, he thought. A long, low planter that he had not noticed before appeared in front of him. The planter was full of evergreen bushes. Tall weed stalks stuck through and above the bushes. This place has no owner, he thought again. Then he recalled Dr. Crawford had said the inside of the units was equal to or better than any private mental ward in the Chicago area. Nash saw no reason to doubt it, and he was a trifle surprised because Crawford had also said the population of Read was, by nature, skewed to the poor or people who had exhausted their insurance or otherwise run out of money.

With a start, Nash realized he had to remember what car he was driving. Dr. Crawford, who was walking him to the car, was jabbering about a friend in college who had majored in journalism. Nash remembered he was driving Gentile's maroon, Chevy Monte Carlo, and relaxed. "Where is he now?" said Nash.

"He's in radio," the doctor replied. "He usually does . . . ."

"Excuse me. I have to change the subject." Nash knew the doctor was talking only from nervousness.

"That's fine."

"Do you try to understand all the stuff Victoria says?"

"Me? No. Not everything," said Crawford. "In the acute state, much of it is word salad—gibberish—or delusional. Linguists are trying to figure out the patterns of schizophrenic speech. At least that's what we think it is. There's some indication of substance

438

abuse. That complicates things. But she makes sense here and there."

"Yep."

"You think it's tough for you and me, Nash. Ninety per cent of the doctors here are foreign born. Many speak English as a second language."

"What?"

"Physicians are not busting down the doors to be employed here."

"Doc, I've got one more question."

"I don't know if I have answers for all your questions, Nash."

"You'll have an answer for this one. This is the car." He got out his notebook and pen again, and he rested the notebook on the roof of the car. "After your technician killed March, everybody here apparently thought it had to be covered up. You say there's a bunker mentality among employees because only bad things ever appear in the media about DMH. Did it ever occur to you or anybody here that the public might approve and think it was a fine thing that you killed Billy March? The governor could have told the press in his best spontaneous style that under his administration, even homicidal maniacs are required to obey the law, and that March brought his demise on himself. Or some such thing."

"We don't refer to people as homicidal maniacs, Mr. Nash."

Nash had felt the phrase jar in his mind when he spoke it. The... patients...were real. Nash still considered Billy March a homicidal maniac, but he could see how the doctor looked at March differently.

"All right. I understand that. But you understood my question, too, I think, doc."

"The way the administration of this department looked at it—and I have no evidence about whether it went beyond this department, well, of course, the state's attorney's office knew—is that the press would attack us from all directions at once. We would be villified for shooting down the patients were are supposed to be treating, the sympathetic point of view. We would be lambasted for

439

leaving the other patients and our employees in danger of physical attack by a known killer, Billy March, or, as you so picturesquely refer to him, a homicidal maniac.

"Since this is a minimum security facility, the neighbors around here would be stirred up to think that an unreconstructed murderer was in their midst without their knowledge. That, in the opinion of the administration, was the worst potentiality. It would cause the federal grand jury report on this department to be dredged up again. The higher ups felt the damage to the department would be severe.

"And that's the way they normally feel around here every day. The election campaign created the usual mass paranoia among the supervisors and the higher ups, and there was pressure from the governor's office long before March got killed. Reporting bad news around election time is always discouraged."

Nash could imagine the situation. He'd seen public employees under election pressure before.

"Let me emphasize, Sam, this place is not a snake pit. Nothing like that. On the other hand, if you make this department into a prison, you're going to get Far View Hospital."

"What's that?"

"Look it up. It's a hospital in Pennsylvania for the quote quote criminally insane. Some of your colleagues won a Pulitzer Prize for exposing it to the fresh air."

Nash liked the idea but had to skip it. The clock was running. Approaching darkness made him extremely conscious of the time. He put away his notebook and opened the car door.

"You've been very open and helpful, doc, and I don't know what's going to happen to you as a result of this story. Victoria, in her way, supported what you said."

"That's nice to know."

Nash was tempted to add, "I believe your story," because he did. But he kept this to himself. He had phone calls to make. "Believe it or not," said Nash, experiencing an attack of reality, "I don't know how much of this will get into the paper. Sometimes it's hard to sell stories on chaotic days. This is going to be one."

Nash had often been in this situation where an individual has expended two hours and cut two years off his lifespan to reveal the biggest secret he would ever have or to explain his life's work. And after the big revelation, Nash had to go back to the office where reports of many other events were coming in from the city and the world. Great stories sometimes failed to get through the meat grinder, leaving reporters drowning in bile and stomach acid and ignored, and leaving the sources of the unprinted stories very confused.

"You come highly recommended, Nash. I'm sure you'll do a professional job."

"Yeah, we'll see. Very little waiting." Nash settled into the seat, closed the door, and put the keys into the ignition, then rolled down the window. "Your friend has a good idea about finding a permanent place for some of these people," said Nash, "some of the career nut cases wandering the streets with shopping bags. I'll see you."

"You got 10 seconds?" Dr. Crawford's face was suddenly by window.

"Aaaah!" Nash wished he had never said anything. Time tension was building up. "Okay, make it quick."

"Let's say it's the summer, and you're driving near downtown. The sun is high. The radio is playing a great song. You come to a stoplight—this happened to me—and while you're sitting at the light, this really special pair of hips goes sauntering across the street in short shorts right in front of you. She kno-o-ws she's special. You lean back and take it in. What kind of feeling do you get?"

Nash had to laugh. The doctor had touched one of Nash's major weaknesses which lately he numbered at about a dozen. "Uhhh," Nash cleared his throat, "you get lots of feelings."

"All right, but among the other feelings, you know what is a principal one? You may not even notice it." Crawford was very earnest, not quite himself, scared, Nash guessed.

"What?"

"Freedom!"

"Hah hah." Nash broke out laughing again. He pointed his right index finger up. "Well..." Still laughing, he ticktocked his head from side to side as if to say, "Maybe."

"I don't mean you're going to jump out and proposition this chick. Not the freedom to grab her. You might even be married. I am now. You're not going to DO anything. I don't think chicks would understand. In fact, I know they wouldn't. It's just the sun and the music, and the sight of those hips going across the street. Maybe the girl feels it in a different way. It's in her walk. She's strolling across the street in the sunlight, doodle-lee-do. I mean freedom as in life, liberty, pursuit of happiness."

"For a man, you just see this chick and lean back and feel good. Freedom." Nash nodded. "Okay, yes." He had experienced this.

"So who decides who should be kept in institutions? Who decides who should be swept up off the streets? Doctors? Police? Partly. Sooner or later, the big question belongs in the political arena: What do we make the behavioral limits of freedom?"

Nash finally understood the doctor was talking about a separate issue. "I'll ponder that, doc." Nash put his hand on the keys and turned on the ignition. "Meanwhile, for the matter at hand," he spoke loudly and held up four fingers. "Four hours."

39

Driving north on Oak Park Avenue he knew that it did not go through to the Kennedy Expressway. Have to get off it and find a different north-south street, he told himself. Got to find a phone before the expressway. Crossing Forest Preserve Drive. Breezed through on green. (It was best to leave Read on a high note before anybody got any second thoughts. When you picked up the phone to call in, it always made them squirm.) Oak Park Avenue was beautiful going for 5 o'clock, he told himself. It was better than Narragansett. But where would there be a phone? This was a residential neighborhood, close to his own neighborhood. Nice song on the radio, he told himself. Heard it a hundred times. No idea what it's about. He turned off the radio. Single family homes. Six flats. No. Eight flats. St. Rosalie's Church. Made the light again. Go back to the rectory. Forget it. Think straight. For a neighborhood disaster. Wish it was. Simple. Here's the golf course behind the fence. How'd it get here in this area? Always wondered that. Going great. But not one store. No neons. Need a damn phone. Residences. Residences. Of course. The street ends. Knew that. Left or right? Harlem Avenue is left. Too busy. Downtown is right. Solves the decision. Drifting, pal. Time moving. Medium sized store coming up. Elliott's Dairy. Been there many times. Feels funny. Haven't been out on a good story in a while. Can I still cut it? Got to stop somewhere. Yes.

Wheels squealed! People think you're nuts! Calm down. Too lucky no opposite car. Relax. Think. Plan. Everybody's doing ordinary things here except you. Think. Purpose. No panic. Watch your walk. Normal. Door pad. Automatic door. Whoomp. Another. Coming home for Christmas from the dusk to the LIGHT in the cold. Warm. Crowded. Turn left. Newspapers in a wooden bin. No, you don't buy one. Why do you always want to buy one? Phone? . . . Phone? Never used the phone here. Empty checkout lane. This here is the food. No phones here. What do I look like? Goofy. Empty checkout lane again. Not empty. Short checker, staring. Missed her, Tunnel vision and thinking.

"Miss, is there a phone here?"

(She adopts a pose.) "There's one out back by the alley." Must be a frequent question. Door pad. Whoomp. Another. Back is . . . back. Nagle along here. Dark. Asphalt. Yeah, at the alley. Two phones. Whatever happened to phone *booths?* Too bad. Kate. How much change in the pocket? Progress. Real progress about to occur. Phones are good vibes. Everything's gonna be allll right. Put the change right here and look at it. Got it. Deenk deenk. (The coins go in.) Yeahhh. Love the sound. Means okay. Means home. Play the tune. Dee dee dee, dee dee dee dee. Lean. Await.

"City desk."

"Nash for the desk."

40

He was put on hold as he expected.

Across Nagle, he noticed another parking lot, long and narrow, behind a row of one-story stores. He wanted to jump once or twice because his whole body was coiled for action, but he shifted on his feet this way and that and looked around instead. A sign across the street, high up on the back wall of the first store, said, "Pratt and Lambert Paint."

"City desk," said a different voice on the other end of the phone.

"Who is this?" asked Nash.

"Mark."

"Mark, who's on the desk?" Mark was a copy clerk.

"Nobody right now. Krolikowski is in the doping. Solomon is in the doping. Kemper's on the phone. Miller's in the doping. He's still here. Youngman is someplace. There's a lot of people wandering around. Nobody's going home."

"There's nobody on the desk to talk to?"

"I said Kemper's there, but she's taking a story. Well, Leamington's there."

"Leamington?"

"He's standing in the slot going through the 'in' basket."

Nash was still looking around. He noticed the trailer of a semi parked to his left in the lot with a big air conditioning unit on the front staring at him. Refrigerated, he thought. Milk, maybe. He assumed Leamington was just being a busy body, and he weighed how useful Leamington might be. Leamington was a special writer known for bizarre feature treatments of local news. He usually expressed an original point of view on controversial subjects because he never quite understood the issues. When this lack of understanding was pointed out to him, Leamington liked to say he did not write about news, he wrote about "ideas." He was Simonet's intellectual. Nash decided it was necessary to talk to somebody.

"Give me Leamington."

"Burt, pick up one!" shouted the copy clerk in Nash's ear.

"Hello?"

"Burt, how are you, old buddy? This is Nash."

"Under the circumstances, fair."

"Did you get a job yet?"

"I haven't started to look yet. Did you want to speak to someone here?"

"I'm told you're the only guy on the desk. I need you to do me a favor. I want you to take a message into the doping session for me."

"I don't work the desk, Sam, so I don't think I could do that."

"This is hot. This is a scoop, Burt. Write it down for me, would you?"

"Beg pardon? Are you sure I should be doing this?"

"Burt, we're pals, aren't we? I've always been straight with you." Nash and Leamington had gone to lunch together once.

"I've got a major story to write, Sam, so I can't help you too much. What's your message? I'll leave it here."

"There was a patient shot to death..."

"There was a patient shot to death," repeated Leamington.

"...at the Read Mental Health Center in January."

"...at the Read Mental Health Center in January."

Nash paused to let him write.

"Is that it?" asked Leamington.

"No. No. There's more. Just a little more. The original story we had about Clarence Bryce was right."

"Who is Clarence Bryce?"

"Don't worry about that. Just write it down."

"Okay...I've got it. I'll leave it right here, Sam. Nice to talk to you."

"No, Wait. Burt! I want you to take that into the doping session while all the editors are there."

"I can't do that."

"Why not?"

"I told you. I don't work the desk. I'm not going to interrupt the doping session. And I'm really extremely busy."

"Burt, trust me. It's okay. Take the note to Georgia or Aaron Solomon. Just hand it to them."

"I've written, 'Great story, says Nash,' and I'm leaving the note right here. The editors will see it as soon as they emerge."

"Burt, can't you just take it into the doping? Why won't you do this?"

"I'm trying to be polite. But since you insist on an explanation: This is just another shooting. The mind swoons. I realize these things are important to you, so I will leave the note on the desk here. I assume you're coming in."

Time was running. There were more phone calls to be made, people to be tracked down. Should he go in, to the chaos in the office, or should he stay out, he thought? Could he sell the story if he didn't go in? He had three hours and fifty minutes to deadline. Two hours of that would be writing, one time through, quickly. He could tell Leamington to give the note to somebody else to take to the doping, but once the passing of the note from hand to hand started, the note might end up in the waste basket.

"Thanks, Burt. You're a helluva guy. Just leave the note there. I'll be in the office in 45 minutes if anyone asks."

Nash hung up the phone. He realized he had been hoping against experience and common sense that the first person he spoke to would be an influential editor who would immediately see how great the story was, and the rest would follow easily. Leamington's reaction was closer to reality. When the editors left the doping, they would be hell bent in their chosen directions, and getting them to stop and listen to something new for page one (other than a plane crash), and then diverting them to the new direction, would be a military accomplishment. A great strain of wits, wills, and emotions was ahead, and it almost exhausted Nash to think of it. In one sense, Nash thought, Leamington had a point. It was another shooting.

Nash was long accustomed to puff ups and deflations, and he knew just to keep going. He also knew if he was going to do his best, he needed a scheme.

He was 90 per cent sure the mystery had been solved, but Nash was not in the business of solving mysteries. Just as cops were in the business of arresting the culprits and making the arrests stick, Nash was in the business of publishing timely, accurate news stories for hundreds of thousands of readers. To have a great story, to solve a mystery, and not get it in the paper, meant nothing. To be beat by another reporter into publication on his own story was worse. It would mark him as a man who failed to compete in the natural world. This concept was scary to Nash, but it was not truely forseeable. His past defeats were suppressed as being separate. And with his adrenalin up, he discovered he was still what he had been.

(A new part of him, which Nash was beginning to tolerate, wondered how long he would be what he had been—and how long he wanted to be.)

Trying to let a plan work itself out in his head, he stared at the

448

traffic going by. His basic idea required quick phone calls, about four of them. The phone was only a few feet from the street, and the cars and trucks kept hammering, ARRRRRrmmm. All that noise would get in the phone. Why couldn't he have found an indoor telephone? Geez, time was going down river. Tense, he turned away from the street. Heyyy, baby. A young woman with red hair, a short jacket, and tight girl's cut jeans of which she was properly proud was walking toward the store, her back to him. I'd say this noise doesn't bother you, does it, doll?

The girl calmed him. She was food and drink he ate with his eyes. He took a deep breath and enjoyed his powerful urge to be obnoxious, even as he controlled it. Then he wanted her; the familiar pain provoking an inner grin. The story had to compete with other things for a moment.

Since his brain fever over women had taken hold, Nash had experienced days when the smell and aura and sight of females everywhere made him lecherously drunk and dizzy, sometimes for half an hour at a time, until he knew full well that the difference between himself and any number of notorious fools and even criminals was balanced on a razor. "I see what happened, guys," he sometimes thought. Then one day he had stayed home with a flu-like ailment, and the following day in public he discovered women had no more effect on him than garages or sidewalks. This unexpected vacancy became a terror, like a sneak preview of death, and made him accepting and nearly grateful when his inner struggle over women shortly returned. He decided he was in for a long haul and that God was a practical joker—who laughed a lot in a way that sounded like, "You'll get by."

Nash did an about face, dropped in a quarter, and phoned the office of the Cook County Medical Examiner.

41

Joe Gentile sat on a barstool in the Billy Goat tavern, and his head was swimming. He could tell that he was swaying a little, counterclockwise, but seemingly side to side, perhaps imperceptibly to observers, and a bartender was holding his glass and saying, "Another one, buddy? It's on this man here." The bartender indicated "here" with a sideways nod of his head, and Gentile understood he was supposed to look and see who was buying the drinks. Gentile did not want to fall down. That was paramount. The bartender was at the moment a white apron and a middle aged head with fat cheeks. Gentile was able to hold up his right hand, palm toward the bartender, and say, "No. Uh. No, thank you. No."

He slid off the barstool to the right, timing it correctly to match the moment he spun to the right, feeling utterly without self consciousness, no concern about who was looking at him and no guilt for having turned down a drink, feeling the righteousness of an inebriated person, secure in a world that extended about a yard in each direction, knowing that in his condition he was permitted to protect himself as best he could, and people of understanding would not be offended if he quit without proper and polite advance notice. Gentile had years before tried to master drinking, but he was one of those who got drunk quickly and often, so he had, for the most part, given it up. Nevertheless, this day was special.

He turned and gazed at the stairs leading up to the exit door. The stairs were about 10 yards away through a maze of tables and chairs and people to be offended. They were not people of understanding. But there was no hurry. He was going to study the paths.

"Joe is blitzed!" said one of his drinking companions, demonstrating to Gentile's mind tasteless boyishness and the excitability of the older nerd.

"Hey, Joe, listen, c'mon now, where are you going?" Someone else took hold of him under the armpit with the same arm extending across his chest, and the fragile grasp combined with the voice put Gentile at a disadvantage. Women did not often hug him in public, even women in their 60's. It was not unpleasant.

"Um, Mary, dear," said Gentile, pawing ineffectually at the arm across his chest, trying to remove it. Mary Stern was behind him.

"You should have a cup of coffee."

"No." Gentile shook his head back and forth, back and forth, back and forth. Then he said, "I'm going back to the office."

"Do you think you should, Joe? Why don't you wait a while. You're unsteady. A group of us will go back in a little bit. . . . Oh, good. You see I need help here with my beau." Her last words were directed at someone else.

The atmosphere of the Billy Goat was, as always, as if it were an old, color photograph of itself. Mellow, dark brown of the L-shaped bar and partial plywood panelling predominated but were enlivened by the numerous, multicolored lights, signs, bottles, and geegaws typical of a long-standing tavern. Indestructible, small, black tables and chairs constituted the furniture. The entire scene was illuminated by the amount of light found in an older bowling alley. The Billy Goat was never deep dark as the old Boul Mich was, and some people found the darkness of the Boul Mich more relaxing.

Sometimes the interior atmosphere of the Billy Goat seemed to have a faint, yellowish tinge which some said was the effect of tungsten light bulb filaments, and others said was due to the accumulation of nicotine on bulbs and walls. This was more common in past years.

From the walls in the western half of the tavern, the faces of elder newsmen looked down. The faces and photo busts, all black and white, 8½ by 11, had been hanging in their frames for decades. Here and there a small, brass "-30-" was affixed to the bottom of the frame, a newspaper symbol signifying "end of story."

Over the long section of the bar where Gentile and Stern discoursed, blown up bylines were pasted this way and that by the management, usually to reward people who had written stories about the Billy Goat. About half the bylines were from newspapers that had gone out of business. Various photographs of the founder, William "Billy Goat" Sianis, posing with beauty contest entrants or with a goat, were behind the bar around the liquor bottles.

The Billy Goat was one of many bars patronized by the Chicago news media, but the family management made an effort to keep news people comfortable and returning. The effort succeeded because the Billy Goat was believed to have the cheapest prices, and a reporter could usually find another reporter there if he was lonesome.

The individual whom Stern was glad to see, and who she assumed would help with her "beau" said, "Bo who? Bo Schembechler? Let me at him."

"I believe this is Bo Jo," said Stern. She was speaking to Bob Wolfram.

Wolfram was under six feet tall, but had big shoulders and always stood erect which made him look larger. His baritone voice was instantly recognizable.

Gentile had ceased paying attention. He heard a cheer go up, but people were always cheering for something in a bar. He was barely aware of such loud remarks as, "Wolfram! Wolfram!" "Hey, the lucky son of a bitch." "He returns!" Gentile's mind was blank. He waited patiently for a thought, feeling very tolerant of himself and detached from the others.

"...under the weather, my friend. Why don't you do what Mary says."

Gentile deduced that he had temporarily tuned out, and someone was speaking to him from in front this time. He opened his eyes and raised his eyes as far as he could to see. His head was hanging, and he had to lift his eyes to see forward. He did not raise his head, only his eyes, wrinkling his forehead to get his eyebrows out of the way. "Well, who do you think?" he said.

"What did you say?" Wolfram smiled. "You can let go of him, Mary. He's not going to fall."

"Well, who do you think?" Gentile lifted his head and stood straighter.

"You having a good time, Joe?" Wolfram was wearing his coat and had just walked in. Wolfram's hand was at Gentile's side holding a fistfull of tuxedo.

"Come on," said Gentile. "It's a fucking shit ass day." Stern had removed her arm, and Gentile was getting his bearings.

"Take it easy, Joe." Wolfram looked at Stern and apologized with his facial expression for Gentile's language.

"Mr. Wolfram. It's nice to see you." Gentile reached out and touched Wolfram. "I'm going back to the office for the last time."

"Not yet, I hope. Listen, I just came here to join you people. How about if I have a couple drinks and then we all go to get something to eat, and then we go back?"

"That's a superb idea," said Stern. "And Joe, my dear friend, you could have a cup of coffee."

Gentile ignored much of this as the prattling of busy bodies who were interfering with his freedom. He didn't consider himself as drunk as they did. In his opinion, he was just babying himself. "You do what you want," he said.

"We want you along," said Stern, bending her head trying to find his eyes. "I suggest we stay another half hour, then about 5:30 we can go to Riccardo's for spaghetti. Right? Okay?" Riccardo's was a block away.

Wolfram asked a waiter in a stained, white apron to pick up his tip lying on one of the small tables and to bring two drinks. He and Stern sat down at the table, leaving Gentile standing.

"Hey, Joe. Joe." Wolfram waved to Gentile and pointed to a chair on the opposite side of the table. Gentile eyed him. "Just for a minute," said Wolfram, pointing to the chair again demonstratively.

Gentile sat down heavily and settled after rocking to each side. "Mr. Wolfram, how's your new job?"

"You're not that far gone. The job is different. A lot more bosses at the Ledger, more people on the desk. I'm pretty sure I'll get my shot at night city editor, but I won't have the one man authority I would have had at the Chronicle."

Gentile was looking at Wolfram through the tops of his eyes, as if peering over non-existent glasses. Wolfram's answer was much too long for Gentile to follow, and he lost track of it. He decided to try the question again from a different angle.

"How's your new job?"

"Whoa." Wolfram smiled. "It's...great." He turned and began talking to Stern.

Gentile's attention faded because he was not receiving an answer. He was not interested in following every conversation. Absorbed in his own world, he thought of a different way of phrasing his questions.

Said Stern, "You wouldn't believe the people who have been calling. Some of them are really shook up. In the midst of it, Joe and his friends were kind enough to call and invite me here this evening. Wasn't that nice, Bob? But I believe they've had a head start."

"That was sweet," Wolfram agreed. "He looks uncomfortable in his tux and without his pipe."

Gentile frowned heavily and appeared perplexed. After a pause, he said, "Wolfram. A minute. I meant, are you black, still, when you get a new job?"

"Whaaat?" said Wolfram.

"Do you get reincarnated?"

"Do you?" said Wolfram sharply.

Gentile shook his head several times, then said in a calm, dignified manner, "I don't have a new job. I'm dying."

"Ohhhh, Joe," said Stern.

"I don't know what to say, Joe, except no, I don't get reincarnated."

Gentile's head dropped again while the other two talked and kept watch on him. His eyes seemed to be closed as he slowly reached inside his tuxedo jacket and withdrew a cigar. He raised his head and offered it, apparently out of politeness, to Wolfram.

"No. It's yours. Cigars today?"

Gentile offered it to Stern.

"No, thank you, Joe."

Gentile held the cigar in both hands just above the table, turned it over and over, then surprisingly and slowly put it back in his pocket.

"Aren't you going to smoke it?" said Wolfram.

"No." Gentile shook his head, took a deep breath, sighed, and added, "I went to the Medill School of Journalism."

"I didn't know that," said Wolfram.

"As I said, I graduated from Medill, got hired at the Chronicle, and worked there 18 years. I never had another job as an adult."

"Joe, it's gonna happen for you. Many people switch jobs once in a while to get ahead. You're going to get a new job and *you* will be reincarnated. You'll be a new man when it happens."

"You're a good newsman, Joe," said Stern. "You're smart. You're very employable."

"Tell me something," said Wolfram, turning to Stern, "Where is everybody? I thought more people would be here."

Only about a dozen Chronicle staffers were in the bar.

"People are afraid to leave," said Stern. "I guess they think the building will close down while they're gone. A lot of old timers are showing up in the newsroom, and there are little get-togethers going on in various offices. I needed to get out for a while."

"Pretty thick?" said Wolfram.

Gentile let his mind relax and felt quite conscious yet content with the absence of thoughts and stimulations and at peace. He knew deep inside that thoughts would resume shortly.

After a long, but, to Gentile, indeterminate time, he said, "Do you know how many times I have defended the Chronicle?" He had interrupted them. "Excuse me. Do you know how many times I have defended the Chronicle, busted my butt for the Chronicle? My relatives think I'm the Chronicle. They ask me about stories in the home repair section. I never read it."

Wolfram and Stern stared at him. "Well, hello, Joe," said Stern. "We missed you."

"How many times exactly?" said Wolfram.

"You're being a wise guy," Gentile responded.

Wolfram pointed to his chest innocently, said, "Me?" then said in a conciliatory voice, "All right. Okay. We're all talking about the same thing you are. It's difficult."

Gentile picked up the full cup of coffee he found sitting in front of him. He sipped it. It had turned cold sitting there, and he grimaced at the sensation.

"The Chronicle had good moments," said Stern. "Some days it was very good. It gave people an alternative when the other papers wouldn't listen. That's important. And I can remember some fine individuals and some interesting scoops."

The two men sat up straight at that. Both asked Stern to tell some stories. She told two from before their time, sketching out the characters with anecdotes within the stories. But she seemed uncomfortable leading the conversation.

The tales of old glory inspired Gentile; and he was starting to regain his senses and ceasing to baby himself. "The news business is a fight," he said. Stern nodded and opened her eyes to listen.

"We went up against the other papers for what, 15 years for you?" said Gentile, looking at Wolfram.

"Ten years," said Wolfram.

"How long for you, Mary?"

"A long time."

"Well, it's 18 years for me," said Gentile, "fighting every day. Beat them. Get beat. Get it right. Get it wrong. Sell lingerie. And we lost! We're destroyed. They won. That's a long fight to end this way. It's painful." Gentile shook his head and looked at the table.

"Yes," said Wolfram after a pause. "I'm glad I got out of there, but it still is for me. I guess we didn't get enough lingerie ads."

Nobody spoke for a few seconds, then Wolfram said, "How long has it been for you, Mary, if you don't mind my asking?"

Stern turned to look at him. Eventually she smiled. She said, "Forty-two years."

"Ho...," said Gentile.

Wolfram blinked. He said, "You seem to be taking it better than some."

"On the outside, better than Joe is," she said. "But I approve, Joe. It's just that after a while—later for you strong young men..." Then she spoke more slowly. "...you begin to lose places; you lose people." Her gaze remained nearly steady. "It's the natural progression. But that doesn't make it any easier. And you have to control your reactions, control yourself. You can't lose yourself. Now I have to decide what I'm going to do every day."

"What are you going to do?" said Wolfram.

"Maybe I could teach if I can find some place that wants me, even a grade school. You fellas know any place? But in the meantime, I want to focus on what I have. You know this is the first time in years I plopped myself down on a bar stool and sat at a bar—with men." She pointed to the bar where she and Gentile had been earlier.

"You can sit at a bar any time you want," said Gentile.

"Nobody asks me." She reached out and touched Gentile's cheek. "Bless you, Joe."

"I thought you'd prefer sitting here," said Wolfram.

"I like this, too. I do. I like both. Thank you for your thoughtfulness." She squeezed Wolfram's hand on the table and held it. She said to Gentile, "My reckless other sweetheart, do you want another cup of coffee before we go?"

Gentile drank the dregs down in one gulp and got visibly dizzy from throwing his head back.

"Take it slow," said Wolfram. "While you do, I'm curious. Did you mean anything special when you asked me if I was still black?"

"I don't remember." Gentile was staring at the coffee cup on the table, hoping the table wouldn't start to move again. "Oh, yes. I remember I said something about your being reincarnated." Gentile looked up. "That's all it was."

"I thought maybe you were making a snide suggestion about ambition. But it would be unusual for a white guy. How's your gyroscope?"

"We can go. I gotta find my coat. Tell me what you thought."

"It doesn't really apply here." Wolfram stood up and stretched.

Gentile and Stern spoke simultaneously. Gentile said, "Wait a minute." Stern said, "Uh uh."

"Joe made his confession of fear," Stern continued, "and I admitted to my fear of becoming a little old lady. You can't just walk away with our secrets."

Wolfram was smiling. "This is not a fear," he said with a broad shrug. "It's an impossibility."

"Losing your blackness," said Stern.

"Exactly," said Wolfram, sitting down again. "Or giving it up. Can't be done physically, not by the vast majority, including me.

Nevertheless, some people would say—and did—that I quit being black when I went to Ohio State. Some people, fewer, would say from the opposite perspective that my father quit being black when he stayed in the Navy in the 1950's when the Navy hardly ever promoted blacks. But he had a job. He raised his kids. The way I see it, nobody quits. I also believe like Sartre, you are what you do. Only Sartre wasn't black. I believe I am what I do, and I'm black, too."

"We never doubted it," said Stern.

This provoked laughter from both Gentile and Stern seemingly to the relief of Wolfram who had appeared self-conscious as if he had overdone his speech.

"And we're happy that you, at least, have no fears," said Gentile.

"That's right," said Wolfram in mock agreement. "None."

Rising, Stern said, "Gentlemen, shall we get some spaghetti then put the paper to bed?" Wolfram began to help her with her coat.

Said Gentile, "Now I lay me down to sleep."

"Joe," responded Stern, grimacing, "you're giving me the chills."

42

Nash ran out of change and headed back to the store. On the side window, one of the many posted signs said, "Milk, $1.19 a gallon." Incredible low price, he thought. He got his change from the short checker and gave her his best smile, intended as a blessing for the whole, female gender. She was too young and was taken aback as if he were a masher. On the way out the doors again, Nash's eyes twinkled and he almost laughed aloud. He decided he was getting to be a dangerous character whom people were going to have to come after with a net. Retracing his steps toward the phone, he told himself, Let's have a little middle-aged deportment here.

Nash had already phoned John O'Toole, the chief administrator for the Medical Examiner's Office, an older man who was at ease answering questions and making decisions and had no fear of the media. O'Toole was gone. His secretary, who would have been the second best choice, also seemed to be gone. Each phone call had cost Nash a quarter because whoever was answering the office's main line never came back on when the extensions were not answered.

That left Doc Baum, the medical examiner. As Nash arranged his change on the metal counter under the phone, he was thinking that Baum could be ideal for the commotion Nash intended to make, possibly a dream because Baum could be aggressive when his terrain was challenged. But Baum could be impatient, had too many irons in the fire, and was often hard to reach.

He punched the Medical Examiner's Office main number again and asked for Doc Baum.

"I think he's gone, too," said the individual who had answered the two previous times and recognized Nash's voice again.

"Ring him anyway." The civil servant wasted no further breath, and the ringing sound came on. Two rings, three. Nash started to adjust his plan with a new idea.

"Doctor Baum's office." It was a secretary. Adjustment ceased.

"Is Doc Baum in? This is Sam Nash of the Chronicle."

"I'm afraid he's on the phone, Mr. Nash. And when he gets through, he has to leave immediately for an appointment with the County Board President. Do you wish to leave a message? He'll have someone return your call tomorrow. He's already late."

"I won't screw up his schedule. This is important, Miss. Tell him it's about a homicide that was never reported to the Medical Examiner's Office."

"Would you rather speak to one of the investigators?"

"No, ma'am. This is Doc Baum's business. He'll want to know. I'm talking about a homicide that was officially suppressed to keep your boss from finding out. He'll want to hear it."

There was a sigh at the other end. "Just a moment, please."

Nash waited.

"Yesss, Mr. Nash." Doc Baum's distinctive, high pitched voice was reminiscent of Hughes in bronchial distress. The doc always sounded as if he were being hanged. Nevertheless, Nash thought he

461

detected exasperation and forced hospitality in only three words. Nash knew he had to score quickly.

"Doc, I wouldn't take up your time without a good reason. I admire the way you run your office, and I think you're good for the city; so I thought you should hear about this." Nash hoped the flattery would sensitize the doc's auditory nerves. Baum was vain, a human quality reporters found valuable in a public official.

"Thank you, Mr. Nash. What is it you wished to tell me? About a homicide that was officially suppressed?"

Nash took a deep breath and organized his speech as he would for his editors. It had taken him years to learn to do this. "There are two agencies involved, the State Department of Mental Health and the Cook County State's Attorney's Office. A mental patient was killed. . . ."

During the conversation, Nash made an instant decision without debate and gave him Dr. Crawford's home phone number which Crawford had given to Nash. He briefly imagined Crawford's shock when the Medical Examiner's Office descended before the story appeared. (At least Nash hoped that would happen.) The necessity could be explained to Dr. Crawford later. Crawford had agreed to let Nash use his name, so Nash was using it.

The phone call to Doc Baum lasted three minutes. Nash hung up feeling that the results were fairly good. Baum had been offended at the revelation and righteous at first; then he had decided to withhold belief because it was only a story over the phone; then he had become practical and promised to put someone on it.

Nash stared through the phone box, thinking and filing away the first move to get it off his mind. He knew he could not control what other people did. He was satisfied with his plan and confident that he would do his part. The familiar moving situation was like a poker game. One had to be content with uncertainty.

He dropped in another quarter and punched Bryce's old office number in the Criminal Courts Building. Campbell, the new occupant of Bryce's office, did not answer. Nash guessed Campbell was still around the office but not near the phone. Nash tried to remember the general, night number for the State's Attorney's Office, but couldn't. His watch said 5:22. He called the city's general number and asked for Area 4 homicide, one out of a hat. A Sgt. Zielke answered.

"Sergeant, this is Sam Nash of the Chronicle. What's the night number for felony review at 26th Street. I'm on the street and I can't remember it." Nash had gotten to know Sgt. Zielke while covering a lengthy trial at the Criminal Courts Building years earlier, but he wasn't sure the sergeant would recall.

"What the hell, are you determined to cover the news to the bitter end, Nash? I thought the Chronicle was through."

"Just about. A few more hours to go. Like a snake, we die after the sun goes down."

"Where have you been lately? Haven't heard from you or seen you?"

"I don't want to hurt your feelings, Zielke, but the murders in area four have acquired a repetitive quality that works against them as news stories. Plus, I do do other things." Large areas of the inner West Side where Area 4 was located had become depopulated, yet crime remained high. Some of the remaining residents were so lost to general society, living in a strange world of their own, that reporters, editors, and readers had difficulty identifying with them. Life was twisted, and biological groups were stupefied on welfare. Murders in the region were sometimes ignored by the major media. Such crimes were the province of the police, the City News Bureau, and heaven.

"Yeah, but our clearance rate (the solving) is one of the highest in the city. So what are you after, Nash? What's the last, hot story?"

Nash hesitated then made another snap decision. "Would you believe the State's Attorney's Office covered up a homicide?"

"I would believe anything, but how could they do that?"

"They got in first. No police. And they just sat on it."

"Nawwww. All those law school graduates? Come on. I hope this is true, though. I love it—assuming it happened far away."

"No connection with Area 4, sergeant. And what do you mean, you hope it's true? The Chronicle just told you it was true."

"Why, sure. That settles it, right? Hah hah. You're okay, Nash. Here's the number. . . . Good luck with your pursuits. You're serious. You're really gonna write this?"

"It will be in the morning Chronicle. You may tell the world." Not specific enough, thought Nash. "You can even tell the City News kid when he calls around for his beat check. Just tell him what I told you." The information Nash had given the sergeant was hardly enough to allow City News to get started. But that was all Nash wanted. He wanted City News making phone calls, asking questions.

"Since when do you guys give your stuff away?"

"I'm not giving anything away. I'm trying to stir something up. Trying to get the garbage to rise to the top. I got no tomorrow, you know."

"I'll tell you what, Nash. In the line of duty, when the City News kid calls, I'll ask him what he knows about this. Police business, you know? I assume this happened in Chicago."

"It did."

"Okay, but I won't vouch for it. I'll tell him I heard it from you, and I'm just inquiring. He can call you."

"That's fine. That's perfect. Thanks, sarge. He won't call me. That's not how it works. He's got to get it himself. See you."

Nash called the phone number the sergeant had given him and left a message that Nash hoped would be discussed among the night staff at 26th Street and that he was fairly certain would be passed on to higher ups. He told the state's attorney's investigator manning the phone to give the message to Campbell, Saddler, and Mrs. Ryan, and added that the Chronicle wanted their response. Nash imagined the investigator would give the message to his own superior or to Campbell. Nash hoped that the message was hot enough that it would keep being passed up the line because no one wanted the responsibility for keeping it to himself.

Ten minutes later, Nash was on the Kennedy Expressway. Despite working himself into a nervous condition in traffic, he got lucky, and it took him only 40 more minutes to get downtown.

. . . .

He parked Gentile's car where he correctly guessed a parking space would be available, "underground" on the third level of Wacker Drive, east of Michigan Avenue. This was the surface of the earth, about 50 feet below the raised surface of the city at that point. He ran up the stairs two at a time driven by the story in his head, but by the last set of stairs his perspective had changed, and survival had assumed importance equal to the story. "I have got to quit smoking!" he said to himself as he hung onto the railing and took the last stairs very slowly, breathing hard and swallowing saliva, one stair at a time. The climb was approximately five stories, and the stairs were steeper than would be found in a building. Nash was in better shape than he had been, but he wasn't ready for this climb.

When he arrived out under the sky into a crowd, he headed for the Chronicle Building on the West Side of Michigan Avenue being careful not to stumble on wobbly legs. Reaching his goal, he passed right by the front door of the newspaper and kept walking all the way around the block, slowly, wasting precious time, bringing his heart rate down, restoring his breathing, and dissipating the fuzziness in his head.

He was getting his legs back by the time he stepped off the elevator on the fifth floor, the newsroom floor. Three women and a man were walking past the elevators, laughing, and drinking out of plastic cups. He recognized all four and knew the names of three of them.

"Want some coffee, Sam?" said one of the women, named Colleen, with a smile. Nash guessed this was not coffee.

"Not right now, Colleen. What's the situation in there."

465

"Oh, just an ordinary day," she said, and all four laughed. "Come on back to the morgue. We're having a little bonfire." Her joke referred to burning the clips, an inconceiveable sacrilege. The clips would be used for research as long as they lasted. "That's not very funny is it? We're having a small get-together, the first reunion of the once-upon-a-time Chronicle staff." She raised her cup as if she had proposed a toast.

"I'm going to try and sell a story," he said with an effort at appearing nonchalant. He turned to go down the hall into the newsroom.

"I think the paper's already printed or something," said Colleen, to more laughter.

Another female voice, sober sounding, said, "They have an early deadline, Sam."

Nash turned quickly. The speaker was Maureen Warmsley who had collected the donations for Sally Bernstein's going away party. "How early?" he said.

"Eight o'clock, I think, for the city desk."

Nash was momentarily paralyzed, trying to adjust. Then he turned without a parting word and walked rapidly into the newsroom passing by knots of reporters around various individual desks, and, in response to greetings, saying, "Hi...Hello," perfunctorily without stopping or looking. As he walked, he felt his chest to find the outline of his notebook underneath his trenchcoat in the inside, sportcoat pocket. He finally stopped at the city desk where Krolikowski was reading a story on her computer terminal with her back to him, sitting stiffly erect, showing the tension of a new editor.

"Georgia, where's Aaron?" he said before she saw him.

She turned the wrong way to look for him, then turned and found him. "I don't know. He's around. What are you up to? I found this note from you a little while ago buried under some things on my desk."

"Did you tell Aaron?"

466

"Yes. We didn't know what to make of it. We asked around. Nobody knew where you went. What have you been doing?"

"Getting the story. You want me to tell you, or you want me to tell Aaron, or you want me to tell both of you together? It would save time to tell it once." He could tell by the sound of his voice that neither his voice nor his breathing was completely normal yet.

Slowing the situation down, Krolikowski inclined her head and looked at him questioningly, and from this Nash knew that his anxiety was apparent. He was violating his own rule and Phelan's example not to show it. Intensity was common; that was okay; panic was not. He took a deep breath through his nose and told himself he was going to have to clamp down and put on the best act of which he was capable, Mr. Authoritative, everything's-in-hand, you-can-rely-on-me, Nash. But he couldn't immediately. He stood there, sensing he might be wild eyed, forcing himself to stand and wait for an answer.

"Tell Aaron," she said somewhat aloofly. "If he says we go with it, we do. Are you okay?"

He exhaled again, found himself relaxing, and reflexively, without conscious decision, started looking at Georgia as Georgia. He noticed her eye shadow, her cheekbones, the glow of her skin. Conscious thought caught up and he realized he was taking a moment to smell the flowers. He continued looking at her for a second or two on purpose. He realized separately he was entertaining a notion about Georgia that did not fit the time or the place.

He smiled a natural smile of appreciation for her looks, felt a little of the calmness he wanted coming from somewhere, and said, "We print the story, I'll be fine."

She looked at him more appreciatively this time. "Can you give me an idea how good this is?"

"Yeah, okay." The story was running before him like a rabbit. He suppressed his latest spontaneous seduction plot to keep it from taking up needed space. (It hovered in a corner of his mind, teasing him faintly.)

He put one hand in each pocket of his trenchcoat and found the tapes in his left pocket. "Here." He showed them in the palm of his hand but held onto them. "I got two tapes. One is full on one side, 30 minutes. The other is about 15 minutes. Have you got two, good, calm people to transcribe them?"

"We've got more people than we need. Give them to me." She stuck out her hand. "What do they say?"

He gave her a brief description, then added, "The governor's race was a factor. This is a confession and an explanation by one party."

That said, he put the tapes in her outstretched hand. "You'll need two machines, and you might need two rooms for these people." Reporters, copy clerks, supervisory editors, rewritemen, copy editors, photographers, graphics editors, photo editors, artists, editorial assistants, and what all else were bumping into each other all over the newsroom as if it were election night, most of them with little to do. The open newsroom was chaotic.

"We'll do the best we can." He could see the shining of extra excitement beginning in her own eyes. Nash put his hands back in his coat pockets and turned one way and another trying to find Aaron Solomon.

"You want us to make any phone calls for you?"

"Maybe. I can't think of what phone calls to make just yet. It's in here." he pointed to his head, "but I've got to dope the story."

"Try back by Simonet's office," said Krolikowski.

"Okay." Nash took off two steps and came back one. "I marked the sides that count with an X. Ignore the other sides. Whoever does this, tell them to *keep going* no matter what they hear. Just keep going until they're done."

Nash marched to the back of the newsroom, skipping sideways sometimes to slip by knots of people in the aisles, saying, "Excuse me. Excuse me," when he bumped into people or had to move them with a touch of his hand. Women who had to arch their backs as he passed behind them or step out of the way took offense and made faces.

From a distance of 10 yards, he could through a glass wall at least three men sitting in Simonet's office. Managing editor Peterson was in a chair with his elbows on the arms, talking and gesturing. Nash stepped a few feet to the right and confirmed that Solomon owned the arm and shoulder visible at the other side of the room. Simonet was behind the desk. Nash walked up and knocked on the door jam. The door was open.

"Excuse me," said Nash, interrupting someone's voice.

"Come on in, Sam," said Simonet from behind his desk, waving with a pen in his hand. "Come in."

Nash walked in and looked for a chair. He sat in one, leaned forward, and made himself count to two. He told his face to assume the proper gravity. Felt all right. Okay. He did not trust Simonet's pose of affability.

"I've got a story for you," said Nash.

"Yes, Aaron's been telling us you left a scribbled note," said Simonet. "That's an interesting practice. Why didn't you dope it with someone?"

"You were all in the doping when I called."

"Send someone in."

"I tried. Dictating the note was the best I could do." Nash raised his eyebrows and pointed at the clock on the wall. "Bob." It was after 6:30.

Simonet accepted this admonishment gracefully and made no response. They were all used to moving quickly. "What have you got?" said Peterson.

"There was a homicide in a state mental hospital which was investigated by the Cook County State's Attorney's Office but was never made public. It was suppressed by two governmental agencies, and the motive appears to be the gubernatorial primary."

Nash gave them approximately the same, brief description he had given to Krolikowski, but more slowly, more calmly, adding, "The original story I did about something fishy going on at Read was basically correct. But this is five times better. A patient was shot dead by a member of the staff. We have two witnesses and lots of background. We've nailed Madame Ryan and she's earned it. We raise a substantial issue about what to do with insane killers. AND we give an inside view of a modern, state mental hospital which is a lot different than people think."

"Did you get any response from the State's Attorney's Office yet?" Solomon cut right to the essential question, as Nash thought he would. None of the editors had ever met the principal witness, Dr. Crawford, and this story had blown up in the Chronicle's face before. Nash expected the editors to be skittish.

"I have left messages for Mrs. Ryan and her top two assistants, but whether they've returned my calls yet, I don't know. I just got here. I doubt it. The messages were explicit, and I think they'll need time to plan their strategy. I think we have more than enough to go on without their response."

"Just a minute," said Simonet. "It seems to me the heart of the first story was that Clarence Bryce, the chief of the State's Attorney's criminal division, was fired over this. But Mrs. Ryan demonstrated quite convincingly, to our embarassment, that he was fired over something else. Have you got anything to disprove what she said?"

"Clarence Bryce got in trouble for two different reasons," said Nash, gesturing with his hands. "That would not be unusual. There was the eavesdropping, and then he tried to take this shooting to the grand jury while Mrs. Ryan wanted it covered up. In this story, we'll explain the Bryce episode again, but Bryce is not the main issue. He's almost the human interest angle. The news is that there was a homicide in the state institution where we said something smelly occurred—even though it appears to be a justifiable homicide—and this was investigated and then covered up by the State's Attorney's Office. That last part is extremely serious."

"Yes, I can see that, Nash," said Simonet slowly, uncertainly, demonstrating to Nash that Simonet didn't see it. "But for the purposes of our story, how big a deal can we make out of this if Mrs.

Ryan's office performed an investigation?" When he saw Nash's expression, Simonet added quickly, "I just think you should be more clear about this." (Nash was squinting, and his mouth had dropped open against his better judgement.)

"Bob," Nash shook his head, an unconscious action. "They simply can't do that. That's not sufficient. If the State's Attorney's Office gets kinky at the top, the whole law enforcement process..."

Nash felt a hand on his knee, saw it was Solomon's, and knew he was supposed to stop. Nash stopped and worked at controlling his face.

Solomon took over, speaking in an upbeat, conversational manner. "You've got a good point, Bob. Sam left out a few steps. All homicides have to be reported to the coroner, or the Medical Examiner's Office, we call it now, and apparently they skipped that. Is that right, Sam?"

"You got it."

"And the Medical Examiner's Office releases a list several times a day to the City News Bureau of the latest cases so all the murders, violent deaths, and accidental and unexplained deaths are in the public domain." Solomon looked at Nash for polite corroboration, and Nash nodded.

"If some doctor slips you under prematurely to steal your kidneys and livers..." Peterson chimed in, speaking out of the side of his mouth. "...you hope that the Medical Examiner will detect it, and the public will be outraged." Peterson chuckled and flicked an ash off his cigar toward an ash tray on the floor.

Simonet glanced at him. "We only have one liver, Pete."

"I always considered that an oversight," cracked Peterson.

Solomon grinned and looked in the vicinity of his feet, then raised his head to continue:

"Sam's case never made the required trip to the Medical Examiner and out into the open," said Solomon. "It was suppressed, kept secret. Why, Sam?"

"The public will have to decide that," said Nash. "It's been widely reported Mrs. Ryan wants to be named attorney general by Governor Beal if our attorney general wins the U.S. Senate race in November. Beal would have to still be in office to appoint her, and Beal appeared to be in danger of losing the primary. It's obvious to me it was the election. People do bizarre things all the time when contests get that close. Everybody gets frantic.

"I got Dr. Crawford on the record today saying the Department of Mental Health was in a state of seige even before the shooting, determined to keep the slightest, negative report from leaking out and affecting the election. He said that after the shooting, his superiors told him to talk to no one but a man from the State's Attorney's Office. They also suggested he go on vacation. He did. He also said his superiors were extremely fearful about the overall effect the incident would have on their department, election or not."

"How do we know this Crawford is telling the truth?" said Simonet. "What if he's a kook?"

Solomon looked at Nash. "Where'd you meet this guy, Sam? You sure he works there?"

"Positive. I interviewed him in his office in the place, and the employees all knew him. He's got his own desk, and he knows what's in it, and he's very sane."

The metropolitan editor shrugged indicating his acceptance. "I think it's a helluva story, Bob," Solomon said. "I honestly don't see how we can ignore what the doctor says even if we can't get Mrs. Ryan to cave in on such short notice. As for the kook thing, Sam said a nurse backed up the doctor; and we have to rely on the reporter's judgement a little."

"Uh huh. Thank you for pointing that out, Aaron." Simonet came to life and leaned forward. "That's exactly what I'm afraid of. We had a version of this on page one before, relying on his judgement. But let's say for the sake of argument that this time Mr. Nash knows what he's talking about." Simonet switched his attention to Nash. "This is a justifiable homicide, you said. Describe it to me."

Nash described Billy March, then described how March got killed, using five sentences altogether.

"It appears he had it coming," said Simonet.

"That's why it's justifiable," said Nash.

"I understand that," said Simonet, narrowing his eyes quickly. "So we have a maniac who had to be killed to save someone's life. This is investigated by the proper agency and deemed to be justifiable, and what they forgot to do is tell the Medical Examiner.... I'm just saying how this will look to the general public. It's a type of story, perhaps." Simonet meant it was minor and going inside, at best.

Nash stared at him, not blinking. He told himself: This guy's nothing. Don't let him get to you. Sit still. Keep your mouth shut. By accident, he has the keys to the pages. Nash told himself that what he needed was a commitment of big space anywhere in the paper. After that, he should allow Solomon to stick around to handle the rest, the struggle over position, in whatever way Solomon chose to do that.

"This belongs on page one." The words came out. Nash couldn't help it.

Simonet seemed to relax a little and settle in his chair. They had entered his arena. "Page one is pretty crowded," said the executive editor, smiling and wrinkling his nose. "I think we may be able to run it inside when we see how the pages shape up." After a moment, Simonet looked past Nash's right ear then sat up to his full height in his chair and said briskly, "How much space will you need for this story?" indicating the conversation had gone on long enough.

Nash wanted 40 inches, an enormous story for the Chronicle, almost two full columns of type. He knew the fastest, absolutely, he could write 40 inches from typewritten notes was an hour and 40 minutes. Working from scribbled notes, it took much longer to find things, and he hoped to get some return phone calls. Both would slow him down. There were other things, too. He looked at the clock. He had an hour and fifteen minutes.

"Thirty inches," he said. Something would have to give or this was impossible. Something would give, he decided.

Simonet looked at Peterson who shrugged and nodded. Thank you, Pete, thought Nash. You know I can do it, and you know it's worth it.

"Go ahead and write your story," said Simonet, "I think you should do somewhat less than 30 inches. Also, we have an early..."

"I already figured that in."

"...deadline. Thank you. We're printing 50,000 extra copies, and the weather bureau is predicting two inches of snow." (Circulation often insisted on early deadlines when it snowed at night because snow on the roads slowed the trucks.) Simonet concluded, "But we'll get it in somewhere, I'm sure."

Nash got up to show he was properly leaving. He moved in slow motion because it was obvious to him he had not sold the story very well, and he was full of distrust for Simonet. With his jaws clenched, Nash debated on the one hand that it was foolish to argue any more and might be harmful; and on the other hand that it was the last day of the paper and Dr. Crawford could give the story to someone else tomorrow. When should one be foolish?

"Mr. Simonet, have you ever heard of the 'disappeared ones?' " Nash was standing.

"Sam, I'll take care of it," said Solomon. Nash avoided looking at Solomon but could see Solomon's hand wave. Nash was referring to the thousands of people in South America and Central America who, for political reasons, have been abducted and secretly murdered, their bodies never found.

"I'm quite familiar with that situation, Nash. I suppose you're going to tell me Billy March was a political dissident or a revolutionary."

"No. He was a nut."

"And Agnes Ryan runs a right wing death squad."

"The point, sir, is not that Mrs. Ryan runs a right wing death squad. The point is that civilizations build up systems, some of which become so commonplace they become part of the wallpaper. We cease to understand them until they are violated. Whatever way this system came to be—the way we make unusual deaths public— we can all see now what it's for. We have to uphold the system be- cause it's our turn."

"Excellent, Nash," said Simonet. "Why don't you go write your story then and let us do what we do. And this is not South America. The Chronicle reports more murders than you can shake a stick at."

Nash guessed he had said as much as would be listened to. He turned and started out the door.

"Have you got the body?" said the voice of Peterson behind him.

Nash whirled. "I can get it."

"Nash!" Simonet with an open hand sliced the air from left to right in front of his chest. "Go write your story now and let us do what we do. It's late." He gave Nash a very clear push-away gesture. "Thank you."

While walking into the newsroom, Nash thought of what he should have said: "We cannot allow people to be killed in secret." That's what he should have said, he thought.

He was 20 feet from Simonet's office, clearing his mind and winding himself up for the final rush, having decided to take his chances on the full 30 inches—he knew he had bitten off more than he could chew—when Solomon caught up to him from behind.

"Sam, what did you mean you can get the body?"

Nash had to think for a second. He was past that. Then he faced Solomon. "I've got the parents' names and phone number. They were supposedly told what happened, and they had a little funeral. If they talk to us, that's the body." (In murder trials, both Nash and Solomon understood that corpses are not introduced as evidence. Instead, a relative is brought in to testify that the victim had been alive and then was observed definitely dead. This testimony stands for the body. Photographs and autopsies are used to show the man- ner of death.)

Solomon grinned. "Do it. Do it," he said.

43

Krolikowski was on the phone, but she saw him coming and cupped it.

"Call it 'Mental,' " said Nash. She wrote it down. This would be the slug of the story. "We don't know the length yet," he added, "maybe 30."

"Kemper and Youngman have your tapes. Can you talk to them yourself?"

"They'll know where to find me. I'll be at my desk."

"You left your hat here." She pointed to it and smiled at him, amused.

"Thank you, dear," he said.

Nash was still wearing his trenchcoat and sportcoat and was hot. He took his arms out of both on the way to his desk and threw them on Gentile's desk, and his hat on top. He turned to face a woman in a black evening dress and pearls who was sitting in Nash's chair with her legs crossed. She was speaking to a well-dressed man sitting on top of Nash's desk. Nash merely stared at the woman.

"Should we move?" she said, getting up quickly. "Jim, I think this man..." The woman did a few dance steps preparing to leave, and Jim also stood up.

"We were looking for a place to sit down. I hope we haven't inconvenienced you. My wife and I used to work here 25 years ago." Jim stuck out his hand.

"That's what I figured," said Nash, shaking the hand. "You're nice, practical people." Nash turned away from them, sat in his chair, and fished his notebook out of the pocket of his coat on Gentile's desk. He immediately started turning pages in the notebook, looking for the phone number of Billy March's parents.

He found the number, dialed it, and got a thrill. It was busy! Then he got a red, felt tipped pen out of a drawer and began skimming his notes, drawing large red circles around sentences and sections he wanted and at the same time refreshing the words in his head. After a few seconds, he called the morgue on the phone and told them to send out the last envelope of clippings on Clarence Bryce. In writing the story, Nash intended to copy some of his own previous words about the Clarence Bryce scandal to save time. He also asked for clips on anybody named Billy or William March.

He went back to his notes, drawing more circles. Time taunted his mind, urging him to jump ahead and write, but he knew he would be fooling himself and the writing would actually move more slowly if he didn't keep his information and his head in good order.

Finally, he turned to the computer and signed on, feeling immediate relief from banging the keys. He took a deep breath to enjoy the drop in pressure and relax for an instant; then he called up a blank story form on his screen, typed in the slug, typed on his byline, and sat back to think of a lead. He looked at his watch. Seven o'clock. He had an hour.

After fifteen seconds, he started to type:

"The Cook County State's Attorney's Office and the Illinois Department of Mental Health have covered up a homicide in a state mental hospital for almost two months, an early report of which State's Attorney Agnes Ryan denounced as a hoax, the Chronicle learned Thursday."

That was too long and too clumsy, he saw right away. He changed it to:

"The Cook County State's Attorney's Office and the Illinois Department of Mental Health covered up a homicide in a state mental hospital for almost two months, a doctor in that hospital told the Chronicle Thursday."

Nash felt he could dream up one or two better leads, but he had no time, and the editors were going to get their fingers in it anyway if they liked the story. He erased the phrase "in that hospital" to shorten the lead and kept going.

"The Chronicle printed a sketchy report six weeks ago of the violent incident involving a patient in the Read Mental Health Center on the Northwest Side, but that report was denounced by State's Attorney Agnes Ryan as a hoax. It was not known to this newspaper at the time that someone had been killed.

"Thursday, Dr. Gerard Crawford, a psychiatrist in the hospital told the Chronicle a hospital staff member shot a patient in the head to save a nurse.

" 'The patient...had killed before and was trying to do it again. It was a life-saving effort by a member of the staff,' said Dr. Crawford.

"Examination of the records of the Cook County

Medical Examiner's Office shows the homicide was never reported to that office, as required by law.

"Concealment of a homicide, even a justifiable homicide, can be a felony in Illinois. Concealment of a homicide by the State's Attorney's Office is unheard of in recent memory...."

Nash knew this paragraph might not pass muster. The editors might demand that some expert declare the offense to be a possible felony rather than the Chronicle. They would also want an expert to verify the second sentence, that the incident had no precedent. Both tasks could be swiftly accomplished by a phone call to the head of the Chicago Crime Commission, a civilian agency. Nash decided it would save time to let the editors figure out the obvious, assign someone to make the call, if they insisted, and fix up the paragraph. These thoughts were simultaneous with the flow of his typing.

"Hey, Nash."

Nash looked up and saw a babyish young man, Brian Forrest. "Go away. Don't say a word. I'm busy." Nash was looking back at the story as he said this, annoyed that his concentration had been dented.

"Georgia told me to help you. Make phone calls. Get you a cup of coffee. Anything you need."

Nash raised only his eyes. "A cup of coffee would be great. Any kind. Go away."

"Sure. Sure."

Nash ignored him. He started typing another sentence: "Dr. Crawford identified the patient who was shot to death as Billy..." He jumped in his chair. "FORREST! Holy shit, get back here!" he shouted, "C'mere. C'mere."

Forrest ran. Nash whipped through the pages of his notebook. "You got a pen? Write down this number." He gave Forrest the phone number of March's parents. "Use that desk." He pointed to Gentile's desk which was to Nash's right when Nash was typing on

479

his computer terminal. "Take my coat off it. Throw it on the floor."
Forrest did.

A copy clerk had occupied Gentile's chair only moments earlier
and was eating a banana. "You'll have to move," said Nash. The
clerk got up, pretending to be docile and sheepish.

"All right. I'm going to type one or two more sentences here, and
that will be the gist of this story. Then I'm going to print it out over
there, number 3." Nash pointed to an office printer standing against
a pillar 20 feet away. "When you get it, Forrest, I want you to read
it, then call that number I gave you. That's the parents of a young
man who was shot to death in a state mental hospital.

"I want you to ask them if it's true that it happened. What did
state authorities tell them? Did the authorities ask them to keep it
quiet? If so, who asked this? Do they remember names or what
agency? (Nash was glad to see Forrest had the sense to write down
the questions, and Nash slowed his dictation to let Forrest catch up.)
And what do they think of all this?" Nash watched Forrest scribble.
"I've only got a few minutes to write a long story here. You're on
your own."

Nash finished the sentence naming Billy March as the dead man
and put in another sentence on March's trial for murder and acquit-
tal by reason of insanity. Then Nash hit the "print" button, told the
computer "#3" and pointed demonstratively to the printer. Forrest
popped out of his chair, ran to the printer in a crouch, and waited
tremblingly for the printing process to finish. "I ordered two printouts," said Nash. "I want you to take the first one to Krolikowski
and tell her to give it to Solomon. You got that?"

"Take the first one to Krolikowski and tell her to give it to Aaron
Solomon," repeated Forrest, turning around to look at Nash.

"You know what to do after that."

"Yes."

Nash resumed writing and erased Forrest from his mind.

At 7:20, a diminutive reporter in a white blouse and gray slacks approached Nash's desk, although all Nash noticed was gray slacks and a voice which said, "This is the first five pages."

"Right there," said Nash. The implication was his desk, but his hands were typing. "Just drop 'em."

"Youngman says he'll be done with his whole tape in a minute. He seems to have the short one, but the batteries wore out in the machine he was using."

Nash only nodded and stared into his screen, concentrating his mind through his eyes. As the reporter walked away, the curve of Nash's concentration dipped for a second, and he flicked his eyes to see who it had been. Kemper. He flicked them a second time to absorb the way Kemper's blouse fit into her slacks at her tiny waist, the mind's many rooms always leaving one open. But his thinking moved ahead non-stop.

As he pushed himself and disappeared into the writing process, Nash's mind sometimes fell completely blank for a few seconds during which he had the aura of racing-, jumping-, chased-by-flames thought but no conscious ideas. The work was in the back of his head where he could not consciously visit. Suddenly, then he would type again, type a part his unconscious mind had worked out and delivered to consciousness.

At other times, his fingers typed simple things without the delay of his mind conceiving them, the thoughts taking place in his fingers. Then he would flit back and read the words for the first time to be sure they were what he wanted.

At 7:30, he had 9 inches; the toughest part of the story was done, the top; and he was getting ready to go faster.

"Nash, they don't want to talk."

"Who doesn't?" Nash had no idea who was speaking immediately or what he was talking about.

"Billy March's parents. They said they don't wish to discuss it or publicize it. They hung up."

Nash turned abruptly to his right. He rapped Gentile's desk with his palm, then pointed at Forrest. "Tell them we're writing the story anyway. It's going to be in the paper tomorrow, about their son. If this story is wrong, they should tell us. If the story is right, what do they wish to say about it? Read them what I gave you and say, 'Is this right, or do you wish to correct it?' Then keep them talking."

Nash turned back to his story, scanned the last paragraph, understood where he was, then raised his hand and added for Forrest without looking at him: "Whatever they say, write it down exactly. Even little bits." He realized he needed one of the red circles from his notebook.

"I gotta ask you one more question, Nash."

Nash's eyes widened, and he spun in his chair. "Forrest!" The abrupt movement startled the young man, and Nash knew he had to keep Forrest calm. "Brian," Nash spoke soothingly, "what is your question?"

"If the dead guy's parents were told about it, why is this a cover-up?" Forrest was holding the printout of Nash's first few paragraphs.

Nash was surprised to see in Forrest's face, in addition to obvious fear, some determination. For this, Nash could give him a break. If Forrest was trying to understand, if his mind was really engaged, he could be useful.

"The State's Attorney's Office can't make private deals on homicides," said Nash, chopping the air. "They have to tell the Medical Examiner. They didn't, and that's the law. And the Medical Examiner has to tell us. We can't let government officials decide to make some killings public and keep other ones private. That would get to be a mess, and too much suspicion would build up. The public knows, Forrest, that WE don't give a damn." Nash pointed to his chest. "We'll print anything, more than they ever wanted to hear. That's their reassurance. And it's your occupation. Make the call."

"We don't print all the murders, do we? Don't we cheap a lot of them out?"

"We could print them all, and people know that, too, like a

threat. Nobody wants to read them all. But this one is special. Somebody tried to hide it. So this one we lay out in the long form."

He turned back to his computer. It occurred to Nash as a strange, almost laughable image, that he was starting to remind himself of Hughes. He shook his head to clear that image then stared at the screen a moment until his concentration returned. Inside the story again, he realized he was at the beginning of a blow-by-blow account of the events the night of the shooting, and he needed the words from his notebook. He began skimming circled sentences while another part of his mind was estimating the story. Considering all the "comments" he had to get in—which Nash thought of as a lump—possibly from the parents, possibly from the Medical Examiner, possibly State's Attorney Ryan, and perhaps the Department of Mental Health, Nash knew he might need more space or Dr. Crawford's helpful and earnest background was going to be left out.

"Sam."

He recognized Krolikowski's voice and was ready to bite her head off for causing another interruption. He held it in. Editors always interrupted. "Yes. What?" He lifted his eyes to her for a moment, then returned to his notebook while she spoke.

"Mrs. Ryan's holding a press conference at 8:15 in the Daley Center."

"I can't cover it."

The answer was pure reflex. Distracted editors often forgot who was doing what and had to be reminded. Nash looked up when Krolikowski's statement finally registered. "Send somebody sharp. This is for us, I'm sure. This is just what I've been hoping for."

He noticed Krolikowski's green sweater went nice with her brown hair, and Solomon was standing next to her looking serious. The last day must be difficult for him, thought Nash whose mind was bounding, a boulder going down hill. "It's related, Aaron," he said. "We got 'em. Get the story on page one now." Nash's plan had been to provoke solid, official reactions before the story broke that would sell the story even if he could not. He felt vindicated and switched to ignoring the editors. Maybe they had time. Nash was up against it.

"We're not using the story for this edition."

It was Solomon's voice.

A white explosion shot upward through Nash straight to the top of his head. He swung away from his desk and rose out of his chair like a fighter coming out of his corner, except his arms were high in the air, his fingers spread, and he was looking up. He kept turning, coming around almost 360 degrees. He took two, big steps around his desk before they could see his face which was fiery like a boy's in the middle of the big game. His arms dropped when he got in the aisle, but spread wider, wide enough to seize both editors together.

Solomon thrust out his chest and looked hard at Nash, and tried to push Krolikowski behind him. She resisted as if this demeaned her. Nash stopped his forward progress. His exaggerated arm motions were actually an effort to control himself. "Aaron...," he said hoarsely, "Be a man now." (Nash meant, or thought he meant, "You have to understand what you're doing to me," but it came out sounding differently.) Nash still had his arms in the air. He croaked, "What?"

"We're not going to use it," said the metropolitan editor through his teeth, trying to hold Nash's eyes, looking from one eye to the other. "Just for this edition." Solomon was still trying to keep himself between Nash and Krolikowski by pushing her with his outstretched left hand. Finally, he said, "Georgia, back up!"

"What in the name of..." Nash raised his arms higher in the air again, his face getting redder and more violent looking. "Gimme an explanation, Aaron." He took another step toward the metropolitan editor.

"They want to see what Ryan says at her press conference," said Krolikowski from behind Solomon.

Nash could not understand what she was saying. His mind was tuned only to Solomon's voice, and Solomon was silent while he and Nash stared at one another.

"You know!...This is bull....This. My." Nash was having difficulty phrasing his speech.

"We'll get it in the next edition," said Krolikowski, her voice strained. "They're afraid of getting trick bagged like before."

It registered on Nash only that a woman's high voice was speaking again. "Do I have to deal with this, too!" he shouted to Solomon and pointed at Krolikowski.

"Georgia, go back to the city desk," commanded Solomon without looking at her.

"I will not!"

"Georgia, use your head," said Solomon harshly.

"I'm involved in this as the night city editor, and I'm staying."

Nash couldn't believe this. He did a pirouette and thrust his right hand out as a gesture when he was facing them again. This was the arm closest to Krolikowski. "Georgia, your fucking..." Solomon knocked down his arm. Nash glared at him. "I'm not going to touch her." (to Krolikowski) "Your fucking woman's lib will have to take a rest. I don't want to hear it." (to Solomon) "I want an explanation."

"I'm on your side!" she shrieked. "I think this is a stupid fucking decision."

Nash's emotions were boiling over in all directions. He was getting confused, and a simple target had turned out to be the wrong target. He didn't know where to strike out, what to say, what to ask, what had happened. And he was afraid of totally losing control because he knew too much emotion would finish him for the night. From the expressions on the faces of Krolikowski and Solomon, Nash could see he was considered the biggest problem here. Solomon was playing some kind of mute game on him, Nash decided. They had to be manipulated. They all had to be manipulated. As soon as he could do it.

Nash did an about face, cocked his head stiffly and looked up at nothing, trying to regain control of his trembling and the storm in his brain. It came to him that he was too old. It was downhill from here. This might be his best story ever. As angry as he was, he was going to rescue it. He was going to take charge. Yes. It could be done. He brought his eyes down and surveyed the section of the city room in front of him. A crowd of people, most of whom he knew in one way or another, had gathered in front of him and at the corner of his right eye, and, he assumed, around to the side and in back of him. The crowd did not bother him. An accidental side effect of being a reporter for years was becoming accustomed to crowds. Farther away, the newsroom noise told him the paper was going to be put out by other, busy people no matter what the idle here and he himself did.

"Are you ready to listen now?"

"Shut up!" He flung his arms out like an umpire then realized that this reaction to a simple question showed he was a long way from regaining control. His mind had been zooming at 100 miles an hour writing the story, and somebody had flipped the car. The engine was roaring, and his wheels were spinning, and he was going nowhere. He looked up at various sections of the ceiling again. It would take a long time to slow his mind and his emotions, he told himself, and he knew he didn't have that much time, so he was going to have to conduct business while he was unstable.

"I need a drink!" he said to no one.

He looked down at the real world again, walked around behind his desk, and tried to sit down. When the chair wouldn't cooperate, he kicked it into position, and then he sat down. He picked up his notebook, flipped to an empty page, picked up his pen, and said, "Okay, what's the program?"

"We're holding the story out for this edition," said Solomon.

Nash already knew this, and he was angry as hell at hearing a repetition. His eyes flashed, but he forced himself to nod. "Go on," he said. He noticed Solomon's face had darkened as if he were the insulted party here, the son of a bitch. Nash feared that Solomon would lose control next, and they'd waste more time.

"This is not my idea," said Solomon.

"I think God must have done this," said Nash, intending to be sarcastic.

But Krolikowski laughed at the remark, and a few of the bystanders snickered, breaking the tension. Solomon even ventured one-fourth of a smile. Nash was not amused and was not going to laugh. If he laughed, he would cry. He hung his head. Please, he thought. To his desk top, he said, "What about the 11:30 edition?"

"Did you call the parents?" said Solomon."

"Forrest?"

"I told YOU to call them," said Solomon.

Nash looked up. "I can't write the story and call the parents! Anyway, the line was busy."

"I got through once," said Forrest, "and they didn't want to talk about it. Now it's busy again."

"That's a good sign," said Solomon. "If they don't want to talk about it, it means something happened. You explained it to them, Forrest?"

"Yeah, I explained what we were calling about," said Forrest.

"I already knew something happened," said Nash.

"And they didn't deny it or argue?"

"No. They just said they didn't want to talk about it."

"Keep at it." Solomon explained the way Forrest should handle it, a different version of the same instructions Nash had given. Then Solomon added, "You get some corroboration, and I'll get it on one, maybe the line, Sam."

"Corroboration?! Aaron, I already have the two principal witnesses, Dr. Crawford and a nurse describing the whole thing."

"I need solid corroboration. What nurse? She's anonymous. Simonet is very leery of this. He's not going to have a screwed up story in the last editions of the Chronicle."

"He told me to write it."

"He doesn't want to deal with you. He's not going to talk straight with you. That's the way he is. He tried to fire you before."

"When was that?"

"The last time. I wouldn't allow it."

Nash stared at Solomon, saying nothing, thinking little. Then he asked, "What about the 11:30 deadline?"

Solomon turned to Krolikowski. "Who'd you assign to cover this press conference?"

"I'd like to send Kemper."

"Well, you'd better do it. Let her read what he's written first. It's twenty to. She's got time."

"She's typing up the transcript of his interviews. I'll get somebody else to finish for her."

"Tell her not to give away too much at the press conference," said Solomon. Krolikowski waved assent.

"I'd like to see this transcript, Sam. That might help."

Nash held up five pages, and Youngman suddenly stepped up with another handful. "Great stuff," said Youngman.

"Thanks," said Nash.

"Copy!" shouted Solomon, holding the papers in the air.

"You wanna use my office?" said Solomon to Nash. A short copy clerk took the papers from Solomon's hand by stretching. "Three copies," said Solomon. "Use my office," he said to Nash again. "It's too crowded out here. The 11:30 deadline is pushed up to 10:30. That gives you almost three hours. You could write a novel in three hours."

"Give me 40 inches."

"Be reasonable. There's no room for that."

"You got a stupid story that says, 'The mayor says goodbye to the Chronicle. The governor says goodbye to the Chronicle. The President says goodbye to the Chronicle.' You got a stupid story like that?"

"We've got a stupid story like that. Leamington wrote it. I think it includes the Cardinal, too."

Nash knew it included many other such worthies. "Throw it out," he said.

"I'm not even going to argue with you. You write the story, 25 inches. Let me do what I do. Go in my office."

"Throw out a columnist on the opinion page and jump it there. That'll help me get 40."

"We can't jump a news story to the opinion page."

"Just once."

Solomon lowered his voice. "Look. Sometimes I understand why politicians refuse to turn on old friends. It's like kicking your own life around. We started out together."

"Pretty much."

"Do you think you need something? Let me know...You don't ...?" Solomon had his hand on Nash's desk and appeared concerned and brotherly as if he were trying to phrase a delicate question. "I could get you one cup of very strong coffee to settle your nerves." He meant bourbon with a little Coke. "I don't want you stiff, though."

Nash seriously considered this proposal, running his hand through his hair and making a few faces. Then he shook his head. "No. I told my wife I wouldn't."

"I should never have brought it up. I apologize."

"You know I'd love it. And you were thinking of the old days."

"The old days, and some of the old guys who were around when we started. And Shatto." Shatto was a reporter of their own generation who had taken up drinking in the newsroom.

Nash was about to ask whatever happened to Shatto, but something told him to ditch the remembering. He reached out and hit a button to sign off the computer terminal. "I'll be in your office."

. . . .

Without too much trouble, Nash got the story up to 16 inches, lifting quotes from the transcript of his interview with Dr. Crawford. He could not tell if the overall structure of the story was holding up because his mind had lost its edge, and the words on the screen were just words. He made a lot of typing errors because his fingers still trembled. The State's Attorney's press conference was on his mind because of the amount of space it might eat up; and March's parents (what was Forrest doing?); and he wondered if Doc Baum had called and nobody had brought the message. Nash's last extra obligation was nicking at his thoughts, but he decided to go to 20 first.

Spread haphazardously across Solomon's desk were the pages of the transcript, Nash's notebook, clip envelopes from the morgue, and loose newspaper clippings. Nash's right leg was jumping. When he stopped it, both legs started jumping. He wanted another coffee. Forrest had got him one. And he was coughing intermittently from too many cigarettes and from nervousness.

Still, it was relatively quiet in Solomon's office. At one point, as he tried to think of a sentence, it occurred to him, Well, you finally made city editor. He smiled to himself and suddenly wanted to go through Solomon's desk. The impulse was easily bypassed because of his steady weight of fear—fear of how the story would read, fear of blowing the latest deadline, fear of not getting it on page one, fear that they would chop it down so small it would be incomprehensible. These were motivating fears which helped him concentrate rather than debilitating fears.

When he got to 25 inches, gas welled up in his chest, and he burped and realized he was hollow. He had been burning calories at a furious rate, and his stomach was pumping out acids waiting for food to appear. He rearranged his shoulders to loosen some muscles, read the last inch he had written, then got ready to re-read the story and throw parts of it out. He had reached the limit of 25 inches Solomon had given him, and some compulsory comments, such as from the parents and State's Attorney Ryan had not yet been included.

At 8:45, Solomon's phone rang and Nash answered it. Krolikowski informed him that Mrs. Ryan had admitted the whole thing in her own way. Mrs. Ryan claimed the failure to notify the Medical Examiner was an oversight. She thought the Department of Mental Health had taken care of this detail and the department thought her office had done it. She said she had just spoken to Doc Baum and apologized to him.

Nash knew her excuse was a transparent lie to anyone at the press conference, but he also guessed a few members of the public would buy it. Mrs. Ryan told the assembled press she had labeled Nash's previous story a hoax because, in her opinion, it hinted a crime had occurred when the shooting was really justifiable and not a crime.

"March trying to kill the nurse was a crime," said Nash abruptly. "So was concealment of a homicide."

"I know," said Krolikowski.

Forrest burst in.

"Where's my coffee?" said Nash, hanging up the phone.

"Oh," said Forrest, stopping in mid-stride. "I already brought you one."

"Cream only. I want another one."

"I got a statement from the family."

"Did you type it up?" Nash had gone back to staring at his computer screen.

"No. I'll do that, too. You want me to go and do that?"

"What's the gist?"

"They think it happened like you said, and they think this is negligence. They were offered a settlement, but now they're thinking of hiring a lawyer. It's a payoff."

"Nah." Nash dismissed that idea with a rasberry and turned to Forrest. "A settlement is legitimate legal business. They could defend that. I'll use it someplace." Nash intended to make the thrust of the story unchallengeable, a homicide that was concealed by the authorities. "The only negligence that I can see here is that some over-optimistic doctors tried to give their wacko son a chance." He looked back at the computer screen. One of the routine hazards of asking people for their comments, in Nash's opinion, was that you were then stuck with foolish comments. But there was no way around it. "Type it up," he said.

By 9:20, despite trying to limit the story to the essentials, Nash had 45 inches, 20 inches over his assigned length. He was finished, and it was time to trim the story to size. Clearly, some of the essential parts would have to be thrown out. The question was, which parts? A daily newspaper had many stories, each of which was important to different individuals or groups, and the stories all had to fit together by staying in their assigned sizes. Nash felt the floor beginning to vibrate as the presses in the basement started up, printing the 3-star edition for home delivery to subscribers. The home delivery edition would lack what Nash considered the Chronicle's best story for the day, the story about State's Attorney Ryan and the concealment of a homicide. But there would be no empty space. All the pages would be full of other news. It galled Nash to be left out of the home delivery.

Nash decided he had stalled long enough. He found he had one cigarette left, lit it, and picked up the phone. The number he knew by heart. He told himself this had to be a short call.

" '. .llo."

"Who's this?" he said. Someone had answered the phone after only one ring.

"Eileen." The little girl who could run fast.

"Eileen, is your father there?"

"I will see. Who is calling, please?"

"Sam Nash." He closed his eyes, picturing the scene this announcement might cause in the house.

"One moment, Mr. Nash."

The family noises in the background were indecipherable after Eileen put down the phone. Nash thought of the many times in the middle of public scandals that rocked the city he had called state or federal prosecutors at home at night and caught them while they were holding gurgling or crying babies. And some of the witnesses were warming baby bottles or complaining about sloppy school work. And some of the crooks caught in high places were worrying about the fancy schools and what the kids and grandchildren would think, and about the damn defense lawyers who were taking all the ill-gotten pile as their payments, every penny. Someone picked up the phone.

"This is who?"

"This is...(Nash tried to compose something clever, but couldn't.)...who you think it is. Howdy."

"Nash?"

"Yes, Clarence. It's Nash. I don't have long to talk."

"You're bold as brass, aren't you, Nash?" said Bryce with a chuckle in his voice.

"Maybe. Now I want you to listen."

"How's the journalism business? Oh, you're going down for the third time, aren't you. A genuine loss to the city. I mean that sincerely. I thought the Chronicle had the best comics." Bryce's voice was lilting with amusement.

"The comics will be picked up by the Ledger and the Post, most of them."

"Wonderful. That's a relief. I never see your byline anymore."

"You may have to get used to that." Nash decided to slow down, quit pushing. He leaned back in his chair. Clarence had to banter, and Nash knew he himself needed to loosen up for the long term good of the story, especially if he had to severely trim it, which was hell.

"No job, eh?" said Bryce.

"You sound pretty good," said Nash, turning the question.

"I'm working. Getting ready to protect innocent criminals from the excesses of our judicial system. I joined up with Harry Schaeffer. It was in the columns."

"I missed it."

"I was hoping to join the attorney general's office and continue putting the mother-fuckers away, but we can't have everything we want, and this pays well."

"I called you for a serious reason, you know." Nash had already smoked almost the entire cigarette and dropped it in the ash tray.

"Now I think I'm offended, Sam. Is that the only time you're going to call me?"

"You wanna hear it?"

"Not really. I was having a nice evening here."

"The Read Mental Health Center story is going to break again. This time we got the whole thing. There was an inmate shot to death by an employee in January. It appears justifiable. The coroner was never notified." Nash lapsed into the old name for the Medical Examiner's Office.

"So what?"

"It's probably going to be on the 10 o'clock news, and people are going to start calling you, or may have."

"My daughter occupies the phone. That's why you called? I'm out of that racket."

Psychological denial, thought Nash. "The whole business of why you got fired is going to be dredged up again. It's all going to start all over again." Nash shifted in his chair. "Some people will say you were an innocent victim or a hero. Other people are going to reexamine the wiretapping thing. I'm telling you in case you want to leave town for a while." Nash felt pretty cold about this. If Bryce had lost flexibility and was going to pretend nothing was happening, Nash was still going to tell him.

"They can all go fuck themselves. I have nothing to say to anybody, not even you—on that subject. But I'll be right here, or in my office. If somebody wants to subpoena me, well, that's different. But I don't think it will happen."

I think it will, thought Nash. The erudite Clarence Bryce liked to sound tough and earthy once in a while. Nash had always thought Bryce was just showing how easy it was.

"...It's Nash." Bryce was momentarily talking to someone else. Nash guessed who it was. "He just called to give me a bit of information. Just wait....I'm back. So, are you writing this?"

"Yes." Nash explained the story briefly and how he got it and mentioned Scott Campbell's involvement. "If you want to comment on the record, be my guest. Otherwise, I gotta write."

"Quote. No comment. Unquote. I heard they really covered themselves in manure. Campbell may slip out of it. He's a slick piece of work, that young man is. If he survives, he might put Hawkins away. He's that clever. It's very chivalrous of you to call, Sam."

Nash snorted. "I'm sorry about the way it worked out, Clare."

"Some other time."

"Yeah. . . . Well, I have to. . ."

"Listen. I want to make sure you do not misconstrue things. I feel I owe you that."

"You owe ME that?" Nash was astonished. "Okay. You have my promise I won't misconstrue things. I think I figured it out. You never knew about the illegal eavesdropping games being played by what's-his-name, the state's attorney's investigator, until it was too late. When you found out, you had him fired. Then he flipped (went over to the side of the defense lawyers)."

"That's essentially correct. He was a hotshot, and a devious one."

"And in the Hawkins case, you knew about it and allowed it to go on."

"That's partly wrong. I won't comment on that. But I knew what I was doing, Sam. I always knew. I chose. . ."

"I know, the good of society."

". . . and I accepted the consequences in advance. Not the good of society! Well, yes. But that's not what I'm referring to. I chose the consequences if you get caught, and I don't wish to evade them now or have people be told silly things about me in the newspaper. That would be dishonorable and make me nauseous, Sam. Suarez."

"Suarez," repeated Nash. "I remember from Ignatius." (Ignatius is a high school.)

"You would, Sam. It's relaxing."*

"But see, Clare, you went too far when you issued the subpoena for Victoria. You knew they had something on you, and you did it anyway. Suarez didn't suggest that after you go through the stoplight, you call the cops on yourself."

"Back up. Irish Catholics perhaps have guilt trips like that. And there is a bit more involved here than going through a stoplight. But I was doing fine; just blowing the whistle on Ryan and Saddler for the benefit of the rest of the people who were staying in the office; a little warning. My luck held until—Shazam!—Dr. Truth came along and wrote that first story in the newspaper."

"Yeah, well..." Nash almost said, "Dr. Half-Truth," but he swallowed it quickly. He was glad to see Bryce still had his sense of humor. In fact, Nash was immensely relieved. Nash still wanted to know why Bryce didn't give him the information he gave to Mike Franzel, but he could guess. He had a picture frame for what happened. Several pictures could fit, all similar. "I have to go."

Nash was interrupted by a verbal struggle at the other end. The struggle ended with a woman's voice on the line.

"Nash?" In the background, Bryce was saying, "Be brief."

Nash dreaded what was coming. "Yes, Joanne." He held the receiver a little away from his ear.

"May you rot in hell. After all my husband did for you, you turned on him like all the rest. Not one good word. May you burn! I mean it."

"Yes, Joanne."

The altercation was renewed at the other end while Nash looked at his watch and grew very antsy, almost hanging up. The dispute seemed to be resolved with Bryce saying, "...be right there," and Joanne saying, "You're crazy to talk to him."

---

*Francisco Suarez, S.J. (1548–1617), author of "De Legibus," was the most prominent in a line of legal philosophers who established the concept of a purely penal law. According to this concept, which is not universally accepted, some civil laws do not oblige in conscience. According to the same principle, a person caught violating a purely penal law is nevertheless morally obliged to pay the penalty that is imposed.

"So," Bryce was back on the line, breathing from apparent irritation. "How's the wife?"

Nash burst into laughter. His tension and the incongruous question were too much. While he laughed, he managed to choke out, "Aha! I was worried about you, too."

"You can't be serious," said Bryce over Nash's continued laughter. "It's just politics and newspapers. I've practiced for this."

Laughing. Relaxing. Letting down. Long day. Tiring mental struggle. Nash sucked in a breath. "I suppose. I was..." He stopped laughing. He had tried to avoid laughing and had failed. His face was tightening. He opened his eyes as wide as he could and breathed through his mouth. Then he squeezed his eyes tightly shut.

"You were what?" said Bryce.

"I was...I thought..." Nash massaged his face hard with his hand.

"What? What were you doing?"

There was silence on both ends for a while. Nash continued to massage his face and his eyes with his hand, and grew angry at himself for emoting. He had another deadline approaching and no time to waste. Finally, he blurted out in a gravelly voice, "I was worried about you, pal."

"Nothing to worry about," said Bryce softly.

Nash let out a long breath. "I thought you might..."

"Might what?"

"...move to California, asshole!" Nash laughed a tiny laugh at his own joke. "Sorry about this."

"Move to California?!...Oh. A morbid figure of speech. Too much imagination, Sam. Probably an occupational hazard. Never! You think I can be crushed so easily? By the fucking news media? Do you think I'd do anything that would please Schuty?"

"I apologized," said Nash, laughing and wiping tears from his eyes at the same time.

"You're going to get me going here."

"I know."

"When I die, you scandal monger, of natural causes, I'm going to heaven, not to California."

"You think you're going to heaven? A lawyer?"

"Shiiit."

They were both silent for a few moments. At length, Nash said, "I gotta go, Clarence."

"Write your story. Thanks for calling."

"Don't forget," said Nash.

"What?"

"Buy the Chronicle."

"For sure." Bryce hung up laughing.

Nash didn't have a handkerchief, so when he wiped his face, he dried his hand on his shirt, and he felt like laughing at himself. After he found his place in the story and in the notes again and typed one more sentence, Krolikowski came in the door.

"Sam..."

He knew what his face looked like, and he couldn't hide it. "Yes, dear," he said, looking up.

Krolikowski froze and turned ashen. "What's the matter?" she said.

"Nothing. It's too hard to explain, but I'm fine."

She showed big, compassionate eyes as if to comfort his apparent sorrow. "They're going to make it the line story," she said. She was leaning toward him a little from the waist as if she wanted to come over and touch him. The female caring instinct, he surmised. Her earnestness forced Nash to smile very broadly.

"You turkey," she said. She straightened up.

"I thought they'd make it the line eventually. Thanks for the hand you had in it, sweet stuff, and thank Aaron, too."

"Sweet stuff," she said with full sarcasm. Then in a more girlish manner, she added, "Whadjyou yell at me for?"

"I guess I was overwrought." He over-pronounced the word "overwrought," rolling it around in his mouth which gave it a humorous side.

498

She nodded several times then made a curious face which Nash could not interpret. Krolikowski said, "When do you think you can let it go?"

"Ten minutes. Maybe 15." Nash pounded the desk suddenly, for effect and because he felt like it. He said, "It's too bad, boss, that our most faithful customers, the home delivery readers, won't get the Chronicle's last big story. That's a crock."

He waited for the proper reaction from her (which would have been, "I know. Damn right.") But Krolikowski was struggling with something, he could see. Maybe, he thought, because he had been her mentor and now he was calling her boss, she had to adjust. Things were passing across her face, puzzles. She bit her bottom lip. Then she said, "Is everything really all right?"

She was still looking at him intently. He looked her back to be nice. Then, as the moment lengthened, Nash started to get a scary idea and he squinted. Looking in her eyes, they seemed oddly open, warm, patient. Because of the great confusion of emotions caused by the last day of the paper, Nash wondered if somehow the most recent of his continuous sexual yearnings had gotten misinterpreted by Krolikowski in the viewing as being more personal than it was. Had an area opened up between them that was never to be opened up? If so, he wanted to handle this without a trace.

Calculatingly, tenderly, carefully, Nash pretended he heard only a simple question. He said, "Yeah, it is, Georgia. Everything's going along pretty good. All I need is about 15 minutes and two columns." He smiled—ostensibly because he was whistling Dixie looking for two columns. On another level, through his eyes, he wished her the best, everything.

Krolikowski furrowed her brow then focused her eyes again. She took a deep breath and let it out. She relaxed. Then she blew him a kiss and turned to leave.

"What's that for?" he said.

"Write your ass off, Sam," she said over her shoulder. "But be prepared to cut it."

It occurred to Nash that one really did live only one time; and there were some things one would never know because one was not supposed to know if all was handled properly. And he was content with that. He turned back to the computer.

. . . .

Simonet had had about as much as he could take. Besides that, his wife had arrived and was sitting near the news desk. She had never seen what he did. It wasn't easy to see, meetings and quarrels mostly, decisions endlessly. And he couldn't describe it. Simonet knew his wife had some idea that journalism at his level was intellectual, and that the debates were high minded, or at least colorful, with a few minutes for reflection. On the editorial page where he'd been hired as a prize winning writer out of Oklahoma, it had been a little bit like that. Long ago.

Since then he had become city editor (a misstep into an inbred swamp, hostile reception, quick escape), eventually managing editor, then executive editor; and for the most part he considered that he had been afflicted with supervisors who, despite fancy titles, were depressingly ordinary. They were unimpressive in appearance or demeanor. The bold ones were given to making mistakes on a regular basis and complaining; the meek ones were dependable but too cautious to stay on top of the news. The politicians among them, both bold and meek, he played off against one another over and over. How, with such qualifications, there could be egomaniacs among this group of supervisory editors was a mystery to Simonet, but there were. He was pleased, once again, with his gift for making decisions in this atmosphere.

What was that sports column that almost ran a few weeks ago? McLaren, the eccentric, wrote that maybe it would be better if one of the city's two baseball teams left town. The sports editor, Girando, said it was a fantasy, a piece of imagination. When pressed, Girando claimed it was freedom of speech. Freedom of frigging speech? "Tell him to get his own newspaper or tell it to his girlfriend. That column is killed." The dufus was a good columnist, too, Simonet thought, but sometimes writers got too wrapped up in their own ideas. The public reaction would have been against the Chronicle, and the paper was then teetering on the edge.

Now yet another disagreement had begun. The night city editor was trying to make him look bad, Simonet thought. Females had that advantage. Solomon was taking her side. Simonet knew he could resist, but the point was respectable, and he told himself that what the heck, he had an itch.

"I understand your position," he said to Krolikowski.

She began to go at him again, and he raised his hand to interrupt. "I said I understand." He turned to Rodriguez who was sitting down chewing a pen. "Manny, remember when you had to show me how to do this?" Simonet moved his hand over three different phones that were close together. Rodriguez took the pen out of his mouth, looked up and stared. What are you so astonished about? thought Simonet. The editor picked up the receiver of a black phone that had no dial and turned to face his wife. He waited a moment for someone to come on the line. Then he said, "Max, this is Bob Simonet. I'll be down in a few minutes to explain this. Keep everybody sober. Stop the presses."

501

44

In the typewriter and paper-and-pencil days, the main story would have been a copy editor's nightmare, circled paragraphs and long arrows on almost every page indicating how the paragraphs should be moved, and large sections crossed out so that some pages had only two or three good sentences. Nash had written a lot of stories like that. In those days, nervous copy editors had to whip out their scissors and glue pots, cut up the stories as indicated, and more if they felt like it, then glue them back together before editing them and sending them to the composing room. The copy cutter in the old-time composing room might have cut up the glued-together pages again and parceled out the fragments to several lineotype operators to speed up typesetting. And the type produced would have been real, lead type, each line a separate piece of significant weight you could hold in your hand.

The scissors and glue pot and lineotype days were over in Chicago. All that work was done in the computer, and what came out were stories on slick paper strips, newspaper columns. The strips were cut and arranged on a cardboard page until the page was full and ready to be made into a printing plate. The results of these technological changes were simplification of labor, some increased efficiency and speed, also a reduced number of jobs and the gradual obsolesence of an ancient skill, the skill of a lead type printer. For comparison, it was as if a new bacteria had made all wood disappear, rendering carpenters obsolete.

Those remaining Chronicle printers who had come up with the old system—even though they had adjusted to the new—feared this was their last newspaper job.

By 11:30 p.m., Lower Wacker Drive and Lower Michigan Avenue were jammed with Chronicle trucks. The trucks arrived from outlying garages at staggered intervals to pick up their papers at the Chronicle docks, but with the cancellation of the 3-star edition, all the trucks had backed up, waiting. Several thousand papers that had been printed without Nash's story were going to be dumped. The faithful home delivery readers would receive the Chronicle's last big story.

The story came out, in the end, pretty much the way Nash wanted it to. Once the editors became enthusiastic, they had decided to give him two stories, one 29 inches long, the main story, starting on page one; and the other, a 14-inch sidebar on the opinion page which Nash used for a summary of Dr. Crawford's description of a modern public mental hospital, the rights of the patients, and how and why mental hospitals had changed. If the Chronicle had been ongoing, Nash could have written that story on another day.

The decisions by the editors were good ones, requiring only that Nash once again push himself into a controlled frenzy, this time to make two stories out of one. He had to move previously written paragraphs, sentences, and sections around with an abandon that would have been impossible without a computer. Simonet had also extended the deadline 15 minutes, to 10:45 p.m. This would not have been enough had not the editors eventually ceased their requests for revisions and allowed Nash to finish. He had learned over 15 years how to meld his intentions with his instructions, how to compromise, and how to argue away orders that were too far wrong to be finessed.

He read and re-read his work in the computer over and over, long after the stories had passed from his control and were moving toward their pages in the newspaper. He saw changes he would make for the next edition. In the back of his mind, the knowledge that he had left Kate to wonder all night nagged at him.

Hours earlier, he had called her as soon as he had sat down at Solomon's desk:

"This is Sam. Stay home, babe. Something happened, and I'm going to be tied up in knots until who knows when. I'll tell you this. My hoax was no hoax. I got the whole story. It's all right."

"Good. Oh, good. Boy. I prayed so you wouldn't take today too hard. So you don't want me to come?" (Their plan had been to meet downtown for supper and then to see the Chronicle through to the end together.)

"I can't talk. Honestly. I don't even know how long I'm going to be here, but I won't be company. I'll wake you up later." He knew that she knew from his clipped tones he was about to hang up.

"I love you, Sam."

"I love you, too."

By 11:30 p.m., Nash thought he ought to find out what the next deadline was—his body was still jittery with stress—and he ought to call Kate. A movement in the doorway caught his eye. He glimpsed a nice pair of legs in nylons rising into a cloth coat. He automatically followed the legs up to the face and got bonked in the eyes.

"Hey! I was just thinking about you."

"I'll bet you were."

"It's the truth. What are you doing here?"

She stepped into the office with her head held high, briefly appraised the decor, turned to him, drew in her chin at an angle, and said, "Do I have to have an explanation?"

"Wouldn't hurt," he said.

She glided in further, continuing to hold herself in a haughty way, looked here and there to see if anything else was interesting, then turned toward the desk and glanced at the surface contents. The contents were scattered pieces of paper, newspaper clippings, some files of Solomon's in a pile, coffee cups, other junk, an ash tray. Her expression was politely disapproving; then she bent down, looked directly in his face, batted her eyes, tilted her head provocatively, and said, with sarcasm, "There was nothing on television."

She blinked twice more.

Nash had followed this because he had no choice, until he suddenly cracked up.

"Wha-a-t?" he said, his chest heaving with his unexpected burst of laughter.

She straightened up, turned her back to him, and looked at Solomon's wall posters. "Who did you think I was?"

Nash's chest was still heaving with laughter at this performance. "Who did I think you were? Uhhh, Minnie Minoso?" He laughed some more.

"Who is she?"

"Who is she?" he repeated, laughing. "He was an outfielder. I really thought you were this Greek chick who's been following me around. She has olive legs and almond eyes and pomegranate something."

"Lips." She looked at a picture and showed her right profile to him.

"And two luscious..."

"I think we should refrain from that." She turned.

"Oh, you do."

"Yes. Don't you have something to do here."

"More than you can imagine. I was doing it."

"I thought this was serious business here."

"Kate, I'd like to continue this, but..." Nash was starting to feel pressure again. If there was another deadline coming up, he judged it should be soon, and he hadn't made any of his changes yet. He wished the editors wouldn't leave him in the dark.

She went to the couch, sat down demurely, and Nash started to turn to his computer screen.

"Is this the way you work?" she said.

He looked up and smiled with incredulity. "I'm not doing anything as you can see. If you want me to work, be quiet. I'm getting up tight."

"You have time."

Instinctively, he relaxed a little. She wouldn't lie.

"How do you know?"

"Trust me. You're looking for changes, right? Any major errors?"

"I try to avoid major errors."

"Did you make any?"

"Not today, that I can see."

"Minor errors?"

"Things that aren't clear," he said. "And matters of emphasis. I think I misspelled somebody's name."

"There are no more editions," she said, crossing her legs.

Nash was stunned. This meant the end. "How do you know? Who said? There should be one more."

"Gentile told me. He said the word has been passed around that it's sports only unless something major happens. Mary Stern told me the same thing. I don't think she would get it wrong. She said if you had any big changes, you better tell somebody."

"You mean they forgot about me?"

"It's a big place."

This seemed bizarre and embarassing to Nash, but he believed it. Any extra chaos added to the normal level of chaos resulted in breakdowns in communication. He pictured the editors all talking to and consulting with each other in a circle jerk until they used up all the time. Self-involved, he thought, as a description for the editors; then immediately recognized this also described him.

Nash decided his changes were mostly cosmetic. A misspelled name they would almost always change, but he knew they wouldn't shut down the presses for one name. Changes of emphasis impressed reporters, rarely editors.

He eyed his wife, "When were you going to tell me?"

"I just told you." Kate tossed her head very nicely and looked at him again. "Mary Stern has offered to watch the kids for a few minutes."

His only response was a quizzical expression—for the revelation about the children—but his wife's behavior was also making him very curious and physically interested. She could do this dizzy, sexy role. Sometimes she could be so, what he considered to be, American, it was disconcerting; and she usually had something up her sleeve.

"They can see where their father works one last time." She spoke this sentence in an unhurried manner, her voice smooth and calm. She nodded at him. "Mary seems to enjoy them. She's very good with them. I told Bobby he was responsible for his sister."

So now she was going to switch, he thought, and play the cool-headed mommy. Nash's mind was released and became a grab bag of confusion. The Chronicle was all through, he thought. It didn't matter what changes he wanted to make in his great story. The computer was useless to him. The building was dead on its feet. When everybody walked out—nothing. He faced the issue squarely. He could not go back through the years. He could not do anything over. He would never be 24 again, the age at which he joined the Chronicle. He would go on, he supposed. He pictured himself in a new job. But then he would die. He really wasn't permanent. Just—zoom.

"You want me to help you with anything here?" she said calmly. He guessed she was tired of watching him meditate.

"I don't know."

"You want me to leave you alone?" She sat up quickly with her legs still crossed and stuck her breasts out, like a cinema secretary.

He couldn't believe it. She was oblivious. But he didn't want her to leave him alone. Not like that.

"What can you do for me?" he said, then guessed. "Or are you already doing it?"

She chuckled. "Are you depressed, buddy?" She waggled her shoulders.

"Are you afraid?" said Nash.

"I suppose if I thought about it, I could be." She let down. "So I'm taking things one at a time, which is what you should do."

Nash sat back and folded his arms. "Did you ever wonder how you got into this?"

She thought about it. "Going places with my sister and my cousin where I wasn't supposed to go—my father doesn't know to this day—and shooting pool with strange men."

"You did that?"

"Yes." She almost seemed to disapprove. "It's too bad, in a way, our daughter won't be doing that."

"How would you know?"

"I will know."

"I'll bet you would never do that again."

"You sure?" She tilted her head and lifted her chest again.

"Damn." Periodically, Nash had to admit that his wife was a stranger to him; and he marveled at her ability to seize control of his mind.

"Sam, what do you want me to do?"

"You wanna put these clips away?"

She moved over and sat in the hard back chair in front of the desk.

"There's dates on the clips and dates on the envelopes," he said weakly.

"I see."

Nash began gathering up everything else. "Forget what I'm going to tell you because everything he said was off the record."

"Of course. Who?"

"Bryce." Nash gave her a summary which she absorbed.

"... The way it looks to me, Bryce can't respond to any of the eavesdropping charges without responding to all of them," said Nash, coming to his conclusion. "So he decided to take the blame for the whole thing. That's the reasonable way. Much simpler. He seems to be guessing that the eavesdropping scandal ended for legal purposes when the courts threw out the evidence."

"Shouldn't that be the end?" she said. Nash had put everything into a pile.

"Have to wait and see. Somebody may want to prosecute. He knows it's possible. I'll bet everybody will leave it alone."

"You said all he really did was eavesdrop on a cop killer."

"Allegedly. More likely the cops did that and presented Bryce with the results after the fact. Then Bryce was stuck with deciding what to do. They knew where the gun and the sweatshirt were. Nobody knew how long the stuff was going to be there. Do they go after it or not? Eavesdropping without a court order is against the law. Bryce understands local officials can't be allowed to do that on their own any more. The techniques have gotten way too advanced. The feds tape people's stomachs gurgling in their sleep. What if our beloved Mrs. Ryan had such authority?"

Kate grimaced and seemed taken aback. "She'd probably bug our house."

"I'll bet she would have. Better we control all local officials who have the wherewithal and the inclination to do the bugging. The feds have taken this to the outer limits. If the feds ever get carried away, I think the people will pull the plugs."

"What was it you said about Campbell, the guy who took Bryce's job? You told me before Campbell was on your side."

"I didn't realize how sharp he was. If a guy understands the media, he can be very dangerous. For the first story, he gave me a little tidbit to cover himself, to make himself one of my sources, in case the shit hit the fan. By becoming one of my original sources, he knows I'm going to go easy on him in the newspaper—if I name him at all—because he's decent and helping me.

"The next day, Campbell saw from my story that I didn't have diddly. Then he knows which side he's on, the side of the winners. So he gives me a line of baloney, which probably wasn't all baloney, but just enough to throw me off for good. And I fell for it."

"Not permanently."

"Today was a lucky break." He forgot for a moment about the sheet metal desk front and absent mindedly looked under the desk to see what the problem was. Their feet should touch. When he looked up again, she was amused at him. Then Nash's eyes went out of focus and his mind started to wander searching for something that was trying to come to the surface. Sentences from the stories he had just written were flying through his mind and leap frogging. Phrases shouted and yanked at his attention. This commotion had to run itself down over several hours. In another way, he was like a horse after a long run, steaming and foaming and trying to let his mind walk, walk, walk.

He turned to look at a wall to help himself search within. He began narrowing his eyes. "Son of a bitch!" He opened his left hand, palm up. "I think I got it."

"What do you got?"

Nash was startled by the sound of Solomon's voice asking the question, but he kept his wits about him. "Uhhh, a way to quit smoking."

"Whatever it is, you should do it."

"He doesn't smoke at home any more."

"How are you, Katerina? You look stunning." The metropolitan editor was a little glassy eyed, and his tie was folded up in his shirt pocket, sticking out.

"Thank you, Aaron. You look stunning, too. How's Lisa?" Kate smoothed her dress and adjusted her posture.

"She's fine. She's here. We're going to stay downtown for the night. Are you guys going to give up my office so I can pack?" He pointed to four, large boxes nested inside one another in the corner behind Nash.

"So that's it?" said Nash.

Solomon plopped down on the couch. "We're running everything as the 5-star, Sam. No 3-star and no 4-star. We'll do a rolling replate for late sports, and that IS the end."

"Too bad," said Nash, meaning the end of the Chronicle.

"Yes."

"How'd you get them to stop the presses? I missed that."

"Georgia did it."

Nash tensed slightly.

"Georgia came up to me and wanted to give it the college try, wanted to know if I'd back her up. She's very fond of..." Solomon's eyes flicked over at Kate for an instant and then back to Nash. "...the story." Nash glanced at Kate and met Kate looking at him.

"Okay, boys," said Kate, making a wry face. "I think we get the point. Go on."

Solomon sat up straight, obviously enjoying himself. He looked tired, too, but confidence and a certain male sparkle were visible.

"I told Georgia it's very hard to get Bob to change his mind on a major matter, especially if you challenge him directly, but that I would back her up. I told her how I thought we should go about it. She said she had a different plan, and she certainly did. It was better than mine," Solomon said smiling.

"What was it?" asked Nash.

"She cried," said Solomon. "I heard she could do that, and she was really good. I was impressed. Bob needed an excuse to change his mind, and she provided it."

"Probably the emotion of the paper closing down helped her," said Kate.

"Sure it did," said Solomon.

Nash was not sure what to make of this.

Solomon snapped his fingers and jumped up. "Damn. I just remembered I have to say goodbye to some people who have to leave. You two can be city editor for five more minutes, but that's it."

After Solomon left, Kate turned to her husband. She moved her tongue around in her cheek and gazed at him slightly sideways. Nash arched his eyebrows and looked angelic.

"So, my darling," she said finally, with a hint of sarcasm. "What was it you 'got'? What was your inspiration just before he came in?"

"Oh, that?" he said, relieved. "I figured out how they might have eavesdropped on Hawkins. I don't know why it keeps running around in my head. Must be because of talking to Bryce. It's another secret."

"So what's the secret?"

"You know the main charge was that the authorities found out where Hawkins hid the gun through either a bug or wiretapping. This was never proved."

"Yes."

Nash rested his forehead on a thumb and index finger as if this were an aid to thinking, and he gestured with the other hand. "Somehow I knew this was tied up with Fred Hughes, but I couldn't figure out how. I just remembered. An old rewrite man who is now retired told me a story about Hughes once that makes the connection.

"One day a long time ago, while Hughes was our chief investigator, Hughes phoned this rewriteman in the office and asked him to perform a strange favor. Hughes told him, 'Just put the receiver on the desk, Jimmy. Ignore it, Wait three minutes. Then hang up.' Hughes said he was going to be talking on the other end of the line, but told the rewriteman not to pay any attention to what he said because it would not make any sense and it was not directed to the rewriteman.

"Of course, the rewriteman picked up the receiver after a while and listened anyway. What he heard was Hughes cussing out and running down police commander somebody or other, attributing all sorts of bizarre sexual practices to him, then starting in on the com-

mander's relatives, accusing them of being thieves, grafters and per-
verts. The rewriteman said Hughes was really in top form. Then
Hughes hung up.

"Remember, Hughes was making a long speech in the telephone
after telling the rewriteman not to listen. So supposedly, nobody is
listening to this.

"A couple days later, the rewriteman asked Hughes what it was all
about. Hughes said he needed some information from the cops at
Area 3, 39th and California, and the commander there told the
dicks not to talk to him. So Hughes got mad and drove out to Area
3 and put a dime in the pay phone on the landing between the first
and second floors. This is the phone the detectives told friends and
relatives of people under arrest to make their calls on, and sometimes the offenders themselves, too. Hughes said the phone was
tapped, and the cops at Area 3 played the tape back every day.
Hughes said his speech so there'd be a little bouquet on the tape for
the commander and to ridicule the commander in front of the other
cops listening to the tape."

Nash laughed and shook his head. "That was 20 years ago. I
don't know if that still goes on, or if they have switched phones. But
Hawkins was arrested in Area 3, and they took him there."

He looked at his wife, and she was still gazing at him. "It seems
like games, doesn't it? But it's life and death."

She nodded several times. "It's games and the other."

"I've got an appointment for a job interview at the Ledger at 9
a.m. tomorrow."

"What?" She put her hand over her heart. "You do?"

"I was bound to score sooner or later." His eyes twinkled and he
laughed.

"You're good," she said. "It was inevitable."

"Yeah, right. There's no guarantee. Wolfram gave me the metropolitan editor's number. The guy was pissed because I called him at
home. But I made a good pitch. I got the name of the shooter from
a nurse at Read with the understanding that I wouldn't print it. But I

can still track him down and interview him. Plus, Doc Baum owes me now, and he'll come through with a story. And a lot of guys in the State's Attorney's Office will look out for me. I offered this all to the Ledger if they hire me. The shooter has immediate potential."

"Great. The shooter," said Kate, partly teasing him.

"You watch. That'll be a good story—and you'll want to read it."

"I probably will," she said, "especially if it gets you a job. Then I'll read every word." She rose and began walking around behind the desk.

"I still have to find out who else in the State's Attorney's Office knew about the coverup, besides Ryan, Saddler, and Campbell, and how close it gets to the governor."

Kate started massaging his shoulders and neck. "And you'll find out, if I know you. What about the eavesdropping?" she said as she kneaded his muscles.

"If the Ledger wants to pursue that again, they can assign someone else."

"Oh? But maybe if you did a few more stories about that, too, dear, you could get Clarence indicted and expose everybody else connected."

He understood she was kidding. "Nobody will ever get to the bottom of that. At least I don't think they will. But you raise the essential, ticklish issue." He looked up at her briefly. "If the Ledger insists I do both halves of this scandal—which I doubt—but if they do, I have to decline. Bryce is my friend, plus I already talked to him off the record about the eavesdropping. I can't investigate it now. I think I can work this out," he said, waving his hand. But he knew he wouldn't be sure until he negotiated with one or more of the editors of the Ledger in the morning.

"We have to go straight home," Nash added.

"I knew that when I came," she said. "The children have to go to bed." She removed her hands and started walking toward the couch.

"Then what did you get all dressed up for?"

"Are you crazy?" said Kate, picking up her coat. "You see all

514

these women around here? You see all these young girls ready to party?"

"I never notice." Nash realized he had inadvertently lifted the wrong lid, and he hoped it would close quickly.

"Gimme that again."

Nash shut one eye and busied himself picking up his pile of papers as if it required concentration.

"Sam, you look at every chick on the street lately as if she were naked."

He took a deep breath, raised himself up, smiled innocently, and said, "You find that unusual?"

When they left Solomon's office a few moments later, Nash knew he had temporarily cooled Kate's affectionate mood by being dense. Nevertheless, he was accustomed to natural ups and downs, and he wouldn't have paid this a lot of thought except for a tiny, disquieting note he detected behind her irritation, a note hinting Kate might suddenly feel inadequate. This he was incapable of tolerating. He was determined that he would fix any such false idea of hers.

Walking out of Solomon's office was a little like leaving the womb, and Nash felt dropped into harsh and uncertain reality. Friendships were breaking up in fact if not in intention all around him. The events of the day, like a table full of pool balls crashing in all directions on the break, left him with the sensation again that the ground was moving. He had felt this way before after a day too full of revelations, rises and falls, and secrets, some of which he had to keep, and weaknesses, his own and others'. This time, for a fact, the floor was rocking as the presses began printing the last Chronicle.

When Kate got caught up in conversation with someone, Nash hauled the kids off to say some goodbyes. Despite the disorder and the time, Georgia was still on the city desk. When he said goodbye to her, his children were next to him fighting, and Georgia's expression was amused, and something else.

"You're very lucky, Nash," she said, leaning back in her chair.

"Yeah, thanks," he said, as he tried to maintain the social contact while pulling Bobby and Kim apart. Their hands felt good anyway. "I'm probably going to see you on the street sometime soon (chasing the news)," he said.

"Not right away. I'm taking a vacation."

"I wish I could. I'm tired."

"Kids look good on you, Sam. I don't know if I can relate to that myself," she said.

"Come off it." Nash thought he knew Krolikowski pretty well. She was a Polish girl from St. Ladislaus parish in the neighborhood around Chopin Park, which was pronounced SHOW-pin. "Feeling your years at the ripe old age of 29?"

"I just turned 30."

"My goodness. To be 30 again."

"Can you see me wrestling with the little darlings? Yours are certifiably cute, of course. Do I look like the Mrs. Mom type?"

"I don't know what Mrs. Mom is, but when the opportunity comes..." He lowered his voice, "...you look like all the mothers I see."

She blushed a little. He wanted to say, "Georgia, marry that copper, or marry some other guy, and have children. Let your children doubt. You cannot doubt!"

He knew if he was drinking, he would have said it. But since he was sober, he was able to think twice. He was even able to wonder if, incredibly, men were letting her down.

He said instead, "Good luck at the Post."

"A reporter again. I'm looking forward to it, I think."

Nothing further was coming from either one of them for several moments. He still hadn't found a way to bring up the stopping of the presses and Krolikowski's role in it. Finally, Nash freed one of his hands, reached out, and shook her hand. "Thanks, Krolikowski."

" 'S'Okay, Nash."

"Dad, she's got my hat," said Bobby, referring to his sister.

Nash looked around the room for Kate. He had seen her watching

516

him talking to Krolikowski, but now he couldn't find her. He let the children represent his apologies to almost everyone for not being able to say more copious goodbyes. People shouted things to him, clapped him on the back, but more than equally had their own concerns. He managed to hug Gentile and Wolfram and kiss Mary Stern.

When he located Kate, she was decidedly off-hand to him and continued a conversation with the wife of one of his co-workers while he waited, with the kids. It even seemed to Nash that Kate became nervous when the other woman moved on. Kate finally turned to him and said, "So?" with studied nonchalance.

"You ready to go?" he said lightly. They were near a little-used rear entrance.

"Sure. Why not?"

"Oh, wait a minute!" said Nash. "I've got Gentile's car keys. Wait for me. I've got to find him." He held out the children to her.

Kate took the children's hands, then said, "Why don't you get a ride home when you're ready, and I'll take the children now."

"No. Wait for me."

"I'd rather go."

"You came all the way down here to get me. Hey." He reached out to touch her face, and she pulled back. Nash saw her distress again, which he knew was unnecessary, and he closed his eyes in frustration.

He was becoming angered by random things beyond his control that kept popping up on all sides and even inside him while he faked being the same as always but feared he was losing his grip. He was even scared of applying for a new job. Now his wife was hurt because she suspected him of fooling around with a girl to whom he had behaved properly, although he had earlier been plotting otherwise.

Who had the map to this maze?

Nash thought he detected the finger of God, the Great Comedian, the Great Practical Joker in all this, teaching who-knew-what.

Okay, What? What? demanded Nash in a fraction of a second. Cling to what?

He frowned, even with his eyes closed, at his own last question to God ("Cling to what?") because Nash did not recall conceiving that question. It seemed like another random element popping up inside his head. But then, after a moment, it seemed it was something from his subconscious or his memory, and he decided it was a helpful question.

He opened his eyes.

"Katerina." He thanked her silently for standing there waiting for him to say something. "Umm, you'd be surprised. You'd be wrong to think what you think. You're my girl. Don't see things where they ain't because the reason they ain't is because of you. You could make ...a gigolo faithful."

She snorted at him. "Why would I want to do that?"

"Well," Nash's mind was working as if he were writing, "if he was just a potential gigolo, you know, he might be intriguing to have around because with your charms you'd own that guy, and you could use him."

Her expression was amazed but narrow-eyed.

"And then you'd have to feed him. But he'd be a heck of a prisoner. And you're the only one who could lock him up. Because you are. Trust me." He nodded.

She seemed to study him suspiciously and weigh him, using unknown factors. At length, her eyes softened. He wasn't sure of things until she turned her head at an angle, looked at him and said, "Did you eat today?"

He loved her through his eyes.

"Sam, there's a media crowd in the lobby, our colleagues. They want to take your picture, and TV wants you to say something." It was Solomon who came from behind Nash. "You know, the last edition and all. They want you to talk about the last big story. Go ahead."

"Oh, no, Sam. The kids," said Kate. "Talk to them tomorrow."

"I know some of these people, honey."

"He should really do it," said Solomon. "You go with him, Kate. The whole family."

"I don't want to," she said.

For a moment, Nash thought of many things, including the possible positive or negative effects on his job interview in the morning. That seemed 50–50. Then he said:

"Aaron, old buddy, having duly considered this, the story is in the Chronicle, and I'll be around tomorrow. Would you give these keys to Gentile and tell him I owe him a couple cases of beer. I think we're going to exercise everyone's well known Constitutional privilege to slip out the back door."

Then each taking a child by the hand, they did.

ACKNOWLEDGEMENTS

I wish to give special thanks to Daniel Greenberg, retired deputy superintendent of the Chicago Read Mental Health Center, and to Dr. Robert Beech, director of psychology there, who gave me hours of their time so that I might be able to write an accurate description of a modern mental hospital. Considering the hammering that public mental hospitals have taken in literature, which is true to some extent in this book, their generosity is amazing. Any errors in this book regarding Chicago Read or the mental health field are solely those of the author.

Special thanks also to Morton Friedman, former chief of the criminal division of the Cook County State's Attorney's Office; William K. Hedrick, former assistant United States Attorney in Chicago; Jeffrey Kent, former chief of special prosecutions for the Cook County State's Attorney, now once again an assistant U.S. attorney; Dick Hill of Illinois Bell; Milton Hansen, my editor, who should be immune from criticism for advice I refused to take;

Richard Lorenz, my proofreader who gets the same immunity; and to Tom and Linda Handschiegel who read this manuscript from its infancy and offered helpful suggestions and support.

No father could write a book without the forbearance of his wife and children for which I am extremely grateful. In this case, my wife was also my principal reader.

For numerous favors in making this book, I am also grateful to Margo Alexander, Betsy Brenner, Alan D. Busch, Fern Schumer Chapman, Steve and Evelyn Crews; Gerard Crimmins, the late Robert Corbet, Cheryl Devall, Katina Alexander Dunn, Denis Ginosi, Don Harris, Tim Jones, John Kass, Anne Keegan, Andy Knott, Kathy Ksandr, John and Marilyn Lux, Pete Makin, Brother Michael McCabe, O.F.M., Charles and Terri McGaughan, Albert V. O'Hara Jr., Clarence Page, George Papajohn, Colleen Crimmins Rosen and Rocky Rosen, Max Saxinger, Barbara Schaffner, Sally Suddock, Father Paul Waddel, C.P., and Ben Yonzon.

This book could not have been completed without Dr. J. David Madsen. And thanks to Mike Sneed for her advice and encouragement and to Bob Greene who said to me, "Why don't you write a novel?"